A NOVEL

THE THIEF

Editing by Maxann Dobson, The Polished Pen http://www.polished-pen.com

❀ Created with Vellum

DEDICATION

This book is for Maree.
You know what you did.
And you know how much you mean to me.
Kelly is for you.

"I loved you the same way I learned to ride a bike; scared but reckless."
Rudy Francisco

PROLOGUE

KELLY DANIELS, 15 YEARS OLD

I'm in my bedroom when it starts. Homework spread out on my bed in a chaotic mess as my head tries to make sense of the algebra equation.

What a bunch of shit.

I'm trying though, just like I try with everything I do. I *try* to be quiet. I *try* to go unnoticed and blend into the walls. I *try* to be a good student. I *try* to be brave and strong like my older brother, Casey.

I turn my head to the frame on my bedside table. The photo inside shows me and Casey in black and white. Mum took the photo when she was in an artsy mood, toying with the idea of photography and earning hobby income. We knew it was a pipe dream though. Dad would never let her have anything. Eventually he tore up every photo she took, but I managed to save this one.

It shows the both us laughing at each other, so similar in looks, down to the blond hair and blue eyes our mother said were brighter than the halos of angels. Casey and I even have the same mannerisms. But that's where it ends. Because my brother is a fucking cunt.

Familiar rage ignites in my chest when I think of him. Four years older than me, Casey left. He got free. He's at Charles Sturt University in Goulburn now.

"Selfish bitch!" I hear my dad roar from down the hall.

My eyes squeeze shut. *Please stop.*

Casey said he'd come back for us.

"Six months," he vowed, grabbing my shoulders and looking at me with fierce eyes. Determined eyes. *"I'll get settled and come back for you. I promise."*

I believed him. Of course I did. He's my big brother. My protector. But it's been eight months now and nothing. I have to accept that he moved on and left us behind. He's never coming back.

My fingers tighten around the pencil in my hand. It snaps in two. *Crack.*

"I'm sorry!" my mum cries in a broken voice. A desperate one. Panicked. As if she has a chance of calming him down with an apology. "I won't—"

"I'm over your lies, Maggie!" My dad's voice is cold and hard. It gets that way. He goes into a rage and becomes a different person. A monster. *Smack.* "Tell me why you bought the damn dress! It's for the new neighbour across the road, isn't it?"

A single man had moved in to the vacant house two weeks ago. A teacher, I think. He looks around forty and kind. He made the mistake of smiling at my mother and saying hello when they'd both gotten out of their cars at the same time and checked their respective mailboxes out front.

"It's not! I swear!" she sobs. "It's for—"

"Shut up!" he roars. "Where did you get the money for it, bitch?"

My jaw clenches tight, and my breathing begins to labour. I start rocking on my bed, not even noticing that I'm doing it.

"You gave it to me."

Of course he did. On a *good* day. But he forgets things on his *bad* days, and today is definitely one of those.

"Bullshit! You *stole* it from me."

Smack.

"Please," she cries.

Crack.

He's yelling in earnest now, and she's crying and screaming. My mother is begging for mercy from the man who's supposed to love her, and he's giving her none. It's almost as if he enjoys her begging. It fuels him.

Their fight builds and I reach a point where I just can't take it anymore. *I can't, I can't, I can't.* It's been too much for too long.

My rocking is forceful now.

I have to do something.

I have to ...

I jump from the bed and crouch, scrambling for the suitcase beneath it. It's already packed, sitting there ready since the moment Casey left. I packed for Mum too. Food, clothing, shoes. Enough to get us through a few days at a shelter until we can get in touch with my brother. But he's not coming and we need to leave. Today. *Right now.*

"No!" she screams and a thundering crash comes from their room. It's followed by eerie silence. I shoot to my feet, dizzy and ears ringing, the suitcase forgotten.

I start for their bedroom, picking up speed when I hear Dad sobbing, the sound like a wounded animal. I've never heard him cry. It sends chills skittering down my spine.

Their bedroom door is slightly ajar. I place a shaky palm on it and push. My eyes find my mother first, and I stop breathing. She's on the floor facing toward me, a crumpled heap of limbs and pretty blond hair. Blood pools beneath her head and soaks the carpet. Its metallic stench is thick in the air, choking me. Her eyes, like the brightest blue in a hot summer sky, are open and sightless. They stare at me with nothing inside them. Empty of life.

Grief rises like a tidal surge. I try to swallow but it won't stay down. My throat aches and my eyes burn as I stare down at her lifeless form.

He's killed her.

She could have left him. She could have had a whole other life. I have hidden photos of my mother when she was young, ones my father never managed to destroy. Photos of her life before him. Before her every breath became a battle. My mother used to be Maggie McIntyre until she met my dad at the age of nineteen. Her hair used to shine, long and pretty, and her eyes sparkled. There used to be happiness and sunshine in her heart until she fell in love with a callous man that sucked the life right out of her. Now there's nothing left except blood on the corner of the dresser above her and the stain of misery and death on the floor.

My father sits on the edge of the bed. He's sobbing, shaking his head in disbelief.

Fury explodes. Its onset so swift and hard it overtakes my body completely, breaking through the shock and horror. The sound of his cries fuel my anger. Hands fisted and knuckles white, I leave the room and make my way down the stairs. When I reach the study, I open the bottom drawer of my father's desk and take out his gun. After checking the chamber and finding it loaded, I walk to the staircase. I take each step slowly, knowing what I'm about to do but unable to stop myself. *Someone stop me, please.* But no one comes. I'm alone.

When I return, my father still sits where I left him, a sobbing pathetic mess.

"I hate you." The words spew from my mouth like venom.

He swallows snot and tears. "I'm sorry."

I walk toward him. There's a storm surrounding me, intensifying, and I'm caught in the middle of it. It takes control, raising my arm and pressing the gun in my hand to his temple. "Give your apology to the Devil."

Sanity screams at me. It claws at the edges of my mind, trying to rip me free from the storm. It makes me hesitate.

"Do it," Dad pleads, his voice a gravelly whisper. He wants to die. He *needs* it. My father is a rabid dog that needs putting down for the good of society. "Do it, Son."

I lift my chin and stare down into his watery eyes, hating that I'm doing him this one favour. And hating my brother for letting it come to this. If I learn one thing from this day, it's to never rely on anyone.

Not even those you love. Because the moment you do, they'll turn their back on you and you'll find yourself alone.

The air around me stills.

"See you in Hell, Dad."

I pull the trigger, ending his torment.

1

I tug at the collar of my crisp white shirt. It's too tight. I can't fuckin' breathe. My eyes scan the room, lighting on Grace Paterson across the room, the fiancée of my older brother. She sees me tugging and the corners of her lips tilt upward. Sadistic bitch. She knows how much I hate playing dress-up. I fix my features in a scowl. It evokes a laugh so beautiful my chest tightens a fraction. Grace is outfitted in a white strapless dress. It highlights the colourful tattoo of flowers that wind down her shoulder and left arm and the fiery waves of hair that hang down her back. Casey is a lucky bastard.

I'm stuck at this fancy place called The Florence Bar, celebrating their recent engagement. Waiters carrying trays of canapes move about the room. Tall bar tables hold vases filled with towering flower arrangements. Their scent mingles with expensive perfume and the sweet tang of champagne. I don't belong here. Not in this place. Not with all these beautiful, high-class people. And not in this ridiculous tuxedo that Grace supplied after I handed over a shit ton of cash. It feels like I'm wearing a damn straightjacket. I roll my shoulders.

Fox shoots me a look of sympathy. He's decked out in a tuxedo for the first time and looks as out of place as I feel. His dark blond hair has grown long and it's tied in a braid down his back. "Another drink?"

I snort. "Is that even a real question?"

Luke Fox is my *real* brother. My brother in the Sentinels MC. They've been my family from the moment I left mine behind, bleeding out on the carpeted floor of my parents' bedroom.

After shooting my father, I walked blindly to my room and sat on my bed. A cop, Morgan, arrived twenty minutes later. She said a neighbour reported hearing a gun shot.

Morgan was a rookie, but she was also an undercover member of a biker gang. The Sentinels. She reviewed the scene. She could see what went down. Morgan saw my struggle and decided I'd been through enough. Rather than take me into custody when I tried to run, she called in her biker brothers. They made the scene appear as a murder-suicide, then they took me in before Morgan reported the incident. I wasn't going to live with my brother. Not after what he let happen. So I chose to remain hidden with Sentinels, and there I stayed.

It didn't stop Casey looking for me. He searched for ten years, choosing not to believe it was a murder-suicide. I know because Morgan told me he was digging into the case. He believed that someone else did it. And that someone else took me away and killed me too because there was no way I wouldn't find my way to him if I were still alive.

Casey found me eventually. A year or so ago. All that digging into our parents' case was causing trouble, to the point where I was left with no choice but to intervene. It was then that he learned the truth. That I killed our father. And how I blamed him for allowing it to happen.

He found out I was runnin' with the Sentinels, and he looked at me as though he didn't know who I was anymore. That kind of thing changes you, though. It makes you harder, and it makes you darker. I was no longer the sweet kid my brother used to know. But the Sentinels did for me what he never did. They looked out for me. They had my back. They never *abandoned* me. Brothers *for life*, not just when it fuckin' suits you.

"Are you going to go and congratulate your brother?" Fox asks as we walk over to the bar.

My lips tighten. "Not yet."

I try to avoid him where possible, despite Grace's attempts at a familial reconciliation. You can't force a relationship where the connection has been irreparably severed. We aren't brothers anymore, and we have nothing in common. I don't know how to talk to him.

I ride with the Sentinels, earning a dollar by tinkering with their bikes and cars. My brother owns a business called Jamieson and Valentine Consulting alongside three of his friends. They work as security for a big name band, *Jamieson,* but they also work with the police, hired on as "expert consultants" for kidnapping cases, ransom, and hostage negotiation. They often get their hands dirty, getting involved in shoot-outs and car chases. But Casey's specialty involves getting children out of abusive situations by whatever means possible.

We reach the bar. "Two whiskeys," I call to the bartender, hoping hard alcohol will wash away the bitter taste in my mouth.

I get it. He didn't get me out, so he spends his life appeasing his guilty conscience by saving other kids. It's fuckin' admirable, right? Except you can't fix the past. No matter how many lives he saves, it doesn't change the fact that I was the one he left for dead. His *own blood.*

"Make them a double,' I add, again tugging on my collar.

The bartender sets our drinks on the counter. We pick them up and toss them back in a simultaneous motion. Fire spreads through my chest. Fox hisses from beside me. It's good liquor. Quality. Expensive. It slides down easy, caressing my throat like a hand over silk. God*damn.*

Unfortunately, it's not a miracle cure as my bitterness holds strong. I set the glass back on the bar with a *clink* and a hard voice. "Another."

"Tying one on tonight, little brother?" comes a voice at my back. Speak of the Devil and he shall appear.

My teeth grind together as the bartender hands over my second glass. I snatch it up and turn. Casey is decked out in a similar tuxedo, though he somehow manages to look smoother than I do. A little more at ease. His hair is short at the back and sides with the top slightly tousled as though he's let his old lady style it for him. She probably did. That's what women do. Change how you look until you don't recognise yourself anymore.

My hair is lighter than his and longer. It's tied at my nape in a short rough ponytail. Beside him I feel as though I've been raised by apes and they're trying to introduce me to civilised society. It won't work. You can take the man out of the jungle and dress him in pretty clothes, but you can't take away the animal inside of him.

"That's the plan," I retort, my lips peeling back in an unfriendly sneer. Grace appears at Casey's side, and I quickly wipe the hard expression from my face. I like his old lady. She may have forced me into a monkey suit, but she has a heart. A deep one. I don't know how my Judas brother managed to steal it.

I give Grace a flirty wink. "Hey, babe."

Casey bristles and I chuckle silently to myself.

"Kelly," Grace says in a stern voice. She knows I'm trying to goad him.

Trouble is, I can't seem to help myself. My eyes scan the length of her in a long deliberate fashion. "Looking hot as fuck tonight, *babe*."

"Daniels," Fox mutters quietly beside me while Casey's knuckles whiten on the glass in his hand, exercising considerable restraint.

That restraint sets my heart pounding with fury, compelling me to goad further. I raise my glass. "Congratulations on your engagement, Brother. Though it's a shame."

"What's a shame?" he asks, his jaw ticking.

"That your old lady didn't choose the better brother. Maybe she'll come to her senses one day soon."

Grace's sharp intake of breath is audible.

"Careful, Kelly," he replies. "You're starting to sound a little jealous."

Damn him. I throw back the second whiskey and enjoy the powerful burn as it spreads wide through my chest. "It's hard to be jealous of a man who walks out on his own family." My gaze shifts to Grace. "Watch out he doesn't do it to you too, Slim."

Casey snatches my wrist, his grip hard and tight. The glass drops from my hand and shatters to the hardwood floor, drawing the attention of the guests around us. "That's enough," he growls through gritted teeth. *Slim* is *his* nickname for her and his alone. That I've just used it is the straw that breaks the camel's back. "I may have walked out on you, but I was coming back. Damn you, I was coming back."

My lips flatten. "Trouble is you didn't."

Casey drops my wrist and steps backward, his face paling. "This is not the time or the place."

"It never is," I retort with heat and look around. Clusters of people surround us—women in glittery dresses and men in sharp suits, their hands holding glasses of champagne and their eyes on us. They're staring, mostly at me. At the wild beast let loose upon their world.

"Perhaps you should leave," my brother says in a flat, monotone voice.

The goading has worked. Casey has given me the *out* I need to get the hell out of here. And it's for the best. It's far better to leave than remain where I don't belong. "Perhaps I should."

Our feet crunch over broken glass as Fox and I walk away. People step out of our path, leaving the exit clear. I don't look back.

Fox and I are jogging down the front steps when a voice calls out, "Wait!"

We both stop and turn. It's Jake Romero. He's an old friend of Fox and Jamieson's drummer. They used to run together, back in the day when Romero was a henchman in the King Street Boys—a gang that has since disbanded thanks to the law and Mackenzie Valentine, his old lady.

He's wearing a suit too, though he's sans tie. I wonder how he got away with that. He jogs down the stairs, reaching us, his voice an accusation. "You barely stayed five minutes."

Fox shrugs. "We got shit to do."

"Yeah?" Romero's brows rise. "What kind of shit?"

"Sentinels shit," is all Fox says. Despite their past friendship, we're a brotherhood and we don't share our business with outsiders.

"Right, okay." Romero nods. He gets it. Then his gaze shoots to me. "I wanted to have a word."

"About what?"

He looks around. "Not here."

My eyes narrow. "Let me guess, it's not the time or place."

"Cool your jets, Daniels. Here on the steps of the Florence Bar where we happen to be blocking the entrance is not the place."

I fold my arms. "Then where?"

"What about Fix?" he replies, referring to a coffee house in Darlinghurst. It's situated across the road from the office of Jamieson and Valentine Consulting. "Ten minutes?"

Curious, I give him a nod. We have nothing better to do with our night. Our so-called *Sentinels shit* was just Fox giving an unquestionable excuse for us to make our getaway. "See you there."

Romero turns and jogs back up the stairs while Fox and I make our way to the parking lot behind the popular venue, taking our time.

"What do you think that's about?" he asks.

"No clue. I guess we'll soon find out."

We reach our Harley Davidsons. I swing my leg over, kicking up the stand. The bike settles beneath my heavy weight with familiarity. I run my hand down her glossy black gas tank in a loving caress. *Hello, my baby. Miss me?*

She responds with an answering growl when I turn the key. The engine vibrates deep down inside my soul, aligning its tune with the beast inside me, soothing it. I liberate the bow tie from around my neck and undo the first three buttons of my shirt. After tucking it inside my saddlebag, I look to Fox. He's doing the same. When freed, his lungs expand, drawing in a deep breath. Then he looks at me and grins. *Let's ride.*

We roar out onto the main road together and my hands relax their hard grip on the handlebars, easing into the ride. Harleys are low and heavy. Riding them is about the journey, not the destination. By the time we arrive at Fix, my hair is mussed and my clothes rumpled, but my heart is lighter.

Fox's eyes are lit as we walk toward the coffee house, having parked half a block down the street. Riding makes him happy too. My brother is a paramedic. He's seen some seriously bad shit. Last night's shift was some dude fucked-up on meth swinging at him with a baseball bat after beating his son unconscious. Fox is a better man than I am. I would've ripped that bat from his hands, splintered it in two, and stabbed the fucker with it. This is why I tinker with bikes and cars and not with people.

We reach Fix and Romero is already there, his Dodge Charger gleaming in its park out front. He grins. "Beat you."

"It's not about the journey—"

Romero cuts Fox off, finishing our habitual spiel. "It's about the destination. Yeah, yeah ..."

"Get stuffed, Romero," he retorts.

They're both laughing as I slap my palm on the glass front door and push it open.

2

ARCADIA JONES.

I look up from my phone when the door of Fix opens. I don't know why I do because I can't hear anything other than my music. I'm at a table in the back, tucked away in a dark corner with my textbooks, earbuds in as I flick through my favourite playlist on Spotify. I'm prepping mentally. Tonight is my last boost before I hit the straight and narrow, so it needs to be perfect. The right frame of mind is crucial. I have to be focused and calm. And it has to be dark and late, but not late enough there aren't any cars on the road at all, because you need to blend in, not stand out.

The instant I see him walk inside it's a physical punch. I flick down my list of songs, tap my *go-to* song "Joker and the Thief" by Wolfmother, and hit play. It's the song I always hit when I see a car I *have* to have. It's a recognition and a craving, all at once. An exciting, pulse-pounding moment that steals the breath from my lungs. A hunger so fierce it forms an obsession that won't leave me alone. I'm feeling all of that and more when he steps inside the busy coffee house, two big burly guys following behind him.

The beat pulses through me as I watch with furtive eyes, knowing he won't notice me looking. I'm dressed in a way that leaves me inconspicuous, with my mass of dirty blond hair hidden beneath a beanie and a scarf obscuring my neck and chin. It's cool tonight, the kind of cool that settles deep in your bones. He seems unaffected by the chilly temperature as he stalks toward the counter like a lion on the hunt.

I push black-framed glasses further up my nose, studying him as my song plays out. He's not my type. I don't *do* suits. And he's wearing a fine one. It's tailored, highlighting a trim waist and shoulders wider than the engine block mounted in my garage. His hair is shoulder length, as though he's growing out a shorter cut. It's tied back with loose strands tucked behind his ears.

I'm good with the smaller details, and he has ones that don't add up. The facial hair isn't a full beard, but it's not stubble either. Wearing a suit like that, his face should be smooth. And his hands ... I watch them as he reaches inside the pocket of his jacket. They're large and calloused. A working man's hands. He pulls out a wallet. It's leather with the appearance of a battered, old work boot. Its age tells me when he finds something he loves, he'll only let it go when you pry it from his cold, dead hands.

My eyes shift to his suit-wearing friends as he pays for their order. They don't add up either. One has long hair tied back in a braid, the other has hair buzzed short, and the hint of a tattoo peeking above the collar of his crisp navy shirt.

The paradoxical trio turn from the counter with coffees in hand and walk my way. I return to my textbook, blind to the words as my heart pounds. The song fades in my ears, and I hear them take the table next to mine. Chairs scrape on the floor and deep voices wrap around me like a warm blanket.

A new song kicks in—"Him and I" by G-Eazy and Halsey—and drowns them out. I try focusing on my subject, something about supply and demand, when the *ding* of a text message cuts through the music in my ears. I flick it open.

Echo: Get a hold of yourself.

Bitch. My eyes dart up, scanning the ceiling perimeter. One security camera is anchored in the top, back corner, facing outward. My table in the back is obscured from its view. Then I shift slightly, looking to the front. *Damn*. A camera sits fixed above high shelving behind the counter, blending in beside ornamental mugs and large mason jars.

My best friend can hack into anything she chooses, leaving no trace behind, and tonight she's choosing to hack into Fix's security and watch me.

Ellington "Echo" Reid is a prodigy. We became friends at the age of sixteen when my ex-boyfriend leaked a picture of my naked boobs onto Facebook. Echo was my new lab partner at the start of the term. She sat beside me, always wearing so many coats that most didn't notice her at all. I thought she was mute until she slid her phone across the table and muttered, "These your tits?"

I jolted at the sound of her rough voice, and my eyes widened on the screen. They were indeed my *tits*. Everyone would know they were mine too. Not because my face was in the picture—it wasn't—but because I was wearing a necklace my ex-boyfriend Johnny bought me that spelled out my name. I wore it every day.

"I'm going to kill him," I hissed, only I couldn't do it right then and there because he cut class early that day.

"Want me to remove the picture?" she asked.

My brows winged up. "You can do that?"

The slow smile that creeped over her face was downright sinister. "I can do all that and more."

But for what price? I come from a long line of thieves, having learned that there's always a cost for anything, even when you steal something that doesn't belong to you. I'm a descendant of the great Racer Jones, not that I advertise my heritage. I can steal anything thanks to the tutelage of my grandfather, but cars are my forte. Their sleek pretty lines and powerful engines are a siren song, and the adrenaline from driving them is better than any drug you can manufacture. "What do you want in return?"

Her eyes darkened with a malevolent glint. "I want Miles Howard's car."

My brows winged up even higher. Not because my lab partner knows my private business, but because it's a big ask. Miles Howard is the school bully. He's renowned for fixating on a particular student and grinding them down until they're nothing but dust in the air, swirling listlessly through the school hallway. The only good thing about Miles Howard is his sweet, sweet ride. "A car for removing my tits from the internet is not quite an even deal."

She shrugged. "You can take it or leave it. But if you decide to leave it, that picture will haunt you for life. You'll find it on social media, porn sites, and blogs. Hell, people will even make memes out of it and share that shit far and wide."

"Okay, okay." My lab partner painted a hideous picture. Not to mention, if my older brother found my tits leaked all over the internet, I was dead anyway. And Miles deserved it. "Deal," I said, holding out a hand.

She shook it. "Deal. I'm Ellington by the way," she added. "But you can call me Echo."

"Ace," I replied.

"Nice to meet you," Echo said as she started packing up her books halfway through our lesson.

"You're leaving?"

"The longer your tits are out there the longer it takes to remove them."

"Good point."

My new friend slunk out of class, leaving me to take notes for the both of us. Two hours later she found me in the cafeteria, having spent the morning pretending to ignore the suggestive jibes and snickering laughter from those around me. It hurt though. How could I have liked a guy who felt it okay to do something like that? I'll never be so stupid as to trust a guy with private photos of myself again. Lesson learned.

Echo pulled out a chair and sat down with a *thump* and a smug grin. "Done. Where's my car, Ace?"

"Out in the parking lot where Miles left it, I imagine," I said mildly and took a bite of my ham and salad sandwich. My parents were health nuts. It sucked to sit there in the midst of winter smelling deep-fried food while I chewed on kale and grainy bread. *"Proper nutrition keeps a clear head and strong mind,"* they liked to say. *"All the better to boost your cars with, darling Ace."* Nice to know they cared about my health but are seemingly unconcerned with the probability of prison. *"You're a Jones. We don't get caught."* Their belief in me was absolute.

Echo snatched the sandwich and took a huge bite. She grinned around the giant mouthful and said, "Well, what are we waiting for?"

I picked up my drink, slurping down cold-pressed cucumber, pink lady apple, and mint juice. "There are cameras in the parking lot."

Her grin evolved into an expression of superiority. "Seems they're suffering a technical glitch today."

Excitement rising, I fist-bumped my new mischievous friend and stood, abandoning my crappy lunch. "Let's ride."

Hours later we had that car boosted and sold to the Marchetti Brokers' chop shop for a tidy sum. Not wasting time, they began disassembling the car that afternoon, selling off the individual parts for a big profit. Miles Howard would never find his ride again.

"What did he do to piss you off?" I asked her later that afternoon as we sat in a local cafe, Echo choosing to drink a coffee and me slurping down a double shot chocolate milkshake.

"Besides being the one who took the photo from your ex-boyfriend's phone and uploading it himself?"

"It was Miles who did that?"

"Yup."

I scowled. Stealing his car wasn't payback enough for what he did, but it would have to do. "You still haven't told me what he did to you."

"I'll tell you one day."

The second song on my playlist ends, and the *clink* of coffee mugs and the *whoosh* of the frothing machine draw me out of the memory and back into Fix.

I tap out a reply to Echo's message.

Me: I do have a hold of myself. I'm focused. It doesn't get more focused than this.

She starts typing an instant reply, seeing through my lie thanks to camera number two. I watch the three little dots flicker across my screen until it pings.

Echo: You're not. Look out the window.

"Stop the Rock" by Apollo 440 starts playing when my eyes flick up. Instead of hitting the window and beyond, they land on *him* at the same time his land on me. I stop breathing. And moving. I sit there, music blaring in my ears, pinned to my seat by the cold, hard gaze of his blue eyes.

They move over me, curious, landing on my textbook before rising again. Then he looks away to his friend with the braid, who's talking. I'm dismissed. I take a deep breath.

Echo: The window, ACE. Not the sex god.

I try again, this time looking beyond the man and outside. My mouth goes dry and flutters fill my belly. It's a Dodge Charger. 1979. Candy apple red with white racing stripes. Mint condition. Holy hell. *Come to Momma, baby girl.*

This is Echo's definitive knowledge that I'm unfocused and off my game. How did I miss that? I drag my eyes away long enough to respond to my friend.

Me: Who does she belong to?

Echo: Sex god no. 2

My eyes land on the guy in the suit with the braid.

Echo: Not him. The other one.

They shift to the suit with the buzz cut. He looks like a man who would hunt you down to the ends of the earth if you so much as touched the gleaming paintjob on that sweet, sweet ride. I crack my knuckles, suppressing the grin. I love a challenge.

Echo: His name is Jake Romero.

Me: What else?

I know Echo's digging deep when it takes ten minutes for her to respond.

Echo: Bounce it. He's the drummer for Jamieson. Too much trouble. Too many contacts.

I don't want to bounce it.

Me: What contacts?

Echo: King Street Boys. Sentinels. Valentines.

The King Street Boys are an old gang and old news. But the Sentinels MC aren't. Neither are the Valentines. I've never met any of them, but I've heard of them. Like bulldogs, they sniff out trouble, and not only do they dig it up, they tear it apart.

Me: Boo. I'm going out for a closer look.

Echo: Oh great. Well done. Yes. Go put yourself on their radar.

Ignoring her froth of sarcasm, I down my last mouthful of coffee —it's cold—and grimace. Standing, I slap my textbooks and papers closed and shove them inside my book bag. Flicking to a new track on my playlist, I tuck my phone into my pocket, sling the bag over my shoulder, and head outside. They pay no attention to my departure.

Cold air hits me like a slap to the face when I step outside. It's worth it to get a closer look at that car. And I'm not the only one drawn by her pretty spell. Two other guys, early twenties, are standing nearby, talking and eyeing her with admiration. I walk to the other side of them, hiding behind their stature so I have more time to stare.

Echo: She's glorious.

I sigh. Of course, there's a camera focused on the entrance to Fix.

Me: She really is.

Echo: Finish up and walk away. Your sex god is on the move.

My sex god? Pffft! But she's right about the first part. I need to get going. My composure is rattled. I won't be boosting any cars tonight at this rate. Maybe I should go home for a power nap. The problem is that I live with my older brother and I'm not in the mood for an inquisition on my whereabouts tonight. Mason is out of the business. He's busy making sure I am too. And I want to be. I really do. I'm studying for a bachelor degree in Business, majoring in Finance. It doesn't get any straighter or narrower than that.

I even try looking the part, making an effort to wear my reading glasses and a smidge of makeup when I usually wear none. I'm dressed in a collared shirt and tailored pants, teamed with a pretty pair of pointed flats on my feet. I do admit to having a pair of Converse in my book bag. I can't boost a car with impractical shoes.

I tuck my phone in my pocket, my gaze returning to the Charger for one last appreciative glance. The next song on my playlist fades when I hear, "She's beautiful, isn't she?" from behind me in a rumbling voice.

My body hits high alert. I pull the earbuds from my ears at the same time messages vibrate their delivery on my phone, one after the other. I shoot a glare to the security camera before turning around.

It's *him*. Of course. Echo did warn me. Perhaps my feet remained rooted to the pavement because I wanted to see him for one last appreciative glance too. It's well worth it. Up close, he's overwhelming. My senses are operating at full capacity as I take in his scent, the warmth radiating from his body, and the enigmatic depth in his eyes. All I need now is to touch and taste and my sensory journey will be complete.

"Yeah, I guess she is," I say in a manner that I hope exudes ignorance. I don't want him knowing I was scoping out the Charger.

He takes a bite of the muffin in his hand. It's oversized and thick with chunks of milk and white chocolate. It looks almost as delicious as he does, and after years of deprivation, I now suffer a powerful sweet tooth.

"You want a bite?"

My breath quickens. "Sorry?"

"A bite. Of the muffin." The fluffy treat is thrust in my face. "You're lookin' at it like you wanna—" He cuts off as though he was about to say something crude.

I'm fascinated. He doesn't talk like a high-class suit. And his voice is deep and smoky like a Cuban cigar. "Like I want to what?"

"Put your mouth on it."

Sweet baby Jesus. My inner thighs clench, and I take the muffin. There's something so oddly intimate about sharing food with a complete stranger. His nostrils flare when I take a bite.

"You got a name?" he asks, watching me chew. Never have I felt more self-conscious than I do in this moment.

I swallow. It's good. Sweet and rich, but not sickly. "Arcadia."

"Arcadia," he mutters to himself as though tasting my name on his lips.

Another message dings as I offer back the muffin. Echo is getting antsy for me to leave. "What about you?" I ask as he takes it.

"Kelly."

Kelly and Arcadia. *Why did I automatically think that?*

He takes a big bite, right next to where I took mine. A shiver of longing tickles my skin. I want that mouth biting *me*. His eyes heat as he watches me. Does he see through me so easily?

I try for a polite smile and gesture a thumb to the footpath behind me. "Well, it was nice to meet you, Kelly. I should get going."

A frown wrinkles his brow. "You got a ride?"

Is that concern on Kelly's face? It's nice and oddly comforting to have a stranger looking out for my welfare in a world where everyone only looks out for themselves. The only problem is that my *ride* is three blocks down, waiting for liberation from her protected spot in a dealership garage. Echo infiltrated their computer system. The BMW is the five series M550i and brand new. The sexy lady was in getting her very first service today. But come tomorrow morning when her owner comes to collect, she'll be long gone.

"I do." A slow smile builds as I start walking backward. "Thanks though."

He takes a step toward me like he doesn't want me to leave. "You sure?" There's a hint of suggestion in his tone. "Because I can give you one."

Hell yes, baby, I bet you could give me the ride of my life. I take a deep breath, drawing in the strength to say no. I *need* this boost. "I'm sure."

He nods. "Guess I'll see you round then, Arcadia."

I bite my bottom lip, drawing it inside my mouth. "See you."

3

KELLY

uck me stupid. Arcadia has stirred a hunger inside me that demands to be fed. Pity she didn't want that ride. Even though she's not my type, I find myself staring after her. She looks studious, like a desk jockey of some sort, with her fancy pants and shoes, and those provocative reading glasses. Her eyes were focused on that economics text book inside the coffee house like her life depended on getting an A-plus.

Catching her gaze had been intense. Her eyes were a large bluish grey, and turbulent, like the seas of a wild storm lived inside them. Those eyes were framed with dark brows and even darker lashes. Sharp cheekbones gave her otherwise pretty features a powerful edge, as if she could turn from sweet to fierce in a single instant.

Fox slaps me on the back, his gaze on her retreating figure. "No dice, huh?"

I take a bite of my muffin and chew. I speak around my mouthful as the dark night swallows her up. "Not even with this stupid penguin suit on. I thought chicks dug this shit."

"Demand a refund."

"I should. The damn thing cost me my left nut."

Romero reaches our huddle. I drag my eyes from the direction she disappeared in and look at him.

"So? What do you think?" he asks, referring to our discussion inside of Fix.

I fold my arms, conveying an unhappy stance. "What I think is that I want to see this place before I make a decision."

Romero nods. "Fair enough." He points down the street, the opposite direction to where Arcadia left. "It's two blocks that way."

"Let's go," I say.

We choose to walk, and ten minutes later we arrive in front of a huge garage in Darlinghurst. An impressed whistle escapes my lips as I stand back and take it in. "You two are buying *this*?" I ask, referring to him and my brother, Casey. I need to double-check because this building, in this location, would cost way more than the left nut I just handed over to Grace for my suit. It would cost your entire cock and balls, and even a kidney too.

"Hell yes, we are."

It appears brand new, as if some poor bastard built it for the specific purpose of operating a garage and went bankrupt before he could get the business up and running. Two enormous black garage doors occupy the left side, the side where all the magic happens. The right clearly houses the office section. Romero walks over to the office entrance and pulls out a key.

"You got a key?" Fox asks, walking over to him while I hang back. My eyes are on the building but my mind is in the clouds. To have a legit business like this, with all the bells and whistles and fancy tools, is a dream, and it's just typical my asshole brother gets to realise it for himself.

"Sure do," Romero replies, unlocking the door. "You can get anything when you know the right people."

Fox steps through the doorway. "Ain't that the fuckin' truth."

Romero holds it open, looking at me. "You comin'?"

"Yeah, yeah."

I walk over, peeling off my jacket as I step inside. I toss it on the oversized reception counter as I inspect the space. It's closed off to the garage area by large glass windows and an automatic sliding door. There are offices behind the counter but none of that interests me. My eyes are fixed on the cavernous space beyond the glass. The building extends right back, leaving enough room for several cars. Multiple restorations. And at the back is a large room, extending from one wall to the other, to house an area for all the spare parts. Racks of stainless steel shelving are already installed.

Fox steps up beside me while Romero goes off to flick on light switches. "What are you thinkin'?" he mutters.

"I'm thinkin' there's drool on my chin right about now. You?"

Fox sighs, his eyes on the cavernous space too. "I'm thinkin' it's makin' my dick hard."

His mention takes my mind to Arcadia and how she made *my* dick hard as I watched her lips wrap around that muffin. It's barely deflated, even after that walk in the cold night air.

"So are you in?" Fox asks me.

"No fuckin' way. If Romero and Casey think I'm going manage this little operation for them while they sit back and rake in a bunch of money, then they've got shit for brains."

Romero's voice is hard from behind me. "Is that so?"

I turn, folding my arms. "Yes, that's so."

"You know this is Grace's idea," he says, referring to Casey's fiancée. "We're looking for a manager who knows what he or she's doing, and she suggested you."

This doesn't surprise me. Grace and her damn meddling. "And Casey went along with it because he likes to do whatever she wants?"

Romero holds up his hands as if surrendering. "I'm not here to argue. I'm just here to ask if you want the job. If you do, it's yours. If you don't, then we'll find someone else." He walks over to the automatic door and it *whooshes* open. He steps through, and Fox and I follow behind him. He stops but I keep walking beyond him, already smelling the thick scent of grease, hearing the clatter of tools, and seeing the beauty of scrap metal transform into works of art. It makes me hungry. *Damn* hungry. I want this. But I don't want to be working this dream for someone else.

I stop and turn. "I'll manage your operation." Romero opens his mouth to speak and I hold up a palm, stopping him. "On one condition."

He nods agreeably. "Shoot."

"I buy in. Become a partner and own this with you."

Fox's brows fly high. "Brother, you got the money for this?"

"Yeah," I reply, the singular word hard enough to shut down any further questions. It's money I never wanted to touch, tainted with death thanks to my mother's life insurance. My chest tightens and I turn away, pretending to inspect the space again while I gather composure. I don't miss the slow grin that forms on Romero's face before I turn. He likes the idea. I do too. It might mean having to put up with Casey's bullshit more often, but for this I could put up with him *and* the entire Valentine crew he runs with. And that's sayin' a lot because I always manage to rub those assholes the wrong way.

Arcadia

ECHO: Your lady is waiting

Her message is code for me to make my move. Echo has the cameras down and she's on standby for potential emergencies. I'm already eyeing the dealership from across the street, hidden in a dark alleyway between two buildings. I can't see her. She'll be out back, detailed and serviced, waiting for just the right person to treat her right. I'm just hoping she's in a position where I don't have to move other cars to get her out.

Me: How does she look?

Echo: She looks bored but prime.

Anticipation heats my blood as I tuck my phone away. Prime is Echo's code for ready to go. It means this boost should be a walk in the park. But now is not the time to get cocky. That kind of attitude can get you into trouble.

Head down, I make my way across the road, armed with security codes and ready to pick the lock from the side entry door. I'm inside within two minutes. The keys are kept nearby—it's standard policy for most dealerships in case the cars have to be moved in an emergency, like a fire.

Prior research leads me straight to the box. "Damn smart keys," I mutter, finding the BMW key without effort. It's a tech gadget's dream. With a digital screen, it even lets you set the interior temperature before you get in. It's a dream car but give me old school any day.

After hitting the button by the side of the garage door to roll it up, I'm inside the car and driving it out onto the street, my heart pounding inside my chest. I've switched my reading glasses for oversized sunglasses, and with my hair hidden beneath the beanie, I'm unidentifiable to any street cameras I pass along the way. There's no time to enjoy the ride. I reach my destination in a roundabout route without opening the car up to enjoy the powerful engine. It's unfortunate, but it's also smart. And I've always played it smart.

The Marchetti Brokers' chop shop, already alerted to my imminent arrival, have the door rolling up. I'm grinning as I drive inside. The door rolls down behind me and the engine purrs for a moment before I hit the button and switch it off, sighing.

My car door opens. I look up from the driver's seat. A girl is looking down at me. I put her age at about mid-twenties. She has wide dark brown eyes and layered brown hair to her shoulders, carefully constructed into messy waves. She's wearing black leather pants and a leather vest, which heightens skin I can only describe as luminescent. How is skin like that even real? "Who are you?"

"I'm Murphy." She grins, revealing even white teeth, and steps back so I can get out. "And this car is gorgeous."

"Ace," I reply, wondering when Tony Marchetti brought her on. It's only been about six months since my last boost, so she must be new. "And it is. If you like this sort of thing."

"This sort of thing?" she asks as I stand and shut the door behind me.

I pull the sunglasses from my eyes and tuck them in my bag. "Cars with no character."

Murphy shrugs, her eyes falling to the car with admiration. "What does that even matter? She's so sleek and powerful."

Pity rises inside me. It's this type of ignorant attitude that irks the crap out of me. "What does it matter?" I roll my shoulders, gearing up for a rant. "There's no significance without character. Her beauty might capture attention, but character captures the heart." I run my hand down the sleek black hood. "This girl here is loyal to no one, but a car with character..." I stop and turn, raising a brow at Murphy "...is loyal to the bone."

She laughs, her gaze moving from the car to me. "You talk like cars have a real personality."

The curious thing about Murphy's comment is that most car enthusiasts believe they do. Why would Tony bring in someone so ignorant? I narrow my eyes, studying the new recruit. "Who hired you?"

"I did," comes Tony's booming voice as he walks out from the back door and toward us. Tony is a big guy with dark curly hair and blue eyes. His demeanour is sweeter than the icing on a cupcake, but falling on his bad side will land you in the fiery pits of Hell. The cops have never been able to put him out of business because he changes his location on a regular basis, leaving no trace behind.

Tony's eyes fall on the sophisticated black beauty. "Any trouble?"

"None."

His eyes gleam with satisfaction. "Because you're the best."

I place the smart key in his open palm. "I *was* the best."

Tony's eyebrows furrow into two sharp lines. "What do you mean *was*?" His fingers curl hard around the device, almost crushing it.

"The BMW is my last lady, Tony. I told you I wanted to retire."

"Yeah, in forty years. You're just a baby, Ace. You've got decades left in the business. And I've a got another job for you. A big one."

The apprehension I've been supressing is realised. He isn't going to let me go as easy as I'd hoped. *Dammit.* "Tony ..." I shake my head as Murphy stands silent, following our exchange. "Thieves are like cats. We only have nine lives and mine are all used up. I can't go to prison, and I can't do your job. It's time for me to move on."

"Bullshit!" His nostrils flare. "It's a lucrative one, and you'll be damn grateful that I'm offering it to *you*. Do you know how many others would jump at this?"

"Let them jump." I hold up my hands and start walking backward in the direction of the exit. "I'm out."

Tony steps forward and grabs my bicep before I get too far. His fingers dig in painfully, and my stomach knots. "You're not out, Ace," he says through clenched teeth, yanking me back toward him. "You're not out until I say you're out."

His response triggers bile in my throat. Was it naïve of me to believe he'd be cool with me walking away? "Don't do this, Tony."

"I don't have a choice. My ass is on the line. And if mine is, so is yours." He lets me go and I stumble. "Do you know what I'll do if you don't do this?" Tony's shoulders are tight, his stance menacing, as he jabs a finger at me. "I'll set fire to your house with your family inside it, and I'll make you stand beside me as we watch it burn to the motherfucking ground."

The threat rocks me like an earthquake, leaving the ground unsteady beneath my feet. "You sonofabitch," I hiss, both fury and fear churning inside me. "How dare you threaten my family."

I know it's not an idle one. Working with Tony has always been a double-edged sword. He feeds my addiction and pays me well, but deep down he's the Devil. I broke all the rules and danced with him. Now I must pay the price.

"If you were a good girl, I wouldn't have to."

My lips press in a line as I stare at Tony. He rolls his shoulders, relaxing. Does he sense my acquiescence already? "I'll do it."

He nods, a smug smile forming. *Cocky bastard.* "You say that like you have a choice."

"There's always a choice," I say softly. Wearily. Because deep down in the darkest recess of my soul resides a hideous shame at the anticipation heating my blood. I live with this nefarious addiction. I know I have to quit. I promised myself and I promised Mason, yet my heart skips a beat at the thought of another job. Just one more. It's lucrative and as long as I do it, I know my family will be safe. When

I'm done I'll pack up and move them all to another country. Starting a new life in this business is not uncommon. It's what you do to survive. And I am a fucking survivor.

Tony steps forward, close enough for his chest to brush mine. I tilt my head up, meeting his gaze with defiance. He brushes his knuckles down my left cheek. "Then you made the right one, baby girl."

"I'm not your baby girl, Tony."

"Sure you're not." His lips quirk as he pulls an envelope from the back pocket of his jeans and thrusts it between us. I shift back, taking it. It's thick and heavy. "Open it."

"I don't need to." He always pay the exact amount. No more, no less.

Tony's eyes flicker with anticipation. "Your list is in there."

"My list?"

I open the unsealed envelope. Inside, amongst a neat bound packet of hundred dollar notes, rests a folded piece of paper. My brows furrow as I pull it out and unfold it.

"Twelve cars," Tony says, folding his arms as I stare at the page. They've been written down with care. I run my eye down the list, my stomach sinking. My job is *twelve cars?* And each one seemingly more impossible than the one before it. "Twelve weeks. The shipping containers are booked." Tony disassembles cars like these. The parts are packed inside containers, hidden amongst legitimately purchased car parts, and shipped overseas. "Miss the final deadline, and we'll be enjoying that toasty bonfire at your house to farewell the winter."

Panic climbs my throat. "You can't hang on to the cars that long. The cops will be all over you. The docks are the first place they'll look. Your plan is pure insanity."

"Let me worry about that, Ace. You do your thing and I'll do mine." His eyes harden. "Memorise that list and then burn it."

Tony turns and walks away, leaving through the same door he came in from. My gaze shifts to Murphy. She hasn't spoken a word through the entire exchange. "Can I walk you out?" she asks me.

"I know the way." I turn and leave through the exit. Murphy

follows. The air outside is frigid, and she rubs her bare arms. It's almost like she doesn't want me to leave. "What do you want?"

"I want you to teach me."

"Teach you what? How to steal a car?" A huff of laughter escapes me. I'm tired and tonight's events have left me delirious. "No. God, no."

Murphy lifts her chin, and there's a flash of toughness in her eyes that I never noticed before. An edge of something a little bit fierce. "Why not?"

Jesus Christ, she's serious. "Did you miss that exchange back there?" I shout, seized with a sudden frustration as I point to the building behind us. "I'm trying to *get out*! And he'd rather burn my family to ash than see me walk away. Is that what you want for yourself?" I shake my head. "If so, you're an idiot and you deserve everything you get for crawling into bed with him, knowing the consequences."

I start walking down the dark street, toward my pre-arranged meeting point with Echo.

"So that's a no?" she calls out to my retreating back.

I give Murphy the middle finger without turning around.

"Dammit," I hear her mutter. "Wait!"

Murphy's feet slap against the cement path as she chases after me. I don't stop. She falls into step beside me like a pesky fly. "Can I see the list? Maybe I can help."

"Sure. After I burn it. And then you can help me by staying the fuck away."

She takes hold of my shoulder and forces me to a stop.

I throw up my hands. "Jesus! What?"

"Please." Murphy holds my eyes, her jaw setting with determination. She suddenly seems older than I originally figured. Maybe a little harder too. "Let me help."

Is Tony using her to watch me? I wouldn't put it past him. I wouldn't put anything past him. "Why are you so eager to get involved?"

"Because I've heard of you, Ace, yet you're not what I expected."

"What did you expect?" I ask, not liking that she's heard of me. I prefer to fly under the radar. It's so much safer there.

Murphy shrugs. "Someone older. Someone with a little less..." she looks away and huffs "...heart." Her gaze returns. "But you're younger than I thought, and you seem like a good person."

"I'm not really anything, Murphy." A lump of remorse fills my throat. My past doesn't make me a good person. There will always be a small amount of darkness in my soul, doing its best to compete with the light. "I'm just trying to live my life. It was nice meeting you, but I have to go."

4

KELLY

I tug at the tie choking my neck. Another week. Another high-end bar. Another lavish party. And another goddamn suit. Why can't my brother and his friends throw a party like normal people? Whenever there's some *momentous* occasion, it can't be celebrated around a fire with a fuckin' beer. No, that would be too relaxed and fun. Instead, it's orchestrated into some colossal *event* that makes you lose the will to live.

This time it's to celebrate our new car restoration business, Rehab. The name fits. We'll be taking on broken cars and healing them, starting Monday. Contracts were drawn up and signed the day after my initial inspection. The rest of our time was spent equipping the workshop and office. I'll be the one in charge full-time, and Romero and Casey part-time. When we start building a reputation and get busy, we'll hire on mechanics. For now it's just Romero and Casey, an office manager, and me. I'll be eating, sleeping, and breathing Rehab, and I'm itching to get out of here and get started. I want to run my fingers over the gleaming new tools, do a last trial of the expensive hoists we installed, and read over the guide on the engine diagnostic tool pads.

Romero's old lady, Mackenzie Valentine, materialises at my side, interrupting my thoughts. She's wearing something that shimmers like the sun and dips to her navel, revealing massive tits. "Fuck me," I say to them.

She's holding a glass of champagne in one hand and a beer in the other. The beer is thrust in my face. "Eyes up here, asshead."

I drag them upward and take the offered drink with no apology. "If you're gonna put them out there ..."

"It's not intentional." Her green eyes scan the room until they land on her old man. That's where they stay. "These goddamn airbags won't fit into anything else."

I splutter into my beer.

"Shut up," she mutters.

"Why didn't you just buy something new? That's what you bitches always do."

"Bitches? Really?" Her gaze shoots to me, hardening. "Have you ever tried shopping with a baby? Fitting rooms in fancy stores aren't designed for prams. Or boobs that leak milk twenty-four hours a day. I tried and just ended up dripping on to the carpet with a screaming baby in a pram that was wedged half in and half out of the door. Not to mention I've gone up a damn size in clothes. All the dresses I did manage to drag inside didn't even—"

"Jesus Christ!" I exclaim, cutting her off. "Too much information, Valentine. Way too much."

Mackenzie had a baby girl three months earlier. Gabriella Mary. They call her Satan. You would think it fitting for a newborn, but this baby is an absolute angel. Even I hadn't minded her frequent visits to Rehab while the three of us were busy outfitting the workshop.

"Typical." She snorts and sips her champagne.

"What's typical?" My eyes drop to the fizzy alcohol in her glass. "And you're not allowed to be drinking that."

"You men. You can handle blood and guts and violence, but the second there's mention of a leaking tit you run screaming like little girls. And who are you? The breastfeeding police?"

"Fuck off." I down a mouthful of beer, highly offended. "I can handle anything. And maybe I should be considering you're not supposed to be drinking alcohol and yet here you are."

"You can handle *almost* anything," she concedes, her eyes falling on Casey. He's walking toward us. My shoulders stiffen as a tidal surge of anger rises. An automatic reaction to his presence. "And besides, I just expressed. That means I can have a drink if I choose. I just wanted to offer you a congratulatory kiss." Mac leans in, rising on her toes to reach my cheek. Soft lips brush against my skin, and she whispers in my ear, "Play nice."

Drawing away, she pats my cheek—*hard*—and walks off, leaving me to face my brother.

"Kelly," he says with a nod.

"Casey," I reply with a stiff voice.

He stands beside me, and we both stare out into the crowded bar. "How are you?"

"Good." My hand tightens around my glass. "You?"

"I'm good too."

"Glad we got that cleared up."

My brother sighs. "We work together now. I think we should try to get along."

"We're partners in business. That doesn't mean we have to be BFFs. Or hang out at parties."

"Kelly ..." he starts and then stops.

Fuck it all. He's trying to be mature here, and my resentful attitude is making me feel like a dick. I want to listen to that small part of my conscience that's telling me to grow the hell up, but my anger is so damn loud it drowns the voice out.

Casey tries again. "Are we all set for Monday?"

The anticipation of my first day at Rehab heats my blood. We have our first car being delivered at seven o'clock in the morning. Romero purchased it at auction with business funds. A '69 Chevrolet Corvette in desperate need of restoration. After turning this car around, we'll make a profit in the six figures. That's if I can bear to part with it when the time comes.

"All set," I reply.

His eyes gleam. My brother is just as excited about this beauty as I am.

"I'll go over the Corvette with a fine-tooth comb first thing," I tell him. "And make a list of everything we need. Some parts will take a bit to ship, but I'll put a rush order on 'em. This girl's restoration will get us good future business so I want her finished as soon as possible."

Casey nods. "Agreed." After sipping his beer, he adds, "I'll be there on Monday to help take delivery. The spray booth should be arriving at some stage too, so we need to arrange the installation."

Fox comes up from behind, wedging himself between the two of us. "Shop talk?" He's slurring. He started on shots within the first five minutes of us arriving. I can't blame him. It's the only way to survive these parties. He puts an arm around both our shoulders, jostling the two of us. "Don't be boring. Look over at the bar."

Our eyes shift in that direction.

"Red dress," he adds, giving my shoulder a squeeze.

I shake my head, looking away. I'm not in the mood. I have too much on my mind right now.

"Jesus, Daniels." I'm jostled again. "The bar," he says again, his words less slurred and a little more intent. "Red dress."

I shrug him off, facing him with a glare. "I'm not in the fuckin' mood, okay?"

Fox holds up his hands and starts stumbling backward toward the bar. "Your loss is my gain." He slurs it with a pitying expression and then hiccups, ruining his little moment.

Arcadia

I HAVE a vodka and soda sitting in front of me, untouched. I'm not here to party or drink. Or hook up. I'm here for a black 1968 Pontiac Firebird. The third lady on my list. She's a wild beast, and resting in the heavily guarded parking lot of this bar. A parking lot only accessible through the back entrance. My thoughts are caught up in her when I'm bumped by someone wedging themselves into the small space beside me at the bar.

"Can I buy you a drink?"

I glance to my left, seeing a suit without looking up. "No thanks." My gaze returns to my glass. "I have one already."

"You'd prefer something a little sweeter?" He leans in and I catch the scent of whiskey and spice. "Like a chocolate muffin perhaps?"

I turn my head, this time looking all the way up. I encounter a dark blond beard, a straight nose, and deep brown eyes that seem to see all my secrets. Jesus, it's one of the guys from Fix. The one with the longer hair. If I didn't realise it then, I'd know by the incessant buzzing of the phone in my purse. Echo is keeping tabs.

The adrenaline in my system revs its engine. Is Kelly here too? I turn my head further, scanning the crowd behind me quickly.

The suit beside me sighs in mock sadness. "Looking for someone?"

My gaze shoots back to him, and I realise I'm giving myself away just that easily. "No."

"Kelly, maybe?"

My brows rise a fraction. "Who?"

He laughs. The sound is deep and rich. Infectious. My lips curve and he stares. "I like you."

"You don't even know me."

He holds out his hand. "I'm Luke Fox."

My phone buzzes again. I ignore it and take his hand, shaking it. "Arcadia Jones."

"Are you here with friends?"

"No," I say without thinking and then grimace. It makes me appear sleazy— some lone girl at a bar wearing a slinky red dress. The outfit was necessary because it's just that type of establishment. I wanted to fit in, not stand out.

"No?"

"I mean, I was," I lie. "My friends left a moment ago. I'm just finishing up my drink, and then I'll be leaving too."

He looks at my full glass. "You don't seem to be in a hurry."

I pick it up, taking a huge gulp. The vodka is strong and burns my throat, even with the addition of soda.

Luke frowns. "And now you are. You know I *did* shower before coming out tonight."

"You smell good," I reassure him.

He grins. "For the record, I smell good everywhere."

Laughter escapes me. Luke Fox is a flirt. He signals the bartender. I catch a glimpse of tattoos on his wrist. A reminder that he's a paradox, like his friends. "What are you drinking?" he asks me. "I'll buy you another."

"I'm good. Seriously, I'm leaving soon."

Luke steals my drink, taking a sip as the bartender reaches us. "Two vodka sodas," he tells him then turns to face me while our drinks are being made. "You can't leave me to drink alone."

"You're a big boy," I say, because he literally is. "You can handle it."

"You know I'm big everywhere too."

I laugh again, shaking my head.

"What? I am." I laugh harder, and his bottom lip pokes out just a little. "Am I just a joke to you? I might be big, but it doesn't mean I don't have feelings."

"I'm sorry." I pick up my drink so I have something to do with my hands. This guy has game. He's like a tsunami. If I don't take a figurative step back, I'll drown. "I'm not laughing at your size."

"Then what's so funny?"

His eyes flicker with amusement so I know he's joking with me. "You flirting with me."

"Am I bad at it?"

"No! No, not at all," I protest, sipping again at my drink. "You're good at it."

"You know, I'm good at—"

"Wait, let me guess! You're good at everything, right?"

"You're a smart girl." Luke's eyes travel down my dress and back up. The material is tight and sparkly, dipping low in the front *and* in the back. It makes me feel like someone else. Someone feminine and sexy, something I'm ordinarily not.

"Smart enough to know I should be leaving soon."

"Come on. I'm selling myself hard here." His winks over the rim of his glass as he downs half the contents in one go. "It's not working?"

"It's …" I pause as he removes the empty glass in my hand and adds the new one. I drank all that? "Are you trying to get me drunk?"

"Only if you want to be."

"I don't. I—" I need to be sober. I need that Firebird. I need … I turn my head again and my eyes find *him* in the crowd. Kelly. He's standing with a group of people, drink in hand. Someone is talking to him, but he's paying no attention. Instead he's staring right at me. Goose bumps rise across my skin, at odds with the heat catching hold of me, as if I'm burning alive from the inside out. I touch a hand to my cheek. It's chilled from the ice in my glass. I'm surprised the contact doesn't generate a hiss of steam.

"I … what?" Luke prompts.

Kelly's eyes are intense. They peel away my dress, leaving me exposed and breathless. I lift the glass to my lips, feeling a sudden powerful thirst. He watches me as I drink the vodka down. I have to drag my eyes away and back to Luke.

"I …"

"You …"

I've lost my wits. I set my drink down on the bar and grab my purse, standing. "I have to go."

He snags my wrist and I pause. "Are you okay?"

"Of course." Which is a lie because my head is spinning, caught in a vortex of vodka and Kelly. "Why?"

"Because one minute you were here with me and the next you were gone."

My brows draw into puzzled lines. "But I'm here."

"Not really." Luke taps a finger to his temple. "You checked out."

I seek out Kelly. Oh Jesus, he's coming toward us, moving through the crowd like a goddamn panther. "I was—" It's too much. I look back at Luke, his palm still wrapped tight around my wrist. I tug lightly, but he doesn't budge his hold. Panic begins to claw at my throat. I was only supposed to be here for a pretend drink before making my way out the back and snatching that sexy car out from under its owner's nose. Echo has probably left a million messages. I have no doubt that most involve her bitching me out. The last one would be telling me to walk away. "I have a big day tomorrow."

That's the truth. The Firebird doesn't make many public appearances and time is not on our side. Tonight was the perfect opportunity. *Was.* But now I have two drinks under my belt, and two people who can positively place me at the scene should it come to that.

Luke shrugs. His palm loosens its grip and I'm freed. "Then I won't keep you any longer, Arcadia."

"Ace."

"Ace?"

"My friends call me Ace."

He winces. "Are you trying to friend-zone me?"

Kelly reaches us, saving me from having to answer, but I'm not really feeling *saved* right now. At least he's not looking at me anymore. His attention is on his friend and that attention is a little hard.

"What?" Luke offers him a smug grin. "You weren't in the fuckin' mood, remember?"

"And now I am."

Luke laughs but I don't get it.

"Well, I should go," I say, interrupting their private joke. "Nice to see you both again."

Kelly's bulk is blocking me. I'm not short, but I still have to look up, even with the heels giving me a few extra inches. "You're alone?"

"Her friends left her here," Luke informs him.

"You have shit friends," he tells me.

"They're not shit." My reply is ludicrous. I'm defending a bunch of people that don't exist. But I don't want him thinking I'm the type who would surround herself with shit friends, which doesn't make sense, because why would I care what he thinks of me?

"They are shit. They left you here alone."

"I'm not alone." I pull the phone from my purse and wave it in his face. "I have this. And I have Luke," I add, waving a hand in his direction.

"Luke's not yours."

I blink. "He's not?"

"I'm not?" Luke adds.

"No."

"You can't say that."

Kelly lifts his brows. "I just did."

"I mean you can't tell me who's mine or who's not."

"I can tell you whatever I like."

"Well, technically that's true, but if I want Luke to be mine, it's not for you to say he can't be."

This conversation is utterly ridiculous. I can feel Luke's gaze swinging back and forth between the two of us. "I can be yours," Luke adds. "If you want."

My eyes shoot to his. "You're just that easy?"

He shrugs. "I can make you work for it if you're the kind who likes a challenge."

"That's enough." Kelly's voice thunders between the both of us, drawing our attention back to him, and confirming my previous thoughts. "Luke is not easy, and he's not yours. I am."

Laughter bubbles out of me. "You're easy and you're mine?"

Luke snorts so hard he chokes on his drink.

"That's right." Kelly says the words with as much seriousness as he can seemingly muster, yet I don't miss the twitch of his lips. "Tonight I'm all yours."

"Your offer is ..." Egotistical. Appealing. Tantalising. "... unwise."

"Unwise? Why?" Kelly's bulk crowds me, making it hard to breathe, to think. "You the type that wants to peel the skin from my body and wear it as a suit?"

I laugh. Again. What is it with these two? I'm trying to pull off an impossible heist, and here I am drinking, surrounded by two delicious man-flirts. Besides, if any skin peeling is going on tonight, Echo is going to be the one doing it to me for missing my chance at the Firebird.

"I *could* be the type," I reply. "That's the issue. You don't know me."

"I do. Your name is Arcadia. You like triple chocolate muffins." My mouth opens to reply, but he continues, leaning in to speak in my ear. "And I'm Kelly." His voice is low. It tickles my skin, bringing shivers of pleasure. "I like eating girls who eat triple chocolate muffins."

"Actually, her friends call her Ace," Luke points out while I work on remembering how to breathe.

"I'm not here to be her friend," he replies, holding my gaze.

I should be offended. He wants to have sex with me and move on. A one-night stand. He's making it clear. With his words. With his eyes. I'm not going to lie to myself. It's tempting. Even with the suit. He's not my usual type, so walking away tomorrow would be that much easier, right?

Back it up. It sounds like I'm trying to talk myself into this. *Fuck you, vodka.* I tuck my purse under my arm and twitch my dress into place. "Time for me to go."

"You got a ride?"

It's the same thing Kelly asked me when I left him at Fix. It was tempting then. It's tempting now. I hesitate. "I'll send for an Uber." He nods and I turn to Luke. "It was nice meeting you."

"See you around, Ace."

"I hope so," which is the truth. I like Luke Fox. There's a depth to him I haven't uncovered, a darkness hidden beneath his cheeky façade.

I turn back to Kelly, not ready to say goodbye just yet. "Walk me out?"

"You got it, babe."

He takes my hand, his palm warm and rough. My fingers curl into his, holding on as he leads the way. I keep my gaze to the ground. Partly because I don't want to stumble in the heels I rarely wear and partly because it's become second nature to stick to the shadows. Keep my face hidden in crowds. Be unobtrusive.

5

KELLY

I tug at Arcadia's hand, so small and unexpectedly delicate in mine. It reminds me she's not the kind of girl I'm used to. My usual encounters are with women who are hardened and rough. Experienced. The kind who can withstand the harshness inside of me with no expectations. I was raised in a household of violence, and from the age of fifteen, I belonged to the Sentinels. Warmth and kindness doesn't come naturally. The only affection I remember is a vague recollection of my mother's smiling eyes, of her kissing my brow at night before I slept, but it's fleeting. When I try grasping the memory, it slips through my fingers like sand.

We step outside. Cold blasts through me, right through the fibres of my suit to my skin. We're smack bang in the middle of winter, my least favourite time of the year.

Arcadia's gaze encompasses the back parking lot with surprise, shivering. "What are we doing out here?"

"Leaving."

She pulls at my hand, trying to free herself of my grip. I automatically squeeze tighter. "But I'm getting an Uber home."

"Not anymore."

"What?"

I shrug. "I'll take you home."

Her eyes narrow with suspicion. "Why?"

Yeah, Kelly. Why? I'm not for the likes of her, so why am I unable to let go of her hand? "Because I'm leaving anyway." It's an honest answer. I can never stay long at these parties. They're a reminder of how little I belong in that kind of world. They make me uncomfortable. I can never say or do the right thing, unless we're talking about bikes and cars. Mostly, I feel like a bull in a china shop, as if I'm going to break something at every turn. I look into Arcadia's stormy blue eyes. *Will I break you too?* Highly possible, but even that isn't enough to relax my hold. "Where do you live?"

She studies me, as if her time is precious and she's deciding whether she wants to spend any of it with me. Eventually, she appears to make a decision and rattles off her address.

I lead her through rows and rows of cars until we reach my bike. It's parked at the back by the gardens. She stops in front of it with furrowed brows, her eyes sliding across the gleaming metal and leather. "This is yours?"

Arcadia sounds surprised.

Now that I know she's not going to run, I release her hand. "Yeah."

"You ride a Harley."

"Yeah," I reply again, tugging at the tie around my neck. I loosen the knot and yank the torturous device over my head.

"But ..."

"But what?" I prompt as I stuff the tie in the side pocket of my saddlebag when I should be tossing it in the shrubs behind me instead.

"N-n-nothing."

Arcadia is stuttering from the cold. I didn't think to ask if she'd checked a coat before I dragged her out into the frigid air. *Stupid!* "You got a coat?"

"No."

I stare at her exposed skin when I've been trying to do anything but. It's smooth and golden, despite the chilly season of winter. I want to trail my fingers over her shoulders and down where her chest rises and falls. I want to feel that smoothness beneath the rough pads of my fingers.

I take a step closer, intending to do just that.

Arcadia's chest stops moving. She's holding her breath as if she knows exactly what I plan to do. "Do I make you nervous?"

"Yes. No." Her fingers clench into fists by her sides yet she holds her ground. "Yes. A little."

I process her confession. I'm surprised at her candour, but I find myself liking it. There are no games with honesty. No need to read between the lines when I struggle to simply read the lines.

I reach up and touch my index finger to her collarbone, where it protrudes sharply. Her eyes flutter closed. Just like that. The slightest contact. I trace a path along her skin. It's soft, like the fragile petals of a flower.

I exhale, my voice rough. "Do you like me touching you?"

Arcadia swallows and opens her eyes. "Yes."

"I should get you home."

"You should."

My finger trails lower, making no move to leave. "Have you been on a bike before?"

She shivers. "I have."

Arcadia's response evokes a vision of her riding the back of some other guy's bike, her hands on his waist, holding him tight, a smile of pure pleasure on her lips. I withdraw my touch, the image a barb.

"My brother's," she adds. "He used to own one. Not a Harley, but a Triumph Street Twin. It was a real retro classic. But he sold it."

"Your brother has taste."

She shrugs like she doesn't want to continue that line of conversation any further, and she wraps her arms around herself, rubbing them up and down. I move to my saddlebag, rifling through the contents for a jacket. I don't find one. I pull mine off and hold it out. "Put this on."

Arcadia shakes her head. "I'm okay."

"That wasn't a question. Put it on." I wave a hand toward her dress. "You can't ride a bike wearin' nothin' else but that."

She takes it, sliding her arms inside the sleeves and pulling it tight around her. The jacket hangs off her like a child playing dress-up, but she seems more relaxed. I grab my helmet next, a full-faced one in deference to the cold, and hold it out. "You can put this on too."

Her eyes fall on it. "No, I'm good."

My brows rise. First, she rejected my initial offer of a ride, then the jacket, and now the helmet. "Do you have a problem with me?"

Arcadia shakes her head. "No. I just don't want to wear it."

"Why not? Worried it's gonna mess your hair?" I tease. The pretty strands are pulled back into a complicated twist at the base of her neck.

"No!" She rolls her eyes, but there's laughter in them. "No ... I just, don't want to wear it."

"Safety first." I step inside her personal space and plonk it down over her head, flipping the visor. "There." She looks ridiculous in the oversized jacked, helmet, and heels. I wink. "Looks hot."

"Kelly!" she shouts, her voice muffled. She yanks it off, panting, hair and eyes wild. "I can't wear it, okay?"

The offending helmet is shoved into my gut. I take it because she's already let it go and turning to walk away.

"Hey!" I grab her bicep. She comes to a stuttering halt with a huff, and I drop my hand. "What the hell is wrong with you, Ace? It's just a goddamn helmet."

Gritting her teeth, Arcadia closes her eyes for a moment. When she opens them, she's glaring with frustration, her cheeks pink. "I suffer from claustrophobia." She gestures at the helmet in my hand. "I can't breathe in those things. I can't breathe in elevators. Or locked rooms. Planes. Traffic congestion." She exhales a slow, even breath, as if trying to find calm. "It's ... debilitating. Sometimes. So maybe I should get that Uber."

"Shit. I'm sorry." She seems embarrassed, so I don't make a big deal out of it by saying anything more. Instead, I jerk my head toward my bike. "Climb on. I'll drive slow. Use the back streets."

After shoving the helmet in my saddlebag, I swing a leg over and sit. As the bike settles beneath my weight, I turn to Arcadia, expectant. She has to hike up her dress a little and hops on behind me with less hesitation than I expected. Her thighs press on either side of me and her front against me as she relaxes into the seat. I stifle a groan.

"Hold on, babe," I instruct, my voice raspy with want.

Her arms slide around my middle as the bike roars to life, her hands linking at my waist. Her hold is firm, trusting. I place a hand on both of hers and turn my head, giving her a sideways glance. All I catch with my eyes is her profile, but there's a smile on her lips. One of anticipation. She's excited.

"You good?" I ask loudly.

Arcadia's smile morphs into a grin. "Giddy-up, cowboy!"

I laugh and shake my head. I've never had this kind of interaction with a female before. Where it's fun and easy. It's not for lack of trying. I'm just no good at it. Perhaps it's the women I hook up with too. They don't want a connection, not with a guy like me, and it never seemed to bother me. I thought I was getting a great deal, fucking around with no strings. But this ... Arcadia makes it easy. She's making me see what it could be like and maybe I want more.

Maybe.

The drive to Arcadia's house isn't anywhere near long enough. Her frequent jostling makes me hard as she twists and turns, taking in the sights around us. I take the scenic route, navigating the beach streets slowly. It allows her time to appreciate the ride and me to appreciate her tits rubbing against my back. Whenever I pull up at a red light, she leans in close to offer directions. Her breath tickles my ear and sends waves of lust crashing over me until I'm drowning in it.

"I don't want this to end," she says at the next red light, her voice loud to be heard and husky from the chilled air. We're almost at her house, having taken an inordinate amount of time travelling north along Sydney's eastern beaches.

"Me either," I reply, but the light turns green, and my words are lost to the wind as I accelerate into the night.

We reach her house and I pull into a paved driveway. It's a quaint style cottage, painted white with navy trim. The lawns are a lush green with overflowing climbers bursting with flowers of pink, most of their petals closed as if sleeping for the night. I was expecting a bland yet sleek apartment of some sort. Probably based on my first impressions of her being a desk jockey and studying books thicker than the pipes on my bike. But this place has charm and personality, much like Arcadia herself.

She climbs off while I'm studying the exterior, and the chill inside of me returns at the loss of her body heat. I turn off the bike. It's late at night and the silence surrounds us, almost deafening in its intensity.

"Thanks for the ride, Kelly."

"You're welcome, Arcadia," I reply, my tone stiff.

She hesitates, and this is where I'm expecting the brush off. The drive would have been sobering, the vodka in her system wearing off and leaving her lucid. Enough to remind her I'm not her type. That I'm not anywhere good enough. I swallow the uncomfortable rise of disappointment. I wouldn't know what to do with a girl other than fuck her anyway, so it doesn't matter.

"You can call me, Ace."

I nod. "Ace." This is the part where I should leave but curiosity has the better of me. "How'd you get that nickname?"

A smile kicks up at the corners of her mouth. "Why don't you come inside and I'll tell you."

"You want me to come inside?"

She shrugs and shifts a little on her heels. "Yeah. I do. I can make coffee?"

Coffee is just a euphemism for *let's fuck,* right? I'm on board with that, though it niggles at me—the thought of this being a one-time thing. *What if I want more than that?* Then I realise I sound like a girl. Fox would laugh his ass off if he could hear what was going through my head right now.

"Sure, babe," I reply smoothly, offering a wink as I slide from the bike. "I'd love a coffee."

Arcadia

KELLY FOLLOWS me up the stairs to the little timber porch. This big hulking hunk of man is right behind me, his steps heavy, his scent surrounding me in a cloud of male pheromones that set my lady parts throbbing. What am I *doing*?

All I know is that I'm not emotionally prepared for him to leave. That ride on his bike was ... freeing. For a small window of time, I had no troubles. I just had someone big and warm to hold on to as we rode through the night. I'm not ready to let that feeling go, which means I'm not ready to let him go.

I flick my gaze behind me as we reach the front door. He offers me an intense stare, unsettling me in all kinds of delicious ways. "You ah ... need to turn around."

His brows rise high on his forehead. "I need to turn around?"

"The key," I say. "It's ah ... hidden near the door and I need to retrieve it."

"Babe." His blue eyes spark with exasperation. "I thought you were smarter than that."

"I am," I reply, a little defensively. "It might be near the door, but it's not in a spot that anyone would ever find."

"Okay, okay." He holds up his hands, surrendering as he turns around. I wait a few moments to make sure he's not peeking, then I scramble quickly for the key.

I have potted plants along the porch, positioned against the weatherboard exterior. Wedged in each are little solar lights. They get hit with the afternoon sun and light up at night. It's pretty. Sometimes I'll sit on the porch step at night with Mason, chattering with a beer as we watch the sun go down.

I yank out the nearest solar light and unscrew the base. The little metal key tumbles into my hand. I re-screw the base, push it back in the pot, and straighten.

"Okay, you can turn back now."

Kelly turns, his eyes searing as they rove over me. It fills my belly with butterflies. So many I feel I may throw up. I spin for the door, jamming the key inside the lock. It twists beneath my fingers, and I open it. It creaks lightly and I wince.

"You live alone?" Kelly asks as we step inside.

The house is dark and quiet inside. I bend, flicking on the switch of the nearest lamp. A warm glow fills the room, illuminating the cosy living area, dining nook, and kitchen. It's small but it's mine. I take off his jacket and lay it neatly across the back of the couch.

"No," I say over my shoulder as I move to the kitchen. Kelly is overwhelming the space, making his shoulders appear even wider than I remember them to be. It's like parking a Mack truck inside my house. "My older brother and I live here."

Kelly baulks. "He home?"

"He was when I left." And I've no doubt he's still here and fast asleep. Mason is not a partygoer. He's a homebody, preferring the company of friends and simple outings, like barbeques and movies. I pick up the kettle and move to the sink. My gaze flicks up as water gushes from the tap, filling it. Kelly appears unsettled, as if Mason is about to charge out from a nearby room with a baseball bat. "He'll be fast asleep, but we can have our coffee outside or ... in my room."

Those searing eyes burn hotter.

Holy Jesus.

I turn off the tap and switch the kettle on, getting out my little coffee plunger. "There's only two bedrooms in the house, but we have a bathroom each. My room is on that side," I say, pointing to his right, "and Mason's on the other side."

Kelly starts toward me like an animal on the hunt, which I believe makes me the vulnerable gazelle right now. My breath catches and I whirl for the fridge, grabbing out the coffee beans. When I shut the door and turn, he's *right there,* his chest in line with my eyes. I grip tightly to the bag of beans and lift my eyes.

"You were serious about the coffee," he utters, his voice low.

"Yes," I croak and clear my throat. "You don't want one?"

Kelly cocks his head, studying me as if the question I asked was more complex than a mathematical equation. Eventually he seems to reach a decision, and a smile tugs at the corners of his lips. "A coffee would be real nice, but right now there's something I want more."

"What?" The word escapes on a harsh exhale because I've forgotten to take a breath.

He ducks his head and a rough palm grabs my jaw, tilting my head up further. "A kiss."

"Just a kiss?"

"Babe. When I kiss, it's not just a kiss."

I grin and bite down on my bottom lip, stopping it from spreading too wide because he's made me a bit giddy. I don't want to let the crazy out too soon.

"Bring it then, cowboy."

Kelly huffs but his eyes are light. "I'm no cowboy."

"You rode that bike like you were born doing it. Like it was just an extension of yourself. It was ..." I can't think of the right word.

"It was what?" he prompts as the kettle flicks off, finishing its boil and returning stillness to the little kitchen.

"Natural. Beautiful."

"You callin' me beautiful, shorty?"

"I'm not short!"

"Shorter than me." Kelly grins and smacks his lips to mine. A fast kiss. One filled with humour and pleasure, as if he's enjoying me. Then he lets go of my jaw and backs up a step.

"So that's it?" I taunt, making my way back to the island bench. "That's your big kiss?"

Kelly leans sideways against the fridge where I left him and folds his arms. "That wasn't a kiss."

I arch a brow as I count out scoops of ground coffee and dump them in the plunger. "What would you call it, then?"

"A meeting of the lips and nothing more."

"Well okay, then." Though my mouth is still tingling from where his lips met mine. The possibility of feeling more than that leaves me antsy. I make the coffee and set out two mugs, trying to focus on the task at hand or risk third-degree burns. "Sugar? Milk?"

"Neither."

"Huh." Same as me. Black coffee. Strong and unassuming. I gesture to the mugs. "Carry those?"

I pick up the full plunger. Kelly follows behind as I lead him toward my bedroom. It's late and too cold to be sitting outside. My room is private and cosy. I flick on the bedside lamp and set the coffee on my desk, pushing aside overflowing papers and books.

Kelly looks around as he steps inside, and I try and see it from his eyes. It's a busy room, but it's oddly soothing. At least to me. Framed family photos are positioned on my desk and walls. Textbooks fill shelves and papers are piled high. Quickly scrawled Post-it notes litter my open laptop, reminders of assignments due and upcoming exams. Being only one of two bedrooms, it's a large space. My bed is a king and smothered with cushions and plush quilts and blankets in colours of grey and pale lemon.

He picks up a heavy textbook and reads the title. "Financial Institutions and Markets. Sounds ... riveting."

Kelly makes it sound anything but. I roll my eyes and laugh. "Be quiet. It's actually not too bad."

He looks at me, aghast. "Babe."

I shrug and sink to the edge of my bed. "At least finance and numbers make sense in world where nothing seems to make sense anymore. They make me feel ..." I hesitate as he opens the text and flicks through the pages, wondering if I'll sound silly, but then I forge on. What's the worst that could happen if he thinks me odd? "... safe."

Kelly pauses his flicking and pins me with his eyes. "Is there a reason you need to feel safe?"

My chest seizes, and I don't know how to breathe around it. How has he read me so easily? There's nothing safe about living life on the edge, even though it calls to me regardless. The anticipation of it. The recklessness. The wild. My heart races just thinking about it. But I'm tired of that same recklessness. And wild.

"There's a special kind of freedom in safety," I answer. "With it you're free to do what you want or be who you want to be. You can have a future."

"So you want to be an investment banker because it's safe?"

He sounds unconvinced and a chuckle escapes me. "Something

like that." I bend and unbuckle the straps of my heels, kicking them off with a groan.

Kelly crouches in front of me, bringing us to eye level. His palms find my knees, his calloused hands scratchy against my skin. The feeling is deliciously welcome. "We all need somewhere where we feel safe."

"Where do you feel safe?"

It's a ridiculous question. Kelly is mammoth. The type no one would dare cross swords with. How would he ever feel unsafe?

He leans in and rubs his nose against mine. "Now is not the time for me to answer that question."

My voice is a whisper. "It's not?"

"No. Some other time though, yeah?"

"Why not now?"

Kelly's lips brush mine and my breath catches at the intimacy and the thrill of it. "Because you're not ready to hear the answer."

We stare at each other for a moment, the only sound the soft breathing between us. Then he kisses me again. This time I agree with him; it's so much more than just a kiss. Kelly's tongue sweeps inside my mouth. I moan deep in my throat, responding, blood heating in my veins.

The pins in my hair fall soundless to the bed when he grabs a fistful, tugging with a gentle force. It sends powerful waves of hunger crashing over me. My lips mash against his, needing more, deepening the kiss until everything goes dark inside my mind. There's only this. Him. An endless pleasure that I never want to end.

Kelly breaks the kiss and stands abruptly, backing up a step, then another, his eyes locked on mine. His chest rises and falls rapidly. "I don't ..."

"You don't what?" I prompt when he trails off. My wits are scattered to all four corners, and I take great satisfaction in seeing that his are too. I'm not the only one feeling whatever this is.

6

KELLY

I *don't know what the hell this is, but it's like nothing I've ever felt before.* I wouldn't ordinarily stop at one kiss. I would have that dress ripped off moments later, my pawing hands all over that rich golden skin. But I can't bring myself to keep kissing her. Arcadia is like fine silver, and my touch feels like a tarnish, dirtying everything that makes her shine so beautifully.

My hands fist at my sides. I'm out of my depth and don't know where to go to from this point. I don't even know what to say. I'm usually confident. I can be a real sweet talker, making moves to get what I want, but this is a move I've never made before. It makes what felt so easy before feel frustrating. I should leave but my feet appear glued to the floorboards.

Arcadia clears her throat and stands, reaching for the plunger. "How about that coffee?"

"I'll do it," I mutter, thankful for the opportunity to get the fuck over myself.

I pour the black liquid into two navy mugs. One has a small chip on the rim. I keep that one for myself and offer her the other. She takes it and resettles on the bed.

I take a seat beside her, sinking into the plush bedding. The quilt puffs up around me as if I seated myself on a cloud. It's kinda ... nice.

"How long have you had your bike for?" she asks.

"That particular one?" I scratch the back of my head, counting time. "I've had her for about eighteen months."

"She's a real beauty." Arcadia says it like she means it, and I like that. How she only speaks words that are truthful. "How long have you been riding for?"

"A long time, babe. Years. Since I was a teenager. It's almost spiritual, you know? Like you're a bird riding the wind," I say, trying to conjure the emotion so I can easily explain it. And I *want* her to understand. She was so open about herself when I asked that it makes sharing that much easier. "There's only one thing in your head the entire time."

"What's that?" she asks, reaching across to set her empty mug on the desk by the bed. Then she reclines back, snuggling into the pillows behind her.

"Joy," I say simply, staring down into my coffee. "I never really experienced that feeling 'til I rode my first bike." I bring the mug to my lips, tipping it back and finishing the last mouthful. "I never looked back after that."

I plonk my mug next to hers and stand, my hands going to the buttons on my shirt.

"What are you doing?"

I pause and wink. "Gettin' more comfortable, shorty. That okay?"

Arcadia's lips curve in a lazy smile. It's compelling and sexy and my fingers return to the buttons, undoing them in rapid succession. I peel the dress shirt off, dumping it happily to the floor. It leaves me in an undershirt and pants. I leave those on but remove the belt. Feeling a little more like myself, I stretch out on the bed beside her.

"Are you tired?" she asks as I settle on my back, resting my hands on my stomach.

"A little."

"Me too."

Her hand comes to rest on my forearm. I suck in a silent breath as she trails her fingers along the skin. "You have so many tattoos. They're unexpected. But they're beautiful." Arcadia reads aloud the words inked on the inside of my arm, near my elbow. "Forget what hurt you, but never forget what it taught you." She turns on her side, looking directly at me. "What hurt you?"

I don't know how to answer her question. I don't want to. To have her know what I came from and the person it made me. I saw the way Casey looked at me when he found out I was a Sentinel. His expression was one of bitter disappointment. He only knew me as his little brother, but the day we reunited after *years,* he looked at me as if nothing could fix the man I'd become. He wanted to save me from myself, but it's too late for that. I'm not ashamed of being a biker brother, but I'm not stupid. We're not considered an honourable lot. And I've done shitty things. I'm not a good person. But Arcadia is looking at me right now as if I'm everything she's been looking for her entire life. I've never had that before and I'm not ready to give it up just yet.

"The past," I eventually answer. "It can be a real shitty place to visit in your head sometimes."

Her fingers stop moving on my forearm for a brief moment. Then they curl around it, warm and soothing. "What brings you joy?" I ask her, wanting to shift away from the dark and heavy path our conversation is heading down.

"Cars."

I turn my head swiftly to look at her. "You fuckin' serious?"

Arcadia grins and deepens her voice to mimic mine. "I'm fuckin' serious."

"What kind?"

"Any kind, but I love originals. Classics. Cars with power and character. I grew up around them thanks to my grandfather's obsession. He taught me how to drive, always saying that I should smoke tyres, not drugs."

"Yeah?" I chuckle quietly. "What else did he say?"

"You want to know his prayer when it's his turn to say grace before we eat Sunday dinner?"

I nod, fascinated at the idea of family dinners. Growing up in my house, we weren't allowed to start until our father sat down at the table. And there was no grace. There was only tension and fear, and that sick feeling of being hungry but not wanting to eat.

Arcadia tells me around the smile on her face, showing an exasperated kind of affection for her grandfather. "As I lay rubber down the street, I pray for traction I can keep, but if I spin and begin to slide, please dear God protect my ride."

I laugh. "I like him. Did he drag?"

"In his younger years. Not so much now. He travels a lot."

"And what's your car?"

She heaves a deep, dreamy sigh, as though picturing it in her head. "A 1967 Ford Mustang Fastback."

Taste. She has it in spades. And I can see why someone would choose that car, but I'm curious as to why *she* has. "Why? Why the '67?"

"Because she's full-bodied and hot-blooded. Because vintage has more character. Sixty-seven was the first redesign of the original model," she says, telling me what I already know, but *she* knows. I let her talk, hearing the passion in her voice and recognising it in myself. "And it's got the big-block V8 engine. I have her in the garage at my parents' house."

"Holy shit. Fully restored?"

"Not even close. I was in Northern California on holiday when I stumbled across her during an eBay search. She looked just like another old junk car in the lot, dumped down in the back because no one wanted her. She's rough. Maybe too rough to restore. The drivetrain is out and there's a bunch of parts stuffed in the boot. She didn't deal well with being shipped here to Australia either." Arcadia's voice turns wistful. "But she could be beautiful. One day."

I like that she can see the beauty in something broken and discarded. It gives me hope that maybe she could see it in me too.

I make mention that it might be worthwhile tracking down the original owner, and we talk cars into the night, until I find I'm talking to myself. She's drifted off. I should leave but instead I find myself drifting too.

————————

It's early morning when I wake, disoriented for just a moment until I figure out my surroundings. The palest light drifts through the sheer curtains that cover the bedroom window. It lights the profile of Arcadia. She's still deep in sleep, but she's moved around during the night. Her hair is mussed and the front of her dress has shifted sideways and up, revealing naked thighs and the full swell of her right tit. A pale pink nipple puckers in the cool air.

I'm only human and it's begging for my tongue. I want the taste of her on my lips, and the feel of her in my mouth to carry me through the day. Instead of giving in, I tug the material across and cover her up.

Arcadia releases a sleepy moan and shifts but doesn't fully waken. I don't have the option of touching her the way I want to. I have so much shit to get done today, so I draw back. Getting to my feet, I leave the bed and grab the blanket that sits folded at the end, pulling it up to keep her covered. I collect my rumpled shirt from the floor and scrawl my name and number on a piece of paper on her desk.

I leave her room, pulling the door closed behind me and tugging my arms through the sleeves of my shirt.

"Who are you?" demands a hard male voice.

I stop short. There's a man seated at the table in the dining nook. It's her brother. They look alike, though his features are obviously more masculine and his skin a little more tanned. And where Arcadia's eyes hold the stormy seas inside them, his right now are holding the burning fires of Hell.

"You must be Mason."

"Yes, but who are you, and what are you doing coming out of my sister's bedroom in the early hours of the morning?"

I was hoping to avoid the wrath of an older brother. Seems it's not gonna be my lucky day. He remains seated as I walk toward him, my shirt unbuttoned. "Kelly Daniels," I say, holding out a hand. He glares at it like it's an insect that crawled into his morning eggs. I drop it to my side.

"You're a Sentinel," he says, spitting the word as if it's a foul and bitter taste on his tongue.

I nod. Mason has been outside and inspected my bike. He's seen the badge of my biker brethren painted on the side. The *opposite* side to where Arcadia stood beside it last night, missing the details.

"Leave," Mason's voice is steel. He rolls back from the table, and it's only then that I realise he's in a wheelchair. He starts toward me, biceps bulging as he rolls the wheels in hard, jerky movements. His eyes are rigid and determined, leaving me in no doubt he's fully capable of throwing me out. "You're not welcome here."

"Ace would beg to differ," I retort unwisely, but Arcadia's brother appears to be an asshole, and I'm entitled to defend myself.

"Ace doesn't get a say."

"She can speak for herself. It's not up to you to—"

He moves further toward me, his eyes narrowing. "I'm her big brother. It's my job to speak for her if I know what I'm speaking is in her best interests."

Mason's words send me spiralling inside a childhood memory.

I'D JUST WALKED inside the back door of our house after school. It was better to sneak in that way in case Dad was home and on a rampage. Casey and I usually walked home together, but he had a free period and got to leave early. He was rushing toward me. At fourteen he was all long limbs and big feet that almost tripped him up. Blood trickled down the side of his face.

Bile rose in my throat, the same way it always did when Dad got violent. Bile and fear. It was a combination that made me dread coming home each day, not knowing if it was going to be a bad day or a day where we could sneak under our father's radar.

"Go!"

Casey pushed at me, propelling me through the door. When we were outside he grabbed my arm and we ran. The yard backed on to an old creek bed. We leaped the low-wire fence and navigated through water and rocks until he deemed us a safe distance away to stop.

When we did, Casey tugged off his shirt and crouched, wetting it in the trickling water.

"What did he do?" I asked.

"I left my shoes in the front hallway. He tripped over them and shoved me headfirst into the wall." Squeezing out the shirt, he rose and touched it to the side of his face, hissing at the contact. "Is it bad?" he asked me.

I swallowed and took a look. It was a split brow and nasty. Tears stung my eyes, causing my nose to fizz and burn. I blinked and turned away. "It's nothing." But it wasn't nothing. It needed a stitch. Or glue. "But maybe—" I bit down on my bottom lip when it began to quiver. "Maybe we should go get it checked out."

Casey's refusal was unyielding. "No."

"But—"

"You want them to split us up? Because that's what'll happen if we go flaunting this kind of shit around town." He pressed the shirt harder to his brow, his voice an angry hiss. "I'm your big brother, Kelly. It's my job to know what's best for both us."

"And *you* are not in her best interests," Mason continues, snapping me out of the memory. He's looking at me like I'm no better than shit on the bottom of his shoe. "So like I said before, leave."

My jaw ticks as I breathe in and out. I can't fault him for playing the over-protective brother card. The same card Casey used to play for me. But the difference in this scenario is that Mason never left.

I turn and walk out, grabbing my jacket where it still hangs over the back of the couch. When I step out onto the porch, I see a ramp on the right-hand side that I didn't notice in the dark of last night. For Mason.

I jog the set of steps to my bike and shove the jacket in my saddle-bag. When I leave, I roll my bike out of the drive before starting it. When I turn the key, the engine rumbles to life, vibrating through every cell in my body. It's a hum that soothes the beast raging inside of me.

7

ARCADIA

*P*hone in hand, I shut my bathroom door behind me with a giddiness that has me doing a booty shake. *Oh yeah, oh yeah.* I pump my arms. Kelly likes me. Kelly *likes* me. I bounce sideways and twerk my butt. *Oh yeah, I got it going on.* Why else would he gift me with his number? But what time did he leave? I fell asleep, but I'm sure I felt the heat of his body during the night. When I woke this morning, the sun was high in the sky and the house was empty. Mason was likely still at his morning swim session, but Kelly was gone. Disappointment had hit me like a brick to the face, until I found the scrap of paper on my desk. Ignoring all the messages and missed calls piled up on my screen, I quickly added him to my contacts just in case the piece of paper spontaneously combusted or something of the like.

Finishing up my dance moves, I turn to the bathroom mirror and shriek.

"No," I breathe with horror. Then I reach up, touching my reflection because I need to be sure it's real. My eye makeup is smeared down my face, and there's a giant puffy ball of hair sticking out the right side of my head, resembling a bird's nest. I'm a freak show. Did Kelly see me like this? It feels imperative that I know.

I open messages on my phone and create a new one. I call up his name from the newly added contact. Then I move to the text section and hover with uncertainty. The cursor blinks at me, on and off, persistent and mocking, pressuring me to come up with some exceptional opener that Kelly will find both amusing and cute, thus compelling him to respond. But what do I say?

"Hell," I mutter as potential approaches flit through my mind. I discard each one as garbage. This isn't supposed to be hard. Maybe I should just keep it simple. *Yes.* I'm trying too hard. Kelly is a cool dude. He'll respond to coolness. Like attracts like, doesn't it? Or does it?

Go figure. I can steal a car, but when it comes to messaging a guy, I lose my marbles. I set my phone down and cross to the bath. After I flick on the taps, I add my special frankincense bath oils and matching bubbles. The scent is supposed to ease stress and anxiety, and I obviously need all the help I can get right now. Then I open the wide window that sits above the tub. It provides a pretty backdrop of the colourful garden and emits fresh air and a little warmth from the sun.

Right. I can do this. I pick up my phone as hot water gushes outward, creating mounds of bubbles and filling the room with steam. Simple text message, come at me. I start tapping.

Me: Hey you!

Oh my god. That sounds so perky, like I'm figuratively slapping him in the face with a hello. Delete, delete, delete.

Me: How's your Sunday?

So. Much. Worse. It reeks of boredom and someone fishing for more information, which I am, but not in a way that I want to be obvious. Delete, delete, delete.

Me: You left your number behind, so I thought I'd use it.

Ugh. I can't even with that one. Delete, delete, delete.

Dammit, Acehole! (That's the name Mason gives me when I'm being a tool, which feels entirely appropriate in this situation). Just be yourself.

There's nothing more myself than something car related, so I attach an image I have on my phone of my sweet Mustang in all her irreparable glory, with a message.

Me: Sending you a sexy pic to start your day off right ;)

Send.

Done.

I sigh, feeling utterly exhausted.

After turning off the taps, I set the phone beside the tub in case he replies. Then I peel off last night's dress and panties and climb in. Heat and frankincense surround me on every level. I surrender to it, tipping my head back against the edge of the bath and closing my eyes.

Then three things happen all at once, as if magically orchestrated by an evil mastermind bent on ruining my day and perhaps my life.

"Oi," Echo barks at me from the open window, startling me into sloshing water over the bathroom floor. Bubbles fly in every direction. My best friend is no doubt here to instigate a new plan for the Firebird, along with bitching me out for last night. Her glare is fiery, at odds with the pink halo of hair surrounding her head. She mostly dyes the pretty crop white, but lately she's been trialling the cotton candy trend. It competes with her dark brown eyes and dark slash of eyebrows, giving her an edgy, sexy look.

Before I can wipe the bubbles from my face, the bathroom door opens with an ominous bang. "We need to talk," Mason growls.

I blink through a soapy haze. My brother is glaring too. "What the hell? I'm in the *bath*. Get out!" I can understand Echo's pissy attitude, but I wasn't expecting an attack from the other front.

Then my phone begins to ring, and my pulse rate kicks up to high gear. My gaze darts to the screen, but it's not Kelly. My hopeful heart deflates. It's Tony Marchetti.

His call sends reality crashing down like a skyscraper under demolition.

What am I *doing*?

I was supposed to deliver the Firebird last night. It was prearranged and they were setup to take delivery. Instead, I delivered nothing. And now I'm here, luxuriating in a bath and getting giddy over a guy, when I also have a paper due on Monday.

I'm ashamed of myself and my behaviour. I checked out last night; Kelly made me forget who I am, and what I have going on, and with what I have going on, I can't afford to check out. This time it's not just about money or the rush of stealing a car, it's about keeping my family alive.

I swipe at the bubbles on my face. Echo has disappeared from the window, no doubt making her way inside, but Mason remains, and his eyes are on my phone. His jaw is ticking, and when he speaks, his voice is glacial. "Are you going to answer that?"

"No, I'm not going to answer that," I mutter, knowing I'm treading on very thin ice right now.

"Why is he calling you?"

Each word he speaks is measured and controlled, making me wince. I'm not fooled. My brother's measured tone means he's reached the point beyond fury.

Mason is the biggest advocate of my retirement. The beamer was supposed to be my last boost, and he knows it. My ties with Tony Marchetti should be severed. So of course I never mentioned *the list* to my brother. He would be furious to know that I'm not out. *Furious.*

Mason *used* to be the best in the business before his disability. Never arrested, no convictions. He could get any car he wanted and always remained one step ahead of everyone, including me. They called him The Ghost.

My brother pushed every limit, and every boundary, but we all know that you can only push so far before your number gets called.

His got called up early last year. We boosted a car together. A 1970 Chevrolet Chevelle. She was a beast, with her sleek black body and white stripes. The guy who owned her, they call him Grinder, was absolute scum. He raped Julianna, Mason's best friend's girlfriend, late one night when she was walking home from the train station after work. Julianna was strong enough to face her attacker and lay charges, but the police couldn't get them to stick and they let him go.

It happened three years ago, but Mason has a long memory, a lot of patience, and a powerful thirst for revenge.

We stole that car but it all went horribly wrong. It haunts me every night when I sleep, and every time I look at my brother, especially now.

"WHAT IS IT?" I asked Mason when he kept glancing in his rear-view mirror. It was late at night, and we were speeding along the M1 Motorway in the stolen Chevelle, heading east. The boost was a breeze, and the car was handling every corner beautifully, making me itch to take the wheel. Sitting on my hands when my brother drove a car like this one made me antsy. But this wasn't a joy ride. This was retribution.

"Nothing," he muttered, shooting me an angry glare.

I'm not supposed to be here, but I wanted the same satisfaction my brother was getting from fucking Grinder over. Julianna was a beautiful person and a friend, but she cut ties with her past. We lost her the day of the attack, and we never got her back.

Five minutes later, Mason sped up. It was not unusual. We were on a mostly deserted dual carriageway. Opening up a ride as beautiful as this one was customary. Except this was Grinder's car, and this was a boost. One of the most important rules on a boost was to drive a fraction beneath the speed limit. Going too fast only attracted attention from unsavoury hoons and the police.

"Slow down," I cautioned.

"I would, but—" He glanced in the rear-view mirror again.

"But what?"

"But we have a tail."

My heart began to thump and a cold sweat broke out across my brow. I glanced behind us, seeing two sets of headlights in the distance. "You said it was nothing!"

"Because I didn't want to say anything when I wasn't sure. But I'm sure now."

"How did we pick up a tail?"

The questioned begged asking because we didn't have one before. We were free and clear. "I don't know!"

"Dammit, Mason." I glanced behind us again. The headlights were getting closer. "Speed up!"

He planted his foot, but not hard enough for my liking. "Harder!"

"Shut your mouth, Acehole, and let me focus on driving. I don't want the police involved."

"I'd rather the police than Grinder and his friends catching up with us." I was reminded of the stories I'd heard about what they did to those who cross them. It made my claustrophobic fear rear its ugly head. "Oh god, Mason, they'll bury us alive in a big dirt hole in the middle of some godforsaken forest. We'll slowly suffocate to death and die."

"They're not going to catch us."

But his voice was grim and didn't reassure me in the least. He planted his foot as we reached the nearest off-ramp. It was more dangerous to navigate the suburban streets, but it was easier to lose a tail.

"Let me take the wheel."

We peeled through the red light of a deserted intersection. "No."

"I'm a better driver than you." It was true. I spent time in the Sydney Rally Car Club while Mason spent his time playing boring sports like cricket and rugby. He might be The Ghost, but I was the Ace. Mason thought the sport was for lunatics, and I admit that most rally drivers were crazy, but it was the ultimate sport. Standard race cars were built for durability and withstanding stress, intense breaking and cornering. Motocross bikes were designed to take a beating, riding over dirt courses without losing speed. NASCAR stockers were over-built. They pushed through the air at crazy speeds, yet needed to be ready to hit the wall or other cars. Rally cars could do all of that at once.

The most crucial skill I learned? You didn't always know what was around the next bend, so you had to adjust on the fly.

"This is not a rally car, Ace."

"No shit!"

We took a sharp turn, and I held on, white-knuckling the dash. The back end slid out and we almost hit the wall. "Mason!"

He oversteered, adjusting, grappling, accelerating. "I got it." The Chevelle growled. "Sorry, baby," he muttered to her.

After two minutes of intense driving, we backed into an alley, switched off the engine, and killed the lights. It plunged us into darkness. A scant second later, motorcycles roared past the main road. They kept going. Then we heard them stop, and my heart attempted to beat its way out of my chest. "Did they see us?"

"No way." Mason shook his head but his tone was unsure. "They couldn't have."

But that ominous roar was coming back toward us, and the flare of headlights got brighter. I held my breath and body still, almost as though they wouldn't see us if I didn't move.

They came to a halt at the alley way entrance. "Mason, fuck!"

Jaw tight, he restarted the engine, and the Chevelle bellowed like a lion woken from sleep. My brother jammed the gear into reverse and slammed his foot on the accelerator. "Sonofabitch." He gripped the steering wheel in one hand, forearm muscles bulging and veins popping, and twisted his head, using his other hand to seize the back of my headrest, speeding backward with his eyes focused out the back window. "They must have a goddamn tracker on the car!"

My stomach churned with fear and frustration and a whole lot of disbelief. "You didn't check it?"

"I did," Mason protested. "I did. I—" He broke off for a moment, his expression horrified. "Fuck. I didn't check."

"Oh no. Oh lordy. Mason. Your nine lives."

His voice was grim. "They're up."

One error. That's all it took. When you were off your game, it was only a downward spiral from there.

We reached the back of the alley. Mason slowed down in anticipation of oncoming traffic. He eased out as fast as he could, spinning the steering wheel in a giant arc as he aligned us in the right direction of the road. But before he could punch the accelerator, bikes pulled up in front of us, blocking our path.

"Fuck." He threw the Chevelle in reverse, cursing again when he checked his rear-view mirror.

I looked behind us. We were blocked there too. A big truck had come to rest sideways on our tail. Mason had made a rookie mistake, allowing them to ambush us with a proficiency we never expected. There was no escape.

I expected my life to flash before my eyes—parts of it that made me who I am today. Like the time when I was five and my parents took me and my brother to my first theme park. I cried for an hour when I found out I was too short to ride the rollercoaster. I ended up on the dodgem cars instead. For *hours*. Mason had to drag me out of the little car, kicking and screaming. Then there was the time my grandad, Racer Jones, began teaching me how to drive a *real* car not long after I turned seven. I remember it clearly, him laughing his ass off when I punched his car into a wall. I'd sustained no injuries on account of the fact that all I'd done was lift the hand-brake. The car had rolled forward two metres and nudged the garage door. Then there was my first kiss with Jamie Hall, a.k.a Dragon, behind the school sports shed where the equipment was kept. He was nicknamed thus because he accidentally set his school desk on fire when he was eleven and Ben Benedict swore the flames came from his mouth. Mason punched Dragon in the school parking lot after final bell and got suspended for three days. It wasn't until two years later that another boy attempted to kiss me, and only because he was the new kid in town and didn't know any better.

I expected all that and more to flash before my eyes, but Mason grabbed my hand instead. His eyes were wide on mine, urgent and panicked. "No matter what happens, I need you to run okay? Don't look back. Just run."

His command sent shivers of dread skittering down my spine. They were really going to kill us. I was going to die today. This was no nightmare. This was *real*. Terror bubbled to the surface. I kept swallowing it down but it was rising so fast I felt myself choking on it.

Mason shoved open his car door, jerking me out with him. I

scrambled across the seats, the gear stick jamming into my thigh. A whimper of pain escaped me but I didn't stop.

He yanked me free and shoved me in front of him. "Run!"

I stumbled, lurching over as I lost my balance. Mason pushed me again, *hard*, propelling me forward before I hit the pavement head-first. Heart in my throat, I righted myself and I *ran*. I heard him right behind me as my legs pumped hard and my lungs gasped for air, his footfalls heavy and breathing harsh. I didn't know what I was running toward, but I knew what I was running away from. There was yelling, then I heard the distinct sound of gunfire.

Oh god. *They were shooting at us!*

"Mason!" I cried, feeling the slide of burning heat across my arm.

"You're fine! You're fine! Just don't stop."

I glanced behind us. Those that had trapped us weren't chasing, they were lingering by their bikes, but Grinder wasn't. He was not far behind us, his expression containing so much rage his face was red with it. He stopped and raised his gun again, aiming.

I turned forward, unable to look.

Just focus on running.

He fired. The shot crackled through the air, a sound I would never forget.

Mason jerked, slamming into me from behind with a grunt. I went down with no time to break my fall. My head cracked against the pavement and blackness embraced me with open arms.

I had no idea how long I was out, but when I came to, my brother was unconscious on top of me, and they were gone, along with Chevelle.

"Mason," I cried, my voice a breathless gasp. I nudged him, yet he didn't move. "Oh god, oh god, oh god."

I managed to twist my body over, dragging it out from beneath him. The back of his shirt was covered in blood. A moan of horror rose from my chest. I pressed shaky fingers to his throat, feeling for a pulse. It was there. "Okay," I breathed, exhaling, shivering from shock. It was cold and dark, and the streets were empty. I had never felt more scared or more alone. "It's going to be okay," I sobbed, reassuring myself before I lost it, not realising I already had.

"WHY IS HE CALLING YOU?" Mason enunciates again, ripping me from the memory as he glares at me from his wheelchair. My brother's spinal cord was damaged from Grinder's bullet, but at least he's alive. Grinder is in prison, charged with attempted murder. We've had to lie low ever since, fearing reprisal from the Sentinels, his biker brethren, ever since.

"I have no idea. So get out, okay?" I say, angered because I'm lying, and I hate having to lie. I promised him, *promised him,* that I would stop after I delivered the BMW. We had needed that last hit of money. The refurbishments to our cottage to accommodate Mason's disability had drained all our funds, and his rehab bills were enormous.

He jabs his finger at me. "Don't you dare call him back."

"Mason! Get. Out."

"No." His jaw tightens. "We still need to talk."

I can hear bustling in the kitchen. Echo is making herself something to eat while Mason badgers me. She *adores* food. She's always shopping for it, cooking it, looking at it, and eating it. "Later," I tell my brother. "In case you haven't noticed, I'm trying to have a bath."

"I don't give two shits about your bath." Mason's voice rises. He's not just angered. He's *agitated.* "You're going to explain to me why the hell Kelly Daniel's was in your room last night! Did you fuck him?"

I stiffen, my chest tight as I try to breathe through the sudden fury. Mason must have encountered Kelly either last night or early this morning. I'm still unsure what time he left, but I don't have time to ponder it right now. "*Excuse* me?"

"You heard me."

My phone dings a message. I break eye contact with my brother and glance down. It's Kelly. He's replied to the message I sent earlier. My pulse skyrockets. I'm itching to open it and see what it says, but not in front of Mason, for obvious reasons. "You're right." My gaze rises, hitting him with a hard glare. "I heard you, but I'm struggling to believe you right now. Who I *fuck*, or don't *fuck,* is none of your business!"

"It is when he's a Sentinel!" Mason roars.

I freeze, my voice lowering to a whisper. "What did you just say?"

"Kelly Daniels is a Sentinel."

8

ARCADIA

*M*y lips pinch, my giddiness over Kelly squashed like a bug on the floor. "Get out."

My brother's eyes widen, his fingers curling tightly around the armrests of his wheelchair. "Did you just hear what I said?"

"Mason, so help me God, get out of my bathroom right this second before I lose my shit."

He folds his arms, refusing to budge. Well, I'm having none of it. Mason is a fool, and along with Tony, he's ruining what would otherwise have been a wonderful morning.

"I said *he's a Sentinel.*"

I unearth the soapy sponge from the beneath the water and toss it at my brother's head. "And I said *get out!*"

After smacking Mason in the brow, the sponge drops to his lap. His eyes glare like lasers cutting through metal as he tosses it back in the bath, half his face now covered in bubbles and his pants soaking wet. If I wasn't so riled, I'd laugh.

He backs out of the bathroom, pulling the door shut as he wheels himself out. With peace now at hand, I submerge myself in the steaming water before rising again and scrubbing at my face. I reach for my exfoliator on the shelf behind me and squirt a dollop into my palm. I'm rubbing it in my cheeks when I hear, "You're such an asshole!" from Echo in the kitchen.

Pots rattle as she slams a cupboard. She's been my champion since as long as I've known her, since *Titsgate* at school. She stands up for me even when I'm in the wrong. A true friend.

"*I'm* the asshole?" My brother sounds gobsmacked.

"I was making bacon and egg sandwiches for brunch but you know what? I'm going to take yours home with me and feed it to my dog."

"You don't have a dog."

"You're missing the point, Mason." Her tone is snide.

"What's your point, then?"

I tune them out, rinsing my face and screwing the cap back on the tube of my face product. When I'm finished in the bath, I get out and wrap a towel around my torso, dripping water as I make the small trek from the bathroom to my bedroom, making sure to bring my phone with me. Kelly's message notification still rests on the screen, waiting for me to open it. I don't waste any more time.

Kelly: She's not as sexy as you

There's no punctuation. No emojis. Just a single gruff line that sends an electrical current through my veins. Three little dots appear as I continue staring at his message. He's sending another one. I lean against the doorframe of my room, eyes pinned to the screen as I wait. It takes an absolute *eternity*.

Kelly: Busy tonight?

I exhale in a *whoosh* and grin, biting the bottom of my lip. He wants to see me again. Me! Little old Ace who lives in worn jeans and black converse with a hole in the toe. Tonight is Sunday family dinner night, but if I turned this guy down in favour of people I see every week, including my idiot brother, Echo would have my full permission to lock me up and throw away the key. I tap out a reply.

Me: What did you have in mind?

"You should see your face right now," Echo says, and I look up from the screen of my phone as the message sends. She's in my room, sitting cross-legged on the bed, plate in her lap as she devours the sandwich she made.

"Why?"

"Because you're grinning like it's Christmas and Santa delivered a shiny new V8 Mustang engine right to your front door."

I purse my lips, quashing the grin as she takes another bite of her sandwich. "I am not," I say as another message hits my phone.

Kelly: In the spirit of being honest, you naked beneath me

Kelly: But I'd settle just for seein' you, babe

All brain function stops. I can't catch a breath. My vision sees the powerful weight of him pushing me into the bed, and I want to know what that feels like.

"Ace?"

Echo is speaking, but I don't hear a word she says. I'm painfully aware of the throbbing between my legs as I type a reply, my fingers moving of their own accord.

Me: Yes please.

Shit. Delete, delete, delete. I pause for a long moment, wondering how to reply with something along the lines of *sign me the fuck up* without it making me sound like an overeager tart.

Oh stuff it. I re-type the same message and hit send before I can overthink it anymore. Then I stare at my sent reply. It says *delivered*, and now I have the powerful urge to run and hide. Texting a sexy man-mountain like Kelly is more stressful than boosting a car, yet the rush is exactly the same. I'm giddy with adrenaline.

"Ace!"

I glance up from my screen. Echo is looking at me as if I've fallen off the edge of the earth. It's accurate because my feet don't feel attached to the ground right now.

"Who are you texting? Kelly?"

"Maybe," I hedge, not feeling quite ready to deliver on all of the details.

I set my phone on the desk near my bed. That thing is a dangerous weapon in my hands. I can't be trusted with it anymore this morning. I turn and wrench open my wardrobe doors. Inside on the left is a small set of drawers. I open the top one and extract a pair of matching white cotton underwear. The bra and panties are plain and boring. Unsexy. They're just what I need to stop me thinking of sexual activities with said sexual beast.

"Maybe? That's all I'm going to get after you blew off the Firebird last night? Ace, you downed two vodkas and let that massive dude lead you outside like a lamb to slaughter!"

I snort, dropping the towel to tug on my panties and snap my bra in place.

"I know he came back here last night," she adds, arching her brow. "Is that why Mason is carrying on like a pork chop?"

"My brother is a fool. A paranoid fool." I jam my legs into a pair of ripped skinny jeans and tug them up my legs, puffing slightly because the return of my anger has me winded. After sliding up the zip, I open another drawer. "Just because someone owns a Harley, he automatically assumes they're a Sentinel."

Echo makes a choking sound. I pause my search for a shirt and turn my head to assess her face. She's trying hard to swallow the mouthful of food that has her cheeks bulging like a chipmunk hoarding nuts.

"What?"

She shakes her head, unable to speak, yet her eyes round in a look of faux innocence.

My gaze narrows. "You're hiding something."

Echo finishes, swallowing. "No I'm not."

"That wasn't a question."

"I know." She picks up the sandwich in both hands and devours another large bite, speaking around her mouthful. "But you're deflecting. I want details, bitch. I earned them," she says, nodding toward the uneaten breakfast resting on a plate on my desk. She made me a sandwich too. Bribery, of course, but I'll take it. I'm hungry, and there aren't many details to give.

"Nothing much happened," I protest, yet I can't suppress another grin as I tug a blue tee over my head and twitch it in place. It's a little worn and faded with big yellow lettering that says: *Buckle Up, Butter-*

cup. "We talked. He kissed me." My mind returns to the feel of his lips on mine and heat travels the length of my spine. "Holy Jesus, Echo, he kissed me like it was the last kiss he'd ever have."

My best friend makes a humming sound. She's processing my information, or lack thereof.

I offer her another crumb as I take a seat at my desk and pull the plate toward me. "I like him."

"That's obvious. I like that you like him, but ..."

"Dammit," I mutter, knowing Echo is about to rain all over my parade. I knew the *but* was coming. I fucked up last night because of my fixation, and it can't happen again.

"The timing is really bad, Ace," she says as I pick up my sandwich and take a bite. An explosion of bacon and barbecue sauce fills my mouth. I chew and moan. It tastes fantastic. "Maybe you should put him on ice until this thing with Tony is done."

I swallow my mouthful and sigh. "I don't want to."

"I don't blame you. He's almost as delicious as this sandwich."

"He really is."

"And big. Like *colossal* big. You could climb him like Mount Everest." Echo is chewing on her bottom lip as if she's contemplating doing just that. Then she shakes her head and returns her attention to her plate. "What are you two messaging about?"

"He wants to know what I'm doing tonight."

She shoves the last bite in her mouth. "*Flund?*"

"What?"

Echo swallows. "*And?*"

"I replied."

"Oh for fuck's sake, it's like pulling teeth." She dumps her empty plate on the bedside table and leaps for my phone before I get wind of her intentions.

"No!"

Her laughter is tinged with glee when I tackle her into the bed, my phone smooshing into the mattress beneath her.

"Give me the damn phone."

"No."

She's still laughing when I rise and wedge my knee into her back. Then I grab a short fistful of pale pink hair and yank. Her breath catches. "Don't make me hurt you, you ... you fucking tutti frutti."

"Seriously?" she wheezes. "We're resorting to name-calling now?"

Echo bucks me off and rolls, gasping.

I snatch up the phone. "Ha!" It rings in my hand, and I check the screen. "Shit. It's Tony."

We share a grim look. "You better answer it."

"And tell him what?"

"I don't know." She throws up her hands in dramatic fashion. "That you momentarily lost your mind?"

I roll my eyes. "Sure. That will work. Thanks for your shitty help."

"You're the one that fucked up," she hisses. "Answer it."

"Fine!" I jab the green button and put the phone to my ear. "Tony."

"Ace. Forgetting something?"

Shit. I run fingers through my unbrushed wet hair and water drips down my neck. It does nothing to cool the anxiety that's currently making my skin hot. "The timing was off."

Tony's voice is harsh. "Your timing is never off. That's why you're the best."

"I'm the best because I know when to walk away. And last night I had to walk away."

"With Kelly Daniels?" he replies in a cutting tone.

Shit. "You're watching me?"

"Of course we are. I never figured you for stupid, Ace, but maybe I figured wrong. Oh, and you might want to check on your grandfather this morning. Seems Racer had a spot of trouble with a fire in his garage late last night. He's lucky it didn't spread."

My fingers tighten around the phone, and I sink to my chair, unable to catch my breath. "What did you do?"

"Exactly what I promised I would do if you didn't get me my cars."

"You gave me twelve weeks," I protest hotly. "Just because I didn't get you the Firebird last night, doesn't mean you aren't going to get it at all!"

"You promised its delivery last night. We were prepared for it, and you wasted our time. You think your time is more precious than mine?"

"Tony—"

"Don't mess up again, Ace. It's not just you we're watching. Get me my cars or your entire family burns."

Tony hangs up.

"Oh fuck," I moan, my stomach roiling sickly as I find the contact for Racer in my phone. It takes only a moment. My grandfather is listed in my favourites. We talk often, mostly about cars, but he's trying hard to take an interest in the new direction of my life. Granted, his eyes glaze over every time I mention the dreaded word *finance,* but at least he pretends to listen, which is more than I can say for my parents.

Echo slides to the edge of my bed, her expression anxious. "What did he say?"

"Racer. He set fire to my grandfather's garage." I put the phone to my ear as it rings and meet my friend's eyes. "Jesus Christ, Echo. What was I thinking last night?"

"You weren't," Echo mutters.

I hiss, a sharp whistle of air pushing between my clenched teeth. "He's not answering. Oh god."

She gets to her feet and snatches up her keys and black aviators, jamming them on her face. "Let's go."

THE SCENERY IS a blur as Echo plants her foot hard on the accelerator, leaving the traffic behind us scrambling to catch up. She's driving a 1971 Ford Falcon GT in midnight black. A car I helped her buy for a ridiculously low price. She only takes it out once a week on a Sunday because it's a massive gas guzzler, but the engine is savage. It's roaring like a wounded bear when the realisation hits me. "How does Tony know who Kelly Daniels is?"

"What?" Echo glances over at me before returning her attention to the road.

"Tony mentioned him. He *knew* who he was."

Her eyes fix in front of her like we're following the yellow brick road. "Tony knows who everyone is," she answers.

"He does not." My lips purse. "You know something. Tell me what it is or I'll scratch your fucking car."

Echo snorts. I would cry like a little girl if anyone marked her ride, and she knows it. "You're as paranoid as your brother. If he's watching you, it makes sense he wants to know who you're hanging around with." Her tone is casual. *Too* casual. But I can't deny that what she says makes sense. "He probably did a bit of digging and found out. I do it all the time, right?"

"True."

"Try calling Racer again."

We're only a minute from his house, but I call up his contact again and dial, putting the phone on speaker. It rings for a lifetime. I'm about to give up again when he answers. It has me breathing a huge sigh of relief.

"Ace, it's like you have a built-in radar when it comes to cars." He sounds crotchety and impressed all at the same time. "How did you hear? I mean, I was planning on telling you, but I was just trying to work out how."

My brows draw into a puzzled line. His words don't make a lick of sense. "Tell me what? I'm calling because I heard there was a fire in your garage. Are you okay?"

"I'm fine, little lass. It takes more than a wee small flame to snuff out your old grandfather. I'm sorry about your car though."

"My car?" We pull into his driveway and Echo switches off the engine, drawing the keys from the ignition as we stare at the ashes before us. Silence reigns, apart from the intermittent ticking of the engine as it cools down.

"Ace? Are you there?"

"We just pulled into your driveway," I whisper, my voice like broken glass.

My grandfather's garage has been levelled to rubble. I'm trying to be thankful the structure is separate to the house, sparing his life, but my Mustang is in there. It's now a burnt-out skeleton of metal, and I'm swallowing with desperation, trying not to hurl all over the dash of Echo's Ford as I stare. Yellow tape surrounds the now ruined structure, advising *caution*.

"Oh, lass." My grandfather's voice is forlorn. "I'm so sorry."

He hangs up and steps out his front door, the screen slapping against the frame behind him as he makes his way down the little porch steps. His white hair is sticking up at the back, and he's clothed in a simple pair of pyjama pants and singlet, as if the fire woke him from sleep, which it probably had. My grandfather has a strong jawline and straight nose. It's a face that tells you he takes no shit, and as he opens my passenger door, I notice it's covered in smears of dark powdery ash.

"I don't understand." My eyes return to the devastation in front of us, my body frozen in the seat of Echo's car. "What's my Mustang doing in your garage? She was supposed to be at my parents' house."

Racer leans his forearm on the open passenger door and bends to look at me. The sympathy in his expression has my eyes burning with grief. "We transferred the car here last weekend because your Dad needed the space. We didn't want to bother you with it because you've been studying so hard, and we're so proud of your ... your ... well, good intentions to earn an honest living. Obviously we weren't expecting my garage to just spontaneously combust in the middle of the night."

My voice is a rasp. "My baby's gone."

"I'm sorry."

"It's not your fault," I say, getting out of the car on wobbly legs. Tony torched the structure because he knew my Mustang was inside. I'll never find another rebuild like this one. It's the death of a dream. And now the shock is starting to work off, anger rising in its place. "I'm just glad it was your garage and not your house."

Echo gets out of the car. "That sonofabitch," I hear her hiss as she starts toward the burnt-out mess for a closer look.

"What sonofabitch?" Racer asks, his gaze skewering my friend down with a flash of intelligence. My grandfather plays the doddering old fool, but he's sharper than a tack.

"The fire. That sonofabitch fire," I say quickly. Racer can't get wind of this or he'll get himself involved. He's supposed to be retired. And though he doesn't like to hear it, he's *old*. He simply can't do what he used to.

"Well, that's true. Fires *can* be a sonofabitch." Racer puts an arm around my shoulders and leads me toward the house before I'm able to inspect the aftermath of Tony's vengeance. "Let's get you a whiskey. Then you can tell me why the Marchettis are playing with matches and what it has to do with you."

"Shit," I mutter.

9

KELLY

$\mathcal{M}$y phone dings and I pull it from the pocket of my jeans as I walk through the front door of the house I share with Fox in Maroubra. It's no sweet cottage like the one Arcadia lives in. It's more of a fixer-upper, but there's potential and the location is great—a fifteen-minute walk to the beach where we indulge our love of surfing most mornings. Fox and I work here and there on renovating the place in return for reduced rent. Maybe I should just buy it outright. Now that I've made the decision to invest part of the insurance money into Rehab, I may as well use the rest for something else worthwhile.

Ace: What did you have in mind?

I don't hesitate with my reply. It's hardly suave or articulate, but at least it's honest. I got the vibe last night that she's not a game player, so maybe she'll appreciate the candid approach. Maybe it will unnerve her a little. Keep her on edge the same way I am right now.

Me: In the spirit of being honest, you naked beneath me.

That would really rattle Mason's bones, wouldn't it? Her brother is probably right; I'm not in her best interests, but it's too late now. That woman has given me a powerful itch, and I need it scratched. I add a follow-up message.

Me: But I'd settle just for seein' you, babe

Dots appear across the screen. Then they disappear. I grunt with frustration and toss the phone and my keys on the shabby breakfast table along with a pack of muffins I picked up from the Grumpy Baker down the street. "Anyone home?"

"Bathroom!" Fox calls back, his voice muffled. "Come check this out!"

"I have zero interest in seeing what genital herpes looks like first-hand, so that's a no, asshole."

"Har, har!" The sound of crashing tiles reaches my ears. I pull a muffin from the pack and peel away the paper as I walk down the hallway. It's all new unpainted drywall and wider than the original design. I reach the bathroom, taking a bite. Fox is sitting on his ass, chipping away at the last of the old seventies tiles, leaving the poky bathroom looking bigger already.

"How the fuck am I 'sposed to shower tonight, huh?"

He spares me a glance. "Who at the club gives a shit if you stink?"

I lean up against the doorframe. He's referring to the Sentinels' motorcycle clubhouse, where we usually head to on a Sunday to drink and talk shit. "I ain't going to the club. I got plans."

"What kind of plans?" he asks, chipping away at the tile.

"The Ace kind."

Fox pauses again to look at me. "You didn't tap that hot ass last night?"

"Are we really going to gossip about my night like a pair of old ladies?"

"Yes, we really fuckin' are. I like Ace. If you don't tap that—"

I jab my muffin at him, crumbs flying in every direction. "You better stop right there."

His grin is smug, the smug sonofabitch. "So tell me all about last night," he says, feigning a high-pitched, girly voice that will give me nightmares for weeks. "And don't leave out a thing."

I toss my muffin at his head. It bounces off, landing in his tool tray. He picks it up and dusts off some flecks of old grout before taking a bite. "Thanks for breakfast."

"Fuck off," I mutter, walking away.

"Just shower at the beach!" he calls out.

"You haven't really left me much choice, idiot!" I yell back. I grab my phone and take it to my room, along with another muffin. After taking a bite, I toss it on the bed and peel off the undershirt I wore last night.

It reveals the Sentinels tattoo that spans the width of my back. I was inked with the image at the age of eighteen. If you stare at it, the red eyes of a grim reaper stare back at you. He stands at the entrance to a rundown pair of gates, one skeletal hand held up, beckoning you toward him. It's dark and ominous, and most believe it represents evil and violence.

But it doesn't. It represents our past. We're Sentinels; guardians to the gates of our own private hell. Only those who dare venture beyond them see the darkness within and feel the bitter chill inside our hearts. We may be sinners, but we're also survivors who've lived hard and rough.

"You goin' for a surf before your date?"

Fox is at my door, demolishing another muffin.

"It's not a date."

He smirks between bites.

"It's not."

Fox shrugs and smirks some more. "You should probably know that she's only using you to get to me. You can't miss the way she was lookin' at me last night. She's hot for my body."

"You're kiddin' me, right?" I peel off my pants and pull on a pair of board shorts, sparing Fox a withering glance. "You were all over her like a bad case of crotch rot. She couldn't get away from you fast enough."

My phone lights up with a notification, and it's then that I notice a text message resting on my screen. Ace replied over five minutes ago and I missed it. Just like that, my itch grows more insistent. Fox checks it too. Nosy bastard. "Oh would you look at that." He grins. "It's our girl."

A whole goddamn bunch of possessiveness climbs my throat and chokes me. "*My* girl."

"I knew it!" he crows and points at me. "You went and caught feelings."

I scowl. "Jesus, Fox. I don't get *feelings* when it comes to bitches."

"She isn't just some bitch."

He's right. Ace Jones is one classy piece of ass. I want inside that beautiful girl. Tonight. Right now.

I flick open her text.

Arcadia: Yes please.

How goddamn *polite* of her. Would she talk that way in bed too? *Please, Kelly, touch me. Please give me your cock. Please fuck me. Please.* Hunger rages like wildfire in my blood. I'm forced to swallow a massive lump of need, yet it keeps rising. My dick stiffens in my pants, and I grit my teeth at the swift ache it gives me. I can't believe a simple text message has me fighting to maintain composure.

"Get out," I croak to Fox before I embarrass myself any further.

Fox leaves without question, though he mutters something under his breath that sounds suspiciously like, "Who pissed in your Wheaties this morning?"

I met Fox at eighteen when he, along with his older brother Leander, joined the Sentinels. Leander used to run with the King Street Boys in Melbourne, but he got out and they moved to Sydney. I don't know how, because the only way you get out of a gang like that is to get dead. It's Leander's story, and he keeps it to himself. If he wanted to share, then I'd know, right? So I leave it alone. But the Fox brothers have been on their own a long time.

Luke Fox joined the Sentinels as a cocky shit. Most in the brotherhood considered me the same, and we naturally gravitated toward a friendship, continually one-upping each other with smart aleck remarks and stupid dares.

I'd never had freedom until the day my parents died. The wild and cocky attitude had come with the new territory. I went a little crazy, overdosing on the liberation like it was pasta carbonara and I hadn't eaten in weeks. It was pure gluttony.

The first thing I did with my freedom was learn to ride. It was an old bike belonging to Bingo, our leader. He said if I could fix it, I could have it. The contraption was an old Harley, tucked away in the shed behind our clubhouse, sentenced to die a slow, rusty death. That was where my joy in tinkering with mechanical objects turned into a powerful obsession.

When I eventually got that bike purring, I took my first ride. I want to say it was everything I expected it to be—glorious, freeing, and badass. Except I accelerated with wild abandon and slammed into the clubhouse fence, knocking down timber posts and bruising my cocky pride. My Sentinel brothers watched on, cheering and laughing, as I got to my feet and dusted myself off.

Not ready to give up, I was about to climb back on when Hammer came at me, face red and yelling, "You little shit, you broke my new goddamn fence!"

Hammer was the handyman of our brotherhood and somewhere in his late thirties. He was big, like a mountain, and outraged— rightly so—because I had indeed toppled part of his hard work. Fear rose up my throat, bitter and vile. It seemed I'd exchanged one life of violence for another, and for the first time I was unsure about the new direction of my life. Then Hammer's fist came at me before I could ponder it anymore, knocking me into the dirt. The sharp punch to my face was like being hit with a two-by-four. The sickening pain was familiar. As was the urge to run and hide.

Then I remembered the vow I made after shooting my father. *No one would ever make me cower in fear again.* So I rose up and took a swing at Hammer. He ducked with ease, side-stepping as I stumbled forward, overbalancing. More cheers rose up from the Sentinels surrounding the clubhouse. They were thoroughly entertained, some even holding fresh beers in their hands as they watched on.

Hammer pushed me from behind, chuckling. My knees and hands hit dirt.

"Think you can take me, little biker wannabe?"

Once again, I got to my feet, and I turned to face him. Hammer's eyes were hard and a smirk lined his lips. That smirk reminded me of my father. It was how he looked whenever he stood over me, watching me cower beneath his fist.

Anger, hot and bright, rose swiftly in my chest. I put my head down, and with a loud roar, I charged. He mustn't have been expecting me to pull such a stupid move, so when I used every ounce of my young, burgeoning strength to shove him off his feet, he went down, right on his ass in front of everyone.

The crowd of Sentinels went silent, and I later learned that no one had ever managed to fell the mighty Hammer before. I stood over him, his mouth gaping, and I held out a hand. There were murmurs from the bikers behind me as he took it and got to his feet. He was tall, but it was obvious I'd be catching him soon.

"You got some balls, Daniels," he said in a low rumble.

It was on the tip of my tongue to agree in some stupid, arrogant tone, but Hammer was watching me with squinty eyes. Curious and careful. Waiting to see how I'd respond. It suddenly felt important to get it right. So I forced an honest reply. "I've been through too much to take shit from anyone."

"Was I giving you shit?" He cocked his head. "You don't think you deserved a walloping for what you did to my fence?"

My chin lifted. "I didn't do it on purpose."

"No, you didn't do it on purpose, but you were unnecessarily reckless, kid. You need a lesson on how to rein that in."

My pride smarted all over again at being called *kid*. "I'll fix the damn thing," I muttered, ducking my head, fists clenching by my sides.

Hammer glared. "What did you say?"

He heard me. He also heard the snarky petulance in my tone. And I realised that I was acting like the *kid* he was me calling me out to be. Suitably shamed, I met his gaze head on, speaking with more respect. "I'll fix the fence."

He nodded, his expression remaining fierce, but I saw an underlying hint of satisfaction from my response. Maybe even a bit of … pride? "See that you do."

He started walking away, toward the clubhouse, then he stopped and turned. He stared at me for a moment, then in a gruff voice muttered, "You ever wanna learn how to throw a real punch, come see me."

Something in my midsection leaped at that offer. Hammer was a respected figure of authority in the Sentinels and apparently willing to look out for me, show me some of the ropes, teach me how to take care of myself. Perhaps it wasn't a big deal to him, but to me it was everything I'd never had with my own father. I was going to grab hold of it with both hands.

I fixed that damn fence, and I got back on that bike. The shine of excitement had worn off but determination had risen its place. I needed to belong. I needed a family. How would any of the Sentinels accept me in their midst if I couldn't ride a Harley? I would show them.

Eventually, riding my Harley became my favourite thing to do. A means of escape. Not just from people and the world but from my head. My evenings were lonely. I slept in a damp room in quarters at the back of the clubhouse. My bed was thin and scrappy. And the slide into sleep brought images of my mother's sightless eyes and the gore of my father's gaping wound after I fired the gun. Nightmares woke me in rivers of sweat, panting, aching, the backs of my lids burning, and the urge to scream so strong in my throat I choked on the thickness of it. I wanted to gouge the memories from my mind, but they were imprinted like words carved in stone, where only the wear and tear of time would grind them down into nothing but a faint shadow.

Hammer had a room there too, though with seniority came bigger space and larger windows. He showed me how to throw that punch, and over time, he showed me more. How to grow into the man I was born to become. My frame began to gain weight and thick muscle. By eighteen I was a powerhouse, bigger than my father ever was, and still growing. But that cockiness was hard to shake. And then Luke Fox showed up with his older brother.

There was contention over their arrival because of their background with the King Street Boys and the trouble it could bring us.

But Bingo laid down the law. We all have a past. Our brotherhood is about who we are, individually and collectively, not where we came from.

Though initially they weren't popular, Luke Fox brought something with him that for me was new. Humour. I was sitting on the outdoor deck of the clubhouse bar, basking in the late afternoon sun with a beer, when he pulled out a seat beside me and plonked his ass down with a deep sigh and a grin.

"Christ," he said, looking me over. "You're a unit. Whatever you're drinkin', I'll have that."

I scowled at his good nature and overt affability. I didn't make friends easy. Casey was always in the back of my mind. How he left and never came back. Not allowing anyone too close was a painful lesson to learn.

Yet I missed my older brother regardless, which felt worse. His loss was a dull ache. It throbbed anew as I reclined back in my seat, eyeballing Fox, because he had that same easy charm that people gravitated toward. A confidence in his skin. In who he was. I'd always admired it in my brother. Coveted it, even. Most people gave me a wide berth. Hammer said it was because I looked ready to beat up the entire world.

"Is this some kind of sad-ass pickup line?" I replied, my demeanour pricklier than a cactus. "Because I don't do dudes."

"You'd be lucky to have me," he said with a snort, unfazed by my hostility, "but unfortunately for you, chicks are more my thing."

"Well thank fuck you cleared that up," I retorted, my tone inferring otherwise. "Wouldn't have wanted to embarrass myself."

Fox laughed, his eyes sparkling with merriment. He leaned over and clapped me on the shoulder, a gesture of camaraderie. "You're a funny guy. How old are you?"

My sigh was heavy at being forced into conversation when I was trying to have a quiet beer. "Old enough."

"Oh yeah?" His brows arch high. "Old enough to what?"

"Drink and fuck," I say, folding my arms.

He laughed again. "Okay, tough guy. Hammer says you're eighteen?"

For reasons I didn't quite understand, this put my back up. Maybe because Hammer was my only real friend and he'd been talking about me to someone I didn't know. "You been talking to Hammer?"

"Yeah, why?" His brow furrowed. "He not cool?"

"Nah, Hammer's cool."

Fox appeared relieved. Biker gangs could be a bit like high school that way, though I'd get smacked up the head for the comparison. But if you make friends with the wrong people, they could change who you are. "Friends shape your soul," Hammer said to me once when the topic came up. We were sweaty and sitting on the floor with beers in hand after a heavy training session. I'd been getting picked on for being a loner and taking my frustration out on the punching bag rather than their ugly faces. "You're smart to be careful about who you let in, Daniels. Those people may be the difference between becoming the best version of yourself or the worst."

I studied Fox. His hair was blond and a little long and wild. I was sure it had never seen a brush. His eyes were dark brown and appeared lit with mirth, as though he saw the entire world and its contents as a joke. He was wearing jeans and a muscle tee, displaying burgeoning biceps and the tattoo of a fox. The image was vivid and colourful, its eyes mirroring Fox's, as though his spirit was inside the animal. It was incredible work.

I nodded at the tattoo. "Who did that?"

"Samuels at *Ink My Life*," he replied. "Good, huh?"

"It's more than good."

"I got it for my sixteenth birthday when we were living in Melbourne. I'm going to get two entire sleeves when I can afford it."

"I want the face of a bear, here," I said, rubbing the outside of my right shoulder.

"Why do you want a bear?"

Bears were the most solitary animals in the world. I read that once in school, and it stuck in my head ever since because I could relate. It didn't mean they were lonely, or melancholy. They were *self-*

reliant. Most animals enjoyed being in groups, herds, or in pairs, but the bear preferred solitude. He walked alone. "Because bears are cool."

"Let's go now."

My brows pulled together in a furrow of confusion. "Go where?"

Fox appeared pumped. "To see Samuels. Get you your bear."

"Didn't you say he was in Melbourne?"

"Yeah, so?"

"Dude. That's a nine hour drive!"

"Yeah, so?" he said again, grinning. "It'd totally be worth it."

I thought about it for a moment. Nine hours on the bike. Freedom. Solitude. The open road. An incredible piece of artwork on my arm that I had a hankering for. An answering grin started to pull at the corners of my mouth.

Fox saw it and nodded. "Hell yeah, Shade."

The name had been given due to my solitary status and the fact that it was known in our brethren that I killed my own father. Bingo said it was where I lived now. In the shade. My life in partial darkness from the smears of black on my soul. I didn't like the name and grimaced when Fox used it. "Call me Daniels," I told him, like Hammer does.

He gave me a nod. "Daniels."

I looked around. Those at the bar weren't doing much of anything except drinking and talking shit. What was the point in hanging around anyway? "Let's go then."

It was the right decision. My bear tattoo was, in Samuels's words, his best work yet. And our journey forged a tentative bond of friendship that I would eventually value for the rest of my life. Fox had my back in all things, and I in his, so I let him in. I had no choice. He was a pesky fly. No matter what I did, he buzzed about, getting in my face, irritating and yet somehow not unwelcome. Fox reminded me to smile sometimes and see the lighter side of life. His was a friendship that helped me find a better version of myself, and if I ever told him that, he'd probably piss himself laughing.

My phone dings loudly, pulling me from the past and into the present. A smile breaks across my face when I see Ace's name on the screen.

It drops when I read the message.

Arcadia: I can't see you. I'm sorry.

What the fuck? Tonight? Or ever? I have a sudden urge to hurl my phone at the wall. "Goddammit."

Fox is walking passed and hears my muttered curse. He stops in the doorway and leans against the frame with a grin. "What's up, Cinderella? Got nothing to wear to the ball tonight?"

"Tonight's off," I growl, tossing my phone on the bed and reaching for a shirt. I tug it on. "I'm going to the clubhouse." The faded black cotton settles around my midsection. After switching out my shorts for jeans, I grab my Sentinels cut from the post of my bed, shrugging it on as I stalk from my room, brushing past Fox. "You comin'?"

My wallet is on the breakfast table. I shove it in my back pocket. Fox trails out, my phone in his hand. "Why is it off?"

I shrug. "Who knows? Chicks and their games."

He flicks open my messages and reads them.

I glare, those messages are private. "You mind?"

"Well somethin' happened between then and now to change her mind."

I pick up my keys, doing my best to sound uninterested as I tromp to the door. "Yeah? Like what? Never mind," I mutter, realising it was probably Mason that happened.

"I don't know. Like somethin' upset her. Or someone. Maybe somethin' came up. Or someone got hurt. It could be anything. Just ask if she's okay, yeah?"

"You sound like a girl." I stalk back and snatch my phone from his hands. "She doesn't want to see me. It's no big deal."

Yet why does it feel like one? Why is there an ache of disappointment in my chest? Once outside, the filtered winter sun provides little warmth as I walk toward my bike. I swing a leg over and settle on the heavy piece of machinery, Fox's words niggling at me. I stare at nothing for a long moment, trying to work out what I'm doing.

Arcadia is just some random bitch who got stuck in my head. So why can't I get her out?

Because you don't want to.

My heart pounds heavy in my chest. I swipe a hand down my face as if to wipe the realisation away, yet it remains. Last night I felt so comfortable with her. Myself. I felt ... confident and yet unsure, a warring jumble of emotion that won't go away, even now as I sit staring at nothing.

Fuck it.

I pull the phone from my pocket, open my messages, and tap out a reply.

Me: Everything ok?

Send.

10

ARCADIA

I stare at the burnt-out husk of my Mustang, having left Racer and Echo in the kitchen drinking hot tea and whiskey. The stench of scorched metal is harsh and unpleasant, and flutters of ash swirl in the air as the breeze picks up. It settles in my hair and on my clothes.

It's a reality check that leaves a bitter taste in my mouth. I've always done a hassle-free trade with Tony in the past. He would demand and I would supply. On good terms. Simple economics. I've never been on his bad side, until now. And being here is no picnic.

I got too cocky, thinking I had it handled. My grandfather could have lost his house. Or his life. I should be relieved it was just the garage along with my car. Instead, hot tears well in my eyes. Selfish tears. I wrap my arms around my middle. This is my karma. Like a rubber band, I've stretched it too far and now it's come back to smack me in the face.

You got what was coming, taunts the scornful voice in my head.

And it's true. I've lived a shady life. Some of my choices may have been warranted—like Miles Howard or the BMW owned by an investment banker who defrauded millions from pensioners—but some not. I've been reckless, deceitful, and my nine lives are up, just like Mason.

A solitary tear spills over and rolls down my cheek. I wipe it away, using the back of my hand in a rough, jerky moment. It's the last one I'll allow. I have an unfinished list of cars to deal with, and time is running out.

With stabby, determined fingers, I send a message to Kelly.

Me: I can't see you. I'm sorry.

The text is delivered with smooth efficiency, and regret rises like a storm surge, making me ache as if I've lost something essential. Suddenly it feels as though I hold the weight of the world on my shoulders, which is ridiculous, because it's just a burnt-out car. But I was just starting to get my life on track, and now it's all gone to shit.

I tuck my phone away in my pocket, telling myself that at least I can focus now, but deep down I know it's a lie because Kelly won't be leaving my head any time soon.

The front door slaps open and Racer pokes his head out. "Come inside, lass. Staring at it won't turn back time and your tea is getting cold."

"In a minute," I call back and turn for one last look at my car. "Bye, little Mustang. I'm sorry our journey ended before it even began." My voice is wistful. "You could have been beautiful."

Once inside, I take a seat next to Echo at my grandfather's weathered breakfast table and sip my tea. He's pottering around in the sink, rinsing plates and wiping the counter. When he's done, he turns his attention on me with a lift of his chin. It's his *I won't accept any arguments* expression, and I brace accordingly. "You should have come to me first, Ace," he says for the millionth time that morning. He leans against the counter behind him and folds his arms. "Now that I have the full story, I'm going to get the Firebird for you."

My lips pinch. "No."

And he doesn't have the full story. At all. I don't want him involved, but considering he knew Tony was behind the fire, I have to give him something. He believes I reneged on the one car last night, not knowing I have a full list of them. Racer would go full Hulk if he knew there was blackmail involved, and I don't want him hurt. He may think himself invincible, and sharper than the blade of a knife, but the reality is that he's old and can't do what he used to.

"I wasn't asking you, I was telling you," he points out.

My jaw tightens. "I don't need you all up in my business."

"Newsflash, young miss, that fire was in my garage. *Mine,*" he reiterates in a growly fashion. "And you are my granddaughter. What part of all that makes it none of my business?"

There's a moment of tense silence where we glare at each other, Echo glancing warily between us. My phone dings, breaking the standoff.

Kelly: Everything ok?

Oh Jesus. I've gone and confused him with my complete one-eighty. My ache of regret intensifies, like heartburn after spicy food.

Echo sees the message. "What the hell, Ace?" she mutters.

"I told him it was all off," I mutter back.

"What are you two muttering about?" Racer interjects.

I stand, slotting my phone neatly in my bag. Echo follows suit, getting my silent hint that we need to leave. "Nothing. Have you rung your insurance company, Grandad?"

He scowls. The only time I ever call him *Grandad* is to remind him that he's old. "Little upstart," he retorts, like he always does. There's something in the normality of it that chases a little of the chill away. My lips twitch. "Yes, I've called. Someone should be here soon."

Echo rattles her keys. "Thanks for the tea, Mr. Racer." She gives him a kiss on the cheek. He appears oddly flustered. I suspect he's always had a thing for pink hair.

"Shoo, now," he tells us.

I kiss his cheek too. "Let me know what the insurance excess is, okay? I'll drop the money over."

He nods. "I'll let you know as soon as I look it up." It's a bald-faced lie, and he says it with a straight face.

I huff.

"Go on, now." Racer gets behind us, herding us toward the door in what seems to be a sudden rush. "I've got things to do."

My eyes narrow and I pause on the threshold. "What things?"

"Look at the state of me, lass." My grandad raises his brows with an incredulity that looks suspiciously fake. "I need a shower and clean clothes before the inspector comes out. Then I have an article due to my editor."

Seems legit. He occasionally writes for *Wheels*—an Australian motoring magazine filled with critical car analysis and blazing testosterone. His journalistic opinions are well-respected. I have a subscription, saving his articles in a little scrapbook of familial pride.

But I'm not fooled. Racer can't hide the spark in his eyes. He's itching to get started on a plan for the Firebird, which is why I'm hurrying out the door. We need to beat him to it.

On the drive to Echo's place, I stare at Kelly's message, musing on what I can say without being too cryptic or giving away my current situation. The fact is I shouldn't reply at all. *Ghosting*, they call it. When you just disappear on someone as though you never existed. I grimace. It's shitty. I refuse to be that person.

Me: Everything's fine. Just bad timing. Sorry.

I chew on the bottom of my lip, hitting send.

Kelly: All good, babe. See ya round

The brush off. The *don't bother me again* message. *You had your chance at all of this and you cocked it up.* My eyes burn. What else did I expect? I've just rejected him. Dammit. I start a reply. I can't seem to help myself.

Me: It's just—

I pause. Then decide it's best I let it go and not say anything more. I'm about to hit delete when Echo bumps me with her elbow as she shifts gears. My finger taps the send button by mistake and my unfinished message pings its delivery.

"Echo!" I yell. "You just made me send half a message!"

She shrugs, her eyes darting between the road and the fuel gauge. "So send the rest."

Kelly: Just what?

I have this wild urge to tell him everything. An idiotic urge. Echo mutters curse words at her gas guzzler, and we pull in at the nearest garage. She gets out to fill up the tank while I sit calmly in the passenger seat, tapping away on my phone.

Me: My mustang was destroyed last night in a fire.

My sanity has left me for greener pastures. It's the only clear explanation for my lack of self-control when it comes to this guy.

Kelly: Shit, babe. U ok?

That his first concern is for me makes me warm. I wind down the window and a cool breeze blusters over my skin, doing its best to chase the foolishness out of me. It doesn't work.

Me: Not really but I will be. It's just a car, right?

That's a lie. It's never *just* a car. Not to me. Her rebuild was a journey and a dream. And now it's dead.

Kelly: I call bullshit. How did the fire start?

Crappity crap crap crap.

Me: No idea.

Oh the lies!

Me: My parents moved her to my grandad's place a couple of weeks ago, and his entire garage burned down.

Kelly: Sorry, babe. Want me to look at it? See if there's anything to salvage?

Me: That's really nice of you, Kelly.

Kelly: Don't call me nice

A small smile plays on my lips.

Me: Why? Am I ruining your badass image?

Kelly: Nice guys finish last

Me: And finishing first is better?

Kelly: Babe

I laugh.

Kelly: U will always come first

My face catches fire, and a steady throb begins to pulse between my legs. I'm thankful that Echo is not in the car right now, witnessing my dopey expression.

Me: You're a gentleman.

I wait for his response but it doesn't come. Just as well, because

Echo opens the door and slams into her seat with force. "I just spent my life savings."

"It's worth it," I say, tucking my phone away in my bag.

"It's not." She buckles her seat belt and turns the key in the ignition, glowering at the steering wheel as the engine roars to life. "You hear me, car? You're not worth it!"

I gasp and give the dashboard a loving pat. "Don't listen to her, girl. You're worth the sun and the moon and all the stars."

"Don't be dramatic." Echo rolls her eyes as we tear out of the garage on a full tank, my hair whipping up wildly. We fishtail out on to the road, almost cutting off a little old lady in a lime green Hyundai Getz. She gives us the finger. I offer a wave of apology before we accelerate with gusto, leaving her well behind us.

The scenery blurs and I tug hair from my mouth. "You would chew through less fuel if you didn't drive like a maniac."

"It's not me, it's the car. She doesn't like low gear."

"*You* don't like low gear."

"Shut up, Aceface."

I snort. "Really? That's the best you've got?"

We bicker the entire drive back to my house, where we load up with snacks and spend a good portion of the afternoon, and into the evening, forming our attack for the Firebird. Time is of the essence, which means our plan is hasty and slapdash, but it has to do.

11

KELLY

"*Y*ou gonna drink that or just stare at it all night long?"

I glance up from the glass of neat whiskey resting unassumingly in front of me. It's later tonight, after my textathon with Ace. I've found myself at the clubhouse, making an attempt to tie one on and failing pathetically.

Leander, or Lee, sometimes Big Fox—Luke's older brother—is beside me, taking a seat at the outdoor table on the clubhouse deck. His dark blond hair is newly shorn yet still remains mussed, as though he runs his hands through it a thousand times a day.

"Yeah, I'm gonna drink it."

He nods, setting a beer down and kicking back with a heavy sigh.

"Big shift?" I ask. Lee is a paramedic like his brother, though where Luke does the job because he gets a rush from its intensity, Lee seems to have a harder purpose driving him. There's a grimness to the job, as if the act of saving lives is absolving him of past sins.

A grimace forms on his mouth. It's followed with a grunt and a hardening of his dark brown eyes. "Bad one."

"Yeah?" It's a question without barely forming one, because flat out asking him if he wants to talk about it is the equivalent of growing a vagina.

"Yeah," he replies and adds nothing more.

We sit quietly, Lee contemplating whatever's going through his head and me contemplating the shit going through mine, which is mainly Ace.

You're a gentleman, she tells me. *Nice,* even. Ace wouldn't be thinking those thoughts, nor texting them, if she knew I was a Sentinel. Why didn't her brother tell her? He spat the word like I was gum stuck to the bottom of his shoe, as if I'm beneath her, so very far beneath her I'm living lower than the deep crusty layers of the earth. Perhaps I am. Perhaps I should stay away. But it seems impossible.

I would be happy to just sit and stare at her, letting my eyes linger on her profile and allowing myself to wonder why every part of her, from the tips of her eyelashes to the dark plum polish on her toes, appeals to me so very much.

Arcadia Jones is a magnet, and I'm a rusty piece of old iron. It's the easiest way to explain this sudden feeling of attachment to someone I've known for such a short period of time.

"Who is she?"

Lee's question pulls me from the trancelike stare at my drink and back to reality. I blink at Lee, wondering how the hell he can see inside my head. "Who's who?"

He rolls his eyes. "The girl. You're brooding all over your whiskey."

"I'm not brooding."

"Yes you are."

"No I'm not."

"Yes he is," Fox adds, flopping into the chair on the other side of me. He sets his own beer down on the table and reaches his arms over his head, popping joints and stretching tired muscles.

"How was your shift?" Lee asks from across the table.

Fox grunts.

"Why don't the both of you just quit?" I ask, picking up my whiskey with determination. *Brooding my ass.* I swallow a decent mouthful. The burn of it tastes like disappointment. Fuckin' awesome. She's ruined me for alcohol.

Lee turns his head in my direction, his brow arching. "Why don't you just quit your tinkering with cars?"

"Point taken," I mutter, setting my glass down.

"Ace," Fox says to Lee.

His eyes crinkle in puzzlement. "What?"

"The girl. Her name is Ace."

"Christ," I mutter, rising to my feet. I'm not going to sit around gossiping about some bitch I have the urge to fuck until my cock falls off from exhaustion. "She's just a piece of pussy." I jab a finger at Lee. "And I'm not brooding over it."

Fox nods. "He likes her."

Amusement sparks in Lee's eyes. "Oh really?"

"Oh for fuck's sake." I hold my palm out toward Lee. I'm going to deal with this right the hell now. "Give me your keys. I'm gonna pay her a visit."

He leans back in his seat, casual and relaxed. I'm not fooled. Lee is planning torment. "Tell me about this piece and maybe I will."

"She's not a *piece*," I bite out.

"You're the one that just called her that." Lee cocks his head, studying me for a moment as he thinks. Then he reaches his conclusion as he rises. "I'll do you one better. I'll drive you. I want to get a look at the..." he pauses to grin "...*piece* that's got your dick twisted in knots."

My jaw sets. It sets motherfuckin' *hard*.

Lee chuckles and Fox lets out a snort as he stands. "You idiots are *not* leavin' me behind."

And that's how I find the three of us in Lee's car, Fox riding front, me in the centre back, and Lee at the wheel, driving to Ace's house so we could all check her out like a bunch of school boys. Truth is, if she doesn't know I'm a Sentinel, I'm not ready for her to know. Rolling up on my bike, she'd likely see the paintwork this time, or her brother would hear me. I peel off my cut and dump it on the floor of the car as we roll up to the kerb near her house.

Fox twists in the front passenger seat. "You gonna peel off your tatt as well?" he asks, referring to the club tattoo covering my back.

"If I fuck her good enough, she's not going to notice anything except how big my dick is."

Lee eyes me from the rear-view mirror, his eyes curious over his younger brother's taunt. "What's going on?"

Fox flaps his gums. "She's got class. Doesn't know he's a Sentinel. Recent events imply she won't like knowing."

Lee twists in his seat. Now they're both looking at me. "If she thinks she's all that, then she ain't worth knowin', Shade."

Shade. He's used the name purposefully because mostly he calls me Daniels, same as Fox and Hammer do. He doesn't use the name in a bad way, but in a factual way. A reminder. Of where I came from. What I did. Who I am.

"I'm just here to get some. That's all."

Lee nods at the car door. "Then get out and go get it."

Bad timing. That's what she said. I'm bad timing. Well, hell. I'm just bad all round, aren't I? It shouldn't stop us from getting what we both want before parting ways.

I'm reaching for the door handle when one of the Fox brothers, I'm not sure which as I'm not looking at either of them and they both sound alike, mutters, "Holy mother of all hot women."

My eyes flick up. A woman is exiting Ace's house. Her hair is short in the back and sides but sits high and thick on top. The cut is bold and dramatic, yet the pale pink colour, like fairy floss, adds an element of sweet and pretty. Her pants are black leather and fitted, her top black with long sleeves. Her collarbone peeks out, sharp, resting below a graceful neck.

"That's Ace?" I'm asked in an oddly tight voice. This time I know it's Lee because Fox knows who Ace is. This girl, I've never seen before. Her eyes are dark, dark brown, and even in the waning light I can see intelligence and a hint of derision inside them, as though the whole world is a joke.

"No."

Another woman follows behind, closing the front door behind her. Same outfit. Her hair pulled into a loose knot at the nape of her neck. Her eyes, usually full of cheek and spark, are severe. There's resolution in her stride as she trots down the porch steps like a woman on a mission. My body tightens into a coil of need. A need that has me remembering the way she looked at me over the bite of that muffin. A need that pulls at me when I think of how warm and soft her lips were. A need that has me wanting to pull down those pants, bend her over the bonnet of the car, rip her panties to the side, and fuck her hard.

"That's Ace," I say, my voice thick with frustration, but it's not *my* Ace. This one is entirely different to the one that emitted a gentle snore beside me last night. That Ace was cute and sexy, someone I could fuck into submission until I'd eventually had my fill before moving on. This Ace is intense and fierce, someone who would rather have her fill of me before moving on to conquer whomever dared cross her path next.

They climb into a Ford that sits in the driveway. A beautiful piece of machinery. The car lights flick on, illuminating the closed garage door as the engine roars to life. After approximately two minutes, where they appear to be conducting an argument, one we all watch with fascination even though we can't hear a word being said, the car reverses out of the driveway with wild abandon and tears off down the street as if Satan himself is hunting them down.

Lee starts his car and takes off, following the apparent dynamic duo.

Fox shoots him a glance. "What are you doin'?"

"Followin'."

I swipe a hand down my face, muttering a curse beneath my breath. "So, we're stalkers now? Because this is borderin' on ridiculous." My voice rises as we take a sharp corner. "No, scratch that. It isn't borderin' on ridiculous. It *is* ridiculous."

Lee flicks me a glance in the mirror. "You'd rather go back to brooding in your whiskey?"

"Yes!" My voice is sharp. "No. Yes." My face fixes in a scowl. "I wasn't brooding."

"You were brooding," they both say in unison.

"Fuck you," is my witty response to the backs of their heads.

"It's not like we've got anything better to do tonight other than drink beer. Besides, it looks like they're up to somethin'. I want to know what that somethin' is."

Lee is right. They were dressed for mischief. "I want to know too, but I draw the line at stalking. Stalking is for creeps, and Ace—"

I stop my rant, assuming Lee has decided to listen to me because we've pulled off to the kerb of a leafy street somewhere in the suburb of Bellevue Hill, one of Sydney's premier suburbs. After taking in my fill of the street—imposing, stately houses, neat and vibrant shrubbery, and a deep awareness of heritage—my eyes fall on the red taillights of the Ford parked several houses down from us.

"Dammit, Lee."

"Does your girl come from old money?"

"I wouldn't know. It's not the kind of thing you bring into casual conversation when you're busy tryin' to get laid," I reply with sarcasm as we watch them alight from the car. I'm choosing to ignore his reference to Ace being my girl. He's baiting me, and I've realised why. It's because I never brood. Not once. So he wants to know how much Ace means to me. I'm not sure why he wants to know. Lee and I are friends, but we aren't the deep and meaningful kind. "Why?"

"Why what?"

"You know what."

There's a deep silence in the car that lasts several moments. During that time, we watch both girls duck quickly across the road and start jogging toward us. "You don't know this, Daniels, but you and I have somethin' in common. And while we aren't bosom buddies like you and Little Fox are—"

Fox snorts with indignation "We aren't *bosom buddies*."

"—it'd be nice for at least one of us to find some kind of peace."

There's no time to contemplate his statement. Ace and her friend are two houses away from us now, both of them pulling black beanies down over their heads. Ace reaches up, tugging the long strands of her hair beneath the woolly head covering. Yet instead of getting closer, their jog tails off to a sudden stop beside a long low hedge of green shrubs.

We watch with open-mouthed amazement when Ace reaches down and plucks an elderly man from the bushy leaves. He, too, is dressed all in black. "What in the fucking hell ..." I breathe. She starts yelling at him. Not in a loud way, but in a hissing kind of way that indicates a battle to keep her fury leashed. Ace is *pissed*.

The old man draws himself up, shoulders broadening under her barrage and features setting into deep grooves of censure. He begins to whisper-yell back.

"It's like a silent movie," Fox mutters from the front passenger seat. "So entertaining yet completely unsatisfying, all at the same time."

Ace's friend appears to be muttering something while tapping into her phone. Then the old dude puts his hand on Ace's shoulder. It's an aggressive gesture. All I see is his fingers digging in to her skin and a red haze infiltrates my vision. I lose all sense of rationality and grab for the handle, swinging open the door.

"Daniels." Fox reaches around, trying to stop me from blowing our cover while Lee simply grins from his position behind the wheel.

My words come out between gritted teeth. "Between this and the fact that her Mustang somehow got destroyed by fire last night, I'm starting to think there's a bigger picture, and I'm not going to sit in a car like a stalker and watch it all play out any longer. That old guy has his hands on her, and I don't care if he's one breath away from the grave, I'm taking him down."

"Her Mustang burned—" I slam the car door closed behind me, cutting off the rest of Fox's question. In my haste, I forgot I hadn't told him about her car.

I stalk toward the arguing trio, my footfalls anything but quiet. Ace sees me first, her eyes cutting my way and her face blanching white. Her words die off. Fairy Floss glances up from the illuminated screen of her phone and stills as she sees me, something like unholy glee lighting her eyes.

"I have every right," the elderly man is saying, not seeming to realise the argument he's still participating in has died a quick death.

My eyes are on his hand, the hand still attached to Ace's shoulder. "*You* have no right," I say, my voice a low growl.

On closer inspection, he's not hurting her. His hand is simply resting there, an action designed to capture attention rather than cause intimidation or pain.

"Excuse me?" The old man turns, his hand falling away before I get the chance to rip it away—regardless of the reason for touching her. His eyes are a dark stormy blue. They fix on me with an imposing glare. One that an ordinary person would perhaps cower beneath. I, of course, don't cower beneath shit. "Have no right to what?" he asks.

"To put your hand on Arcadia."

"Is that so?" He eyes me carefully, taking me in with imperial curiosity. I'm not sure if I'm found lacking or not, when he's finished his inspection. His expression gives me nothing more. "And you are?"

Ace finds her voice. "Kelly. What are you ..." She trails off, taking a step forward and then changing her mind. My presence has thrown her completely. I can see why that would be. My best bet, besides flat-out admitting we were stalking her fine ass, is to deflect.

"What the hell is going on here?" I fold my arms, staring all three of them down like they're a pack of naughty kids with their hands caught in the cookie jar. "The three of you all dressed in black, outfitted for mischief and skulking about the neighbourhood. You think you're all Ocean's Three or something?"

The old man draws himself up to his full height, outrage his expression of choice. "Skulking? Young man, whomever you are, this is a private matter. Your..." he pauses, as though searching for the right word "...defence of my granddaughter is admirable, however it is unwarranted. And although she seems to have your acquaintance, I do not. You may now get back to whatever it was you were out doing in this neighbourhood on this delightful evening, resting assured that her safety in my care is more than adequate."

Christ. Her grandfather. And he knows how to deflect better than I do. A master. Fairy Floss turns her head, failing to hide a snicker. His eyes narrow in her direction. "Echo," he chastises.

"Sorry, Mr. Racer," she mutters.

My brows rise. Fairy Floss is Echo? And Grandpops goes by Racer? Who *are* these people that orbit Ace's inner circle? My eyes find hers. She shrugs, indicating she's at a complete and utter loss.

I hold out my hand to her grandfather. "Kelly Daniels. I'm a friend of Arcadia's."

He takes it, his grip firm as we shake, eyes still narrowed. "Racer Jones." He lets go, eyeballing me while he talks to Fairy Floss. "This the one, Echo?"

"Yes, sir, Mr. Racer, it is."

Ace lets out an audible gasp. "You two are a pack of gossiping galahs!"

Racer assesses the width of my shoulders, ignoring the outrage from his granddaughter. "He's a biggun."

Echo smothers a laugh. "That's how she likes them."

"Would you both stop it?" Ace hisses, and if her face was blanched white before, it's now pinker than her friend's hair.

My brow arches in her direction. "You have a type?"

"I do not! Don't let them drag you down to their level, Kelly, because once you're there, there's no climbing back out."

I want to pursue the topic, but her embarrassment is high. I make note to question her later. I'm not sure I like being her *type*. It doesn't sit well, as if I'm one of many. I don't want to be one of many. I want to be—

You want to be what, dickhead? Her one and only? Don't be stupid. You're lucky to get her into bed at all now, after materialising out of nowhere, making it more than obvious you were following her. You're on her list of crazed lunatics to avoid from now on.

I decide for the cool, cocky approach to hide my idiocy. "There's no level deep enough I can't climb back out of, babe."

Her mouth opens and closes, seeming at a loss to my response.

"We should talk," I add.

She shakes her head, not even pretending to hesitate. "I don't think—"

I take a step a forward and grab her hand. "No thinking."

She has no choice but to follow me, stumbling behind as I drag her away from the huddle and in the opposite direction of the car holding Lee and Fox. I hear her huffing sharply behind me, revealing her irritation. At me.

We arrive at a spot I deem acceptable enough to be outside of hearing distance and turn to face her. Her cheeks are pink from the cold. Honey-coloured strands of hair have escaped the edges of her beanie and blow across her face. She swipes them away with an impatient gesture, her stormy eyes dark in the shadows of the night. I want to stare and just gulp her in, like she's fresh air after being trapped below ground, but something akin to *hurt* is rising. No, not hurt. Because that would make me a baby. Offence. I'm *offended*. I'm damn good in bed. I want to know what the fuck she has going on in her life because no female in their right mind would ditch all of this.

"This is why you blew me off tonight? *This...*" I wave a hand to encompass the outfit that's so wonderfully tight she may as well be naked "...is your bad timing? What the hell are you up to?"

Her brows snap together. "We barely know each other, so whatever it is I'm up to, it's none of your business. Or your friends," she mutters, glancing across at the car.

I look over. Lee and Fox have eyes on us, their car windows down to hear us better. My gaze shifts to the left. Racer and Fairy Floss are watching too, with what appears to be utter fascination. We're like bugs beneath a microscope. I roll my shoulders to disperse the discomfort. *Fuck this.*

I take Ace's arm and lead her over to the car. She stumbles slightly behind and to the side of me, muttering more curses. We come to a halt beside the open window, and Fox grins at Ace. "So lovely to see you—"

I cut through his flirty pleasantries. "Ace and I need to talk."

"Is that what they're calling it these days?" Lee interjects, his voice mild and amused.

Ace leans down to better see him through the window. "You're a funny guy."

His lips twitch. "I'm a lot of things."

My breath escapes in an exasperated huff. "Get out."

Both pair of eyes hit me. "What?" Fox asks.

"Get out of the car," I enunciate slowly.

"But ... it's cold," he bleats. "You want us to just stand out there so you two can chat in the car?"

"Yes. That's exactly what I want to do." Which is a lie because I plan to do more. *So much more.*

12

ARCADIA

I watch Luke and his friend get out of the car. Both of them big, and despite their obvious amusement, an aura of intensity surrounds them, so palpable I can almost taste it on the tip of my tongue.

The passenger door is left wide open. Kelly nods toward it. "Get in."

Said the spider to the fly. At least that's how it feels. "Please," I rebuke.

"Please," he adds.

Against all better judgement, I climb inside the car. Kelly wastes no time shutting the door behind me. He moves around the front of the car and opens the driver's side door. One leg goes in, then he folds the rest of his body inside the car and shuts the door behind him.

His presence fills the entire space so that I can't breathe, despite the open window beside me. I wait for him to talk. God knows, I'm not volunteering anything. *So ... I steal cars* is not really the opener I want to run with, so I remain silent. Except he doesn't say anything either. He doesn't even look across at me. He simply turns the key in the ignition and starts the car. We pull out, roaring off down the street.

My mouth falls open. "What the ..."

I glance behind me. Luke is standing by the kerb, next to his friend, slowly shrinking as we eat up distance on the road, his arms splayed out wide as if to say, "Duuuuude."

My eyes shift to Racer and Echo. My mouth falls open further. He's waving. A goodbye gesture. Echo is beside him, holding tight to her phone with one hand, the other clutching her gut, laughing. Good. I hope the amusement gives her a hernia.

I turn back, facing the road in front of me, wondering where we're going as we turn right at a set of green lights.

Kelly's lips pinch as he drives. He clearly has no idea. He simply continues to focus on the road ahead, one hand on the wheel and his forearm resting on the open window. If I had a camera, I would capture the moment—the shadows on the hard set of his jaw and straight nose contrasting with the light blue of his eyes. Strands of blonde hair whip about his face, and the light of the dashboard has the short beard on his face glinting in the night. There's beauty in his harsh expression, in the roughness of his edges, and an honesty that simply says, "This is me, take me as I am or fuck off." It makes me ache with longing to touch him.

He looks across at me, and he must—*must*—see the ache in my eyes because I feel it so deep in my bones I can barely take a breath. His voice is gruff as he turns back to the road. "You want to tell me what's going on, Arcadia?"

Everyone calls me Ace. I like when he uses my full name. But not enough to admit I'm just a two-bit thief. Someone he's better off without. It doesn't matter that I'm trying to leave it behind me. I'm starting to realise a stark truth. It's inside of me. A part of me I'll never shake loose. *Will you be something I'll never shake too, Kelly?*

"No." My voice sounds rusty. I clear my throat. "You want to tell me where you plan on taking me?"

"Yeah." His eyes gleam as though he's thought of something. He executes a swift U-turn and drives down a back street, heading toward the city. "Somewhere special. You're gonna love this."

We're in Darlinghurst when he pulls into the customer parking lot of a large mechanic's garage. The building is unobtrusive and size-able, the outside brickwork painted charcoal. There's a large sign spread across the front in distinct, vintage lettering that simply says: Rehab.

I stare, confused. "What *is* this place?"

His eyes are on the façade as he answers, "My business."

I look from him and back to the building, more than impressed. "You own this? Rehab? What kind of business is it?"

Kelly shrugs. "Car restoration."

He says it as though it's something inconsequential, but there's something bright in his eyes, maybe pride. "Get the fuck out. Kelly!" I squeal a little—just enough that I should be embarrassed—and punch his arm, grinning. "You never told me that last night!" I turn back to the frontage, taking it in as we both step out of the car and shut the doors. Hands on hips, I bite my lip, eager to get inside. "This is amazing. This is ... unexpected."

My enthusiasm must be infectious because a grin tugs at his lips. "It's only new."

I'm the one grabbing his hand this time, pulling him toward the entrance. It's closed, obviously. The lights are off and the doors locked. "Let me at it, Kelly. Please, please, please." I pout my lips and flutter my lashes teasingly as we stand by the front door.

He laughs. "You're a goof."

"A goof that you're going to let play with all your toys though, right? Say it's so, Kelly. I'm not above begging." I take a step toward him, my front brushing his, tantalising and close. I hook my index finger over the front of his jeans and tug suggestively. "Whatever you want."

His brows rise, yet his eyes are on me like I'm everything he's ever wanted and never dared ask for. "You're whoring yourself out now?"

I grin happily at the thought of getting to have a look and play. "Yes."

Kelly's nostrils flare. "Goddamn, you're pretty," he mutters, seemingly to himself, before his hand snakes around my neck and yanks my face to his, kissing me. His tongue thrusts inside my mouth, his passion intense, his hold on me tight.

My hands grip his shoulders as he backs me toward the brickwork by the side of the front door, pushing me against it, his erection obvious. It presses into me, throbbing, getting harder with every second that passes.

Kelly draws back, panting, staring into my eyes. His are glazed, just as I imagine mine are. "Only for me."

"Only ..." I suck in a breath. "What?"

"A whore. You can be a whore. But only for me."

"I'm not ..." My hands drift down, pressing against his chest. "I don't ..."

He kisses me again, his hips pushing against mine until he's all I can feel. "You don't what?" he says against my lips before moving his mouth across my cheek and down my neck, an urgent caress that makes me shiver.

Oh god, why do I have to be so awkward? My head tilts back to give him better access and collides with the bricks. I barely notice. "I don't usually sleep around. This ... is not something I do."

He stills and draws back slightly, meeting my eyes with humour. "Me either."

"Kelly!" I laugh, even though I'm trying to be serious, and smack a hand against his chest. It's so vast, an endless expanse that needs to be studied in further detail. Irrational need overtakes me, and my laughter dies a quick death. "Take off your shirt."

"Babe, for someone who doesn't usually do this, you seem in an awful hurry."

I snatch a quick kiss, biting his bottom lip, which elicits a groan from deep within his chest. "Don't be a tease."

"You make me feel so cheap, forcing me to strip outside in the cold, without even letting me get you inside first."

His tone is teasing and makes me laugh. Again. "This from the man who said I could be his whore!"

"That's different," he protests as I slide my hands beneath his black tee, encountering ridges of muscle, as if his belly were the Great Dividing Ranges of Australia's east.

I sigh with navigational pleasure as my palms traverse the warm skin. "How is it any different?"

"You're just using me to get inside that door beside you," he says against my neck as he kisses a path upward, toward my earlobe.

"And you're not using me?"

Kelly's lips draw back from my skin, and he lifts his head, his eyes finding mine. His expression is puzzled, as if I just randomly presented him with a Rubik's cube. He presses both palms on the brickwork behind me, just above my shoulders so it feels like nothing else exists outside the two of us. "Can I be honest?"

I tug on the belt loops of his jeans. Of course I want him to be honest, but the sudden weightiness surrounding us leaves an uneasy lump in my throat. For him to give me that when I've given him nothing feels unfair. "Please," I say, swallowing the unease in an attempt to make it go away. It doesn't.

"I'm not sure."

My brows draw together. "Not sure?"

"If I'm using you or not. What if ..." He looks away, exhaling a frustrated puff of air. He shakes his head and looks at me again. "What if once isn't enough?"

It won't be. I know it. "So then we do it twice."

"What if twice isn't enough?"

"So then we do it three times."

His lips quirks at the corners. "What if three times isn't enough?"

I chuckle and palm his cheeks with both hands. "Then we do it a million times."

"Babe." Kelly kisses me. "A million? The chafing would be a bitch, but points for enthusiasm."

He smothers another of my laughs with his mouth, his hands leaving the wall and finding my hips, pulling me flush against him as we kiss. "Kelly," I whisper when he gives me a bare moment to breathe.

"Mmm?"

"Let me inside or lose me forever."

He throws back his head, wrapping both arms around my neck and smooshing my face into his chest, and he laughs *hard.*

Oh god. This man. *This man.*

Kelly eventually lets me go and tugs a set of keys from the pocket of his jeans. Shifting to the door, he slides in a key and turns it. The lock *clunks* in the quiet of the night, and he turns the handle and opens the door wide, gesturing for me to walk inside.

We're in the front office. The counter is sleek, the timber floors fresh with varnish, yet there's an unmistakable scent in the air— motor oil, chassis grease, solvent, and brake dust. It's the scent of my childhood. Of my grandfather, my father, my brother. It's home. I breathe it in, savouring it as I look around. "Where do we start?"

To my left is a set of automatic glass doors that lead to all the action. There's only one car inside. It's concealed, tucked in like a little baby for the night with a car cover. I want to start with her.

"There." Instead, Kelly points down the hallway beside the counter entrance. There are three doors on the right as you head along, which likely contain private offices and washrooms, but he's indicating a set of stairs at the very end.

"Ok. Lead the way."

"Babe." Kelly shakes his head, indicating that's a negative. "You go first on the stairs. Always."

"And there's the gentleman side of you again."

He shakes his head again. "Not a gentleman. Just a pervert. Want a bird's eye view of that fine ass."

My cheeks flush pink at the thought, but he wants me to lead the way, so that's exactly what I do. There's a lot of stairs, and when we reach the top, it's high and not a vast area. On my left is bunch of lockers, a bench seat, and an en suite-sized bathroom. To my right is a big uncovered window and resting beneath it a bed. A large one. King size, at least. It's dressed with nothing but white sheets and white pillow covers. It makes sense, because when you're working late into the night, your body gets stiff and tired, and crashing somewhere close by always feels like heaven. And white sheets mean you can regularly bleach them to remove grease stains.

Still. Here we are. Standing beside a bed with no one else around. I turn and face him. "I see you've led me to your lair."

"Au contraire, babe. You led me."

"Touché." My lips form a smirk. "Now take off your shirt."

Kelly grabs the back of the neckline and tugs it off, mussing his hair. He tosses it to the corner and walks backward toward the bed. He reaches it and sits on the edge while I stand there and stare.

His chest is what dreams are made of. *My* dreams. It's a hard chest, but not just with muscle. With scars and tattoos. With chest hair and thick veins. With *life*. It says, "I've worked and I've lived." It also says, "I'll protect you from any storm." It should also come with a sign—warning: Touching this is an experience that will change your life, forever.

"Your turn," he eventually says, after waiting out my extra-long gawking session with unexpected patience.

Ugh. Do I have to? I'm pretty sure beneath this long-sleeved high-necked fitted black shirt lurks a granny bra. I tug the neckline away from my skin and take a peek down.

"Are they still there?" he quips.

Fuck. It's the granny bra. I want to weep. I let go, the stretchy cotton snapping back into place as I look at him. "What?"

"Your tits. You seem worried they upped and disappeared on you."

My gaze sweeps the length of him again. He has all of that, and I have heinous unmentionables that my neighbour's dog wouldn't even chew—and that dog chews everything. He broke through our fence late last year and into our yard and ate his way through my brother's putrid old boots that he's owned since 1985.

This is supposed to be a sexy and passionate encounter, one I've been imagining since the moment he stepped foot inside Fix. My daydreams pictured me shaved, with smoky eye-makeup and heels, and the kind of black lace so scrappy you needed to invest in a microscope just to find it in your underwear drawer. And Kelly would drop to his knees in gratitude just seeing me in all my dazzling glory.

"They're still there," I croak, miserable. I suck. I fucking suck so bad.

"And that makes you sad because?" he prompts.

"I'm not sad. But you should turn around."

"What? And miss the show? Babe." He folds his arms. Muscles bulge. *Christ.*

"Just ... trust me."

Kelly crooks a finger. "Come here."

I press my lips together, my feet glued to the floor.

His eyes narrow and he starts to rise. "Don't make me come over there."

I splay my hands out, warding him off. "Wait," I blurt out, knowing I'm ruining the moment, but I seem unable to get over myself and my manky underwear. "Just ... close your eyes for a second."

"Ace—"

"Please?"

His sinks back to the bed and closes them. I waste no time. I reach around, unsnapping the hooks on my bra. Diving up through my sleeves, I yank out the straps, rip the damn thing up and outside the neckline of my shirt, and toss the offensive garment to the corner where I send out a hopeful prayer for it to spontaneously combust.

"You can open them now," I inform him, slightly out of breath.

Kelly's eyes open and he looks me over, his brows rising. "You look ... no different. What did you do?"

"Let's just do this, okay?"

"You're making it sound like laundry. Is sex going to be a chore for you?"

Ace, you're so good at this, laughs my inner voice. *You should totally be a porn star.*

"Shut up," I mutter to myself.

"Shut up?" Kelly echoes.

Oh my god. *Fuck it.* I take deep breath and peel my shirt over my head. After it drops to the floor beside me, I remove the elastic band from my hair and give it a quick shake, letting it fall down the naked length of my back.

Kelly rises, soundless, staring. My heart stops. There's hunger in his eyes, a craving that makes everything that came before this moment just ... fall away.

"Babe," he says. "Come here." His voice is sandpaper, his words a rough command.

I walk toward him and he takes my hands, tugging me flush against him. The heat of his body is vivid, the press of his naked skin heady. I slide my palms upward on his chest, winding them around his neck. He responds by trailing the rough pads of his fingers down my ribcage, his thumbs brushing the sides of my breasts. Shivers erupt.

"You like that?" he murmurs.

I can only nod and moan when he does it again. "Oh god," I say with a shaky breath. The torment is delicious.

Kelly sinks back onto the edge of the bed, bringing me down with him. I straddle his lap, and he ducks his head, licking a small pathway between both breasts. I hold still, my hands on his shoulders. He kisses his way across my chest and slowly draws a nipple inside his mouth. Pleasure shoots straight between my legs, sharp and sweet. My head tilts back and my hair spills down. He takes the strands in his fist and tugs, arching me back further, forcing my breasts to rise higher.

When Kelly's finished giving them all his attention, my panties are soaked. He lets my hair go and his hands move to the waistband of my leather pants. *Oh god, yes.*

He glances up at me. "Stand."

I fumble from his lap, my legs unsteady like a newborn foal. Kelly's hands encircle my hips, supporting me as I find my feet. Then they shift to my pants button. He undoes it and slides my zipper down, his pace excruciatingly slow.

He slides his hand in, outside of my underwear, and I know he can feel how wet they are because his eyes close and his nostrils flare. I don't know what panties I'm wearing. I'm past the point of caring. *Just touch me.*

As if he hears my plea, his hand pushes its way inside the fabric. His calloused fingers rub against the slick skin. I sway, lightheaded, and he retreats and stands, the size of him towering over me.

"Kelly."

He shoves my pants down, bunching them beneath the cheeks of my ass. Then he turns me and nudges me down, so now I'm the one seated on the edge of the bed. I fall back on my elbows when he takes my pants and tugs. I lift my legs, and he peels them clean away, leaving me in just my panties.

"Pull them to the side."

My breath hitches. "Kelly."

"Do it, babe."

I do as he asks, revealing the swollen, aching flesh beneath the thin layer of fabric. I'm more exposed to this man than I've been to any other in my entire life.

His eyes burn and he groans as if in pain, his hand going to the bulge in his jeans and squeezing. "Prettiest fuckin' sight in the world."

"It's your turn to come here now," I tell him.

Kelly takes a step forward. I open his jeans and shove them down along with his boxer briefs, leaving them to bunch around his strong thighs. His cock is thick and juts out. I take it in hand, feeling the silky hardness. It jerks at my touch, and his hands fist at his sides.

"Think I might explode if you lick it," he mutters, gruff, so I touch my tongue to the head, licking my around the tip. "Shit."

Kelly yanks off his pants and steps out of them. Then he's on me. Determined hands wrenching at my panties, pushing me up on the bed until he's between my legs, kneeling. He doesn't bring his mouth to me. He lifts my hips, bringing me to his mouth as though I weigh less than a feather.

"Oh god." My palms are sweaty, shaky, as he tongues my clit, licking and sucking with a savagery that sends my pulse through the roof. It's so intense. So good. There's nothing delicate about it. His beard scratches the sensitive skin, his mouth relentless. His fingers dig in to the backs of my thighs. The night is quiet except for the panting of my breath and the sounds of him devouring me.

He drops me back to the bed and slides a thick finger inside. I suck in a sharp breath and an orgasm builds. His mouth returns, sucking hard as he slides in another, stretching, thrusting, curling.

"Kelly," I pant, rubbing against him, riding his tongue. He groans. "Kelly. God."

Then he's gone. I turn my head, my eyes fluttering open. He's crouched over his jeans, facing my way, frantic, tugging a foil packet from his pocket. He tears it open with his teeth, and I watch as he rolls it on with quick, jerky movements. Then he's back on me, surrounding me, pushing his way in.

He's thick. Big. It's uncomfortably good. I bring my knees toward me, and it seats him deep, so deep I feel the pulse of him inside me. I close my eyes. He thrusts and my clit throbs to the same beat as my heart.

"Ace. Look at me."

Kelly moves again. A harder thrust.

My eyes open.

"That good?"

He rocks his hips, watching me.

"More," I whisper, my own hips rising to meet his, feverish and needy, my clit aching and my need for friction desperate.

Kelly rocks harder. My hands clutch at his back, fingers digging in, impatient. I expect him to laugh at the torment he's subjecting me to and enjoy my frustration, but his brow is creased and his breath is erratic, as if he's barely holding on.

"Fuck," his mutters, his voice gravel.

He draws out and punches back in. I gasp, the bed bouncing from the force.

"Yes." I suck in a breath. "That."

Kelly ducks his head, his teeth nipping the sensitive skin of my earlobe. "So fucking good," he rasps, pulling out again.

"Mmm." I'm delirious and shaky. He pounds in again. And again. The bed judders. My skin burns and he watches me fall apart. It's intense, and raw, and so good. "Don't ever stop."

His thrusts come faster, harder, and his brow creases tighter. "Don't ever want to."

My legs lock around his hips as pleasure builds. Sweat sheens our skin. The sheets beneath me are damp and strands of hair stick to my neck. Every sensation is heightened, every breath harder to take. Then I'm coming, and he's sweeping me up in his arms as lights dot my vision.

For a moment I'm weightless, and then Kelly's seated on his knees with me straddling him. Thick biceps wrap around me, clutching me to him, one hand against the back of my head, the other my lower back. He thrusts upward, holding me tight, rutting into me with powerful force.

Waves of pleasure wash over me as I ride out the aftershocks. His lips find mine, kissing me as his body goes hard. He groans into my mouth, rocking and straining, every muscle rigid as he comes.

I'm dizzy when we end the kiss. He presses his forehead to mine, our breaths harsh and ragged.

Kelly's eyes are closed but mine are open.

I'm crazy for you. Just like the song. Exactly the way Madonna croons it. *Crazy, crazy for you.*

Rather than drawing away, his head ducks into my neck and his arms pull me tighter, a steel band locking me close. His lips brush my skin as he speaks. "Only nine hundred thousand, nine hundred and ninety-nine more of those to go."

Laughter bubbles out of me.

Eventually we peel our sticky skin away from each other and flop to the bed. My eyes close. "This place, I haven't even had the tour yet, but it's like a dream, right?"

"Yeah, babe."

"You're so lucky."

Kelly grunts. "Would give it all back if I could."

I peek open one eye, turning my head to look at him. His gaze is on the ceiling above. "What do you mean?"

"Nothin'."

"Kelly?" I prompt, because his statement doesn't feel like nothing. It feels like a whole lot of something.

His voice is harsh. "Leave it."

"You brought it up."

"Not gonna argue about it."

My eyes close and I leave it be. For now. I feel the bed dip as he rises. The bathroom door closes. The sounds of the toilet flushing and tap gushing filter through, and then the bed is dipping again. My eyes peek open. He's on his side now, facing me, naked, every inch of him glorious.

"Tell me about your Mustang," he asks.

My lips turn downward. "There's nothing left of it."

"I'm sorry, babe," he says and rubs my arm, his voice drowsy.

We chatter softly and drift off. I don't remember falling fast asleep until I'm woken by someone talking.

"Please, stop."

It's a whisper. Pained and thick with fear.

My eyes blink open. It's still night, and the light of the moon filters through the window. I rise up on one elbow, rubbing at my face. Kelly hasn't moved from his side. *"Make it stop."*

He's talking in his sleep? I jostle his shoulder. "Kelly."

"Please. I'll do anything. Just stop. Stop. Please."

"Kelly," I say again, firm and loud, a sick knot forming in my belly at his words.

He doesn't wake. Instead, a solitary tear tracks down from the corner of his eye and plops to the pillow. *"You left and it wouldn't stop. You left and never came back. You left. I had no choice."*

"Kelly." My pulse races with distress. Make what stop? *Kelly, what happened to you?* "Wake up."

My panicked voice gets through, and he rolls over sleepily, facing the other way. My eyes drop to his back, and my heart stutters before it comes to a complete stop.

"No."

Bile rises, climbing my throat as I stare at the Sentinel tattoo laid bare before my eyes. A trembling hand rises to cover my mouth.

"Oh my god, no."

13

ARCADIA

I scramble from the bed, grabbing at my clothes that are scattered about the floor, all the while my chest is tight. I can't catch my breath. I can't think, because if I do, I'll throw up, or scream, or pummel him with my fists, and I can't do any of those things. I can't wake the sleeping beast. Looking into those beautiful blue eyes—traitorous eyes—will hurt too much.

I shove my feet inside my panties and yank them up my legs. My pants go on, one leg at a time, my bra ... well, just fuck that thing. I'm tugging my shirt over my head as I double-time it down the stairs on silent feet.

I'm running down the hallway when my eye is caught by the covered car inside the workshop. I come to a stuttering halt, and a slow, determined, angry smile forms on my lips. Fuck you, Kelly, and fuck the Sentinels.

After searching for the button that activates the automatic doors, I punch it. They *whoosh* open. I step inside. The space is beautiful. His equipment is top notch, the tools tucked away, gleaming in their compartments. Wonderful things happen in this workspace. Amazing transformations. I swallow the lump and grab the car cover in my fist, yanking it away in one fell swoop. It flutters to the ground behind me and I stare, my mouth falling open.

The Dodge Charger sits there in all her glory—glossy candy-apple red paintwork and wheels black and wide, their tread wider and bigger than Australia's national debt. The white stripes through the middle proclaim her hotter than shit.

Who does she belong to?

I run my palm along her curvaceous sides, a gesture of worship.

His name is Jake Romero.

My breath puffs out through my lips as I make my way around her front, caressing, my mind racing.

What else?

I reach her front and turn, staring.

Bounce it. Too much trouble. Too many contacts.

Right then, at that table in Fix, I knew, *I knew* that we'd meet again, me and this beautiful lady. And here we are. I stare her down, letting her know who's boss as if she were a living, breathing creature.

What contacts?

King Street Boys. Sentinels. Valentines.

All the signs were there. Right there in front of me. I just refused to see them. Mason has been so overly protective since the shooting, so overbearing. He smothers me with it. And every person he saw riding a Harley was eyed with suspicion and a tight jaw. But he was right. This time he was *right*, and like the little boy who cried wolf, I discounted his declaration with scorn, thinking only of myself and what I wanted. Thinking only of how Kelly made me feel—desired, alive, vital—and how I wanted more of it. *Greedy bitch.*

I hiccup. A sob. What I've done is building inside of me, a wild storm that I know will unleash soon, faster than I can contain it. My eyes flick to the board by the door. The keys are right there, making it appear so easy, but only a fool would swipe them. The gleaming Dodge Charger in front of me is a brumby—a wild Australian horse found in the Northern Territory. She'll let you get close, draw you in, nostrils flaring as she slowly lulls you into a false sense of security, but the moment you climb on for a ride, she'll buck you so hard that every bone in your body will shatter the moment you hit the ground.

I have to move fast. Once I press that button to open the garage door and start the car, Kelly will wake.

With keys in hand, I slide them in the ignition without getting in. Once I've hit the button by the entrance and the garage door begins to *whir* upward, I run, scrambling around her side, almost sliding across the bonnet. I'm inside and the engine roars to life as freedom reveals itself in front of me. Wide open road beckons.

The clutch goes in, I drop the gear, and my foot hits the accelerator, punching it to the floor. The Dodge Charger surges forward, her back-end skidding left ... right ... left, before righting as I hurtle through the front parking lot. I jerk the steering wheel sideways and fishtail out onto the street.

My heart is pounding right through my chest when I take a glance in the rear-view mirror. Kelly is running out through the open garage door, his chest bare, hands on the fly of his jeans as he yanks the zipper upward.

"*Fuck!*" I see him yell. Then he turns, running toward the car we drove here earlier that night.

This is it. This is the part where I get broken into a million pieces. But I can't seem to care. Instead, I seize the gearstick and punch my foot on the clutch, jerking it up a gear. Like a horse smacked with a riding crop, the Charger howls and gallops forward. I wind the window down and air rushes in, circling the small space and blowing my hair in every direction.

"*We have a tail.*"

It's me and Mason all over again. My palms form a sheen of sweat. I take a sharp turn, and my hands slip on the wheel.

"*Your nine lives.*"

Mason glanced across at me then, fear forming in his eyes, the kind of fear I'd never seen before. Not for himself. For me.

"*They're up.*"

Blood spilled over his back, soaking his shirt and dripping down his sides. It puddled beneath the both of us, the metallic scent so thick in the air I choked on it. The shrill sound of sirens in the distance haunt me every time I hear them.

Mason was always an over-protective brother, but after that night it became my turn take care of him. When he was in the hospital, I never left his side. I slept curled in a chair. When he woke and learned his fate, he died. My brother died because the one I have now is not the same. There's no more laughter or wild abandon. There's no more teasing. My brother doesn't live anymore. He just exists.

His anger in the bathroom this morning was more emotion than I've seen from him in years.

"Kelly Daniels is a Sentinel!"

The rage and the pain I've been holding at bay surge forward. A sob breaks free, and another, and I punch through another gear before swiping at the tears on my face.

"My brother is a paranoid fool."

That's what I believed. What I told— Realisation hits me. Echo's face. Her *face* when I told her what Mason said. She knows. She fucking *knows.*

I grapple with the wheel as I yank for the phone in the back pocket of my leather pants. She's listed in my favourite contacts. I waste no time dialling, putting the phone on speaker, and shoving it in the centre console.

She answers, sleepy, humorous. "Did you get to the boinking?"

Rage squeezes the breath from my lungs. "You bitch!"

"What?"

"You knew!" I suck in air, another sob escaping. "You knew. I let him touch me. I let him inside me." *His hands trail down my sides, rough and delicious, caressing. My skin erupts in shivers.* Bile rises. "And you *knew!*"

"Ace—"

I don't understand it. My best friend. The one person I thought I could count on above all others. "What is *wrong* with you?"

"Ace—"

"Don't." Her betrayal tastes bitter on my tongue. "Just ... don't."

"Ace, where are you?"

I laugh. I tip my head back as the car roars along the windy road toward Bondi Beach, and I fucking *laugh* hysterically. "What, you don't know?" My hands grip the steering wheel, my sarcasm thick. "I'm in the Charger."

"What Charger? What ... Oh my god. Ace."

I glance in the rear-view mirror.

"We have a tail."

Kelly is roaring up behind me. I inhale a shaky breath and let it out. "This is on you. Whatever happens next is on you."

Echo's voice is hard. "Don't you dare."

"Fuck you, Echo!" I yell.

"Fuck you too, Ace."

We go silent, my chest heaving because I haven't taken a proper breath since the moment I woke in Kelly's bed. Hair blows across my face, and I shove it away.

"You didn't see it." Echo's words are a bare whisper that I almost miss.

Kelly flashes his lights behind me. *Pull over.* Ignoring him, I take the next turn hard, the Charger's rear-end careening out behind me.

"See what?" I bark.

"You!"

"What are you talking about?"

I've reached the winding road along the cliff tops by the beach. The scent of the salty ocean invades the car, and the temperature drops several degrees, meaning an easterly wind is blowing in hard. A storm is coming.

"I'm talking about you, Ace!" she yells. "You go on about how your brother 'died' after the shooting, but you don't see."

"Oh my god, Echo! See *what?*"

"You did too."

My foot slackens on the accelerator and the Charger slows.

"You don't laugh anymore either. Instead, you ... you walk around wearing goddamn beige skirts and flat shoes and those ridiculous reading glasses, with your nose stuck in some finance book. You're hiding from life, Ace. Hiding like a fucking coward! Neither of you died, and yet you both act like you're buried six feet under. I'm sick of it. Fucking sick of it."

"I laugh." My mind travels back through the last two years, scrambling to remember the last time I laughed, really laughed, and I can't. No. Wait. Kelly. He makes me laugh, and the realisation sinks my heart, because Kelly is a lie.

"Not really. I mean it's there on your lips, and in your voice, but it's not there in your soul, Ace."

"Don't give me any philosophical bullshit," I interject.

Echo keeps talking like I never spoke. "I saw your face when you met Kelly. You came to life. I saw you look at that man like you had a goddamn vagina again. So I decided not to tell you he's a Sentinel, because I knew you'd shut back down. You need to start living again, Ace. Stop punishing yourself for what happened to your brother! You put every cent you owned toward his medical bills, and his rehabilitation, and outfitting the house to cater to his disability. And when he told you to stop stealing cars, you went and enrolled in the most boring university program alive because it was *safe.*"

"There's nothing wrong with safe!"

"Says the girl who's driving a stolen Charger with a motherfucking Sentinel on her tail!"

A parking lot looms ahead, overlooking the crashing waves of the beach. It beckons. I'm tired. Drained. I'm the best car thief in the business, but I can't outdrive Kelly. Stealing this car is the dumbest thing I've ever done. But what Echo did was dumb too.

"Did you think I'd never find out? That I'd exist in some little bubble with Kelly and live happily ever after? He's a Sentinel. They're rapists. And murderers!"

I pull in and stop the car. Kelly roars to a stop behind me, sideways, blocking me in. Putting the gear in neutral, I tug the handbrake on and turn the key. The heated engine shuts down, *ticking* in the still of the night.

"They're not. I researched them, Ace. Did you think I wouldn't do that? Grinder was an exception. He was the one that came after you with a gun, the others were just trying to get his car back, but I couldn't tell you that. You wouldn't listen even if I tried. You both just painted all of them with the same brush."

I glance in the side-view mirror through my open window. Kelly is stepping out of the car, slamming the door shut behind him. My breath rasps in the silence as his feet crunch on the gravel, the sound getting louder.

"Grinder was kicked out of the MC. They took his cut and burned the Sentinels tattoo from his skin. The fact that he's still alive in prison is a miracle."

My eyes meet Kelly's in the mirror as he gets close. The anger in them is bright, but there's hurt in there too.

"Kelly's not some polite, respectable guy. He's got a lot of rough edges, and a past that ... that ..." She seems stuck. "But he's not Grinder, Ace. None of them are."

"What hurt you?"

"The past," he answered. "It can be a real shitty place to visit in your head sometimes."

I swallow the lump of unease in my throat. Is it possible that Echo speaks the truth? I should believe her, right, because she's my best friend, but it's too much to process right now. I need somewhere quiet to think and here, with Kelly approaching, is not that place.

He reaches the driver's side of the car. I'm treated to hard, bare skin, and a trail of hair that leads down to the low waistband of his worn jeans before he crouches, laying both forearms on the open window.

Mere mortals would cower beneath the blazing glare in his eyes. And because I am, in fact, a mere mortal, I do. Just a little.

"I have to go," I say to Echo, and without moving my gaze from his, I fumble behind me, hitting the 'end call' button.

Kelly sets his jaw. He looks like he wants to speak but doesn't know where to start.

"Do you know who I am?" I ask, because I'm not sure how he can be who he is and not know who I am. Has he not put the pieces together?

His tone is flat. "You're Ace Jones."

"That's right. Do you know who Ace Jones is?"

"I was trying to learn," he grinds out, "but then the bitch fucked me and left, stealing this here Charger, and now I'm wishing I never knew her at all."

I bite the insides of my cheeks, holding back a heated retort, because after my conversation with Echo, I'm starting to think that maybe I deserve that, and that maybe he deserves an explanation.

"My grandfather is Racer Jones," I say quietly.

"I met him already, remember? So yeah, I know."

"And my brother is Mason Jones. The Ghost."

Kelly's face is blank for a moment, and then he stiffens, every muscle turning rigid. He studies me as comprehension dawns. "You're Ace Jones."

My lips press together.

"Dammit." He rises, slapping his hand against the side of the Charger. I can't see his expression now, but his anger is palpable. He stalks two, three, four steps away, swiping hands through his hair before turning to look at me. "I'm falling for a fucking car thief?"

Did he say falling? "Wait, what?"

"You stole Romero's car!" he yells.

"Yeah. I did!" I fumble with the door handle. It flings open and I step out, slamming it behind me. "And I'd do it again," I yell back, stalking toward him, my finger jabbing in the direction of his chest, "because I went to bed last night with a hot, sexy man..." my voice rises to a shriek "...and I woke up with a fucking Sentinel!"

"Yeah?" He gets in my face, not holding back. "Well, I went to bed last night with a hot, sexy woman and woke up with a thieving whore!"

My gasp is so hard and swift I choke on it.

"You weren't lyin', were you, babe?" he says with a sneer while I wheeze and splutter. "You'd do *anything* to get what you want!" He waves a hand at the car I stole right out from under his nose. "Even fuck some guy from the same MC that shot your brother in the back and paralysed him for life."

I stumble backward, his words a figurative punch to the face. "I can't ..."

"You can't what?" he growls.

My belly heaves. I turn and bend at the waist, hands on my knees as I throw up. Torturous heaves rack my body until there's nothing left. I'm gasping and wiping tears from my face when a warm palm slides along my lower back. I flinch.

"Babe," Kelly says quietly.

"Don't touch me."

"You didn't know either, did you? That I'm a Sentinel."

I turn around, stumbling on weak limbs and face him, shaking my head. "Not until I woke and saw the tattoo."

Kelly grabs me and pulls me against him. My face mashes to his chest as his arms circle tight around me, a shackle I can't escape from. "I'm sorry I didn't tell you. Figured you'd think I wasn't good enough."

I struggle, my hands pushing against him. "Don't—"

"I'm sorry." His arms tighten further, and the fight leaves me. I still, turning my head to face the crashing of the waves. "Grinder is ... what he did was fucked-up and it's on us, because we let him in. We made him one of us and for some reason he thought that was licence to do whatever he wanted. He might be in prison, but we made him pay for what he did," he says, his voice a rumble in his chest as he holds me.

"How?" I croak.

He swallows. "We ... emasculated him."

"You what?"

"Babe. We cut his motherfuckin' dick off."

My stomach pitches all over again. "You did that?"

"Not me, personally. But I condoned it."

I struggle again and Kelly loosens his hold. I shift back so I'm able to tilt my head upward and look him in the eye. His brow is furrowed. Is he worried what I think of him now?

"It's not enough. He's still alive."

Kelly

MY INSIDES DO A DOUBLE-TAKE. I was expecting revulsion, and yet she's still here, talking to me. Club business is something I do my best to stay out of. Although I'm a member of the MC, I'm still that same solitary bear that walks alone. All I knew was that he raped a girl, and he shot a man they call The Ghost, a man who stole his car. Ace's name maybe came up once, but it was not something I paid attention to—nor added two and two together after meeting her. She was wearing glasses that night in Fix and studying finance for fuck's sake. That is *not* the persona of a car thief, though she certainly fits it now with her black outfit and sticky fingers.

"Unfortunately, yes, he's still alive," I say eventually.

"Echo says..." she pauses to grimace "...she says that you burned his tattoo away?"

"We did."

"So you basically tortured him."

My lips press together. What am I supposed to say to that? It's not something enjoyable, to physically brutalise another human being. There's a grimness to the task. A knowledge that it's something that has to be done. And after, you walk away a little heavier in the soul. Mine has more than enough marks on it now. Too many to count.

Ace steps further away from me, hugging her arms around her middle. "Where do we go from here, Kelly? I'm a ... thieving whore and you're a—"

My brow arches. "Fucking Sentinel?"

"Yeah." She gives a weak laugh. "That."

"Maybe you can tell me what your plan was after stealing Jake Romero's car."

"There was no plan. I woke up and I panicked. And she was there, under that cover like a beautiful red treasure. From there ... I don't know, I lost my mind a little, I guess." She shakes her head, and there's a beat of silence between us that makes my chest tight. I want her all over again. Even the crazy parts. Because she sure as fuck is crazy, getting in that car and handling it the way she did. If I hadn't been so mad, I would've stopped to admire it. Ace takes a step backward, bringing her closer to the Charger. "I should go." Her voice firms. "I need to go."

She turns and walks. My eyes drop to her ass, just for a moment, but it's a long enough moment that she gets her hand on the handle of the door before my brain catches up.

"Whoa, whoa whoa!" I call out. "If you think you're getting back in that car and driving away, then you've got a screw loose, lady."

Ace pauses. "I promise I'll drive it back to Rehab."

"Yeah, like I'm gonna trust you."

We end up driving back to Rehab together in the Charger, Ace in the passenger seat. Lee's car is locked up tight at the parking lot. Considering it was his brilliant idea to stalk the girls in the first place, he can go get it tomorrow.

The drive is quiet, the only sound a deep purr from Romero's car. He brought it in early yesterday for a simple oil change. Even the tiniest hairline scratch on the immaculate paintwork will give him a stroke. The fact that it's still in one piece is the only reason I'll still be breathing tomorrow when he comes to collect it.

We're only a few blocks away when Ace finally decides to speak.

"Sooo ..." she drawls, glancing at me sideways. "You're falling for me?"

Dammit. She had to remember me saying that, didn't she? "Nope."

"You can admit it, you know." She waves her arms to encompass the interior of the car. "This is a safe space, and I am an ... an empathetic person."

"Har! Empathy my asshole."

Amusement emanates from her smug face. "You like me."

"I used you. Remember when I said I wasn't sure?" I point out, out-smugging her smugness. "Well, now I'm sure. Consider yourself used. Your pussy was wet and tight and very accommodating, but now my dick and I must move on to other pastures, ones of the non-thievin' variety." A light-bulb *dings* on in my head. "Holy shit!" We pull into the parking lot. I don't have the automatic garage door key on me—it's inside—so I park it out front and switch off the engine.

"That's what you were all doing out there last night." And I say *last night* because dawn has begun to break over the horizon, a riot of orange and hot pink that makes the bonnet of the Charger blaze like fire. "You were going to steal a car!"

She gasps and the sound is phoney as fuck. "We were not!"

"Save it." I open the door and step out. Turning, I bend to look at her, my eyes narrowing. "I'm on to you."

14

ARCADIA

*M*y phone vibrates a message. I glance down at the screen from the lecture hall in front of me. Professor Braune, or Professor Yawn as she's known in student circles, is waxing on about the beauty of quantitative analysis to make informed financial decisions. It's her introduction, and she's been talking for ... I check my watch ... approximately twenty minutes. And rather than being seated near the front by the exit (the thief in me is always looking for an easy getaway), I was late and had to make my way up the stairs to the three vacant seats near the back row. The sea of students in front of me are all surreptitiously checking their phones, their heads tilting downward at random intervals.

Echo: Where are you?

Me: Hell. I'm in hell.

It's Friday afternoon, a week after I lost my mind and stole Romero's Dodge Charger. Kelly went inside Rehab after we returned. I (wisely) chose to stay outside and message Echo for an extraction. He may have been waiting for me to eventually follow him inside, but instead I was collected twenty minutes later, and that was that, apparently. I've been lying low since then, and my interaction with Kelly has been non-existent. I know, because initially I checked my missed calls and messages every ten minutes. Eventually, it reduced to every hour. And then just once a day.

Today I haven't bothered to check them at all because the sexual spell he had over me has lifted. That's right. It *lifted*. No more lust. Sex dreams be gone. Kelly and I were nothing more than a departure from reality. We simply veered from the road at the same time, causing a collision. A collision of naked limbs and sweaty skin, and his thick, heavy cock thrusting inside my ...

I bite my bottom lip before I moan aloud.

Now we're back on course, following our separate paths. Kelly with Rehab and me with Professor Yawn and the delights of mathematical investigations. My sigh is loud and heavy.

Echo: You're on campus, then.

Of course I am, though her message is unusual because she always checks my phone to track my whereabouts. She's great at invading my privacy that way.

Me: Yes. Being all cowardly.

I can almost see her eyes rolling at my jab. Did she think I would quit my degree overnight because of her revelatory opinion? I'm not *hiding from life*. This is my future. A chance for a respectable career. I'm doing the right thing, *dammit*.

Echo: What subject are you in right now?

Is pretending to take an avid interest in my course load some sort of weird, roundabout apology for telling me I look ridiculous in my banker attire and reading glasses? I'm still wearing said glasses today instead of my contact lenses, but I chose my outfit today without any thought at all. Pale denim jeans, so worn down there are rips at the knees and beneath both butt cheeks, and a beat-up brown leather jacket that I cast to the empty seat beside me because the heat is on.

My underwear is the only thing I chose with care. My cheeks burn, thinking of the offensive bra I ditched back at Rehab. So I may be sitting here in a ten dollar grey-ribbed tank top with a lace up tie at the bust, but my breasts are encased in the finest lace and pushed up somewhere near my chin.

Between that and my messy bed hair, most students are staring at me like I'm the new girl. Ignoring the rubbernecking gawks at my chest, I push my glasses up my nose and stab my fingers on the screen, texting a reply.

Me: The subject is how to choose better friends, so stop messaging me because I clearly need to pay attention.

Echo: I'm so totally butthurt.

She's not butthurt. The bitch is probably shoving a donut in her face while she flicks her gaze between the twenty thousand computer screens (give or take) in front of her. She consults for a computer security company, sometimes at their offices in the city and sometimes from home. Echo has her finger on the pulse of Sydney. She's basically the Eye of Sauron. And unfortunately, she gets to work her own hours, so that leaves her free to harass me at any given moment.

Me: There, there.

Echo: Is Mason still away?

Mason flew to Melbourne on Tuesday. He's spending a week undergoing tests with a specialist, and Echo knows it. The intent is to discuss the possible treatment of electrical stimulation on his spinal cord. It's impossible to remain optimistic. Every day he visits the doctor, or the physical therapist, he returns home in that damn chair with his head hanging a little lower than it did the day before.

Me: Your inquisition is ruffling my suspicious feathers.

Echo: Calm your mind, little bird. Just making sure we're still on for sex tonight.

My lips twitch. *Sex* is code for steal a car. You can't actually text *let's steal a car*. If the authorities ever got their hands on my phone, they'd simply think me a lesbian. And because Echo is basically hotter than a stripper on a pole, it's unquestionably believable.

Me: We are. Think you can manage a double orgasm?

Code for boosting two cars in one night. This deal with Tony Marchetti is a noose around my neck. Every day it squeezes a little tighter. The sooner I can deliver the goods, the sooner I can breathe again.

Echo: I can. Because I am a sexual God.

I snicker quietly to myself and tuck my phone away. The next hour and a half finds me tapping my fingers against my knees, impatient to leave. We already planned for one car, but two requires extra time and brain power. When the lecture ends, I'm already packed up, tote bag dangling from my shoulder and jacket in hand. I shoot from my seat. Unfortunately, so does every other student in the room.

With us all leaving en masse, it feels as though I'm caught in a landslide. We're a veritable surge of people rushing the exit. The doorway isn't wide, and it seems there's some kind of blockage outside causing everyone to slow down.

I'm elbowed in the side. "Ouch," I grumble to the guy who did it, but he's already pushing forward.

I reach the doors and sunlight hits my eyes. Shading them with my hand, I discover the cause of the traffic jam. My pulse leaps and my feet freeze to the ground, causing those behind me to stumble. Kelly is leaning against the outdoor column by the exit. One leg is drawn up, his foot pressed casually against the wall. He's wearing a sleeveless white tee and jeans, along with his motorcycle boots and Sentinels cut. His hair is tied back and arms folded, expression hard and flat—a warning not to get close.

Students have slowed down and flick wary glances his way. One of the girls in my study group, Solange, is walking out ahead of me. She fluffs her artful golden curls and heads his way.

"Are you lost?" she asks, her expression indicating she's more than happy to help him find his way, preferably up her stupid short leather skirt.

Kelly pins her with a direct stare.

"Because I can help you," she adds.

He doesn't reply. Instead his eyes lift from hers in dismissal, searching before they eventually hit mine. They do a visual scan, pausing on my chest for a considerable length of time. He rubs the back of his neck as if he doesn't know what to make of the display. His expression seems to evolve into a glare. When his gaze returns to my face, his eyes are intense. My skin flushes with heat and my pulse leaps.

Kelly pushes away from the column, ignoring Solange mid-sentence because she's still talking, trying hard to evoke some kind of response. He starts toward me. Suddenly Echo's mini interrogation becomes clear. She was trying to pin down my exact location so Kelly could find me. Is her plan to push us together? Because I was of the opinion she believed him a distraction from The List.

"Hey," he says, reaching my side, his unexpected presence wonderfully unsettling.

"Hey."

"I ... uh ..."

It's the first time I've seen him stumble over his words. For some reason, I seem to like it. For once, it's not me being awkward. "Stalking me again?"

I'm jostled from behind, making me aware I'm blocking the exit. I start walking along the path that leads to the busway. Despite my slight obsession with cars, I don't actually own one. Mum and Dad own a van that Mason and I borrow all the time. Otherwise, I usually catch the bus or get an Uber, when I'm seriously tired.

Kelly falls into step beside me, close enough that his arm brushes mine. Electrical zaps shoot through the limb. "In your dreams, Ace."

"Then why are you here?"

Students crowd the stairs by the library. Kelly walks ahead of me, and they basically part like the Red Sea. I walk through with ease behind him. Huh. That was ... kinda badass. "Because we need to talk."

We fall back into step beside each other. "About how much you like me?" I say, deliberately obtuse, because I've been expecting this. He wants to know—

"Why were you out stealing a car that night?"

That. He wants to know that. He must really want answers to be visiting me out here on campus. "You came all the way out here just to ask me that? Have you forgotten how to text?"

I pick up speed. His long strides keep up with ease.

"You sayin' you'd answer me if I messaged?"

I snort, almost at a gallop now. "No." *But I probably would've read your message a thousand times over like I do all the others.*

Kelly grabs my bicep. I come to a stumbling halt, eyeing his man-handling paw with a glare. That hand has touched me intimately. Those fingers have been inside me, his skin rough and calloused, scraping my sensitive skin. My cheeks flush.

"What's goin' through that head of yours, babe?"

"You," I blurt out, thoughtless and maybe a little breathless.

He exhales. "Jesus."

His eyes are blistering. I look away before they burn me to ash.

"Once wasn't enough," he mumbles.

"Sorry, what?"

"I said, let me give you a ride."

My mouth falls open but inside I'm trembling. *Kelly is naked on his back on my bed. I'm straddling him, his cock inside me, and he's thrusting upward. I'm barely hanging on. I'm ...* Yeah, that foggy haze of lust clearly hasn't lifted. I can barely see through it.

"Home," he adds with amusement, as though he can see inside my head.

I start walking again, giving him no response. I can't do this. I have sex planned tonight. And two orgasms. *Two.* The bus schedule is on a sign post up ahead. I head toward it with quick strides.

My bicep is grabbed again. "Kelly!" I huff, coming to a halt for the second time. "I don't need a ride."

Titters erupt from the students loitering in the busway.

His grin is all-knowing. "Oh, I think you do."

My lips pinch. "I don't. I have a bus to catch."

He lets me go, his brow furrowing. My stubborn attitude is wearing him down. Good. Let it wear him down to dust for all I care. At least that way he'll stop harassing me. I can't have him involved in my business.

"No girl of mine catches the damn bus."

"No girl of ..." I trail off, madly trying to supress the wild flush of pleasure. Along with it comes a bit of annoyance. We've had sex once. It doesn't make me his property. Though the thought of being his property ... "I'm not *your* girl. You..." I jab his chest "...might be falling for me..." jab, jab "...but I'm not falling for you ..." Jab.

He folds his arms, brows arching. He's looking at me like I've been placed here for the sole purpose of his amusement. "Because I'm a fucking Sentinel?"

"That's right." I add a sneer to emphasise my point. "Because you're a fucking Sentinel."

Kelly outright laughs. Then in one smooth, easy motion, he winds his arm around my waist and herds me from the busway. "I forgot how entertainin' you are."

His arm tightens when I wriggle for freedom. "I'm not your private circus performer."

"Babe. Don't give me ideas."

I'm being steered toward the huge student parking lot, Kelly navigating the pedestrian crossing as cars slow down to let us pass. I shift out of his hold but remain close to his side as we walk, as if he has a magnetic force field that keeps pulling me in. "I should push you into oncoming traffic," I grumble, halfway across the road.

He snorts. "Not if I push you first."

"You wouldn't—"

Kelly grabs me around my lower waist, lifting me into a fireman's hold before I can blink. I shriek and flop against him as he strides along. Traitorous laughter bursts from my lips.

His voice is so very deep and masculine and amused. "I would."

A lipstick escapes from my half upturned bag. It drops to the ground and rolls away. "Oh my god. Kelly." I smack my fist against his back to make him stop. "My lipstick."

We're over the crossing now. Cars surge forward. I gasp, watching my tube of glossy Ripe Peach Bellini roll under a wheel and break into a thousand pieces. My fist whacks him again. "You heartless bastard!"

"So get a new one."

"They don't make that colour anymore."

He sets me down and I realise we're at his bike. I forgot the motorcycle parking lot is closer to the lecture halls. It's how almost a quarter of the students get around. There's a mountain of bikes as far as the eye can see, but there are none like his. Kelly's bike is an eagle amongst a flock of pigeons. My eyes roam the gleaming black paint-work with longing, remembering our last ride together being a biblical experience.

I give one last feeble protest. "Mason—"

"Is in Melbourne."

"Echo has a big mouth," I mutter.

For obvious reasons, Mason is unaware of my encounter with Kelly over the weekend. It's not like I can say, "Oh hey, remember back when you accused me of sleeping with a Sentinel? Well, you were right. I did. My bad."

My brother would blow a gasket, but his anger would pale in comparison to the hurt and disappointment it would cause him. I don't want to disappoint Mason, even though technically I already have … he just doesn't know it.

No amount of reasoning will make him see Kelly any different. Echo may have gotten through to me with her "all Sentinel's aren't Grinder" spiel, but where I'm stubborn, Mason is like the Immove-able Object.

I stare at Kelly, knowing my brother won't see him in the same sexy light I do. Kelly is hotter than a heatwave, the kind that blows through unexpectedly, its humidity sucking all the oxygen from Earth's atmosphere. But he's also kind, and funny, and he treats me like I'm his favourite candy. It's hard for a girl to resist all that.

"Wake up, Ace." Kelly is clicking his fingers in front of my face, his lips curved in a smirk. He's caught me in a trancelike ogle.

"I'm awake," I snap hotly.

"Well, somebody's frustrated. Don't worry, babe. I got what you need."

His comment is loaded with sexual innuendo. My eyes drop, expecting to see his hand on his junk in a lewd gesture. Except he's not. He's holding out a helmet. Momentarily forgetting my claustro-phobic tendencies, I snatch it from his hands and plonk it down on my head. Then the world goes dark and my lungs squeeze.

Kelly rips it from head. My hair goes everywhere, and I gulp in some air.

"Well that's not gonna work, is it? I'm an idiot for not remembering about your phobia." His voice is gruff as he brushes wayward strands from my face. "You okay?"

His concern overrides my embarrassment. I swallow a heated retort. "I'm fine. Really. I'll get the bus."

With one hand, he takes hold of mine and pulls me close, with the other he tugs his phone from his back pocket and starts tapping. "Just give me a few." He sends a message and it *pings* an almost instant reply.

Kelly puts the phone away and looks down at me. "Now, where were we?" His lips touch mine, the contact brief but it's enough to have my thighs clenching together. "Oh, that's right." Setting my hand free, he palms my cheeks and kisses me again. "I was giving you what you need."

I draw backward, just a little, so I can meet his eyes. And when I do, I can't help divulging more than I should. My voice comes out a whisper. "I don't steal cars, Kelly. Not anymore."

Kelly's exhale is so deep it flares his nostrils. He's looking at me as if doesn't know what to make of me. And I get it. Because it's pretty obvious we were out stealing cars, and there was that whole ... incident with the Charger. His hands fall away from my face.

"My grandfather taught me the life. I inherited every skill he has and more. And I love it. The rush. The ride. God! My heart beats so hard in my chest I think it will explode." Shame rises, heating my cheeks. "It's all I'm good at. But I can't do it anymore. I can't. I don't want to go out in a blaze of glory or end up in prison." I wave a hand at all the buildings behind me. "*That's* my life now. Education. Finance. I'm trying to grow up. Be responsible. I'm trying to go straight, Kelly."

"Okay." He looks away, rubbing his lips together for a moment, contemplating my admission. Then his gaze returns. "So tell me, and give me the respect of an honest answer, what were you all doing that night?"

My head drops. Having to be honest sucks. It sucks so fucking bad. But I can't lie. Not now. Not after that. If I do, there'll be no coming back from it for us and for some reason, I'm not ready for that. I lift my chin. "We were stealing a car."

"Dammit, Ace!"

Kelly turns away, hands on his hips.

"You don't understand."

He spins back around, eyes hard. "So explain it."

A motorcycle thunders toward us. We both turn our heads. The rider is a Sentinel, wearing a cut and a black helmet, his beard long enough to hit his chest. He rolls to a stop beside us and cuts off the engine.

"Great timing," Kelly mutters to him as the guy peels his helmet off, revealing salt and pepper hair and crinkles at the corners of his eyes. And though Kelly's tone is sarcastic, I couldn't agree more.

The man smiles at me. "You Ace?"

It's a lovely smile. I can't help but return it. "I am."

He holds out a hand. "I'm Hammer."

I take it in mine. It's scarred and calloused. "Nice to meet you, Mr. Hammer."

"No. Just Hammer."

He gives my hand a quick squeeze and lets go. Then he thrusts a helmet at me. It's smaller. Feminine, with an open face, yet it's still black. "Thanks."

Hammer smiles that genuine smile at me again. "You're welcome, pretty lady." His gaze shifts to Kelly. "All good?"

Kelly nods. "All good."

Hammer's bike roars to life. "I like her already," I hear him say to Kelly before he drives off, disappearing down the slope of the parking lot the same way he came in.

15

KELLY

*T*he ride to Ace's house is sweet. Sweeter than the last time because there's less inhibition in Ace this afternoon. Her arms wind a little tighter and her chest presses a little harder against my back, as if she's remembering our skin-on-skin contact. I sure as shit am. There's an ease to being with Ace I've never had before. A friendship that makes me relaxed enough to be myself but also pushes my emotional boundaries to a breaking point. It's intense.

I park the bike behind Echo's Ford and no sooner are we inside then she's upon us, her pink hair reaching impossible heights and her eyes grim. Echo messaged me a week ago as we drove off, leaving them all standing in the street staring after us. It was a sweet message that went along the lines of:

Echo: Take care of her as if she's the Queen of England or your life is over.

It didn't faze me. It was more reassuring than anything. If you have friends like that in your corner, then you're doing okay.

The Charger Incident in the early morning hours gave me a whole new perspective. Ace isn't just sweet and funny, she's wild and unruly. She has a heavy heart, a messy soul, and a reckless mind.

She's an all or nothing girl. If I want to take this any further, I have to either back off or dive in and swim my ass off.

So like an idiot, I dove.

It started with me going by her house this morning at the risk of another run in with Mason ... only no one was home. Undeterred, I messaged Echo after I finished in the workshop just after 2:00 p.m.

Me: Where is she?

Echo: I don't know who you're talking about.

I called bullshit. Echo appears to be rather protective. Not in a mama bear protecting her cub kind of way because Ace is no defenceless animal, but in a lion guarding his herd kind of way. The ferocious protecting the formidable.

Me: Whatever she's got going on, I want in.

The purpose for Ace, Echo, and Racer's late-night outing was nefarious. Of that I was sure. Add to that a burnt-out Mustang and it became dangerous. Ace had trouble on her doorstop, and there was no helping her if I lacked all the information.

Echo's reply took twenty minutes.

Echo: Sydney University. East Wing. Lecture hall 2B. Bring her home instead of the damn bus, and I'll wait for you both there.

Echo: PS Mason is in Melbourne.

Echo: PPS Delete these messages #orelse

I didn't delete the messages. Ace isn't stupid enough to not realise how I found out her exact location. I didn't reply either. Mostly because I don't have a vagina. And I don't do hashtags.

Now we're in her house and there's nowhere for Ace to run, and nowhere to hide. I think she senses an ambush because her face takes on an overly bright expression. After dumping her bag and jacket by the small table near the door, she all but hurdles the living room couch to reach the kitchen.

"Coffee anyone?" she sing-songs, lifting the electric kettle from its placeholder.

Echo shakes her head and points to the coffee table that rests in the middle of the living room. It's a sturdy dark timber affair decorated with a bottle of whiskey and three glasses. "Ace, we're going to need something stronger than coffee."

Ace ignores her friend and looks at me. "Coffee, Kelly?"

"I'll take the whiskey." Obviously. I know Ace well enough already to know I'm going to need it.

"Well I'm having one," she declares to the both of us and fills the kettle from the tap. While she's busy putting her coffee together, Echo takes a seat on the armchair. I follow suit, seating myself on the double sofa, the coffee table between us.

"So ..." Echo drawls, casually unscrewing the cap on the bottle and pouring generously. She shifts the bottle to the next glass. Pours. The cap goes back on and after returning the bottle to the table, she nudges one of the glasses toward me.

I lean forward and pick it up, expectant, elbows resting on my knees. Echo is about to overshare, and I want to hear all of it.

She downs half her whiskey in one gulp, makes a face, and continues. "Ace is being blackmailed by Tony Marchetti."

Sonofabitch. I reel backward in my seat at the same time I hear a mug smash to the tiled kitchen floor.

"Echo!" Ace shouts.

Ace's friend reclines back in her seat, glass in hand, an expression of self-satisfaction on her face.

"What are you thinking?" Ace shouts again.

She races toward me like the kitchen is on fire and snatches the glass from my hand. She downs it and erupts in a coughing fit. The empty glass is thrust back in my general direction. I take it back, managing to maintain a mild expression while anger rises inside me like hot lava.

When she's finished wheezing, she pins watery eyes on Echo, oblivious to the tension beginning to emanate from my body.

"You can't go blathering my personal business to all and sundry!" My jaw ticks. I'm not *all and sundry*. "This is my situation. Not yours." She points at me. "Not his. Mine! I fight my own battles. I don't drag other people into my mess for them to fix it for me. If you think for one second—"

"I did think!" Echo shouts over the top of her. I reach across the table for the bottle and busy myself pouring a whiskey while they duke it out. "This is me *thinking*! I'm not telling Kelly so he'll fix this. We'll get Tony his cars." His cars? I take a sip and swallow with disapproval. It's not the good stuff, but I'm definitely willing to overlook it in this particular situation. "But if we have the goddamn Sentinels behind us, then—"

"They're not the goddamn Sentinels," Ace interrupts. "They're the Fucking Sentinels."

Echo huffs. "If we have the *Fucking Sentinels*," she enunciates loudly, "behind us, then Tony's going to think twice about burning any of us to the ground."

My eyes narrow as the final piece of the puzzle slots into place. And it figures. That's the Marchetti modus operandi. They like to burn everything and everyone who fucks them over.

"Have you lost your mind?" Ace's decibel level is high enough to make me wince. I take another sip of whiskey. And another. The cheap flavour improves with each mouthful, probably because it's burned my taste buds clean away. Ace splays her arms out wide. "The Sentinels aren't guns for hire!"

Well ... technically that's true. We aren't contract killers, but if a Sentinel brother or their family has trouble, then that becomes *our* trouble.

Echo looks to me, an expectant expression on her face. *I've done my part,* she's telling me. *Now go do yours.*

My jaw ticks. *Nice try, Echo,* I tell her with a hard, silent response while Ace perches her butt on the edge of the couch as far from me as possible, her arm stretching to impossible lengths to reach the whiskey bottle, *but that's not how this works.*

After a considerable amount of strained quiet, in which I'm reviewing their argument in my head, I set down my offensive glass of alcohol, stand, walk to the kitchen bench, turn and lean against it so I can eye them both from above, and fold my arms.

"Kelly—" Ace begins.

I cut her off. "Let me get this clear. You steal cars—"

"Used to."

My nostrils flare. "You *used* to steal cars. Considering Tony Marchetti is involved, and yes I know who he is," I add before Ace can interrupt me again, "that must make him the chop shop you delivered to. But now you're busy trying to put that life behind you, workin' hard at gettin' yourself a quality education, and Tony Marchetti has decided he doesn't like that—the business is too lucrative and he's got a reputation to maintain. So he's asked you to steal a bunch more cars, and I say *cars* because Echo mentioned it was more than one. You refused. So instead of gettin' someone else to do his dirty work, he's makin' *you* do it—because you're the best in the biz—by threatening to burn you..." my hands curl into fists "...and everyone you care about, to the motherfuckin' ground if you don't."

"Kelly—" Ace tries again.

"I'm not fuckin' finished," I bite out.

Her eyes narrow.

"Now I'm figurin' you did somethin' since then that he doesn't like, because your Mustang, along with your grandfather's garage, are charred beyond repair. Not only that, you were out last Saturday night with Echo *and* your grandfather, trying to get the cars he's blackmailing you into boosting, because he lit a fire beneath you. Literally. This means he's impatient, so you must be on a deadline."

"Like I said before, this is not—"

"What? My problem?" My eyes flatten and every muscle in my body goes rigid. "Because if it wasn't before, it is now."

Echo nods her agreement, her expression smug. Ace is sitting stiffly, fury radiating from every pore of her body. Tough shit. She is *not* going to deal with this on her own.

"Give me the list."

"What list?" Ace asks.

"Really? After all that, you're still going to feign ignorance?"

Echo stands and walks over to me, a sheet of paper in her hand. I take it, scanning the ten cars (two are marked off so I'm assuming those have already been delivered) with disbelief. Marchetti is expecting the impossible. Surely Arcadia 'Ace' Jones is not that good.

I tuck the list in my pocket and glare at both girls. "Neither of you are gonna do a damn thing from here on out without my say so. I don't want you talkin' to Marchetti, or answerin' his calls, or plannin' any kind of boost, until I work out the best way to deal with this."

I can tell by both their expressions that my orders have not been well received. It's quite clear that Echo wants me solely for protection, having endorsed me as a *hired gun*. And Ace ... well, Ace doesn't want me involved at all.

Unfortunately for them, I don't get involved unless I have full control of the situation, and in this, I sure as hell am getting involved.

"Ace. Walk me out."

She doesn't hesitate, rising from the couch and walking to the front door. I'm not fooled by this sudden acquiescence. Ace is spoiling for a fight, and I'm more than happy to deliver her one.

It's not until we're out on the porch facing each other that she lets loose, though not in the way I expected. She does it in a way that throws me completely.

"Kelly, I know why you're doing this." She tucks her hands in the back pockets of her jeans. "Why you're trying to push me out completely and gain control of this mess I'm in. It's because you care, and you don't like that you care, but you care anyway. And that makes you scared. I get that, because I've been there, with Mason. No one wants people they care about ending up injured, or in a wheelchair, or dead. But you can't help me. You can't do what I do. You're a Sentinel. A biker. If you do anything at all, the cops will be all over you like flies on shit. Tony Marchetti promised me that once I deliver this list, then this will all be over. No more cars."

"Bullshit," I mutter. "When it comes to guys like that, it's never over."

"Maybe. Maybe not." She looks away. "But that's my risk to take."

"Not anymore." I tuck a thumb beneath her chin, drawing her attention back to me. "It's our risk now." I duck my head, kissing her. "It's ours."

I'M SEATED around a table at the club later that night, along with Hammer, Lee, and Fox. We're outside, tucked in a dark corner, where I've gathered them all and explained Ace's situation.

The girls might have laid the story out to me—in a roundabout fashion—but it doesn't mean I know how to go about fixing it just yet, short of shooting Marchetti in the head. Ace is basically tied to him for life until something is done. So whatever it is, it has to be a viable solution that won't ricochet back on her—and on us.

Hammer rubs at the hair of his beard, thinking it all through.

"Can't we just shoot them all?" Fox says, sitting forward, his fingers tapping away at the arm of his chair as if he's itching to go out right now and do just that.

Lee gives him a hard glare. "And risk an all-out war?"

He shrugs. "We can take them."

I shake my head. "Shootin' them all dead is tempting." My mind recalls the way it feels to end a life. To see blood and brain matter splatter up the wall. It's the kind of thing that sticks with you in everything you do, even the mundane. Like when you're fixing a car and you slice your finger on a sharp piece of metal—there it all is, the loud *bang* of gunfire and blood spraying over your face. Or sitting with your brothers, shooting the shit, and you look up at the bright blue sky and it just slams into you like a fist to the gut—your mother's brilliant blue eyes and how the life faded from them so damn fast. That's why I ride, and why being with Ace is so good, because they both make it all go away. "Real tempting, Fox. But the repercussions are too big."

"I agree." Hammer nods his head, taking it in. "I have a better plan. One that doesn't involve guns and warfare."

All eyes slice his way.

"You still friends with the Valentines?" he asks me.

My lips press into a flat line. The Valentines are a force to be reckoned with in Sydney. Of the three brothers, two of them, Travis and Jared, are co-owners of the consulting business with Casey. So no, we're not *friends*. However, just under a year ago, their sister, Mac, who's always up in my business, and everyone else's business for that matter, got in a spot of trouble with the King Street Boys. Mac, I consider a friend. So her troubles became ours. I got the Sentinels involved, and the situation evolved into a shoot-out that ended the life of the eldest Valentine brother's girlfriend. But our actions helped save Mac and Romero's life.

"I was never friends with them, you know that. We're not tight."

"Maybe not, but they do owe you a favour."

I nod my head. "That's true. Why? What are you thinking, Hammer?"

He rubs his beard again, his mind visibly ticking over. Appearing done, he leans forward in his seat. "Right. This is what we're gonna do."

Hammer lays it all out, and I can't deny it. His plan makes solid sense. "We can't tell the girls, obviously, so we'll have to work around that. Otherwise, I can't see any other issues. This could actually work."

"Damn straight," he replies.

"The plan is solid," Lee agrees.

Fox disagrees, mostly because he's pissed. "I prefer the guns."

I shake my head. "For someone who spends his time patchin' up the wounds of the bleeding, you're pretty damn eager to go out and put a few holes in some people."

"Just those that deserve it," he counters.

"Well, not this time." I stand, clapping Hammer on the back before I head to the bar. "Drinks are on me, you cheap assholes," I tell the lot of them.

16

ARCADIA

*I*t's after midnight. I can't sleep. There was no sex tonight after all. No double orgasm. After Kelly left earlier, Echo declared mutiny by taking his side. Considering I can't boost any of the cars on the list without her, I had to sit at home and *not do a damn thing* just like Kelly ordered.

It irks me that she got him involved. I'm independent, which makes relying on others difficult. There's never been an easy way out for me. But if I'm being honest, I'm a little relieved too. Now that he knows everything, I feel less of an obligation to push him away. There's no need now that I have nothing left to hide. And there's also the fact that I don't want to.

When he said that it was now *our* risk to take, it made me want to cry. It made me want to tell him yes, I need you. But admitting that to myself makes my insides knot with dread. Already, I can't imagine him not being in my life. He can't be another Mason. I can't go through that again. I even admitted that to Echo, though she knows me well enough to figure out what was going through my head anyway.

She told me, *"Everything in life that matters requires risk."*

Sick at heart, I roll to my side beneath the heavy covers. Kelly matters.

"But this is different. This is me putting him at risk," I told her.

"It's not, you imbecile." She took a frustrated breath. *"It's him putting himself at risk. There's nothing you can do to stop him, Ace. So let him do this. Let him in. Let him help you."*

So here I am, not doing a damn thing until Kelly's say so, and I don't like it. If I'm agreeing to his involvement, then he needs to learn he's not in charge. I am.

I roll to my back, my eyes hitting the ceiling. Sleep is proving more elusive tonight than a Mustang rebuild.

My phone vibrates a message from my bedside table. Sitting up on one elbow, I reach over and grab it, squinting at the sudden bright light as I read it.

Kelly: On my way

My pulse leaps like a horse at the starting gate. I'm not ready. I need space. Time. To ... to ... I don't know. I'm just so *wired* right now. Kelly being here will ramp that up further when I'm doing everything I can to centre myself and think things through. I tap out a quick reply.

Me: Pretty sure I didn't invite you.

There. That's about as welcoming as a fly in your sandwich.

Three little dots appear on the screen. I stare at them, waiting, biting down on the smile trying to form on my lips.

Kelly: And I'm pretty sure I don't need your permission to step over the threshold. I'm not a vampire, babe.

Me: You wouldn't dare. You're not the one in charge here, despite what you seem to think.

Kelly: We'll talk about it when I get there

Fifteen minutes later I hear the rumble of a motorcycle from down the street. It gets closer and closer until it's in the driveway and all I can hear. My windows judder a little as does my heart.

Next comes the heavy footfall of boots on my porch stairs. Is he going to just barge his way in? With the covers drawn up to my chin, I hold my breath with anticipation, waiting to find out.

The doorknob rattles. Does he seriously think I wouldn't lock the front door before going to bed? What shower does he think I last came down on?

I wait for the knock, whereby I will calmly walk to the door, open it, tell him that it's too late for visitors and to return at a more suitable hour tomorrow morning. However, that doesn't happen. Instead, there's a jolt and a click, followed by the sound of my front door swinging wide open.

I jerk upright, my heart a jackhammer behind my ribcage. *He did not!*

Scrambling from my bed in just my panties and oversized tee, I stalk from my bedroom. Goose bumps rise on my skin because it's *freezing*. Ignoring the chilly air, I find Kelly stepping inside my house. My eyes roam the full length of him. He's wearing the same thing he wore earlier, though this time he's added a black motorcycle jacket. I lean against the doorframe of my room and fold my arms, brows arching high enough to fly right off my face.

Kelly hasn't noticed me yet. He's setting his helmet on the floor by the door. His eyes land on me as he's shrugging out of his jacket. He tosses it over the back of the armchair, ignoring my expression of incredulity. "Babe, what are you doin' out of bed?"

"Well, when someone breaks into my house, I think it's best to greet them at the front door and offer a welcoming coffee, don't you?" My voice is thick with sarcasm. "It's only the polite thing to do."

"Awesome. I'd love a coffee," he replies, remaining deliberately obtuse.

"I'm not making you a coffee," I hiss. "You just broke into my house!"

"You're right. My bad." Kelly holds up both hands as if surrendering, his lips twitching with amusement. He's like a cat toying with a mouse, and I'm the mouse. "I'll wait here while you call the cops."

I push off from the doorframe and stalk toward him until we're nice and close, my eyes narrowing. "Don't ever break into my house again."

He takes my hips, pulling me against him. My arms remain

folded, making our joined pose awkward and uncomfortable, but I refuse to yield. I'm not in the wrong here.

"I wouldn't have to if you gave me a key," he points out, as if it were the logical thing to do—which it isn't!

"You're not my boyfriend. You don't get a key."

"Babe." His palms caress my hips beneath my tee, the gesture warming me like a heated blanket. "I was trying to be quiet and let myself in because I didn't want you gettin' out of bed. It's cold as all fuck. Now go." Kelly turns me around until I'm facing the direction of my bedroom and slaps my ass. "Get back in bed. I'll go make coffee."

I'm already at the door to my room when I realise I've just blindly done what he told me to do, but how can I not? The man didn't want me to be cold. He was looking out for my welfare. I can't very well be rude and kick him out for that now, can I?

I pause by the open door and half turn. Kelly's in the kitchen, opening cupboards, looking for the mugs. He finds them on the shelving above the electric kettle.

"Can you make mine a chamomile tea?" I call out softly. "The teabags are in the canister by the coffee. I can't have caffeine so late at night. I won't sleep."

His back is to me when he replies, "Sure thing, babe," and it makes me smile, so I return to my bed, pull the covers back up to my chin, and drift off listening to the sound of Kelly moving about in my kitchen.

I rouse a little from my doze when the bed dips. The covers resettle when he slides in behind me. His arm snakes around my middle, and I'm dragged backward until I'm the little spoon to his big one. Heat surrounds me. I turn, burying my face in the warmth of his chest because my nose and cheeks are cold. He's shirtless and smells like cinnamon soap with an underlying hint of chassis grease. It's my kind of heaven.

"I'm awake."

He shushes me quietly. "Go back to sleep."

Another order. One I'm happy to get on board with, except we haven't settled anything. "We need to talk," I mumble against his chest.

"Tomorrow."

Ah yes. Tomorrow. I burrow further. "Wait. It is tomorrow."

"In the morning then."

"It's okay." I rub my face sleepily. His chest hair tickles. "All I wanted to say was…" I pause to yawn "…that I decided you can help." His arms squeeze me tighter. "But I'm the one in charge."

Suddenly, I'm cold again. I open my eyes. Kelly is glaring, having pushed me away so I'm better able to see just how much my statement bothers him. I'm starting to feel a little more awake though my eyes feel bleary.

"I know what I'm doing," I point out.

"And I don't?"

"Look, we can argue about this until the cows come home, but the fact remains I'm the expert here. Therefore, I call the shots."

Kelly sits up in my bed, the sheets pooling to his lap. It's definitely an unfair advantage in this argument. He certainly knows how to fight dirty. "So exactly how do you envisage me 'helping' you?" he air-quotes.

I pause for a moment. Well, I boost the cars and drive them to Tony. Echo does all the intel, and works as a virtual lookout. Kelly could … could … "You can pick me up after I deliver the cars."

His nostrils flare as he draws in a deep breath, as though he's trying to put a leash on his rising anger. My eyes drop, watching his chest rise and fall. "*That's* how you envisage me helping you?"

"Huh?"

"Ace?"

My eyes rise to his. Yep. Totally unfair. I whip off my shirt and toss it to the end of the bed. Goose bumps break out across my skin. I shiver and hug my chest, feeling ridiculous and exposed.

He appears baffled by my behaviour rather than the mesmerised and distracted I was aiming for. His brows pull together. "What are you doin'?"

"Trying to make this argument a little less one-sided," I mumble, *and failing miserably*. I scowl, reaching for my shirt.

Kelly scoots down on his back and pulls me down on top of him before I can get a proper hold of it. Unprepared, I land in a mess of limbs, hair everywhere and shirt tangled in my fingers. I brush wayward strands from my face as I straighten, straddling his lap. It's then that I feel something very, very hard between my legs. Kelly ditched his jeans before climbing into bed, making his erection impossible to miss. Flinging my shirt to the floor, I instinctively place both palms on his lower belly and rub against him, my breath catching.

Kelly stops me, his hand on my arm. "You want to be in charge?"

"Well, duh."

He tucks both hands behind his head and smirks. "Then go for it."

I tilt my head back and laugh. "You're impossible."

"And you're beautiful."

My laughter dies away as my gaze returns to his. He's looking at me like he means what he says. My heart thumps hard and heavy in my chest. *You're in trouble,* it's trying to tell me. *So what?* I reply with unhealthy abandon. *I'm always in trouble.*

I scoot my way down his legs, peeling his boxer briefs away as I go. Reaching the end of the bed, I stand and drop them to the floor at my feet. He grabs his cock, watching as I peel my panties down my legs. I kick them away and climb back on the bed, making my way back up until I reach his erection. It's long and thick and pulsing heavily in his fist.

I remove his hand and replace it with my own, caressing the hard silky skin in my palm. His breath quickens as the head of his cock brushes my cheek. Sweeping my hair to the side, I duck my head and lick along the length of him.

An inarticulate groan leaves his mouth.

I take the head inside my mouth, giving a light, experimental suck. His hips buck, driving him in further. So I take as much of him as I can.

"Ace," he breathes.

I pull out slowly before going back down. This time I use my hand along with my mouth, sucking and fisting, slow and teasing, up and down. Each time I draw back, my tongue does a small swirl around his head. He growls with frustration and fists my hair.

"So good," he groans, writhing on my bed.

That I'm managing to drive him crazy fills me with need. There's a deep, heavy throb between my legs. It's building, begging for relief.

"Ride me, babe," he rasps.

I give one final flick of my tongue before letting him go. Straddling his lap again, I position his cock and slowly lower myself down until I'm full. There's a brief sense of relief until need hits harder and hotter than before.

His groan is strangled.

"Babe."

I rise up. *Yes.* And sink down, my head tipping back.

Kelly grabs my ass cheeks, his fingers digging in. "Condom," he spits out with a harsh breath.

Dammit. I go to draw up and off him, but he holds me in place. "Kelly—"

"Just …" He hisses. His muscles are rigid, his brow furrowed tight with concentration. "Don't move."

So of course my hips wriggle instinctively.

"Christ." Kelly groans, his hips thrusting upward, once, twice, slamming into me. "Get off, get off, get off." He practically throws me off him and moments later, he grunts and spurts over his own belly. "Dammit, Ace." He fists the bedsheets, veins thick and body straining.

My cheeks heat. "I'm sorry."

Kelly stretches his arm out, breathing heavy as he reaches for the tissue box on my bedside table. He fumbles and it falls to the floor. I scramble from the bed to help him, grabbing the tissues in tufts as I return the box to the table. I turn. He's stretched out on the bed, swiping a hand down his face, appearing bothered and sated all at the same time.

I wipe at the sticky mess on his belly, and he takes the tissues from my hand. "I can do it." His voice is thick and gruff. He rises and seats himself on the edge of my bed. "I've never gone bareback before. It feels fuckin' incredible."

Kelly's right. It was intense and overwhelming, and so beautifully intimate.

He stands and walks naked from my room, the used tissues in hand. I watch the glorious sight, my thighs trembling because my body is impatient for more. The toilet flushes and the tap goes on, water gushing loudly for several moments before it switches off. I'm adjusting the sheets, about to climb back in bed, when I'm seized from behind.

I shriek, Kelly scaring the absolute shit out of me. He lifts me. My feet leave the ground, then I'm flying through the air toward my bed. I land softly on my back, bouncing once, twice. I rise up on my elbows to find him looming over me.

"See what happens when you put yourself in charge?"

I press my lips together. Shit on a stick. I really stuffed that up, didn't I?

He puts a knee on the bed. The mattress dips. He leans forward and both hands land on the bed on either side of my face. It brings him closer to me.

"It's not my fault you have zero control," I declare rashly.

"Oh, woman." Kelly shakes his head, eyes narrowing with heat. "Don't make me spank you."

Lust flares like a lit match.

He ducks his head and kisses me, his tongue thrusting inside my mouth. It's hard and messy, and it's not enough. I moan into his mouth, pulling at his hair, starved of oxygen yet holding him to me so he doesn't stop. I'm drowning but I don't care. I don't need to breathe.

Kelly draws away and I'm gasping. So is he. But he's also relentless. His mouth is on my neck, nibbling at my earlobe before trekking downward. His lips traverse my collarbone and down further, until he sucks a nipple in his mouth. He swirls his tongue before sucking deep.

Sweat dots my brow, and my chest heaves upward, begging for more. My nipple pops free, the tight bud left abandoned and cold.

"Kelly," I murmur, a soft plea.

He shifts to the other, and once more I'm engulfed in flames.

"How wet are you for me, Ace? Hmm?"

His fingers trail down, closer and closer. I wriggle, impatient. *Yes. Please. Now.* They trail through slick heat. "Mmm," I mumble.

"Oh you want me bad, don't you, baby?"

A thick finger thrusts inside, twisting, curling.

I cry out.

"More?"

"More," I plead.

Another thick finger joins the first, and he kisses his way down my belly. It quivers with every press of his lips, with every thrust of his fingers. He slides his way down, continuing his torment. I feel the tickle of his chest hair on my thighs and then his warm breath puffing against the slick heat of me.

"I'm not just your taxi driver, Ace," he says.

My mind scrambles to make sense of what he's saying. "What?"

His tongue flicks my clit. I gasp. "You heard me. I won't be the guy who sits back and waits for you." He flicks me again, his fingers wriggling inside me. "We're in this together."

"Kelly—"

He licks me in one long stroke. I moan, my hips rubbing against him.

"Say it."

I lift my head. "Kelly—"

"If you wanna ride my face, then say it," he commands. "We're in this together."

My head falls back. He's asking me to compromise. To include him properly. To *risk his life*. I swallow thickly, sadly. "We're in this together."

And with those four words, I seal his fate.

Kelly grunts his satisfaction. He licks me again, and again, nuzzling and rubbing with his tongue, his beard chafing my inner thighs. The sheets rustle as my hands fist them, my back arching. He uses a third finger to rub against the entrance to my ass. My inner walls clench, and I writhe on the bed.

It's sensory overload. He's sucking my clit, fucking me with his fingers, and massaging that tight ring until it's almost too much.

Pressure rises. My hands find his shoulders, my fingers raking the skin, digging in as whimper after whimper leaves me.

He sucks hard and I come with a strangled cry.

Pleasure pulses through me, seemingly endless. I can't move. My heart is a jackhammer, and my hair sticks to the back of my neck.

Kelly draws away slowly, giving one last lick, a final taste, before I'm swept up, boneless, and placed carefully on the bed.

17

I wait for Ace to drop the gear and punch the accelerator. That's how a boost works. You get in and you drive that car like death is on your tail. Except she doesn't. She drives the stolen black Porsche 911 GT3 out of the restaurant parking lot like she learned all her skills from the movie *Driving Miss Daisy*. Her feet perform a balance between the clutch and the accelerator, slow and delicate.

It's been a week since our argument over my involvement in this. Arriving at the decision to simply steal the cars together was no walk in the park, but it's all part of the plan. Now we're about to find out just how good we work together.

Not well, apparently. My chest tightens with impatience as Ace inches her way through the rows of parked cars. I wind the window down a fraction. Tiny cars get hot very fast and this thing is a matchbox. Cool air rushes in, offering minor relief.

"Is this a boost or what?"

"Patience, grasshopper," she mutters as we move forward another inch. The parking lot is situated behind the building, with valet parking. Enormous shrubbery lines the entire location, making it the perfect opportunity to swipe the Porsche.

During the week, Echo placed a small tracker beneath each car left on the list. It's a risk, but it can help us track the car's schedule and activities. And with Echo's intel on tonight's dinner reservation at The Lily, we decided the simplest option would be to create a diversion, swipe the valet key, and just drive on out. Simple in theory. Except if we don't speed it up, one of the valet's will come around the corner any moment and bust us wide open.

My arm rests on the base of the passenger window, fingers tapping impatiently. "I'm pretty sure I can get out and walk faster."

She snorts, her hands on the wheel and her eyes focused like a cat. "You males and your blazing testosterone. When you think about boosting cars, you picture *The Fast and the Furious*, with rubber burning and cars drifting through corners. Ninety-nine percent of the time, this is how it's done. Quietly. Below the speed limit. I'm the best because I fly under the radar, Kelly." She takes a hand from the wheel to jab a thumb in her own chest. It's a very exposed chest. She's wearing a long-sleeved black dress with a V that opens to her navel, her eyes smoky and hair in wild waves down her back. The black heels were changed out to her lucky black Converse before we got in the car. "Trust the expert."

All she had to do was *drop* her handbag by the valet and let the contents scatter everywhere. He would stoop to pick it up while she swiped the key. The idea sounded ridiculously cliché, but the girls had it right. The male brain can barely focus on more than one thing when a) a female has her tits just about hanging out, and b) she's in distress (no matter how minor that distress may be). After seeing her in action, I fear that one day the male species may very well become extinct.

We reach the driveway entrance. Ace looks left and right with care. Then we hear a shout. "Hey, that's my car!"

Our heads swivel to the left. There's a silver Mercedes GT-R in the valet drop-off zone. The driver's door is open. A man was obviously standing just inside it, chatting with the occupant. Now he's looking at us and his mouth is hanging open.

"Fuck," Ace mutters.

Damn straight. *Fuck.*

I don't need to tell her to fuckin' *drive*. With eyes flat and jaw hard, Ace slams back to first gear and punches her foot to the floor. In an instant she becomes fearless, revealing the wild inside of her. And the sin.

Ace is no fairy tale, but I'd take the real any day. Her real is about being brave in the face of fear, and her sexy isn't in how she looks but in how she acts.

Damn this woman. I'm fallin' like a tonne of bricks.

I glance behind me. The Porsche owner is flying around the back of the Mercedes. He jumps in the passenger seat, the car squealing from the drop-off zone before he even gets the door shut.

Ace grips the wheel with one hand and wrenches it to the left. The Porsche flies out into traffic, and my adrenaline spikes. With her other hand, she's punching through gears and grappling with the back end just before we oversteer. I grab the holy shit bar so I don't body slam her from the force of the turn.

"I guess this is that one percent!" I shout over the roar of the engine.

Her expression is grim. "I don't have time for jokes right now, Kelly."

"Oh, this is no joke."

We're duking it out between a Porsche and a Mercedes, but we have it in the bag. I have no doubt. Not only does the Porsche have better cornering and handling, it has enough power to make you piss your pants. Not only that, this car has Ace, and she's driving like she's in the Dakar Rally.

"You really are good," I say with some surprise, because there's a difference between someone telling you they're the best and witnessing it with your own eyes.

"Stop talking," she barks, her eyes on the road. "Dammit, I need my headphones."

We rise over a small crest and speed through a green light. The Porsche goes airborne. For a moment we have wings, then the car lands with a screech, more rubber burning as we fishtail down a side street.

"We're are you takin' us?"

"Back streets." Her voice is short, her eyes shifting to her rear-view mirror every few seconds. I glance behind me. The Mercedes is on our tail. Ace accelerates and their headlights grow smaller as they fall behind. "Less cars and people and no traffic lights."

"Good thinkin', babe."

"Can you get Echo on the phone?"

I tug my phone free from my pocket and dial. After putting it on speaker, I set in the centre console. It barely dials once before she answers with, "I'm tracking you. What's happening?"

"We have a Merc on our ass," Ace tells her, shifting gears and turning down another side street. This one is wide and straight, giving her room to open up the car a little. "Give me the safest route to Marchetti's."

Echo gives directions and within five minutes we lose the tail. We're free and clear. Another five minutes and Ace slows right down. "We have to be careful. We might have lost the Mercedes, but they would have called the cops. There'll be an APB out on the car now."

They don't find us. We coast down the final back street toward Marchetti's chop shop. A location I didn't even know until now. The garage door starts rising before we even hit the driveway. We glide right in, smooth and easy, and the door lowers behind us.

Ace switches off the heated engine. It ticks over for a moment in silence while she pauses, swiping a hand down the side of her face. Then she looks at me. Her cheeks are flushed pink, her eyes over-bright, and a sheen of sweat dots her brow. That's when I realise that boosting cars is her drug.

I relax each muscle, not realising how tense each one was until we stop. Even my cock is hard, throbbing in my pants from the moment her foot hit the accelerator.

"We need to fuck," I growl.

Her hands clench briefly then release. "Yes."

After taking another breath, we open our doors in simultaneous motion and step out. I'm closing it and walking around the front of the car when a girl steps out from a door situated at the back of the garage.

"Murphy," Ace says, holding out the keys.

She grins and takes them, her eyes running along the sleek lines of the Porsche. "Another gorgeous car, Ace."

"She's already hot. We were discovered coming out of the parking lot."

"No tail?" she asks.

"Not anymore."

Her eyes shift from the car to me. They're dark brown, like her hair. She's dressed in leather—some kind of vest and pants—though it seems all wrong on her. She looks like a babe in the woods. A sweet, timid Bambi being led astray. "Who's this?"

"My co-driver."

Ace is short with her words and information. But that's how you have to be when you're dealing with people like this—even Bambi has her dark side.

Murphy gives me an "oh well, I tried" shrug. "How many more cars on the list?"

"If you don't know, we're not telling you." Ace gives me a glance and nods toward the front entrance. "Our ride is waiting. Let's go."

I walk behind Ace, only moving ahead of her to open the door. She steps through and I follow, shutting it behind me. Echo is waiting for us in her Ford, the engine idling.

"How'd you go? All done?" she asks when we slide inside, Ace taking the front passenger seat and me settling in to the middle of the backseat.

"All done," Ace confirms.

Satisfied with the response, Echo accelerates hard. It's unexpected and my head whips backward, putting a kink in my neck. I rub the back of it. "Who taught you to drive?" I say in a tone that implies whoever it was, they were clearly unqualified.

"I taught myself."

"Figures," I mutter.

"Don't start with me," she warns. "I get enough complaining from Ace."

"Ace knows how to drive though, so maybe you should think about listening to what she says."

Her eyes narrow on me in the rear-view mirror.

I smirk.

Then I direct my next question to Ace. "Tony wasn't there?"

"It's not usual for him to be there unless there's a major problem. He considers taking the deliveries beneath him. He has his little lackey in Murphy apparently, so I guess she does all his dirty work now."

"Well they can't be too tight. She didn't seem to know much about the list of cars," I point out. "But she seemed interested in finding out."

Ace sighs, her head tipping back against the headrest behind her. "She wants me to teach her all I know."

"What?" Echo glances sideways. "You never told me that."

"Because I'm not going to. I have enough on my plate without worrying about the fate of a little wannabe car thief."

Echo snorts. "How jaded you've become."

With both girls occupied, I pull my phone out and tap a brief message to Fox.

Me: The Porsche is delivered.

He knows what to do from there.

18

ARCADIA

*I*t's Tuesday night, and I'm stuffing my bag with clothes for another boost and an overnight stay at Kelly's.

The scuffle involving the Porsche seems to be a one-off. We boosted two more cars the following week without incident. And another two the week after that. But Mason is growing more suspicious with each day that passes. He's keeping a closer eye on my schedule and asking outrageously probing questions about my daily activities. I'm peppered with them whenever I return from being out. He's not just asking where I've been, he's following it up with questions about my subjects that day, and what did I learn, or what did you eat for dinner at Echo's house … I've told him that's where I've been staying because I still haven't brought up the subject of Kelly. I just can't. Even thinking about it makes my stomach knot.

I'm stuffing my headphones in my bag when a tap comes at my open bedroom door. I pause and turn my head.

Mason is there, his chin is jutting out, which means he's prepping for an argument. "You're going out?"

I keep my voice light. "Yep."

"Where?"

After zipping my overnight bag, I sling it over my shoulder and face my brother.

"Let me guess," he says before I can answer, sarcasm thick in his voice. "Echo's."

I shrug, tucking my hands in the back pocket of my jeans. "Good guess."

"Bullshit."

"I don't want an argument, Mason." I leave my room, walking around his chair to get to the front door. "I'll see you tomorrow."

My hand turns the door knob.

"Don't you dare walk out that door!"

His voice cracks through the room like a whip. I flinch, pausing to take a deep breath before I turn around. Mason is facing me, fury painting red slashes high on his cheeks.

"Enough," I bark. "I shouldn't have to account to you for every minute of my day. You're my big brother, not my warden." My voice rises. "This house isn't meant to be a prison!"

"You're right. You shouldn't have to account for each minute. But ever since you met that Sentinel," he spits with heat, "you've changed." He waves a hand at me. "You have shadows beneath your eyes. You've lost weight. And you're failing subjects."

"I'm not failing—"

"You are!" he roars, wheeling toward me. "I opened your online university account and saw it for myself."

My jaw sets. "You're snooping on me now?"

"Yes! Because you don't talk to me anymore. Your life is falling apart in front of your own eyes and you don't even seem to care! Ever since *he* came on the scene. Are you still seeing him?"

"Mason." My voice catches.

My brother stares at me, breathing hard, seeing the torn expression on my face. I can't stand how we don't talk anymore. That I have to hide parts of my life from him. Mason and I have always been close. Ace and The Ghost. Together we were wild and crazy. Now we're just broken and estranged.

"How could you?" he whispers.

I swallow, miserable.

He jerks forward on his chair, angered by my silence. "How could you?" he roars.

My eyes drop, staring, my mouth falling open. "Mason." Chills travel over my scalp and down my arms, tiny hairs rising in their wake. "Your toe."

"What?" His gaze lowers, seeing nothing. "What are you talking about?"

I drop my bag, moving closer, staring like my life depends on it. "It moved."

"What?" he whispers again.

Now we're both staring. Several long moments pass.

When he eventually speaks, his voice is flat. "You're seeing things."

Maybe I am. Mason is right. Dark shadows rest beneath my eyes. I'm tired, but it's almost a manic kind of tired. Kelly and I can't keep our hands off each other. Along with planning and executing boosts, and trying to pay attention in lectures—not to mention study and work on assignments—I'm burning the candle at both ends.

"Try doing it again," I say.

"Do what again?" he says, his voice rising. "Wriggle my toe? Because I'm trying to wriggle it, Ace. You standing there staring at it isn't helping!"

"There!" I point at it. "You moved it again."

This time he sees. After a charged silence, he lifts his head. His hands are gripping tight to the arms of his chair, and his lower lip wobbles. "Ace," he whispers.

Suddenly it's just the two of us again. Ace and The Ghost. And then we spring into action. "Right, you call your doctor," I tell him.

He's already wheeling toward the dining table where his phone sits. "On it."

"I'll get the car."

"What car?" he asks distractedly, his eyes on the screen.

"Echo's." I open the front door, scooping my bag up as I walk out. "She left it here yesterday. We can go in that."

The minute I step outside, I'm on my phone. Kelly answers after two rings.

"Babe."

"I can't go tonight. I have a ... a thing."

"What thing?" he asks as I jog down the porch steps.

"It's nothing."

"It's not nothing if you aren't comin'. We're supposed to boost another car tonight. It's all planned," he points out as if I didn't know.

"It's just ... Mason moved his toe."

He sounds incredulous. "And that's *nothing*?"

"It's not nothing. It's just ..." I open the back passenger door and toss my bag in.

"It's just what? He doesn't know the two of us are seein' each other so you feel like you can't talk to me about him?"

My sigh is heavy as I shut the door and move to the boot, popping it open in readiness for Mason's chair. "Maybe a little."

"Then he needs to know."

"I'm pretty sure he already does."

"And?"

"And nothing! We were arguing about it and then his toe moved. So now we need to get to his doctor and get him checked over."

"Ok. Was that so hard to tell me?"

"Yes!"

"Jesus, babe. Ok. Go do your thing. Echo and I will deal with the car."

Surprise hits me hard in the chest. "You need to cancel our plans. You can't do this without me."

"Yes we can."

"No."

Mason exits the front door, looking happier than I've seen him in over a year. He turns his chair and starts wheeling down the ramp.

"I have to go," I hiss into the phone. "Do not steal that car."

"We'll be fine, babe," he says and hangs up. I'm left with dial tone in my ear and a sense of foreboding in my belly.

After helping Mason into the car, I stow his wheelchair in the boot and slam it closed. "Where are we going?" I ask, reversing out the drive.

"The hospital. My doctor's there on call. He said to come straight in to the ER and they can page him."

I take one hand off the wheel and reach blindly for his, giving it a squeeze. "Mason."

He squeezes back. "I know. But it's just my toe and it hasn't moved since ... so don't get your hopes up, okay? I remember what you were like during my physical therapy. It wore you down to a shadow."

"You never worked hard enough," I mutter.

"Maybe I didn't, but you can forgive me for being a little bitter. I'm working hard now."

I let go of his hand and return it to the wheel. Maybe it's time while we're both feeling positive. "About Kelly—"

"Not now." He holds up his hand, cutting me off. "One thing at a time okay. Let's just do this, and later, when we're home, you can try and explain why you're with a man who's ruining your life. A man whose biker gang shot me in the back."

"Mason—"

"Later."

"That's unfair," I mutter.

It's not until we're inside the ER that things go pear-shaped. Mason and I are by the front reception of the emergency department. His doctor has been paged and we remain by the counter, waiting patiently. It's busy for a Tuesday. Most beds appear occupied. Doctors and nurses scurry, moving beds or pulling curtains. Potential patients sit in waiting room chairs, their expressions either pained or miserable.

We turn from the depressing scene when Doctor Edie arrives, an elderly man in his mid-sixties who's seen a lifetime of patients like my brother. They chat for a moment, catching up while I pretend to pay attention. My mind is on Kelly. He shouldn't be doing this. He's going to mess it up without me. I need to call him again.

"Ace?"

My eyes refocus. Doctor Edie and Mason are moving toward a hall that leads away from the emergency department.

"What?"

"I said did you want to just wait for me in the cafeteria? You should go get yourself something to eat."

"No, I'm good." I start toward them. "I'll—"

The entrance doors to the ER burst open behind me. A groaning patient is being stretchered in by paramedics, along with a doctor and nurse. They converse in urgent bursts, yelling stats and moving fast. My eyes shift to one of the paramedics. I jolt in shock. It's Lee. *Sentinels* Lee. *Kelly's friend* Lee. I didn't know he was a paramedic. Actually, I don't know anything about Kelly's friends. Or his life. Suddenly it seems imperative that I find out.

Lee looks at me. I know he wants to nod an acknowledgement of my presence because it's in his eyes. But I see his gaze shift to Mason in the hall. It comes back to me and then it moves on. Moments later they're gone.

It's all over in a split second.

"Actually, I think I will grab something to eat," I tell my brother.

He appears relieved. They disappear out of sight, and I pull out my phone, dialling Kelly. He doesn't answer.

Me: Dammit. Answer your phone.

I try calling again. Nothing. Ten fidgety minutes pass. I try again. Nothing. So I dial Echo, who *always* answers. Nothing. My panic ramps up a notch, my sense of foreboding reaching greater heights.

Lee and his partner burst out of the back doors, wheeling an empty stretcher. His eyes return to me. Then they look for my brother. When he doesn't see Mason, he gives me a nod.

"Lee." I put a hand on his arm, pausing their momentum. "How are you?"

"Busy." Then he must realise how abrupt that sounds because he offers a brief smile, one that hints at concern. "You okay?"

"Well … It's just … I can't get hold of Kelly."

His eyes zero in on me. "You worried?"

I am, but I can't tell him why. I don't know what Kelly may or may not have divulged. "Yeah."

"You got good reason to be worried?"

Lee's radio crackles to life. He holds up a finger, pausing our conversion to listen. It's static noise to me. I don't know how he hears it properly.

"... car gone over cliff ... rescue chopper ... extraction. Need you onsite."

Lee replies. "On our way. ETA ten minutes."

"What car?" I mutter, swallowing bile. "What car, Lee? What car?"

He gets back on the radio and asks.

"... Firebird ... smashed ..."

My knees give out. I lean back against the ER counter behind me, taking slow, sickening breaths. Were we planning on stealing a Firebird tonight? I'm too panicked to remember.

"Ace?" Lee sees my struggle and takes my shoulders, standing close enough that I can't look anywhere but in his eyes. "You are *not* okay. What's goin' on?"

Kelly's friend seems so big and capable, and caring. It's almost enough to have me falling apart all over him, but then my phone comes to life in my hand, saving me from an embarrassing display. It's Kelly. *Oh my god.* My eyes burn and the sudden relief leaves me shaky.

"I'm fine. Kelly's fine." I gulp in air and force a smile, showing him the ringing phone so he can see that Kelly is calling me.

"Are you sure?"

"I'm sure, Lee. I'm worrying over nothing. You should go."

He grasps my chin and lifts my face, looking in my eyes as if he needs to make sure I speak the truth. Then he nods, appeased. "Take care of yourself."

"You too," I reply as he steps back toward the stretcher behind him. I answer the phone, watching as Lee and his partner push through the entrance doors, and then they're gone.

"You're okay."

"I'm fine, babe. What's the matter?"

I go to answer when I'm hit with an earth-shattering realisation. The Firebird was the car that we caught Racer trying to boost for us. After that night, we'd told him we'd since taken care of it, which we hadn't because it's now sitting in the *too hard* basket. We told him the matter was closed so that he would leave it alone.

Maybe he didn't believe us.

Maybe he went to check for himself and found out we lied.

Maybe he took the car.

My anxiety rockets through the roof of the building. I can't get any air.

Racer.

"Nothing. I just ... nothing. I'll call you back," I tell him and hang up.

19

ARCADIA

I call up the contact for my grandfather with trembling fingers.

Please answer the phone. Please answer the phone.

The chant runs through my head as I put the device to my ear and listen to it ring.

"Ace?"

He answers the phone. My eyes flutter closed, and once again I sag against the reception counter behind me with relief.

"Hello? Is everything okay?"

I clear my throat. "Yes, Grandad. Sorry. I think I butt-dialled you."

"Young people these days," he complains. A slight hysterical chuckle escapes me. "The only time I ever hear from my disrespectful grandchildren is when I get butt-dialled!"

"I call you all the time," I protest.

"Never. And I never see you anymore."

That's true. I can't remember the last time I attended a Sunday family dinner. "I'll see you this Sunday," I vow. Racer may be fine, but the thought of almost losing him makes me realise how important it is to spend time with him. My grandad isn't getting any younger.

"I'll believe that when I see it, lassie."

We talk for a bit more. I mention Mason's big toe, and he sounds cautiously optimistic. He tells me his garage has finished it's rebuild. He's joined the structure to the house so now he can access the space from inside. He's also getting the builders back on Saturday to help build a greenhouse in the yard for his vegetables.

We end the call and I walk on unsteady legs to the waiting area, moving past the ill and the bored without seeing them at all. The adrenaline from tonight's events has worn off, and I need to sit down. I find myself a quiet corner and curl up in the seat like a turtle retreating to its shell.

My hands are still trembling, and my stomach is churning. I can't remember when I last ate. I can't remember when I last had a normal day. My life is a rollercoaster, and I want to get off. *Let me off.*

Anxiety is an insidious emotion. One that lingers inside of me like a virus. It slowly wanes as I breathe through my belly, staring out through the automatic glass doors of the ER entrance while I wait for Mason. There's not much to see. Just an acre of concrete with a few leafy trees dotted in between to decorate the urban jungle.

"Ace?" I turn my head. My brother is in front of me. "I looked for you in the cafeteria."

"I got held up talking to Racer on the phone," I croak and clear my throat. "How did you go?"

He shrugs and backs up his chair as I rise. We start toward the exit together. "He wants to increase my physical therapy and do more scans. There might be more surgery in my future."

Initially we were told that Mason's recovery would be a long road, but they never told us the road was endless. The idea of him dealing with months back in hospital makes me ache.

We reach the Ford. I take a breath. The urge to crouch so I can meet his eyes properly is strong. I resist because he finds it demeaning. "We've got this, Mason."

"No, Ace. *We* don't."

"That's unfair."

"Not being able to walk is unfair."

"You're right. It *is* unfair. You saved my life that night, Mason, but the price you paid was painfully high." My voice wobbles. "And I'm so sorry for that."

"Damn straight I saved your life. And now you're pissing it away on a Sentinel," he spits.

"Mason—"

My brother turns his head, his mussed hair ruffling in the breeze. He's giving me the silent treatment. I'm a little relieved. I can't argue anymore. It's been a long day and my tank is empty.

I open the car door and wait, allowing him his independence. Watching him struggle to slide inside a car when it was something he used to do with joy is so hard. It's *so* hard.

It's NOT until I climb into bed that night that I remember my essay on national and foreign markets is due the next day. So Wednesday finds me in the quad on campus, seated at an outdoor table in the sunshine near my lecture hall because the library tables are full, furiously typing on my laptop. I can't fail another assessment. It will mean failing the course, making this entire semester a complete waste.

My phone rings. It's Echo.

I ignore it. My paper isn't due for over two hours, but I only have twenty minutes of free time to finish it before my next lecture begins. I need every last one of them.

It rings out and she immediately calls again. I switch it to silent and return to my computer.

When it goes off a third time, I snatch it up and answer with a huff. "Echo, I'm busy."

"This is important."

"It better be."

"The Firebird is gone. The tracker is no longer operational. So I did some digging and—"

"Found out it went over a cliff?"

Confusion is clear in her voice. "How did you know?"

"I was at the hospital last night when the call came in. I had a gut feeling it was the same car."

"Well ..." She huffs. "It's a problem because ... Wait, what? You were at the hospital?"

I run through the explanation about Mason's big toe and I do it quickly because my mind is on my paper. "Now I have to go, okay?"

"Don't you want to hear about the problem?"

Not really. "What's the problem, Echo?" I ask, my voice flat.

"It's completely totalled. I can't find another."

I lower my head until my forehead touches the table. "So figure it out!" I growl.

Echo pauses at my burst of frustration. These cars are *my* problem. She doesn't need to be helping me. No one's going to burn her family to the ground if I don't deliver. Yet she's helping me regardless and here I am yelling at her for it.

"Echo—"

"Okay, I'll figure it out," she snaps and hangs up.

I lift my head, setting my phone down as I focus on the sea of rolling grass beyond my computer screen. There are piles of students everywhere—talking, walking, laughing together, sitting on the ground in clusters as they eat lunch—all of them oblivious to my inner turmoil.

My eyes burn as I return to my essay. The urge to give up is strong. I want to throw my laptop across the quad and watch it smash to a million pieces. Then I want to get up and just walk away ... you know the way Keanu Reeves does at the end of Point Break. He tosses his badge in the water and goes on to live a whole other life. But I can't do that. This is my future. I need to fight for it.

Just breathe, I order myself and jam my earbuds in. After choosing a song from my phone, I hit play. "Dusk Till Dawn" by Zayn and Sia begins to play. The music winds slowly through my heart, soothing my ruffled feathers.

I start typing again when my eyes lift above the screen, caught by someone moving toward me. Kelly is manoeuvring his way through the student clusters. He doesn't go unnoticed. He has a presence that commands attention and a body that's impossible not to notice. Students pause their conversations and laughter to watch.

He's carrying a bag in his hand. *Oh my god.* He's bringing me lunch. My vision blurs. The way Kelly is trying to take care of me makes me ache in the best possible way. He reaches the opposite side of the bench. I blink rapidly, bringing him into focus as I pull my earbuds out.

"Hungry, babe?"

My lower jaw trembles. I lock it down for a moment, fighting back tears. "You brought me lunch."

"Yeah." He dumps the bag on the table between us and looks at me, his brow furrowing with confusion. "That makes you sad?"

A tear spills over. *Dammit.* I swipe it away with the back of my hand before it rolls down my cheek. "It's just been a ..." I was going to say rough day, but it's been a rough few weeks. "It's just really nice of you." I sniff. "I'm so hungry," I add, though my voice comes out sounding like I'd rather chew broken glass because I'm not sure if I can eat.

Kelly walks around the table and straddles the bench seat next to me. Then he pulls me to him, wrapping his arms around me like a tight band. My face smooshes into his chest. It's hard and warm, and he smells of sweat and grease from working all morning. I don't care. It's more comforting than chicken soup on a rainy day.

"What's wrong?"

I feel the rumble of his voice against my cheek. "I have a paper due in..." my eyes flick to the time on my computer screen "...two hours and ten minutes. It's not finished, but my next lecture starts soon, and I can't miss it when I'm already behind." I pause, intending to end my complaint there, but I find myself on an unstoppable roll, like a snowball gathering momentum down a mountain. "And I'm tired, Kelly. Mason is furious with me. He's giving me the silent treatment, so he won't listen to anything I say. He's facing more surgery, and I don't know how I'll get through all that again, which makes me feel *horrible* because he has to go through worse. And Echo is probably not talking to me. I yelled at her. I didn't mean to. I'm stressed and not thinking straight. Last night I spoke to my grandfather for the first time in weeks, and he thinks it's because I butt-dialled him. He went through the garage rebuild without me, and now he's building a greenhouse, and I don't even have the time to help him do that." Then I remember the Firebird. "Racer could have died last night!" I declare hotly, swiping away more tears as he holds me close, his large palm rubbing soothing, warm circles on my lower back. "And you!" I push away from him, glaring. "I told you last night not to do anything and you didn't listen. I thought you were dead too! Kelly ..." I swallow and take a shaky breath. "My life is falling apart, and there's nothing I can do."

Kelly grasps my chin and looks at me. "No one's dead. And your life isn't fallin' apart, babe. You're going through a rocky patch, but it'll get better. You got this." He smiles and kisses me. "And you got me."

"I got you," I whisper.

"Yeah." He kisses me again.

"You've got me too."

This time when he smiles it doesn't quite reach his eyes. I can't make sense of why. It's like he doesn't believe me. "Kelly? You've got me too."

"Okay, babe." I'm not appeased by his response, but I don't have time to ponder it right now. "Now here's what you're going to do. You're gonna eat your lunch with me. Then I'm gonna get back to work while you organise for someone to record the lecture for you. Then you're gonna finish your paper, upload that sucker to wherever it's supposed to go, and after that you go home, listen to your lecture, eat dinner, and have an early night."

Kelly's arranged the chaos from my head into a solid plan, and I breathe a sigh of relief. It's a plan I can work with. "I can do that."

"See? I knew you could."

We eat our lunch together, Kelly keeping one hand on my knee and me chatting about what happened last night with Mason. He and Echo boosted that car like I asked them not to. I'm grateful, though I can't bring myself to admit it. It's one less car on the list. But it doesn't make what they did okay because if they get caught it's on me. I'm not sure I can live with that.

When we finish, he scrunches up our sandwich wrappers and stands. "Babe, I gotta get back to work." He bends, ducking his head to kiss me.

I palm his cheeks before he can draw away, stealing another one, and another. His mouth is warm and his beard scratchy. It's the perfect combination, sending shivers of delight skittering down my spine. I add another kiss. "I won't see you tonight."

He straightens. "We can catch up on the weekend."

"But ..." The weekend feels a lifetime away. "We need to plan." We have our next boost to organise, but I can't specifically say that in a crowded public place.

"And you need a break. Spend the rest of the week catching up on study and sleep. I'll see you Saturday." He bends, kissing me again. This time my mouth opens beneath his and his tongue slides inside. I almost forget we're in public. His arm snakes around my back and lowers until he's got a hard grip on my ass. He groans just a little bit. He's the one to break the kiss because I have no plans to. He shifts his mouth to my ear when he speaks, his voice low and thick. "You'll need your rest because I'm gonna fuck you until you can't move. And when you can't move, I'm gonna eat you out until you lose your voice from screamin' my name. And after that..." he draws back and smirks "...we'll have a nap and do it all again."

Kelly starts walking away, and I'm left sitting there, mouth open and body craving his touch. "Hey!" I call out, my voice raspy. He turns and starts walking backward. "How am I supposed to write my paper after that?"

"I told you, you got this!"

He turns back and I watch him walk away until he's nothing but a speck. Then I shift back to my screen with a sigh and pop my earbuds back in. This time I choose a song that's been in my head from the moment I met him: "Crazy for You" by Madonna.

I get home in the late afternoon to find Mason cooking an early dinner. His back is to me, his eyes on the stovetop as he stirs something in a saucepan. It gives me hope. I slam the front door behind me so he knows I'm home.

He doesn't turn at the sound. He doesn't acknowledge me at all.

"I'm home," I declare loudly.

Radio silence.

I dump my bag on the couch and walk to the kitchen. "You can't just pretend I don't exist."

Nothing.

I know he started a more gruelling physical therapy process today. They wipe him out, but it's no excuse for his behaviour. *I'm trying here.* "You're acting like a child," I mutter, opening the fridge door. There's an unopened bottle of wine in the side door. I grab it out and set it on the island benchtop behind me. The kitchen was upgraded when we moved in. The cabinetry is Shaker style in white, and the bench that runs along the wall behind me is marble Caesarstone, which houses the range hood, pantry, and fridge. The island counter is "night sky" Caesarstone; it's midnight black with little white flecks that resemble stars.

It's a beautiful kitchen, but Mason is making it ugly with his tension. I take a wine glass from an overhead cupboard behind me. "Would you like a wine?" I ask.

He sets down his stirring spoon and wheels to the pantry.

Right. My lips flatten. "I'll take that as a no."

I set the glass down on the starry counter and pour a generous amount. After screwing the cap back on the wine bottle, I push it to the side and bring the glass to my lips.

"I don't want you seeing him anymore," my brother says before I take a sip. His back is to me. The pantry doors are open and he's facing the shelves, unmoving.

I stare at him, willing the anger to rise, but it doesn't. I can't be mad at him. I'm just sad. Tired and sad when earlier today I was hopeful.

"You don't know him," I say quietly.

"I don't need to know him to know what he represents." Mason grabs a container of pasta from the shelf. He puts it in his lap and turns. "I don't want to know him. It makes me physically sick to think of you both together. That he's..." my brother swallows "...touching my little sister with his dirty corrupt hands." He shakes his head. "How can you even ..."

"Enough. Please." I hate hearing Mason talk about Kelly that way. And I hate having to go against my brother this way, but he's giving me no choice. "I won't stop seeing him."

Mason gives me a filthy expression as though I'm tainted too. He wheels back to the stovetop and sets his container on the bench. "Then we have nothing to talk about."

Great. Just ... great. I swipe my wine from the bench, my appetite gone, and I take it to my room. Shutting the door behind me, I set my glass on my bedside table and flop down on the edge of my bed, rubbing my temples.

There's no getting through to him. He barely gives me a chance to try. I have no idea where to go from here. If only he could just get to know Kelly in person rather than me trying to get it through his thick head. Mason needs to see the good in Kelly for himself.

I pick up my glass and take a sip. The chilled wine cools my frustration, and like a magic elixir, it gives me an idea. I leave the sanctity of my room to grab my bag from the couch. Mason is still in the kitchen. He's pouring himself a wine.

My lips purse.

He shoots me another filthy look, and I retreat back to where I came from. I dump the bag on my bed and root around inside for my phone. Finding it, I take it out, unlock the screen, and type out a text to Kelly.

Me: Thank you for lunch today.

I need to ask him a favour, and I can't just text it outright. I need to work my way up to it. After another two fortifying sips of wine, his reply comes through. I like that about Kelly. There's no need to wait an appropriate amount of time between texts. No worry about looking too eager or playing it cool or hard to get or keeping a girl hanging.

Kelly: Ur welcome

Me: I can bring you lunch on Friday?

Kelly: Maybe. Casey will be there.

Right. His estranged older brother ... even though they own and operate a business together. Kelly's mentioned him in passing but doesn't talk about him.

Me: I could meet him?

Kelly: It's your funeral

That sounds ominous, but the way Mason is right now, Casey could hardly be worse. I'm living in a house with Elsa the Snow Queen the way he keeps freezing me out. I'll likely snap at any moment—a violent psychotic outbreak where I smash every plate in the house and dig up the garden beds or something.

Me: Actually I want to ask you a favour.

Kelly: Shoot

I take another fortifying sip of wine because he's going to say no. He's going to say *hell* no. And if he does, then I'm all out of ideas. I'll be up shit creek with no paddle.

Me: Will you come to family dinner with me on Sunday night?

There's a long wait between his next message. I get up and pace back and forth. Then I use the toilet. I sip some more wine. It's almost empty, but I'll have to face Mason again if I want more.

Kelly: Your parents will be there?

Me: Yes. And Racer.

Dammit ...

Me: And Mason.

Kelly: Okay

Seriously? Is he for real?

Me: Are you sure?

Kelly: You tryna talk me out of it now? Is Mason gonna come at me with a carving knife?

I cringe because it's a possibility. Who knows how my brother will react, but we have to try, right?

Me: Maybe.

Kelly: All good, babe. I'll be there. Don't want you losing ur brother because of me.

Of course. He knows what it's like to be at odds with your brother. To lose them as family. It warms me inside to know he'll do what he can to make sure that doesn't happen for me.

Me: You're the best.

Kelly: The best u ever had

My head tips back, and I laugh. Once again he makes me feel lighter. That I've got this because I've got him. Stuff it. I'm going to brave the kitchen again for another wine.

20

ARCADIA

I pull Echo's car into the parking lot of Rebab on Friday. I haven't returned here since the Charger Incident, so it brings back a flood of memories. Most of them involve what happened upstairs. My cheeks flush wildly as I step out of the car, remembering my forsaken bra. I'm just going to pretend it never existed. Kelly has never mentioned it, so I'm hoping that's what he's doing too.

I walk around to the passenger side of the car and grab our lunch from the seat. I'm shutting and locking the car when my eyes are caught by a redhead on stilts. She's walking out of the office door and toward a white Tesla Model X that's parked two spaces down from me. I reserve all judgement on her small electric vehicle. At least it's a P90D, which means it's the performance model *and* she's saving the earth. Echo and I can't say the same with her gas guzzler. She complains about me using the Ford, saying I should just buy it from her, but I'm pretty sure I used a quarter of tank just in getting here. I can't afford her car, just a few brief trips in it here and there, whereby I refill her tank before returning it. Maybe I should just sell it for her, but Echo secretly loves that lady. She'd be heartbroken to lose her.

The redhead eyes me curiously as she gets closer, her blue eyes bright and sharp. She's wearing a white tank with black skinny jeans, high heel boots, and a blue jacket. It's a simple look, but she's managing to rock it with ease. And that's how I recognise her.

I gasp. "Grace Paterson."

Her stride falters and she smiles. "Do I know you?"

It's a dazzling smile. I wince, embarrassed because I'm fangirling. "Umm no." I clear my throat. "I've seen you on a few magazine covers." And catwalks. She's a famous international model. Well, *was*. There was a news snippet somewhere in a gossip rag about her retiring due to illness.

Grace doesn't look sick. Her skin is radiant and happiness exudes from her like rays from the sun.

"Oh nice." Her smile holds and she offers a hand for me to shake, sounding sincere.

"I'm Arcadia," I say, shifting the lunch bag from my right hand to my left and shaking hers. "Arcadia Jones."

"It's nice to meet you."

We let go and she takes a step back. There's an awkward silence.

"So, I should just—"

"Actually, it won't be—"

We both talk at the same time to fill it and then stop, giving small laughs.

"You go," she says, car keys jingling in her fingers.

"No, it's okay. You look like you have somewhere you need to be."

"I was going to say that it won't be Grace Paterson for much longer." She glances at the engagement ring on her finger as if she can't believe that it's there. "That's where I'm headed. For a dress fitting with my girls."

Holy shit. Whoever put that rock on her finger is either rich or madly in love. It's a princess cut blue diamond surrounded by smaller white ones. I admire it for a polite moment. "Congratulations. When are you getting married?"

"Thank you." She bites her bottom lip as she grins as if she's trying to contain a little giddiness. "I'll be Mrs. Daniels in two weeks."

I draw backward, shock stealing my breath. And then I realise ... "You're marrying Casey?"

Her head tilts to the side, the glossy red strands of her hair glowing like fire in the midday sun. "You know him?"

"Well, no. But Kelly's mentioned him."

Grace gasps audibly and she seizes my arm. Her fingers dig in and I wince, though I don't think she realises she's hurting me. She seems oddly, and intensely, excited by my comment. "Kelly's mentioned him?" she reiterates. "To you?"

"Umm ... yes?"

Her fingers loosen their violent grip, and she links her arm in mine, herding me toward the office entrance of Rehab. Only one of the three large garage doors are open. There's a car parked inside and faint music coming from somewhere beyond that. It's a beautiful car. One I haven't had the pleasure of seeing up close before. A vintage Corvette Stingray with a gleaming gunmetal grey paintjob. My fingers literally tingle to touch it, but I'm in the clutches of Grace soon-to-be-Daniels Paterson, and it seems she doesn't want to let me from her sight.

"Won't you be late for your dress fitting?" I ask, taking one last lingering glance of the Corvette before she opens the office door and nudges me inside ahead of her.

"I'll call the girls," she says, stepping in behind me. There's no one manning the front counter, but there's paperwork scattered every-where. "Let them know I'll be a little late."

"Seriously? It's your *dress* fitting." Isn't that supposed to be impor-tant? "I don't want to hold you up. I only stopped by to bring Kelly lunch."

"Lovely. I'll direct you to the lunch room."

"Honestly. It's okay. I know where it is."

Her eyes gleam. "Of course," she mutters, almost to herself. "You've been here before."

We're inside the lunch room, which is basically just a kitchenette with a round table and six chairs, and I'm setting our lunch down on the counter when she says, "So you and Kelly are ..."

"Are?"

Her eyebrows waggle suggestively.

"Oh. Oh!" My laugh is a little nervous because my heart is doing a few flips while I think about what Kelly and I *are*. "We're seeing each other."

"Well, that's wonderful!" Grace picks up the kettle and flicks on the tap, starting to fill it. "Kelly doesn't really uh ... see girls. Much." She turns off the tap. "Or at all," she mutters to herself, but I still manage to hear it. When the task of the kettle is complete and it sits there to boil, Grace turns and leans against the counter behind her, folding her arms. "So, I'll get straight to the point. I need a favour."

"You ..." My eyebrows fly up. We don't even know each other. Just ten minutes earlier, Grace was some dreamlike creature that featured in magazines, someone I would never know. And now she's here, in Rehab, asking *me* for a favour. Don't get me wrong, Grace seems really cool, the kind of friend I'd probably love to have, and of course I would do her a favour ... it's just so very *surreal*.

Her bottom lip pokes out a little. "Please?"

"I ... sure. Of course."

She sags a little, as if my response has relieved her greatly. Just how big is this favour? I scrape a chair back from the table and take a seat. Grace follows suit, taking a seat opposite me. The lunch bag rests between us. Burgers from Mary's. They're double-wrapped. First in foil then in paper, so hopefully they're still warm.

Her eyes drop to the bundle of food and the logo brandished across the front. "Those are burgers from Mary's," she says.

"Yes. Mary's are the—"

"Best," she finishes and presses a hand to her flat belly. "I have a dress fitting. Not to mention a wedding in two weeks." Her eyes slide to the lunch bag with longing. "I can't eat burgers."

I shrug. "I can share?"

"You would share your Mary's burger with me?"

"Of course. I don't mind."

"Mac and Evie would never share," she mutters beneath her breath.

"Sorry, who?"

"My girls," she says. "The ones waiting for me at my dress fitting. They're probably all starving because they're worried about looking good in their bridesmaid dresses."

On that note, Grace gets up and opens a kitchen cupboard. She takes out two plates. I rise to help, taking one of the burgers from the bag and unwrapping it on the counter. I pass it across to her. She sets it on the plate and cuts it in half. Then she pauses, taking a deep sniff. "Oh god, it's like crack, right?"

I laugh and we take our plates back to the table. "I should probably get Kelly."

"In a minute?" she pleads, sitting down. So I sit too. "I just want to ask you this favour first."

"Okay."

Grace takes a huge bite of our shared lunch and chews hurriedly, her eyes unfocused with pleasure. "So good," she mutters around her mouthful. Swallowing, she looks at me. "So ... IneedyoutogetKellyto-cometoourweddingforme."

"Sorry?" I lean forward in order to hear her better, though hearing isn't the problem. It's her rushed jumble of words.

Grace takes another bite. Chews. Swallows. This time she slows it down. "I need you to get Kelly to come to our wedding for me. Well ... for Casey."

"Wait ..." My brows pull together. "Kelly isn't coming to your wedding?" I knew they were estranged, but I didn't realise just how much. Not going to your brother's wedding is a big deal. It speaks of a huge rift, a gaping wound between two brothers that has never healed.

"What the hell?" The words are an angered growl spoken from the kitchen entrance behind me. "What is going on in here?"

I half turn in my chair. Kelly's wearing full mechanic's overalls, except he's removed the top half and left it dangling around his waist. A fitted white shirt covers his chest, and he's wiping at his hands with a grease rag, a thunderous expression on his face.

"Crap," Grace mutters. "He wasn't meant to hear that."

Kelly's eyes shift between both of us, landing on Grace. "I see you've met Arcadia."

She lifts her chin. "I have. And she's lovely. I didn't know you were ... seeing anyone."

"You know now." He walks into the kitchen, tossing his rag to the counter before turning around to lean against it, folding his arms. "So your plan is to recruit her to your cause? Because I'm not going to your wedding."

Her lips purse as if this is a battle she's been fighting with him for a long time. She turns her attention on me. "Ace, would you like to come to my wedding?"

My brows fly up. Grace seems quite happy to be throwing me right in the middle of this.

"Don't you dare put her in the middle of this."

Grace keeps her attention on me as if he didn't speak. I clear my throat. "Well ... Ordinarily I would love to champion your cause, but..." my eyes flick to Kelly then back to Grace "...I don't know why they're estranged. I'm sure Kelly has a good reason, right, Kelly?" I look back to him, shifting uncomfortably in my chair.

This is not how I imagined our mini date going. I was hoping there might be a quickie involved upstairs, followed by a hurriedly eaten lunch before he got back to work and I headed back to the library.

Another guy pokes his head in the door, and I'm struck dumb. "What's going on?" he asks, flicking a glance at his watch before looking at Grace. "Aren't you supposed to be at your dress fitting?"

"I'm leaving soon," she tells him.

"Hey," the guy says to me, as if he just noticed I was in the room. He walks in a little and leans toward me, holding out a hand. "I'm Casey."

"I know." And that sounds strange because we haven't met, but Casey and Kelly look so much alike that it's impossible for me to not know who he is. From the same hair colour and flirty blue eyes to their height and presence. Casey's hair is kept short in back and the sides and a little longer and mussed on the top. He's a little trimmer where Kelly has more bulk, and he's clean shaven, but their resemblance is eerie. I take his hand, shaking it before letting go. "I mean ..." My brow furrows. "Are you twins?" Because Kelly mentioned he was older, but that could mean years or just mere minutes.

"We're not twins," Kelly answers before Casey can. "Grace can I talk to you for a minute?" His tone is icy. "Outside?"

Casey's expression begins to harden, and I shiver at the similarity. "What for?"

"None of your business."

"Grace *is* my business."

"Grace is her own person," Grace says loudly. "And can not only speak for herself, she can actually do what she likes."

She stands and they both leave the room. It leaves just me and Casey, and because I don't know what caused their divide, it makes me wildly uncomfortable. He walks to the counter as if my presence doesn't bother him and flicks the button to boil the kettle that Grace had just boiled and abandoned earlier.

Once that's done, he gets out a mug and half turns. "Coffee?"

"No, I'm good. Thanks."

He nods and goes back to making one while he talks. "You're dropping off a car? I saw you arrive in that Ford. Seriously cool car. I'd love to take her out, see how she handles."

"No, I'm not dropping off a car. The Ford isn't actually mine. I just borrow it sometimes. I'm here to see Kelly."

Casey pauses his stirring and turns, looking at me again as if seeing me for the first time. After studying me for a long moment, he cocks his head. "Sorry, I didn't catch your name?"

"Arcadia."

"Arcadia ..." he prompts.

"Jones."

He nods slowly. "You're friends with my brother?"

"I am."

"How long have you known him?"

"Ah ... not long."

"Enough with the inquisition," Kelly barks, re-entering the kitchen. Alone.

"Where's Grace?"

"She left in that goddamn little electric car."

I agree with the sentiment in his tone. "She's saving the environment at least," I offer. "But still, it's not safe. She'll be the one coming out worse off if she's ever in an accident." I'm warming up to one of my favourite subjects—cars—so I can't seem to stop the verbal diarrhoea. "That's why the old vintage cars are so good. They're built like tanks."

Casey's brows rise slowly as I speak, his head nodding. "I like this girl. Maybe you can talk some sense into Grace."

Kelly doesn't even acknowledge that his brother spoke. He walks to the table, collects my plate and the bag, and says, "Let's go eat upstairs."

I want to tell Casey it was nice to meet him, but the whole situation is awkward. Based on my surface-value opinion, he's really nice, a lot like Kelly, but a little more refined, I guess. I much prefer the rougher edges.

I follow behind Kelly until we reach the upper level. He dumps our lunch on the small table beside the bed. Then he turns and grabs me by the hips. He pulls me close and ducks his head, kissing me. There's no passion. He kisses me hard, as though using me to forget something.

My chest tightens with unease. I press my hands to his chest and push him back a fraction. "Is everything okay? Did you want to eat lunch?"

"Everything's fine, babe. I don't want to eat lunch. I just want to eat you."

He goes to kiss me again, and I draw back. "How long have you and Casey been estranged?"

Kelly's jaw tightens. He lets me go, taking all the warmth with him. I hug my middle as he grabs the lunch package and seats himself sideways on the edge of the bed, busying himself with unwrapping it. I'm starting to wonder if I'm now getting the silent treatment from him too when he finally speaks. "Since I was fifteen."

My body stiffens. I wasn't expecting that answer. Kelly was just a boy. He's twenty-eight now, so I do the simple calculation. "That's thirteen years."

"I know that, Ace."

Kelly

ACE WALKS to the bed and climbs on, seating herself cross-legged and facing me. She looks cute today in her skinny blue jeans and pale pink tee shirt. Aviator glasses are tucked into the neckline and her hair is tied in two long braids. I know she's classified as a mature-age student, but she looks like she belongs. More so than the office-type attire she sometimes gets around in—though she seems to be wearing those outfits less and less. It's as if she were trying to fit into the finance world and is slowly realising she doesn't need to change herself in order to do that.

"Do you want to talk about it?" she asks me.

Do I want to talk about how my mother died? Or how I shot my father in the head and watched his blood spray over the wall and sheets? And how it would never have happened if Casey had just sent for us like he promised? No. Though, I like how she asks rather than demands. Her eyes are dark with concern, and maybe a little turbulent, as if she's ready to unleash a shit storm all over my brother if I just say the word. I almost chuckle. She appears so petite and calm, but I've seen her wild side. It would be entertaining to watch her go toe to toe with him, but I can fight my own battles.

"It's in the past," I say, taking a bite of my lunch and swallowing.

"It's not in the past," she says quietly. There's no argument in her tone even though she's disagreeing with me.

"It is." I set my burger back on its wrapper. I wasn't real hungry anyway. Casey doesn't work in Rehab often as he has his consulting business to operate, and it's fulltime. But he comes in every other

Friday. It makes for a tense day, and I'm usually left with a headache at the end of it. "It was a long time ago."

"Thirteen years ago or three weeks, it doesn't matter. If it's still sitting between the two of you like a festering wound, then it's not in the past."

I swipe a hand down my face, scratching at my beard. Ace is right, and I hate that she's right, because it means the pain is still there despite my best attempts to not acknowledge it. But what am I supposed to do?

"You can't fix what's broken."

Her eyes fill and I know she hears the pain in my voice. It's not an easy thing to hide sometimes, especially with this girl.

"You can." Ace drags my lunch across the bed, removing the barrier between us. Then she shifts up on her knees and moves toward me until she straddles my lap. I don't have any choice except to give her my full attention. "You *can* fix it, Kelly. It might not go back to what it was before, but it would be better than what you have now, right? Think of it like an engine cut down the middle. You would have to weld it all back together, and replace a few parts here and there, but you'll get it running again. Maybe not as smooth as it used to be, but it would still work."

My nostrils flare. "That would mean forgiveness."

"Kelly." She brushes a hand on my cheek, tucking loose strands of hair behind my ear. "What did he do that needs forgiving?"

I lift her up and off me, rising to my feet. Familiar anger surges. "I don't need soothing gestures, Ace," I snap. "I'm not a fuckin' cat."

Ace mutters something beneath her breath and goes about packing away the lunch I barely ate.

It's an insult, I'm sure. "What did you say?"

"I said," she enunciates, turning to face me as she bunches the wrapper in her hands, "that I wouldn't have come today had I known asshole was on today's lunch menu instead of burgers."

Christ. I turn and kick one of the locker doors. It dents slightly and doesn't make me feel better.

"Real mature, Kelly." Her tone is snide enough to make my eyes water.

"You wanna know what he did?" I shout, my hands fisting at my sides. "Do you really want to know?"

"Yes!" Ace shouts back, getting in my face. "Get it out there, god! Because if you don't, it might start festering between us too, and I don't want us broken!" Her voice cracks and she lowers it to a raspy whisper. "I don't want us broken too."

We're shouting at each other and my heart races. I hate this. I hate what this is doing to us.

"He left."

The words hurt like little razor cuts across my skin. My arms hang limp by my side, my body feeling like a wrung-out rag. "He left and when he came back it was too late. Everything was broken."

Ace starts toward me, her steps wary like she's approaching an injured animal. "What was broken?"

"My mother." I swallow, my throat raw and heart thumping inside my chest. "Her body was twisted on the floor and there was blood in her hair. Her eyes were blank. Nothin' in 'em." The image is torture. I blink it away, knowing it will return again soon enough. "Can't fix what's dead, can you, Ace?"

"What happened?" she asks quietly.

"My dad. My dad happened."

Her step falters. She opens her mouth and then snaps it closed.

"Didn't expect that, did you?" I swallow the bitter lump in my throat. "He hit her so hard she smacked her head on the side table in the bedroom. She went down and she never got back up." I start sucking in air through my teeth, willing myself not to lose it. "He killed her."

Ace flinches. She actually flinches. It makes my stomach churn to have her know. I shouldn't be dumping this on her so bluntly, but it's not the kind of revelation you can wrap up in a pretty pink bow and hand over to someone.

"And you were fifteen?"

I nod.

"Did he …" She exhales a shaky breath and tries again. "Did he hit you too, Kelly?"

A heavy beat of silence passes before I nod again, my body stiff, the movement jerky.

"And Casey?"

"Yeah," I say, making myself look at her. Anger is blazing from her eyes.

"That sonofabitch," she hisses.

"Ace—"

"People like that don't deserve to live. They don't deserve to have kids. They don't deserve to see the sky and the moon and the stars. They don't—"

"He's already dead."

"Oh." She exhales another shaky breath and places a hand to her belly as if she feels sick.

So do I. My stomach is twisted in knots. And this is why it's better to never share bad shit like this. I don't tell her that I shot him dead. I can't. Not today. Maybe not ever. Whatever this is that Ace and I have, neither of us are ready for that. I walk to the bathroom, grab a glass, and fill it from the sink. After drinking it down, I refill it and bring it to Ace.

"Thanks," she murmurs, taking a sip. Her hands are trembling. My abrupt confession has sent her into shock. I shouldn't have said anything. Everything was fine and now I've wrecked it. There's an awkwardness growing between us that I should have anticipated.

"You should go home."

"No, I—"

I snatch the glass from her hand and set it down by the bed.

"Casey left you with him?" Ace shakes her head as if she can't fathom it. "He just left and never came back?"

"That's right. He left. He promised he'd come back for the both of us, but he never did."

"That's a damn lie."

We both turn. Casey is standing at the top of the stairs, grease rag in hand and face pale. "I came back."

"You came back later than you promised," I snarl, my eyes hardening, "and by then it was too late. In this instance, it wasn't a case of better late than never, right?"

"I've apologised more times than I can count." Casey's lips twist. "You need to accept it and move on because I'm done with it. I'm fucking done."

My fists itch to punch him in the face because I never *asked* for his apology. I don't want it. And it was a mistake to setup Rehab in a partnership. I can't work with him. And I can't do this right now. Not in front of Ace. Not with this bitterness sitting so heavy on my chest I can't breathe.

My eyes cut to her. "You need to leave."

Ace folds her arms, shaking her head for emphasis. "No."

"Get out, Ace!" I shout, my body vibrating with frustration.

Her lip quivers, tears pricking her eyes. It makes me ache all over. "I'm not leaving you."

"Go!" I bellow, my arm thrusting outward to point at the stairs. "Leave!"

"Kelly—" Casey starts.

"You don't get to speak!" I yell at him, beginning to unravel like a pulled thread. "You weren't invited up here. Both of you just fuckin' go!"

I can hear myself yelling like a maniac, but I can't stop. Ace picked at my wounds and now it hurts too much. My throat is raw and my stomach is pitching as if I'm on a rollercoaster ride that won't let me off. I don't want either of them here to witness it.

I need to get on my bike and ride it out.

"Fine," Ace says quietly, her eyes dark and sad. She collects her phone and keys from the bed. My eyes track her every movement, grief splitting me open, because I'm the one making her go, and I know she won't come back. It leaves me hollow.

She makes her way down the stairs, disappearing out of sight, and my eyes cut to my brother. "You sonofabitch."

"Me?" Casey nails me with a savage glare. "Did you not just see that? You just shoved that girl from your life like you do everyone else who gets too close."

"What I do is none of your business!"

"Yeah?" His brows rise and his snide expression enrages me. Like a wounded beast, I duck and charge, knocking him off his feet. He slams into the wall by the side of the stairs, his head smacking backward.

I stumble back a step, and he comes at me, fist slamming into my face with a *crack*. Pain explodes. I grab the neckline of his shirt and yank. We both go down, wrestling on the floor. My vision blurs. Blood fills my eye. The metallic stench is thick and vile, and makes my heart race with sickening memories.

"Stop," I growl, shoving him away, breathing heavy. "I'm not my father. I won't fight with you this way."

Casey shifts to a seated position on the floor, leaning himself against the side of the bed. He holds a hand to the back of his head, grimacing. "You started it."

I wipe at my brow, blood smearing across my palm. "No, you started it the moment you walked up those stairs and stuck your nose in my business."

"Christ, we're fucking mature," Casey mutters, swiping a hand down his face. "Mum would be pissed if she could see us right now." After a long moment of silence he snorts. "Do you remember whenever we fought, how she'd send us to the old folks' home down the end of the street for our punishment?"

"Yeah." I forgot about that. Somehow all the good memories got lost along the way. "You always got stuck playing "The White Cliffs of Dover" on their musty old piano, and you were shit at it, but they were all so bad of hearin' they didn't even notice."

Casey chuckles and it's an odd sound, because it's the first time in years that we've actually talked rather than argued. "And you had to read those Mills and Boon novels to old Mrs. Stapleton with the moustache because she was losing her sight."

I shudder. If the guys at school had found out about that, they would have plastered my locker door with pictures of dicks. "She always slipped me cookies after, though."

The bell at the front counter of Rehab peals down the hallway and up the stairs, startling the both of us out of the memory.

"Oh fuck," Casey mutters. "That's why I came up here. That dude, Richard, is here to collect the EH Holden you were working on." He scans my face. My eye is swelling, and I can feel blood crusting on my face and in my beard. "So yeah, I better handle that one."

21

KELLY

My head throbs as I lie in bed early the next morning. I press my fingers against the tender area around my eye, wincing. It reminds me how much I messed up yesterday. Bitterness and anger spew from my lips every time the touchy subject of my past is broached. Time might have dulled the edges down to a worn blade, but it still cuts. I don't know how to let it go, but I do know I can't go on like this. Carrying all this hate around is fuckin' exhausting.

My phone beeps. I glance at the screen with surprise. It's Ace. The thumping of my heart increases as I read the message.

Arcadia: Come pick me up. Bring your bike. And a hammer.

My chest expands as I breathe in, exhaling slowly with relief. I feel a stupid smile forming on my face as I waste no time replying.

Me: Be there soon

The heavy weight I was carrying lifts when just moments before it was crushing me into the bed. I honestly thought she was done with me after yesterday. I wouldn't have blamed her, but knowing that it takes a lot more than that to rattle her cage gives me hope.

I set my phone aside and after a nice hot shower, I dress in jeans, boots, and a tee. With her cryptic message, I decide to just throw my whole tool belt in my saddle bag before sticking my head in Fox's door. His head is tipped back. It's hanging half off the bed and he's snoring—not loud enough to bring down the roof, but he's definitely sawing a few logs. I grab the pillow from the floor by the door and peg it at his head.

He stirs and mumbles, "Fuck off."

"Goin' out," I say.

Fox rolls over, facing away from me with a growl. "So fuckin' go already."

"I'll leave you to get your sleep, princess."

He turns his head, cracking one eye open to glare. Then they both fly open and he rises up on one elbow. "What happened to your face?"

"Casey happened."

Fox rolls his eyes and flops back down on the bed. "Fuck's sake," he mutters, over it in much the same way I am.

I leave him to get his beauty sleep. The ride to Ace's house eases the throbbing in my head a little, though I imagine the ibuprofen I took before heading out helped too. It's a beautiful Saturday. No clouds, just endless blue sky and less chill in the air as we near the end of winter. I pull in the drive and idle the engine, thinking it best not to go inside in case Mason is home. One confrontation in twenty-fours is pretty much my limit.

Ace jogs down the porch steps at my arrival. She's wearing worn jeans and old boots like me and a tight tee that reads: *My car is hotter than your car.* She reaches the bike and I tug my helmet off. After setting it on the handlebar, I switch off the engine because what I have to say can't be shouted in her face.

The silence is deafening as Ace sees my eye. Her expression turns sad.

"I owe you an apology," I mutter gruffly before she asks me about it. I reach out and take her hand, giving it a squeeze before letting go. That she's allowing me to do this bodes well for me.

"You do."

I exhale deeply, hating that I've upset her. "I'm sorry."

Her chin lifts. "I'm not leaving you."

My brow wrinkles. "Sorry?"

"Yesterday, when you yelled at me to leave. I might have gone, but only because you needed alone time to cool off. I'm not going to leave you."

I shake my head. "They're some pretty words, babe, but you can't promise shit like that."

Her eyes narrow, not liking my response. "I can if I mean it."

"Okay." I hold my palms up as if surrendering. I know the ice between us is thin right now. No good can come of me skating across it.

"You should come inside so I can fix your face. It's a mess."

My gaze flicks to the house beyond her.

"Mason went out drinking last night with two of his friends," she tells me. "I just checked on him five minutes ago and almost passed out from the alcohol fumes. I left him a barf bowl and got the hell out of there."

"Ouch," I mutter, swinging my leg off the bike while Ace starts toward the porch steps. I snag her hand and she stumbles to a halt. "Come here, babe. Need a proper greeting."

Ace shifts closer and tilts her head, leaning up and kissing me on the lips.

"We okay?"

She nods. "We're okay."

Once inside, I perch on the back of the couch while she comes at me with a first aid kit. After dipping a cotton bud in some betadine, she steps between my spread legs and touches it to the split on my brow. It stings like a motherfucker, but only for a moment because she leans in, blowing gently against the wound to ease it. I study her face as she tends to me. There are a few freckles on her nose, uncovered by makeup. Her lashes are long and dark. She's wearing mascara. And her lips are slick with peach gloss because I can taste it from her kiss.

"What are you staring it?" she mutters, drawing back to dab a bit more.

"You."

Her breath puffs gently against my cheek as she goes about her task. "Why?"

"Because you're right there. And I can."

She snorts. *Dab, dab.*

"How am I lookin'?"

"Like a guy who's going to get a nasty scar if he doesn't get a couple of stitches in this cut."

I shrug as Ace draws back, gets a fresh cotton bud, and adds more betadine. She comes at me again. *Dab, dab.* She pulls back to inspect. *Dab.*

"Chicks dig scars."

Ace snorts again, moving out from between my thighs. "Maybe. It depends."

"On what?" I ask, watching as she rummages around in her little kit. Finding a package of butterfly strips, she takes out two and steps close again.

She gently places one on my brow and pauses to admire her handiwork. She puts the second one on with care as she speaks. "On how said scar was acquired. If you were pushing a little old lady out of the way of an oncoming car and it hit you instead, then yeah, a girl would dig that scar, provided you lived, of course. But if you were out being a drunken idiot with your friends, spewed the contents of your stomach everywhere, then proceeded to slip in it and crack your head open, then that's just a permanent reminder that you're a dick."

I laugh. Her eyes drop to mine and she laughs along with me.

"But this..." her brows arch in question as her laughter slowly dies off "...I'm assuming came from Casey?"

"You assume right."

"And is he just as banged up as you?"

"Worse." As if I'd admit to anything less than that.

Ace packs up the first aid kit. "So you punched it out and now all is forgiven."

"Pfft. Hardly."

She pauses to look at me. "You know it's not your brother you want forgiveness from, right?"

"Ace." My brows snap together and it pulls on the tape. I hiss. "He left."

"Yeah, he did," she says softly, tucking the little kit beneath her armpit, "but so did your mother. You're angry at her because she died, and you're blaming Casey instead because she isn't here and you have to blame someone, right?"

I wrap my arms around her middle and pull her close, resting my head against her belly. I'm unable to refute her words, but they turn my stomach. "What kind of sick fuck blames a dead person?"

"I'm sure she was a beautiful person inside and out, and that you loved her very much, but it doesn't make you a bad person for being mad at her. It shouldn't have been up to Casey to get you out. He was young too, and he tried, right? You said he came back, but he was too late? What was stopping her from taking you and leaving?"

My arms tighten. She loved him. My father. And what kind of person loves the man who beats on her and her kids? *Christ.* Ace is right. I'm angry at her. So fuckin' angry. She brought us into that shit storm life and rather than get us out of it, she died and left me to deal with the fall out alone.

"She was a great mum," is all I say on the matter and push it from my head.

───────

After a forty-minute drive, we pull up outside an older-style house in the outer suburb of Merrylands. It's white weatherboard with a red tiled roof and lush gardens. I'm surprised to see Racer emerge from the front door at our arrival. He's dressed in a white singlet and an old pair of navy work pants, coffee mug in hand. Ace had only given me an address and asked me if I could handle a little hard work today. Naturally, I said yes while flexing my biceps to prove my point, and now we're at her grandfather's house.

I switch off the engine, still wondering what we're doing here. He walks over as Ace removes her open-faced helmet and climbs off the bike, setting it on the back.

"Racer," she exclaims and gives him a hug.

He returns it with one arm, his brows rising as I remove my own helmet and he sees my face. My black eye and cut brow are shit timing. First her grandfather this morning then family dinner tomorrow. It won't help Ace's cause in getting Mason to accept my presence in her life. It's only going to make it that much harder. Another reason why I'm an idiot.

"Nice shiner," Racer comments when Ace lets him go.

I shrug. "Brothers."

He nods. "Yep. I never had one of those, but I raised two boys. Thought the damn kids would kill each other the way they went at it sometimes."

His understanding is sharp relief, so I climb off the bike and retrieve my tool belt. "I believe we have some work to do today?" I raise my brows in question to both of them.

"Racer is having a greenhouse built in his backyard. I thought we could help. And ..." she says, rummaging around in her bag. She plucks out a bottle of whiskey. I wince. It's the cheap stuff from her house. "I brought you this."

He grins with delight. "You're up to something. Helping me with the greenhouse. Buying me whiskey. What's going on?"

"I'm glad you asked." Ace links her arm in his, and they start toward the house. "I'm bringing Kelly to family dinner tomorrow night—"

"You guys go ahead. I'll be in in a minute," I call out.

Ace waves to indicate she heard me and continues chattering with her grandfather as they walk inside the house. The screen door slaps behind them as I set the tool belt down over the seat of my bike and pull out my phone. Calling up my messages, I send through a quick text.

Me: Need you on a job today.

I include the address and hit send. A reply comes almost instantly.

Hammer: Be right there.

When Ace told me to bring a hammer, she should have told me which one, because this one will be a damn sight more helpful, and being a Saturday, I know his only plans today were to hang out at the clubhouse. Tucking my phone away, I retrieve my tools and head inside. It's definitely an older house. The walls are panelled with pale pine slats, and linoleum lines the floor of the little kitchen. It's clean and tidy, and a thousand pictures decorate the wall in the living area beyond.

"Hello?"

Curious, I start toward the pictures when I'm caught by the sight of Racer tucking his whiskey bottle into a blond timber cabinet in the corner of the living room. He's adding it to a large collection of identical bottles, all of them unopened and gathering dust.

He sees me and starts. Then he puts a finger to his lips, warning me to keep quiet. I almost chuckle. Old Racer finds the whiskey just as nasty as I do, yet rather than hurt his granddaughter's feelings, he feigns delight and then hides them away. "Pretend you never saw me do this."

"Saw what?"

He chuckles and shuts the cupboard, following behind me as I walk over to the pictures. There are family photos and photos of a young Ace and Mason, and another kid I don't know, maybe their cousin? There's a school picture of Ace, hair in pigtails and two front teeth missing, a crazy smile on her face. Pictures of her around fifteen years old at the wheel of a dusty banged-up rally car. There are framed articles published in Wheels magazine. I look closer. The by-line says Jonah Jones.

I turn to him, incredulous. "Your name is Jonah Jones?"

He nods. "Great name, huh?"

"I follow your column in the magazine. Had no idea you were the infamous Racer Jones."

"Not many people do. I've lived a somewhat nefarious life. And while it's been one hell of a fun ride, I don't like to advertise it. Especially for Arcadia," he says, scratching at his chin as he looks at all the photos alongside me. "She's working hard for a respectable future." Racer turns and gives me a sharp look. "I won't have you ruining that for her."

"I have no plans on doin' that."

"Good to know." He claps me on the back and starts for the kitchen. "Coffee?"

"Please," I call back, taking one last look at Ace's school picture before I turn and follow. "Oh, and if you have builders coming for your greenhouse, you can call them off. You've got me and Ace now, and I've got a friend on the way. He's a builder by trade and his work is top notch."

He nods, his expression pleased. "Well, I appreciate that, Kelly. Thank you."

Ace steps inside from the back door, stomping her old boots against the mat while Racer spoons ground coffee into a plunger. "It's a great spot for the greenhouse, Grandad," she says. "You'll get lots of morning and midday sun."

"And you'll get lots of vegetables," he replies, adding hot water.

"Ahh, this is just your secret plan to make me more healthy," she teases.

He gives us both a stern look. "It wouldn't kill you young kids to eat a vegetable or two."

We drink our coffee, and Racer shows me the greenhouse site and plans. And after Hammer arrives, we drink more coffee, review the site and plans again, and then we get stuck in. The frame is cut and up by midday. We mostly use nail guns, though Racer uses his old-school hammer. I took a turn at banging nails into wood and found it more labour-intensive but so much more satisfying.

We pause for a lunch break after Ace orders pizza delivery, and that afternoon I staple in the green mesh covering while Hammer builds raised vegetable beds made of Cyprus sleepers.

At the end of the day, we're all tired and sweaty and covered in dirt, but it feels good. The hard, physical labour has chased away the events of yesterday.

Racer and I sit on the back steps of his house, with Ace cross-legged on the grass and Hammer leaning against the outdoor cladding, beers in hand, as we talk and survey our work.

Ace's grandfather clinks his beer to mine. "Welcome to the Jones family, Kelly."

I look to Ace, wondering what she makes of his comment.

She simply grins, and I'm happy that she's happy. She needs to bank that emotion because she'll need to draw on it for Sunday family dinner. Racer wasn't difficult to win over, but he's older with more patience and acceptance. Mason is a hothead like me, so I need to be on my best behaviour or tomorrow night will be a total shit fest.

22

ARCADIA

"*O*h hell no." Mason's face is twisted in anger, having wheeled himself inside our parents' home to find me and Kelly sitting on the sofa, me with a wine because I was bracing and Kelly with a soda water because he drove. Mum and Racer sit opposite us with Dad perched on the arm of the chair beside Mum. It's a cool night and the three of them are enjoying aperitifs of hot buttered rum. It's a Jamie Oliver recipe. Mum is obsessed with the famous chef and watches every cooking show as if it were the American Super Bowl. She waxes on about his use of fresh, healthy ingredients from the garden, and she's currently making her way through his *Everyday Super Food* recipe book that I bought her for Christmas. Dad happily tolerates her obsession—much like me, he finds cooking a chore so he eats anything she makes.

Dad was talking with Kelly about cars when Mason entered, and Racer was chatting with Mum, sharing photos on his phone of our greenhouse build yesterday. I was sitting there quietly rubbing sweaty hands down my dark denim jeans. My parents have been very accepting, particularly considering Kelly is the first man I've ever brought to Sunday dinner.

I phoned my mother earlier this morning to inform her I was bringing someone.

"Ellington, darling?" she asked. "Because I wanted to ask her about that new pink hair colour. I saw a picture on Instagram and it looks gorgeous. I was wondering if perhaps I'm too old to go pink."

"Rubbish, Mum." My mother could absolutely pull it off. Her dark brows and large grey eyes would complement some lovely pastel highlights. "You're never too old."

"I don't think your father shares your view," she whispered into the phone so he must have been nearby. "I showed him the photo. He said she looks like a damn cupcake and well, I don't think it was a compliment because you know how sugary those things are. They give him a toothache. Don't tell Ellington though, honey, because his opinion doesn't matter. He's a man. They don't get it, and I wouldn't want her feelings hurt."

Mum was sweet but Echo's feelings were plated with armour. Bullets couldn't penetrate that hard exterior. "I won't tell her, I promise, but it's not Echo I'm bringing."

"Oh?" she prompted.

"I'm seeing someone."

"Ohhh," she drawled with sudden understanding. There was a pause while she waited for me to expand on my announcement. My parents weren't Mason. I knew they'd be okay once I gave them the full story, but I hated having to do so. I'd rather them just get to know Kelly for who he was, except I didn't have the luxury of time on my side. They needed a little warning. So I explained the situation over the phone, which was difficult because she kept repeating everything to Dad, who was asking questions in the background, which I heard, yet Mum repeated anyway.

They suggested we turn up a little late, making it more difficult for Mason to leave, except he was even later than we were. We beat him here and now it's an ambush.

He glares at me. "I thought that was Kelly's bike out front but I didn't want to believe it. You're such a bitch, Ace."

Mum gasps. "Mason!" Her voice is a whip. "I understand this is difficult for you, but insulting your sister in such a fashion is uncalled for."

My brother doesn't have the grace to look suitably ashamed. He's too angry. His glare shifts to Kelly. "Is this what you're trying to do? Crippling me wasn't enough, so now your plan is to drive a wedge between me and my entire family?"

I fumble blindly for Kelly's hand, squeezing it while I return my brother's glare. "That's an outrageous accusation. Kelly did *not* cripple you, Mason, and he's here because I asked him to be."

His lips pinch so tight a screwdriver couldn't pry them loose. "Fine. Then I'll leave."

"You're not leaving." Setting down my wine glass on the coffee table with a *clang*, I let go of Kelly's hand and stand, fury making me hot. "You won't talk to me at home, Mason, so you can talk to me here. I understand your bias. I do," I stress while he sits in his chair by the front door, his hands white-knuckling the arm rests. "But Kelly's done nothing wrong. He shouldn't have to defend himself to you, or anyone else."

"Babe," Kelly mutters.

I pause to look down at him. His expression is both serious and gentle. He's hurting for me when he's the one being attacked. Emotion clogs my throat, making my voice thick. "What?"

"Don't need you defendin' me. You can put your claws away."

"Maybe you don't," I declare hotly, "but I'm going to anyway. This falling out is not on you, Kelly, it's on me, and it's on my brother." I look at Mason though I'm speaking to the room. "I've never been so scared the night you were shot. Julianna might be alive, but she died inside the day she was raped. We were all hurting and wanted justice. I know stealing that car was reckless. When I realised we couldn't outrun Grinder, I thought we were going to die. But you protected me. You pushed me in front of you, blocking me, and you got shot instead." Tears burn my eyes. "And rather than healing and moving on, we let the wounds fester, and I can't live like that any longer, Mace," I tell him. "Meeting Kelly made me realise that holding on to all that hurt and anger is exhausting." My voice lowers to a pained whisper, my heart thumping with emotion. "I can't do it anymore and neither can you."

Dad stands from his seat on the couch, drink in hand. He gives me a pat on the back, a high level of affection from my father. "You're a good girl, Arcadia," he mutters near my ear before shifting away.

Then he collects the aperitif from the table that Mum had set aside for Mason and walks to my brother. "Let's go outside for a bit, Son."

Mason stares at me for a long hard moment before he follows Dad out the front door. Mum clears her throat when it shuts behind them. "Jonah," she says, because she doesn't believe in nicknames. Real names are given for a reason, she insists, and aren't meant to be butchered or shortened because people are too lazy to speak an extra syllable or two. Dad respects her wishes but calls us Mace and Ace behind her back. "Help me make some more drinks."

Racer swirls his nearly full glass. "I don't need a refresh, Lydia."

She stands. "Well I do, and I want to hear more about your greenhouse, so you can come with me."

"I've already shown you the pictures," he booms, getting agitated because he hates repeating himself. "No need to see them again."

"Jonah," she hisses beneath her breath, though I can hear, and I know Kelly can too because he's biting back a smile. "Don't be obtuse. The lovebirds need a moment alone."

"What for? You think they want to suck face under your roof?" He sounds incredulous.

"Grandad!" I shout, my cheeks hot. "Go and help Mum."

"Okay, okay!" He rises with a groan, making it appear as if he's ancient and the simple task of standing is more than his frail body can take. "Kick an old man out of his chair then. Young upstarts," he mutters as he follows my mother into the kitchen.

Kelly and I are alone. I have no idea what he's thinking. About running, maybe. I wouldn't blame him. My family is definitely not for everyone. I turn sideways on the couch, leaning into the smattering of cushions. "You okay?"

"No," he quips, setting down his soda water and turning to face me. "But I will be if we can suck face."

I snort at his jest. "Stop it."

"I'm not kidding, babe." He grasps me by the chin and kisses me.

"Kelly," I gasp, pulling away.

"Shut up and kiss me, Ace."

"Well, when you put it like that..." I lean close, my mouth near his "...how can I resist?"

"You can't," he replies with a smirk, and his words flash through my mind as I press my lips to his with tenderness.

You can't fix what's broken.

You just watch me, Kelly. I might not fix you, but I'll help you put your pieces back together the same way you're helping me to do mine.

"You're a fool for me, Ace," he adds.

I smack my mouth to his grinning lips. His big warm hands grasp hold of my hips, tugging me closer. My pulse quickens as he takes charge, deepening the kiss into something so much more. His tongue plays with mine and a deep groan vibrates through his chest. I inch closer and his fingers dig in, welcoming the press of my breasts and the heat of my body. "Fuck," he draws back, "You're gettin' me hard."

Kelly's words are fuel to my flame. He makes me forget who I am when he's kissing me. He tangles his fingers in my hair, holding my face close to his as he looks at me. "It's funny how life works out sometimes."

"What do you mean?"

"I don't know." He kisses me before loosening his fingers, letting me go but still keeping me close. "I've made a lot of mistakes in my life, but every single one of them led me to that moment outside of Fix where I met you, and ..."

"And what?" I prompt as he stares blindly over my shoulder.

He looks back to me. "And you make every one of them worth it. You make me a better person without changin' me into someone else."

Tears blur my vision. My hands tremble as I palm his bearded cheeks, my heart thumping furiously with both panic and wonder. *I think I'm falling in love with you.*

"Told you they were going to suck face, Lydia!"

Racer's loud comment is a bucket of cold water to my face. "Grandad!" I shout, my cheeks flaming as I let Kelly go.

Both his and Kelly's laughter ring out through the living area.

"Sorry, lass," he says, not sounding sorry at all. He sets a plate of nibbles on the table before sinking back into the sofa that Mum bullied him out of earlier. "Did I interrupt a tender moment?"

"You're a poophead," I tell him, getting to my feet. "I'm going to help Mum in the kitchen."

Mum is at the counter when I walk in, sprinkling feta over a colourful salad. I snatch a cherry tomato and pop it in my mouth. The fruit bursts open when I bite down, filling my mouth with a rich earthy flavour. "Mmm, yum. What are you making?"

"Roasted honey-glazed duck with a grilled corn and quinoa salad," she announces proudly, finishing her sprinkle with a final flourish. Her Jamie Oliver cookbook is open to the recipe and resting against the timber stand that Mason made her in grade-eight wood-work class. There are love hearts punched through the timber at the top and burnt edges to give it an aged feel.

On the surface, we're pretty much your average family, except our hobbies involve cars—working on them, racing them, admiring them, writing about them, and yeah, an exceptional talent (passed down through the generations) of stealing them. It's not something done for sport. It's a special request made through trusted third parties and something done rarely. Except now our entire family is retired. Apart from me, because you know, Tony.

"Can I help?" I ask, snatching up a sliver of grilled corn. It's hot in my mouth. I garble and pant as if in labour. "Arrgghh!"

Mum ignores me as she sets out plates. "You can get the bread rolls from the oven for me."

Grabbing the oven mitts, I turn around and bend, cracking open the wide oven door as I chew. I'm blasted with heat and the fresh yeasty scent of baked bread. My stomach growls. Dinner at my parents' house is always a treat. Usually one of us brings dessert, but after I informed Mum about Kelly coming, she insisted on making something herself. She's in her *I want to make an extra impression* mode because she cares about me.

"You're the absolute best," I tell her, setting the tray of hot rolls on the stove top.

"I know. Don't ever forget it."

"As if."

"How are your studies going?" she asks as I use tongs to transfer the rolls to the little side plates Mum set out.

I grimace as we work together side by side. "Not great."

"Why's that?"

Well, I'm being blackmailed by Tony. You know of him, though you don't approve of him because he lacks appreciation for *real* cars. Not to mention his reputation is downright dirty. So now I'm stuck stealing a whole bunch of expensive machinery. On top of that, there's a man in your living room that I'm tumbling head-first into mad crazy love with. He's not perfect, but then neither am I, though I know you'd refute that because I'm your daughter and you're biased toward me. So I spend most nights in his bed and my days planning boosts. Somewhere in there I squeeze in study time, but my heart isn't it.

"It's hard, Mum."

"Well, nothing worth having is ever easy, is it," she tells me, trying to be helpful.

"I want to do well. I want to succeed in this, except ..." I trail off, pushing the plates across the counter because if I don't I'll grab a roll and start chewing on it, and that will give Mum a fit because she likes the table set *just so*. One less roll will ruin the effect.

"Except what?" She transfers pieces of the sticky duck to the dinner plates but she's doing it at a slow pace, so I know she's listening carefully.

"Except it's boring!" I burst out, because while there's safety in numbers, there's also tedium and monotony. "I can do the work if I put my mind to it, but I think I'll slowly lose the will to live if I have to do this for the rest of my life."

"So don't." Both our heads turn. Kelly is standing at the entrance, leaning against the kitchen doorway. His size overwhelms the space, making me a little breathless.

"I have to."

"You don't *have* to, Ace."

"I do."

Mum huffs beside me. "Stop being stubborn and listen to Kelly, Arcadia."

I huff too, because my mother only just met the man and she's already siding with him.

"Ace, you just gotta listen to your heart, because if you don't, you'll spend the rest of your life wishin' you had."

"What he said," Mum quips, spooning sauce over the duck with care.

"Sure!" I exclaim, sarcasm thick and voice rising. "I'll just listen to my heart and keep stealing cars for the rest of my short life!" *Fuck it.* I stretch my arm for a roll, ripping off a piece and shoving it in my mouth, chewing furiously. "Because I'll eventually end up in prison..." rip, chew, swallow "...and I can't go to prison because I'll die! I'll have a claustrophobic attack and pass out and *die!*"

The bread gets stuck halfway down my throat. It fucking *hurts.* I thump a fist in my chest as Mum exclaims, "Don't be dramatic, Arcadia. You're retired." I rip away another piece and put it my mouth so I can push the stuck piece down. "You're not going to prison."

I pause my mad chew, my left cheek bulging with bread as my eyes lift to Kelly's. He knows what I'm thinking. He's shaking his head, his expression stern.

"You're not going to prison," he mouths silently. "I promise." He traces the pattern of a cross over his heart.

"You don't know that," I mouth back as my mother continues plating on the other side of me, oblivious to our silent communication.

"So if finance isn't your thing, just choose something else," she says as though it's as easy as putting the wrong item back on the shelf at the supermarket and picking another.

"Cars are my thing," I point out. "And that's your fault, Mum." Mum has a talent for makeup and works part-time slapping faces on models for runways. She's in high demand because she has a reputation for being unflappable in the face of divas, and her following on Instagram is ridiculously high. But the majority of her time is spent working with Lloyds Auctions in their classic car division because classics are her passion. "And Dad's." Dad is the crew chief for V8 Supercar racer, Jordan Haze. "And Racer's." Because Grandad taught me everything he knows. "You all made it my thing, and now I'm stuck not liking any other things."

"Get an automotive trade, then," she says.

"Working on other people's cars is not my interest, Mum. Sure, I wanted to rebuild my own with the Mustang, but that was going to be a project of time and love."

"Okay, so what else?"

"I don't know! That's why it's better to just keep doing the finance thing rather than nothing at all. It's a solid, respectable career."

Mum hands off two plates to Kelly. "Put those on the dining table, love."

"Finance is not you," he says, leaving with plates in hand.

"Arcadia—"

"No more." The topic is making my head hurt. She hands off two more plates to me. "I can't change now. I have student loans. I can't go spending all that money for nothing."

"You'll work it out. You're destined for greatness, honey," she says, picking up another two plates and following me out. I falter and almost drop my load when I find Mason seated at the dining table beside Dad, who's at the head, with Racer on his other side. I catch my Dad's eye and mouth, "Thank you."

He gives me an imperceptible nod as Kelly takes a seat beside him with me opposite Mason and Mum at the opposite end of the table. My brother keeps silent during the meal, but he stays and he eats and offers the occasional mutinous glance toward me and Kelly. That's progress in my book. Kelly and Dad monopolise the majority of the conversation with talk of Rehab.

"And you manage that with your brother?" Dad asks him.

"Mostly," Kelly replies and points to his eye. "We're still working out some kinks."

"Oh, Mum," I say, loading a huge mouthful of duck on my fork because it's delicious and I can't eat it fast enough. "Kelly's brother is getting married in two weeks. Guess who to?"

Obviously Mum would never guess, but she takes me literally. "Meryl Streep."

I roll my eyes. "Mum, he's not ancient."

"He'd be lucky to have her," she counters. "Meryl Streep is a queen."

"Well, it's not her."

Mum tries again, listing her second favourite actress. "Kate Winslet."

"No, it's not her either—"

"Susan Sarandon," she shoots out, pointing her fork at me. My brows rise. "Oohh Helen Mirren."

"Mum!"

"I adore that woman," she says like we don't already know. She has Pinterest board dedicated to her different looks and hairstyles.

"It's Grace Paterson. I met her yesterday when she was at Rehab visiting Casey."

"Shut the front door!" she shouts, her gazing shooting to Kelly. "I love her. I've done her makeup a few times. But last I recall she was living in Melbourne. She's living here now?"

He nods. "She is."

"Where are they getting married?"

Crap. My mouth ran away with me. I offer Kelly an apologetic glance. His hand squeezes my upper thigh, where he's kept it resting throughout the entire meal. It's not a squeeze of reassurance. It's one that says "I'll get you for this later."

"I don't know," he replies. "The invitation is on my fridge, but I haven't really looked at it."

Then Mum dives right in to the deep end. "Got your best man speech ready?"

Kelly pauses a moment before picking up his soda water. "I'm not going."

Silence falls across the table. *Fark.* I place my knife and fork on my empty plate with a *clatter* and reach for my wine glass. Thankfully Dad refilled it just moments earlier. I take a huge gulp before setting it down and removing the napkin from my lap. "Thanks for dinner. This was absolutely delicious. We should get going though."

I start to rise from the table.

"Oh," Mum says, ignoring me, her brows pulling together. "Is it a destination wedding?"

"No." Kelly stiffens beside me, every muscle rigid as he sets his glass back down. I sink into my chair, feeling lower than low. I want to punch myself. I actually want to punch myself in the face for introducing the topic. "It's here in Sydney."

"Oh, love." She offers him a sympathetic expression as he picks up his knife and fork and pushes a piece of corn around on his plate. He's trying to make an effort but his appetite is gone, and I don't blame him one single bit. My gaze narrows on my mother with warning. Don't do it, Mum. Do *not*. "Why aren't you going? Do you not get along?"

My eyes lift to the ceiling. This is all my fault because I don't know how to keep my mouth shut. Instead, I drag Kelly to our family dinner and spew his private business across the table. And my mother, being the intrusive yet caring person that she is not only picks it up, she fucking *runs* with it. "Mum."

"We don't," Kelly answers.

"That doesn't surprise me," Mason interjects, finally speaking for the first time since he arrived to the table.

Mason's biting comment makes my throat burn. It *burns*. Kelly doesn't have to be here. He doesn't have to give a shit about Mason or my relationship with him. And yet he's here. Because I asked. And the only reason I know he would agree to this awkward family dinner is because he cares. Of course he *cares*. He's wearing charcoal-coloured dress pants with an ironed crease. His collared shirt is crisp and white and features a few discreet wrinkles that he missed while pressing it. But he made that effort. We arrived here with Kelly carrying a bottle of wine. And not the cheap four-dollar crap that I usually buy because it's all I can afford. He brought the good stuff. And he gave it to my mother when we arrived with a polite smile, because just like she wants to make a good impression on my behalf, so does he.

During dinner he spent his time fielding probing questions from my father and inappropriate ones from my mother because I was a thoughtless idiot and brought up his brother's wedding. He also fielded glares from my brother, who is so entangled in his own bitterness there is no cutting him free.

And I am done. I am *so* done with my brother that the insides of my nostrils fizz from restrained fury and my heart pounds so fiercely I can almost imagine what a heart attack feels like. I can barely choke out his name. "Mason. Enough."

"Let me guess," my brother adds in a snide tone, ignoring my thickly-voiced reprimand. "You shot him in the back?"

"Mason!" My fury unleashes, my hand slapping against the table, causing glasses and plates to rattle. Kelly inhales deeply to the right of me. He's trying to keep calm. I can feel it. He's trying *so hard* and it almost breaks me apart because he deserves the *world*. He grew up physically abused—hurt and hated on for no other reason except he was there. At the age of fifteen his brother left and his mother died before his eyes. Somewhere along the way he found the Sentinels, a new family, and knowing now that Grinder is the exception and not the rule, I thank God that they were there for him. They were *there* when no one else was. And somehow, despite the horrific childhood he endured, he's still a good person. A person who is still willing to take a chance on life, and hopefully, if I'm lucky ... love. And my brother ... I take a breath. My brother is treating him like an absolute piece of shit. And while he's busy doing that, the man beside me is not only taking it, he's breathing air deep inside his lungs because he doesn't want to lose his shit and cause a scene.

My eyes burn and my throat aches. It *aches* so goddamn much. I'm ashamed of my brother. So *hurt* and so ... so fucking defeated. "You are done," I tell my brother.

Kelly sets down his knife and fork with so much care. The task done, he looks at my brother with an expression so cold it chills my blood. "No, I didn't shoot my brother in the back," he says, his voice forged in iron. "Casey left me with an abusive father when I was fifteen. A man who killed my mother with a single blow to the cheek. *He's* the one I shot, though not in the back. I shot him in the head. And I didn't cripple him, Mason. He died. Instantly. So yeah, now my brother and I don't get along."

His words take my breath away. He shot his father. *He shot his father.* He ... he ... Oh my god. Bile rises, burning my throat. The entire table is silent, and I sit there unable to breathe, unable to think, and about to be sick. I have to do something, but I don't know what— because Kelly shot his father. I spent my time in the kitchen complaining about some stupid degree and ridiculous student loans, as if my life were hard, and he let me go on about it as though it were important when all the while Kelly had *shot his father.*

He's breathing heavy beside me. The admission has cost him. Rather than unleashing on Mason like he deserves, Kelly has shared something about himself that's not just huge, it's *enormous*. It's ... I don't even know what it is.

All I know is that I'm an asshole. I put Kelly in this position where he got backed into a corner like a wild animal, and rather than lash out, he rolled to his back and exposed his belly.

"Kelly ..." my voice is a cracked whisper.

Except he doesn't hear me. His hands are fisted and resting on the table, his eyes on my brother. "I came here tonight because I care for your sister." Oh god, Kelly. I blink back tears. I *will not* cry at this dinner table tonight. I *will not*. "So you understand why I have to tell you this. If you *ever* call Arcadia a bitch again like you did earlier tonight, I will hurt you." My throat aches. After everything I put him through tonight, he's still defending me, and it's wrong. It's fucked-up and all twisted around because *I* should be the one defending *him*.

"She has stood by you through everything. She would take a bullet for you the same way you did for her. She shouldn't have to give up what she wants to make you happy. She shouldn't have to push herself through a finance degree when her heart isn't in it because you decided it was the only future safe enough for her. That's why she chose numbers. *You* told her they were safe, didn't you? And now she feels she owes you because the bullet you protected her from put you in a wheelchair. And now you're telling her who she can and can't have in her life. You're making her choose, and I'll tell you something, Mason. In this, everyone will lose." Kelly draws a deep breath in and lets it out. "Being in a wheelchair is no excuse for being an asshole. And until you can start treating your sister like a human being, you can fuck off out of that house you share with her and move in with your grandfather."

Finished, and only when he's finished, does Kelly rise. He waited until he was done before standing because he didn't want to loom over my brother unfairly. He spoke his threat at eye level.

"Get your bag. We're leaving."

My eyes are fixed to the table. I'm so ashamed of myself. Of my brother. I can't even look at him because I'm scared of what I'll say. *Words can never be unsaid*, I remind myself.

"Ace, let's go," Kelly tells me.

I rise, not knowing where to look, so I look at no one. "I can't even look at you," I whisper to my brother, turning blindly for my bag.

I thought tonight would be hard, but this? This is horrendous. It's a like a bad dream, and I want to wake up. Kelly may care about me, but after tonight we're done. I know we are, because *no one* would ever choose this. Especially not Kelly. And I'm not sure which pain is worse—the shock of what happened tonight or the ache for what never will.

23

ARCADIA

Kelly doesn't speak in the driveway of my parents' house. He puts his helmet on silently and hands me mine. I don't say anything either. I don't trust myself to speak without the words coming out choked. And I don't know how to apologise for what that was back in there. Sorry just doesn't seem enough.

He climbs on the bike and turns the engine. It roars to life and he waits. My stomach is knotted as I climb on, trying to hold myself together when I feel ready to fall apart. My arms slide around his waist, wondering if it will be the last time I get to touch him and feel his warmth. Kelly always, *always*, puts his large hand to mine where it rests against his midsection before we take off. This time he doesn't. He doesn't and it says more to me than any words ever could. He revs the bike a little, both hands gripping the bars as he reverses us out of the drive.

I hate this. This coldness. It's as if a giant black abyss sits between us and crossing it is impossible. My eyes sting and my arms wrap tighter. If he notices, he doesn't let on. He simply draws to a stop at the red light before us and waits, his body stiff as if he can't wait to get me home and off his bike.

"I shot him in the head. He died. Instantly."

My throat grows tighter. I'll never forget those words. Or how he spoke them, as if he simply did what he had to do. I try to picture a fifteen-year-old Kelly with a gun and it steals my breath. What he had to do ... The strength it must have taken. He lives with the knowledge that it was too late for his mother. *But you saved yourself,* I want to tell him. *And I'm pathetically grateful you did.*

We arrive at my house far too soon. He idles the bike in my driveway, and I don't want to get off, so we sit there as the minutes tick by, his feet on the ground holding us upright and my arms so tight around him I don't know how to let go.

But I know I have to. He doesn't switch the engine off or remove his helmet. And when I eventually unlink my arms and slide to the ground on unsteady legs, and after I tug the helmet from my head and tuck it beneath my armpit, he reverses from the drive.

I watch him go and my heart aches. It aches so fucking much. He disappears down the street, brake lights red as he slows before turning the corner, the bike roaring as he accelerates away. Then he's gone.

The street becomes quiet with nothing but the sound of leaves rustling in the breeze. Then, and only then, do the tears start to fall. Faster than I can wipe them away. I have never, *never,* felt more like a piece of shit than I do right now.

I'm not sure how long I stand there, sucking in air and wiping at my face, but it's long enough for Racer to pull up in his car, Mason in the passenger seat, his window down and face pale. He's quiet as my grandfather switches off the engine, opens the car door, and goes to the back end to collect my brother's wheelchair.

My jaw tightens as I choke back another sob. Fuck. *Fuck.* I want to throw my helmet at his face. *Hard.* I want to scream at him. Yell how much I hate him until my throat is raw and my body aches. Instead I look at him, unable to speak, disappointment and hurt laid bare across my face because it's too much to hide.

"Leave it," Mason says to Racer through the open window, his eyes on me. "You can pack me a bag from inside. I'll wait here."

So he's leaving then, like Kelly told him to do.

"Are you sure?" my grandfather asks, coming around to the passenger side to eyeball him properly.

"I'm sure."

I turn on my heel and race up the steps, knowing Racer will follow behind at his own pace. Heart in my throat, I go to Mason's room and open his wardrobe doors wide. A suitcase sits on the shelf above. I stretch high for it, nudging it with my fingers until it shifts enough that I can get my hands on it properly.

I yank it down and slam it on the bed, unzipping it quickly and flipping open the lid so that it falls back against his pillows. Turning, I open drawers and seize his things, blindly tossing them toward the open suitcase because my vision is blurred. When I've cleared them out, I zip it closed and drag it to the floor where it falls sideways with a thud.

"Let me get that for you, lassie."

"Do *not!*" I caution in a shout, my chest heaving and eyes puffy. Grandad's lips press tight, and he doesn't get in my way, which is really fucking awesome because I'd hate to topple him over in my haste to get Mason's stupid bag out the door.

Jerking it upright, I roll it from the room, past my grandfather, through the living area, and straight out the front door. I stomp down the stairs and it follows behind, *clunk, clunk, clunk,* as it goes over each sharp edge and hits the ground.

I'm tossing it in the back seat of Racer's car by the time he catches up, because it won't fit in the boot due to Mason's chair. "There's your bag," I huff, breathing heavy from rage and exertion.

Mason opens his mouth. I spin on my heel and start back up the stairs before he can speak because so help me god if he does, I will wallop him in his stupid face.

I slam the front door behind me and pause, hearing Racer's car back out of the driveway, the sound slowly diminishing until silence reigns once again.

"I'll tell you something, Mason. In this, everyone will lose."

My breath comes out choppy. Then I hiccup, staring at the living and kitchen space. It's empty. Void of life. Waves of sadness hit me, one after the other, until it sears me from the inside out.

I lost.

Kelly

ECHO: Ace isn't answering her phone. What happened with you two?

I ignore the text that *dings* on my screen. It's Friday morning and I'm at the shop, my head stuck beneath the hood of a car. It's Hammer's. I'm replacing his leaky radiator after he did a solid for me with the greenhouse build.

I haven't spoken with Ace since Sunday family dinner. It's best if I don't. Not after I overshared my past with her entire family. Not after I threatened her brother. And not after leaving halfway through a spectacular meal that her mother, Lydia, cooked with such obvious care. Ace has a loving, caring family. Something that any decent man would kill to be a part of, especially me, because I've always wondered what that was like. To even get a glimpse of it Sunday night made me feel like the little boy reaching for the cookie jar and getting smacked on the hand for his efforts.

"I can't even look at you."

The words Ace spoke flay me alive.

Echo: Do you read me?

Echo: Hello?

I switch off my phone.

Casey walks past my line of vision, here for a second Friday in a row. His wedding is in a week, and I know he's catching up on paperwork before they embark on a four-week honeymoon around Australia, caravanning like a bunch of hippies. Grace has been at me again to attend. Badgering me. And for what? We're not brothers anymore, not in the figurative sense of the word, so I don't get it. I don't get why she keeps trying to push a relationship that's beyond repair.

"Why?"

My brother falters, slowly coming to a stop near me as he tries to work out if I actually just voluntarily spoke to him or not. I turn my head, looking him straight in the eye. "Why?"

"Why what?"

"Why does Grace want me at your wedding so much?"

He ponders the question for a moment then gives me a shrug. "Because you're family."

I straighten from beneath the hood. "The Sentinels are my family."

My answer grates on him. I see it on his face. In his tight jaw and grim eyes. "And so are we."

My brows rise coolly, pretending like I don't give a shit when I ask my next question, when deep down, if I looked more closely than I dared to, I know I do. "Do you want me there?"

"It would make Grace happy to have you there, and I want Grace happy."

I don't know why I push the issue but I do. "You didn't answer my question."

He looks at me while I wipe my sweaty, greasy palms on a nearby rag. "Yeah," he says quietly, nodding, his expression sad and resigned. "I do."

"Why?" I push again. Because I know I'm not easy to be around. My resentment and bitterness are heavy, and I throw them in his face at every opportunity.

"Why do you want to know why?"

"Because weddings are supposed to be happy occasions. I don't ..." *Dammit.* I take a deep breath and say what I'm really thinking, "I don't want to be there and ruin all of that."

I've done enough damage to those around me. My blame toward Casey is a noose around his neck. I know, because every time he's nearby, I yank it, choking him with it just that little bit more. And each time it chokes him, his expression grows a little sadder and a little more resigned. And each time I feel no better. I just feel worse.

"So don't ruin it."

Is it really that simple?

I return to my task, sticking my head back under the hood to loosen another hose clamp. I see Casey start moving again from my peripheral vision when he realises the subject is closed. Though it isn't closed. Not quite yet. Because my mind is on Sunday dinner, and Ace, and how time and again she made an effort with Mason, no matter how much it hurt, because it was the *right thing to do.* The least I can do for her is to be the man she makes me want to be.

"I'll be there," I mutter to Hammer's radiator.

"Excuse me?" Casey says from somewhere to the right and back of me. There's shock in his voice.

"You heard me."

"What about Ace?"

I grunt, yanking at a stuck clamp. "She won't be coming."

"Why not?"

"Don't fuckin' push me, asshole."

Then I dump the wrench beside me with a *clatter* and pull back out from under the hood. After wiping grease from my hands again, I pick up my phone and switch it back on, impatient when it takes too long. I stab in my passcode and send a message to Fox.

Me: Do me a favour and go check on Ace.

Fox: Why can't you?

Fuck's sake.

Me: I'm working.

Fox: I'm on shift in an hour.

Me: It won't take long, shithead. Just make sure she's ok.

His reply comes in forty minutes later. I see it instantly because I've kept my phone right there beside me, eyeballing it every few minutes.

Fox: What did you do to her?

Me: Christ. Why?

Fox: You're the shithead, Daniels. You better close up shop and fix it or I'll fix your fucking face.

Me: I can't.

Fox: Why not?

"I can't even look at you."

I don't answer my friend. Instead, I set my phone aside and go back to yanking Hammer's radiator free, my stomach in knots. How can I fix it when I'm the fuckin' problem?

An hour passes. And another. I've dropped an entire bucket of bolts, accidently kicked the drain pan and spilled coolant across the work shop floor *and* fuckin' slipped in it, landing on my ass, and lost my favourite flathead screwdriver.

Fuck. *Fuck.*

My phone *dings* again, running hot today. Most of my messages used to come from Ace. Now it's everyone *but* her and that stings. I pause my work to glance at the screen.

Grace: Thank you, Kelly. Thank you so much.

Huh. Casey must have filled her in. Probably because they need to find the furthest table from the bridal table to squeeze me in at on such short notice. The shit table. But mostly the shit table is full of drunks, the ones who RSVP for the free food and booze, so that works. Either way, I don't want her makin' a big deal about it. I'll show up, eat some food, drink some good shit, and get the fuck out.

Me: Whatever.

Grace: Don't forget, it's black tie!

My face forms a scowl.

Me: You suck

Grace: Bahahahahahahaha! Love you too, brother.

I stop for a moment. Staring at her message. Blinking. There's no time to absorb it because another one comes in straight after it.

Echo: I backed you like a winning horse.

My brows pull together in a puzzled furrow. Seriously. Women. They talk as if you can read their minds. I should turn my phone back off but her comment niggles at me. I want to know what it means. She responds again, answering my question before I can figure it out for myself.

Echo: When she found out you were a Sentinel, she lost her shit. I backed you because I thought you had what it takes. So get in there like the prized stallion I made you out to be and sort your shit out #orelse

My mouth falls open. I don't know whether to laugh or tell her to go suck a bag of dicks. So I do neither. I pack up the workshop, taking care with the tools and making sure the floor is swept and clear. Hammer's radiator is done anyway. I'm just stalling because I'm not in the mood to go home to an empty house or face my brothers at the clubhouse on a Friday night where it's rowdy and loud.

Upstairs, I purposely ignore the bed—and the way Ace made me laugh on it and how she made me feel somehow invincible—and turn left for the bathroom. After a hot shower, where I scrub at my nails with a brush—something I got used to doin' when I was with Ace because I didn't like touching her with dirty fingers—I get dressed in jeans, a tee, and Sentinels cut, and for a moment I stare at myself in the mirror.

My beard looks scruffy, my hair hangs to my shoulders, and my eye is turning varying shades of green and yellow. I'm basically an unkempt beast. I tie my hair back from my face and jog my way down the stairs, keys in hand. Casey is in the front office when I pass by. "Done for the day," I mutter his way.

"Have a good weekend," he calls out to my back because I'm already halfway out the door. He's never said that before. *Never.* And he's sayin' it now as if we're suddenly friends because I'm attending his wedding.

I bite back my automatic reply of, "Save it," and try something new, though I don't pause and say it to his face. I mumble it just moments before the front office door shuts behind me. "You too."

Lo and behold, I don't combust into flames by saying something nice to my brother. The earth didn't stop spinning. The sun didn't fall from the sky. And a tsunami did not rise up over my head and wash me away. I also didn't feel like a bitter piece of crap either.

24

ARCADIA

I drive the car inside Tony's chop shop, and the door lowers behind me. My head is throbbing and I'm seeing two of everything. I have no idea how I made the boost, or I how I even got the '67 Impala Fastback here. My body switched to autopilot, and I'm glad it did because it's now one less car we have to worry about.

Taking a shuddery breath, I open the door and step out, blinking once, twice. There are two Tony's walking toward me when I was expecting one Murphy. It's the first time I've seen him since our inter-action over the initial list of cars so his appearance today does not bode well. He's outfitted in a navy suit that looks more expensive than Echo's Ford with a black dress shirt open at the collar. He might look like a respectable businessman, but some people are just beautifully wrapped boxes of shit.

"Three cars to go," I croak, the sound making my ears ring.

Two steps out of the car, and he's on me. If I were more alert, I would have been prepared. He seizes my bicep, his fingers digging in so hard I wonder how the bones don't snap. "Tony!" I try pulling free, but I'm too weak. Dizziness crashes over me in waves. "What's going on?"

"I'll tell you what's going on," he growls, frog-marching me to the back office and through the door. It opens up to another hallway with doors on either side and I'm pushed inside the one on my right, stumbling. The room is small, housing a desk with two chairs positioned at its front, or maybe it's just one chair, my vision is so fuzzy I can't be sure. He throws me into one of them like a rag doll, and I'm so relieved to be sitting down I almost don't care how I got there. My eyes flutter closed, just for a moment. It feels good, like I want to keep them closed forever.

"Ace. Wake up!" he barks.

"In a minute," I whisper, my throat feeling like I've swallowed a mouthful of broken glass.

His open palm cracks against the side of my face. My eyes fly open and my head snaps backward, pain exploding across my cheekbone. Biting back a moan, I hold my hand against the pained area, expecting nothing less than shattered bones. I'm surprised when everything feels intact. My eyes rise sluggishly, blinking at Tony. He's coming at me again. I raise my arm to ward him off. "Stop. Please."

He actually stops, his hands fisting by his sides. "You're a stupid bitch, Ace."

"What are you talking about?" I croak.

"It's one thing to fuck Kelly Daniels, but it's a whole other to get him involved. I thought you were smarter than that. Not only do you now have the Sentinels on your ass, you have them on mine!"

Oh Jesus Christ. "You're the stupid bitch, Tony. Kelly is helping me, which in turn means he's helping you."

Tony doesn't like my retort, not if the veins popping in his neck are anything to go by. He takes another swing at me, and I can't ward him off this time. His knuckles slam into my jaw and stars explode behind my eyelids. I try lifting my head but it lolls forward, my neck no longer strong enough to keep it upright. I blink, my lap slowly coming into focus. Drool and blood trail from my mouth, leaving a wet red swirl on the pale denim of my jeans.

Tony drops to a crouch in front of me. Grabbing a fistful of hair from the top of my scalp, he yanks my head back until I can't see anything but him.

"He's not helping you!" Tony yells. Bile rises as he gets in my face. "He's using you to gain intel! The Sentinels plan to either muscle in on our deal or bring us down, and he's using you to do it. You're so mesmerised by his goddamn dick you can't even see it. Open your eyes, slut."

He lets me go, shoving my head back as he rises.

"Fuck you, Tony," I whisper, and my jaw throbs with every word. If I wasn't so uselessly delirious, I would go full *Kill Bill* on his ass by getting up off this chair and jamming that pen from his desk into his neck. "Kelly wouldn't do that," I say, but inside my mind races ... because would he? For all my shit talk about the Sentinels in the past, what do I really know about them?

"You cannot be that stupid," Tony spits, running a hand through his hair. "Last year Kelly waged a goddamn war with the King Street Boys, and those who didn't end up dead are now spending the rest of their days rotting in prison."

I blink. I didn't know that. There's so much about Kelly I don't know, and my chest aches because I doubt I'll ever get the chance to find out. "He won't. We're not together anymore, Tony."

"Don't bullshit me, Ace. I'll be watching you like a hawk from now on."

"We're not."

He grasps the front of my shirt and yanks me to a standing position, my legs almost dangling from the ground, and he glares right in my eyes. My head whirls like I've been spun in circles before having to pin the tail on the donkey. If Tony didn't have hold of me, I know my legs would give out beneath me and that grates. "If I ever see him on a boost with you again, Ace, he's dead. Do you hear me?"

My nostrils flare at his threat. Fucking *sonofabitch*.

"Do you hear me?" he repeats, shouting so loud in my face that spittle hits me on the cheek and in the eye.

"I hear you loud and clear," I bite out.

"Good." He drags my face closer, if that's even possible. "What do you see in him anyway?"

"What I see is none of your business."

"Stubborn. Always stubborn," he tuts. "Tell me. I really want to know."

"I see good."

Tony releases me, tipping his head back to laugh. It bursts out of him as though I'm the greatest comedy act on Earth. I grasp the edge of the desk before I tip over, holding on for dear life. "If Kelly Daniels is *good,* then that must make me Mother Teresa."

Kelly

THE LIGHTS ARE off when I pull in the drive of Ace's house. It's late—I took care of a few errands after work and before I knew it, the sun was going down and traffic was a shit fest—but it's not late enough for her to be asleep in bed, so she must be out because there's no indication of movement inside the house.

I heard Mason is staying at his grandfather's house, so I make the decision to stay. After switching off the engine and tugging my helmet from my head, I slide from the bike and collect the Chinese takeout from my saddle bag, making my way up the porch steps.

"I can't even look at you."

Jesus. Her words reverberate in my head and I turn, starting to leave. Then I stop and turn back. *Fuck it.* She'll have to just grow a ball sack and figure it out because I'm going in. Though this time I knock on the off chance she's hiding behind the door, baseball bat at the ready. It hasn't been a half bad day. I don't want to end it by being clobbered for breaking inside her house.

There's no answer after three hard knocks, so I fiddle with the lock on the front door and let myself in, shutting and locking it behind me. I check her bedroom after setting my helmet on the floor by the door and the takeout on the kitchen counter. It's empty, the bed unmade. *Where are you, Ace?*

I know I could message, but I'm not sure if she'd reply, and being here without her knowledge gives me the element of surprise. I could message Echo, I suppose, but that's at the risk of getting chewed out again, and I'm not in the mood for a female rant.

Instead I open the fridge, my eyes roaming the shelves and finding four beers left of a six-pack. It's Stone and Wood Pacific Ale, which is not cheap, and I know it's not cheap because Fox buys it all the time. I don't know which surprises me more: that Ace has expensive beer in her fridge or that she has Fox's favourite beer in her fridge. He was only supposed to check on her, not sit on her couch, talking his flirty smack-talk while they drank his hipster alcohol.

I grab all four beers out and carry them with me to the living area. Fuck him. The least he deserves is for me to drink every last one of them. I crack one open, flicking the cap to the coffee table. Taking a deep pull, I settle back into the couch with the remote and a carton of sweet and sour pork with special fried rice.

Friday night football is on, and considering my least favourite team is playing—and losing by an embarrassing margin—it puts me in good spirits. It's not until after I finish another beer after my dinner and the football ends, that I realise how late it's getting. I make the call to message Echo.

Me: Where's Ace?

Echo: Why? Where are you?

Why do women always answer a question with another question?

Me: I'm at Ace's house and she's not here.

Echo: I'm at the disco picking her up.

The what the fucking fuck?

Me: The disco?

Echo: Yeah. She went out dancing with the ladies ;)

The penny drops and anger burns so hot and quick I almost lose focus. I press my thumb and forefinger to the bridge of my nose, knowing I'm going to lose my shit in a minute if I don't rein it in. I reply, my finger stabbing every key so hard I keep making mistakes and having to hit delete.

Me: You're not supposed to go dancing without me, Fairy Floss. You get her ass home right this minute #orelse

Yeah, I hashtagged, but sometimes when you issue a command,

you have to word it in their language so it can't be misinterpreted. At least, that's how I choose to see it.

Echo: Who's stupid rule is that?

I take a deep breath and pray for calm, then I set my phone aside, knowing better to engage any more than I already have. It takes another half hour of waiting, me with my head tipped back on the couch, staring at the ceiling rather than checking my watch every two minutes, before I hear a car pull in the drive.

Rising to my feet, I walk to the front window and take a peek through the slatted blinds. A white Toyota Corolla sits out front. I'm not sure who it belongs to but I know Echo sometimes switches up her ride, not always using the Ford. The driver's door opens, illuminating her pink hair.

The blinds clank against the window as I draw away and walk to the front door. When I open it and step through, Echo is at the passenger door, wrestling with something.

"A little help," she gasps over her shoulder.

I jog down the steps to the car. It's not until I'm right behind her that I realise she's wrestling with Ace. "What are you doin'?"

She stumbles to the side when I push my way in. I pause when I get a good look at Ace, my stomach lurching with fear, its onset so swift and so strong it steals my breath.

"Baby?" She's unconscious, her body sagging backward after I shunted Echo sideways. I reach out, grappling for purchase before her head hits the gearshift. "No, no, no, no, no," I rasp softly, almost too scared to touch her for fear of doing more damage. I manage to get one arm beneath her shoulders and slide her forward. My other arm slides underneath her knees. "What the hell happened?" I snap at Echo as I lift her from the car.

Ace's arm drops limp and her head falls back, hair trailing down as I carry her up the stairs. Her cheekbone is swollen and there's blood on her face and clothes. I know the rational part of my mind has taken charge because I'm functioning, but the irrational part is banging its fists against the door I've trapped it behind, burning with rage and fear because seeing Ace like this is terrifying. It's my mother all over again.

"I don't know," Echo says, a little breathless as she jogs up behind me. "She delivered the car and was taking too long coming out. She wasn't answering her phone so I got out and found her like this by the side entrance."

She opens the front door wide, and I pass through, turning sideways so I don't bump Ace's head or bang her feet. I carry her at a fast clip into her bedroom and lay her on the bed with care. Her head slumps sideways, and I brush hair from her face, the pads of my fingers skimming her forehead lightly. It's hot and beaded with sweat, her face pale. "Ace? Baby, wake up."

Nothing.

My stomach is in knots.

"Babe."

Nothing. *Jesus.*

"Did Tony do this?"

Because if he did …

"I don't know anything, Kelly. I didn't even know the boost was happening until she sent me a message late this afternoon."

My hands are shaking when I check her pulse, fumbling as I press fingers against the delicate skin of her wrist. My eyes find her face and memories assault me. I'm twelve again and hiding in my room, unable to fight back. Casey is late home from school, but Dad is home early from work. There's yelling and screaming and my chest is tight because I can't breathe. Later I find Mum in the bathroom, her blond hair mussed, her body dressed in winter clothing despite the heat of summer. She's leaning close to the mirror, trying to cover her bruises with foundation and a sponge. She catches me watching her through the mirror's reflection and a smile forms on her face. I don't have it in me to smile back. I can't, because hers isn't real. My mother is trying to hide her feelings from me, but she forgets how much her eyes speak.

"It's okay," she says, dropping the fake smile and turning. She's been subjected to so much relentless brutality, yet she takes hold of my chin with gentle fingers and lifts it with excessive care, as though I were the most precious gem in the world. "I'm okay, Kelly."

But her voice cracks.

That was the first time my thoughts turned dark.

I was getting older. Stronger. Bigger. I was starting to realise it didn't have to be like this, and I remember what I had read recently. *The enemy doesn't stand a chance when the victim decides to survive.*

It was right then and there that I knew my father would die. We would leave, and I would come back and kill the man who broke my mother.

I just didn't know he would kill her first.

"Kelly."

I shake my head, returning to the present. My heart is beating like I've run a mile. The supressed memory has wrecked me.

"Kelly. She's shivering so much."

Ace is almost convulsive, her limbs twitching and jerking of their own accord and her jaw trembling. She moans. "We need to get her under the blankets."

Working together, I lift Ace up and Echo rips the quilt down. When I set her back down we pull them up to her chin.

"Get me some ice." Her cheekbone is swelling further and her face is pale beneath the rising bruises.

Echo runs off and I get my phone out, calling Fox.

He answers in five rings. "Yeah."

"I'm at Ace's house. Need you here."

I hang up.

Wherever he is, whatever he's doing, he knows I'd never make the request if it wasn't urgent. He'll be here.

I sink to the edge of the bed, brushing at Ace's hair. Her eyes blink open and she winces. "Kelly?" Her voice is like sandpaper. I lean closer and she reaches up to cup my face in her palm, her touch whisper-soft before her arm flops back to the bed. "You cut your hair."

She's sick and bleeding in her bed, and she worries over my hair?

"Yeah." I rub a hand over my freshly shorn head, not used to the shorter strands. "It was time."

"Time?" she whispers.

With our features so similar, keeping my hair longer stopped me from looking in the mirror and seeing my brother looking back at me. But when I looked in the mirror after finishing work today, all I saw was a man I didn't recognise. So yeah, it was time. And as I sat in the barber chair after work today, hair falling to the ground around me until it was short, rather than see Casey staring back at me, I saw me. And for the first time in forever, I didn't feel the urge to smash the mirror into a thousand pieces.

"Stop worryin' about my damn hair," I say gruffly as Echo comes back with ice wrapped in a tea towel. She hands it to me before leaving in search of the first aid kit.

I press it gently to Ace's cheekbone. She lets out a hiss at the cold contact and her pain makes me sick. "Babe."

"I'm okay," she whispers, trying for a smile.

I fight for air as she looks at me the same way my mother did. A million emotions punch through me: helplessness, frustration, rage, grief. It all wars with the need for vengeance. I'm not a scared little boy anymore. I grew up. And no one I care about will ever be a victim again.

My jaw tightens. "You're not."

"I am," she croaks.

"Don't argue with me, woman."

"Then don't argue with *me*, man."

She's ridiculous and stubborn and for fuck's sake, how can she make me want to laugh in the midst of this hell? I shift the ice pack down to her jaw. Another hiss escapes.

"I found my mother's diary once," I tell her. "I read it."

"You did not," she says, taking my change of subject in her stride. Her croaky voice sounds scandalised.

"I did. But I forgot until now."

"What made you remember?"

I keep talking, not answering her question. I'm not tellin' her this just because I have an urge. I'm tellin' her because I need her to understand something. "She used to believe in magic and fairy tales. Even at the age of forty, when she died. I remember it underlined three times in her book: No one is too old for fairy tales." How her handwritten words are so bright after having pushed them deep into the abyss of my mind, I don't know. But they're right there, and I can't blink them away. My eyes burn.

"Kelly?"

I look at Ace and it hurts more. "Fairy tales are hope, babe. They're hope. But her hope rested on the shoulders of a man who would never change. A man who beat her because she was foolish enough to love him. A man who never let her go, no matter how many times she tried to leave. So she stayed, and eventually he killed her. And maybe you can't bear to look at me because of what I did—"

Her indrawn breath is sharp. "Kelly—"

"But you need to know this. Tony is just like my father. It's not just about this one list. You'll try to leave, but he won't let you. He'll always want more, and he'll do whatever it takes to get it, even if that means never letting you go. Even if it means hurting you in more ways than you ever imagined possible. Do you hear what I'm saying?"

Her eyes search mine for a long moment, and I know she can see my heart in my eyes because they're the same as my mother's, and in hers I saw everything she could never hide. I can't hide from Ace. Everything inside me is exposed.

"You're going to kill him."

25

KELLY

a knock comes at the front door. Fox has saved me from tellin' her exactly what I plan to do to Marchetti. Echo comes in with a glass of water and the first aid kit while I rise from the bed.

"I'll be right back."

I open the front door and find both Fox and Murphy on the doorstep. Fox is still on shift because an ambulance is parked out front and he's in uniform. Murphy is dressed in black leather pants and a white tank top. She's talking to Fox, and he's glaring down at her, appearing unimpressed. I miss her question as I stand there propping the door open with my body, but I don't miss Fox's reply.

"I don't know you, lady, so I ain't tellin' you shit."

His reply is short and not his usual flirty bullshit, but he knows something's up, and he's worried.

My eyes narrow on Murphy. "You need to leave before I make you leave."

"Who is she?" Fox asks, his eyes not moving from hers.

Murphy's expression is mutinous. Great. Another stubborn bitch digging in her heels.

"Marchetti's minion," I tell him.

"I'm not leaving," she declares. "Not until I know Ace is okay."

Fox shoots his gaze to me. "What the hell happened to Ace?"

"Good question. We don't have the full story." My eyes narrow further on Murphy. "What happened to Ace?"

She looks between the both of us, breathing deep and nostrils flaring as though she doesn't want to talk at all, then she says the one thing I wasn't expecting her to say. "You happened."

My mouth opens and closes. "Excuse me?"

"You got involved and Tony doesn't like that. Trust me when I tell you that you need to get yourself uninvolved."

Fox and I share a glance. Neither of us factored this into the plan. Stupid. So damn stupid. "So what you're saying," I reiterate to Murphy in an eerily calm and controlled voice, "is that he smacked her around because of me?"

My brother freezes for a moment, my words catching him off guard. "He touched her?" Fox barks in a loud voice. "Marchetti fuckin' touched her?" He shoves past me and inside. "Where is she?"

"In her room."

I'm alone on the front porch with Murphy. She shifts on her feet, and while her stature is small, she appears in no way intimidated by my size or my cold expression. "You need to leave."

"Kelly—"

"Leave!" I roar, unable to restrain my anger any longer. "I don't need you here deliverin' Tony's threat in the one place where Ace is supposed to feel safe, not when he's already delivered it all over her face!"

"He doesn't know I'm here!" she yells back.

I press my lips together for just a moment, surprised to find little Bambi has a backbone. It makes me wonder if her clueless exterior is a calculated façade. What is she hiding beneath those childlike brown eyes? I cock my head. "Then why are you here, Murphy?"

She huffs. "I'm here because I want to make sure Ace is okay."

I fold my arms, still propping open the door. "What do you care?"

"I care."

"Yeah? Well go care somewhere else."

I shift back inside, the door starting to close behind me when she calls out, "Wait!"

I let the door close. Ace needs me. "Kelly!" she pounds her fist against the wooden frame and doesn't let up. Frustration bubbles in my chest. I turn and wrench the door back open.

Murphy blinks and steps back, but there's determination in the lift of her chin.

"What?"

"You and your Sentinels are planning something. I know. I hear things. You need to stop using Ace and rethink those plans."

Using Ace? My mind reels backward as if punched. "Tony's little rat hears things, huh? Well hear this, bitch. I'm in this to help Ace. I'm in this to get her out from under him *for good*. And if that means putting a bullet in his head and having to live in prison with that mark on my soul for the rest of my goddamn life, I'll do it with fuckin' bells on."

I know I shouldn't have said what I just said, but it's too late now. I can't take the words back, and I can't control what Murphy chooses to do with them. It was a conscious decision to hide in plain sight with this car deal. I thought—we all thought—it would offer Ace protection. Is Marchetti really so narcissistic that he can't see how putting his hands on Ace would affect me? That I wouldn't react? But then again, if he actually believes I'm using Ace, it's possible he would assume it wouldn't affect me at all.

Murphy's eyes go flat. "Don't do it, Daniels."

Who does she think she's talkin' to? My brows rise coolly. "You can't stop me, Murphy."

"Maybe not," she says in a quiet tone. "But I'd hate to see you rot in prison."

"Oh, you'd hate that, would you?"

"Yeah. I would."

I shake my head, hiding my confusion. I don't know what game this bitch is playing, but it's gettin' old. "I'm not going to tell Ace you were here, Murphy." She doesn't need to know that trouble has followed her to her doorstep. "Go. And don't ever come back."

Arcadia

I DON'T KNOW how long I'm out. There are vague recollections of things that happened while I was sick, though they could just be figments of my delirious imagination.

I remember at one point Kelly propping me up in bed and Echo shoving a large bowl in my lap as my belly heaved. I blinked at it once and then twice—because it was my grandmother's and could they not find a bucket?—before hurling the entire contents of my stomach into it. She gave me that bowl five years ago, not long after being diagnosed with cancer. It came in a set of three and was lovely, sturdy, handcrafted crockery with a beige inside and eggshell blue exterior.

None of us had any inkling my grandmother was sick and neither did she. Then all of a sudden she had six months left, and we were making bucket lists, hot air ballooning, swimming with whale sharks off Ningaloo reef, and watching the sunrise from the peaks of the Snowy Mountains. It all happened so fast. It wasn't until after she was gone that her diagnosis sunk in. Grandad held it together. He still *is* holding it together, somehow.

I think I might have rambled all this to Kelly after throwing up. I remember him laying me back down, wiping at my face with a deliciously cool cloth, while I told him to make sure he sterilises the bowl before using it to bake me a cake.

His chuckle was just as delicious as the cool cloth. "You want me to bake you a cake?" he asked.

I don't remember replying. I was out.

Then there was the time Kelly stripped in my room. I definitely remember that. My eyes were weighted with bricks, but goddamn, I lifted those suckers like a champion weightlifter so I didn't miss a thing. Then he stripped me too, muttering as I flopped about on the bed—as useful as a landed trout. He carried me butt-ass naked into the bathroom where a cool shower was raring to go. We sat on the cold tile beneath the spray, me propped between his spread legs while he lathered me with my favourite whipped soap and a sponge. The chilly water beat down over my chest and legs, washing the thick suds away.

It was magical, until I leaned forward and threw up down the drain. I don't remember much after that, for which I'm exceedingly grateful.

Echo was in my room at one point, holding up dresses on hangers. "What about this one?" she would ask, holding up an evening gown in navy silk. After tossing it to the bed, she grabbed another. I remember catching a glimpse of horrid pink satin. "Or this?"

"What the fuck, bitch?" I mumbled, trying to work out if this was some kind of hideous nightmare or real life, because who gave a crap about dresses when I was lying there dying?

"Pick a dress, Ace!"

My ears rang at her waspish tone. "That one," I mumbled, not even bothering to open my eyes.

"The silver one it is." I heard the rattle of hangers and the low rumble of Kelly's voice. "She's going to need jewellery, Kelly. You best take care of that."

"What else?"

"Hair, makeup, bag, shoes, underwear," she rattled off.

There was a pause in their conversation and then, "Can't you do all of that?"

"Nope." I sensed a hint of glee in her tone. Then there was another pause. I could almost feel the tension and heat of Kelly's glare. "Fine," she snapped. "I can arrange to have someone come here and do her hair and makeup, but the rest is on you."

"Fine."

"Fine," she retorted because maturity had officially made a mass exodus from the house.

The next thing I know I'm waking lucid for the first time with absolutely no recollection of how I got home or in my bed, though my head feels clear and my stomach is growling. The sheets on my bed smell freshly laundered, and the late afternoon sun is filtering through my room via the sheer white curtains that billow out gently from the open window.

I lie for a moment, just breathing. Everything aches, but my face aches most of all. My hand prods the injured area. The pain is a steady throb, focused mainly around my cheekbone and jaw. I blink. My vision in both eyes remains unhindered. I poke around at my right eyelid. It doesn't feel swollen. That's good. I bet it's barely bruised at all. Kelly won't even notice.

I know he's been here, nursing me through this virus. Caring for me when I'm too sick to care for myself. It was stupid of me to think he would run in the opposite direction after being subjected to that family dinner at my parents' house. Kelly isn't a coward. His spine is truer than an arrow pointing due north. He may hide it behind a hardened disposition, with his leather cut and tattoos and his long hair and scruffy beard, but beneath that massive chest lies a heart as deep and as wide as the ocean.

"If I ever see him on a boost with you again, Ace, he's dead. Do you hear me?"

I shift on the bed, my belly forming knots. I never wanted Kelly involved. He's fought too hard to be where he is today. His life means too much. He deserves happiness. He deserves so much more than I can give him, but what I give will have to be enough because I'm not letting go. He's stuck with me now. Like a barnacle on a rock.

"You're awake." My eyes shift to the doorway of my room. It's Echo. She's wearing a short cotton dress in black and white stripes with white Converse on her feet, wiping her hands on a tea towel. "Chortle Chunks is awake!" she calls out to someone over her shoulder.

"Chortle Chunks?" My head pounds as I rise up on one shoulder. "Urgh." I sink back down.

She laughs. The demonic sound grates against my throbbing ears.

"That's the name Kelly bestowed upon you after you blew chunks in your bed before laughing and passing out."

Oh Jesus. I did that? I raise a hand to cover my eyes, wondering if my mattress would be so kind as to swallow me whole.

"He just calls you Chunks now, mostly."

"How long was I out?" I rasp, my cheeks burning with embarrassment. There is *nothing* sexy about throwing up, especially not in front of the guy you have the serious hots for.

"Five days." *Five days? That long?* "Yes that long," she says, answering the silent surprise she can see on my face. "I'm making dinner. You hungry?"

"Does a bear shit in the woods?" I retort.

She leaves as Kelly appears in the doorway. He's shirtless and barefoot, his legs encased in pale worn jeans. He looks warm and sleepy, like he's been lazing the afternoon away on the couch. It's unfair. I'm positive I look like crusted-over mould and he's standing there like a giant cookie I want to shove in my mouth. My eyes rise higher. His hair. *His hair.* "You cut your hair." My voice is an accusation. And his beard is trimmed short. I don't know what to think. His black eye has cleared, and he appears a little less hard, maybe. He grins beneath my stare, and I suck in a breath because a dimple lies beneath the beard. A little diamond in the rough. *No way.* "You have a dimple," I breathe in wonder, mesmerised by the new man that stands before me. "It's ... fucking adorable."

Kelly swipes a hand down the lower half of his face, wiping away the smile and the dimple. "Don't you remember?"

"Remember what?"

He steps inside my room, walking over to my bed as he talks. "Getting home. I carried you inside. You yelled at me about my hair and then you passed out."

"She used to believe in magic and fairy tales."

"He'll always want more, and he'll do whatever it takes to get it, even if that means never letting you go."

I raise a hand to my face, covering my cheekbone with the flat of my palm as it all comes flooding back in waves. What was I thinking with the whole *Kelly won't even notice*. I'm an idiot. I forgot how he placed that ice pack to my jaw with such care, his lips pressed in a fine white line.

"I remember." *You're going to kill him.* "Don't kill him."

Kelly seats himself on the edge of my bed. The mattress sags beneath his weight and my body dips toward him. "I can't promise you I won't," he says, trailing gentle fingers down the side of my cheek.

His reply fills me with sick dread. "Kelly—"

He puts a finger to my lips. "No more. We'll talk about it next week. Right now you need rest. I need you better because I told my brother I was going to this damn wedding on the weekend and you're comin' with me."

The dresses. It all makes sense now.

"Do they know I'm coming too?"

"They didn't but they do now."

My vision blurs and I reach blindly for his hand, giving it a squeeze. I don't want to make a big deal of it but him going is a big deal. It's a *massive* deal. And now I understand the hair and the beard. He's not trying to hide the lion within, he's just learning how to harness it.

"That makes you sad?" He looks away. "Because if you don't want to go, you don't have to."

"Why would I not want to go?"

"The family dinner, Ace."

My face remains blank.

"I can't even look at you?" he prompts.

A beat of silence passes before the penny drops. "At Mason!" I burst out. "I said that to Mason. Oh my god, you thought I said that to you?"

His jaw tightens.

He did. Anger rises swiftly. "Fuck you." I punch him in the thigh but this virus has made me weak. My fist merely deflects off of his leg. "Don't you know me at all?"

I go to thump him again, but he grabs at my hand. He grabs the other too, just in case, and he looks me in the eye. "I killed my father, Ace, while my mother lay bleeding out on the floor. I went downstairs and I got a gun from the locked drawer of my father's desk. I took it out, making sure it was loaded. Then I went back upstairs and I put that gun to his head, and do you know what he said?"

"What?" I croak.

"*Do it, Son*. He wanted to die. He couldn't live with what he did. I should have forced him to, but I couldn't walk this earth knowing he still breathed the same air and saw the same stars as I did, all while my mother was buried in the ground, alone in the dark, where she would never breathe the same air and never see the same stars again."

His voice chokes and tears start rolling down my face. My heart aches. It *aches* for him. It aches for his mother, who will never know the man her boy grew up to be. Someone who's fighting so hard to let go of the hurt, and the guilt, and the bitterness. He's fighting for happiness, and I want to be right there beside him, fighting for it with him.

"Do you know what I said to my father just before he died?"

"What did you say?"

He lets go of my hands and cups my face, brushing my tears away with his thumbs. "I told him I'd see him in Hell, but I was too young to understand. When I got older I realised it isn't a place where you go after you die. Hell is somethin' you carry inside you. It's dark and heavy and fuck it, Ace, I'm tired of carryin' it around."

"Kelly—"

He shakes his head. "So when you said I can't even look at you, I believed you meant it for me because when I look in the mirror I see that very same Hell in the eyes starin' back at me."

Jesus. I pull him toward me, wrapping my arms around him. I can't hug him tight enough, or long enough, but I hold on as hard as I can, love bubbling up inside me so big and so bright it's a wonder I can see. "Kelly," I choke out, lost for words. What can I say to the boy who suffered so much pain and the man who carries it around with him every single day? I don't want to fail him.

His arms slowly wind their way around me, until he's holding me so tight I can barely breathe, and maybe that's enough. "Let it go. Take the good memories and let the rest go."

"How?" he asks, his head tucked in my shoulder and voice muffled.

"I don't know." Because fuck it, I don't, but I wish I did. "But I'm not going anywhere. We can work it out together."

26

KELLY

*W*e're driving to my brother's wedding when my feelings for Ace hit me. It isn't like a brick to the head. It's a slow realisation. Something that's been building in intensity until I feel it through every inch of my body, and it's just in that moment I recognise it for what it is.

I had picked her up from Echo's apartment in the newly painted bright blue '67 Mustang Fastback we've been re-furbishing for an old friend, leaving both windows open because the afternoon was warm and the sky was bright and cloudless. She was a beautiful car, with thick white stripes down the middle that I knew Ace would love. This is what her car could have been, and I wanted her to have this chance to ride in it before the car was returned to its owner.

Ace came out wearing a floor-length silver dress that shimmered in the late afternoon sunshine, which contrasted with the warmth of her skin—a colour that always looked tanned no matter what the season. The shoulder straps were delicate—thinner than my shoelaces and criss-crossing in a complicated pattern at the back where the dress dipped down to her ass. I know her hair was done by a professional because Echo arranged it for her, but it honestly looked as though she'd dipped her hair in the ocean and left it to dry in the sun. It was long and tousled, the ends golden as if she'd spent the day at the beach. Her eyelids had a light dust of what looked like bronze glitter, and her lips were the glossy colour of a ripe peach.

She'd somehow dressed for a black-tie event while still managing to appear earthy and natural at the same time. By some miracle, I managed to open my mouth and speak so I could tell her just how beautiful she looked.

The words didn't seem enough because I didn't see her at face value. I saw all she was on the inside reflecting outward, and it was more than beautiful. It was real. It was everything.

We were halfway there. I was accelerating after the light turned green, changing gears as I told her about how I first learned to ride a bike, because yeah, it's funny now. Back then, when I was a young hothead with a bruised ego, not so much. Her body was twisted toward me, and she was laughing, her smile wide and hair whipping about in the breeze.

That's when it hit me what that bright hot jittery feeling was.

I loved her.

My smile must have dropped clean away, my foot relaxing on the accelerator. The car started to slow.

"Kelly? Is everything okay?"

I don't know. Is it? Suddenly I feel stupid. As if I should have known what these growing feelings were from the start. But had I known, what would I have done? Run the other way? Fucked her once and left? It takes only a moment for me to realise that running was impossible. She was under my skin from the start. You can't run from that.

But now I don't know what to say. Or how to act. Or what to do with how I feel. It's actually true that love makes you stupid.

Arcadia

"Everything's fine," he replies.

It doesn't feel fine. There's an odd vibe in the car, as if I've somehow made Kelly uncomfortable. "I'm not going to throw up all over this beautiful upholstery," I reassure him if that's what he's worried about. The virus has cleared. And while I'm fatigued from doing the smallest of things, my stomach is making up for what it lost over the last week.

"It's all good, Chunks. I know you're feeling better."

"Then you can stop calling me Chunks."

Kelly glances across at me, winking. "Where's the fun in that?"

He's brushing me off and rather than just letting it go like I should because we're on our way to a beautiful wedding, and I want to enjoy just being with him and riding in a beautiful car. I push, and pushing never works out well for anybody. "Is it Casey? I know you didn't want to go to the wedding."

"It's not the wedding." He shifts gears, accelerating as he changes lanes.

"It's Tony, isn't it?" His lips twist. The subject is a touchy one, and I shouldn't have broached it, but since getting better, I have a vague recollection of Kelly and Fox arguing in my room while I was out of it. He was furious. It's why I remember because I've never heard him so angry. It sounded as though Fox were talking him down from a ledge. He mentioned something about sticking to the plan. And that comment has niggled at me ever since. "What plan were you and Fox talking about in my room?"

He doesn't react. There's no widening of his eyes. No jerky moves on the steering wheel. Nothing. And his non-reaction is almost a reaction in itself. "We weren't talking about a plan."

"Really?" *Liar!* "Because Tony seems to think you have an ulterior motive at play."

And if I wanted a reaction, that got me one. His hands white-knuckle the wheel as he wrenches it sideways. We veer off the road, tyres screeching as he grinds the car to a skidding halt just five minutes out from the ceremony venue. He switches off the engine and turns to face me, nostrils flaring and perspiration beading on his brow. "What are we doing here, Ace? Huh?"

He's mad. Sweat begins forming beneath my armpits. "What do

you mean?" I ask, reaching for my little evening bag. I need tissues. The last thing I want to do is ruin Grace and Casey's wedding with bad body odour. I open the silver clutch.

Kelly slaps it from my hand. Its contents spew across the matting of the car floor. "What is the point of us? You and me?"

I stutter, my eyes shifting from my discarded bag to his face. "Well ... we ..."

"I don't know what the hell you're doing with me if you're going to give credit to anything Tony says. I mean, Jesus Christ," he spits. "He thinks I have an ulterior motive at play and you believe him?"

I rub my peach-gloss coated lips together as everything he said sinks in. "I can see now that I worded that wrong."

"Worded it wrong?" His brows fly up and almost off his face. "*Worded it wrong?*"

"Forget I said anything."

"Forget ..." He trails off, an expression of amazement on his face. Irritated amazement, as if he can't believe the words that are coming out of my mouth. Then he huffs.

"I didn't say I believed him."

"Yet it made you doubt me."

"You're hiding something from me. So maybe you don't have an ulterior motive, but something is going on and keeping me in the dark is just putting me in danger."

Kelly rubs a hand over his face while my eyes glance to the clock on the dashboard. The last thing I want is for us to be late to his brother's wedding because we're sitting in a car arguing by the side of the road. I stare ahead, unhappy, the air between us soured like curdled milk. This is why you never push. "Can we just go?"

A beat of pained silence passes between us, and without another word, he starts the car and pulls out into traffic. We arrive at the venue in time, finding a park not too far away. I'm thankful because I'm wearing heels, which is rare for me. Kelly walks around the front of the car. I know his intention is to open my door for me, yet I beat him to it. Not because I'm deliber-ately trying to be a bitch. I'm angry at myself more than anything. It's bleeding over into my attitude, and I can't seem to stop it.

I crouch, reaching for my clutch and its scattered contents.

"Let me get that," he says quietly and gently nudges me aside. I straighten while he collects my clutch. I don't know what it is about watching him put my lip-gloss inside the little bag with care, followed by my little tube of eye drops because when I wear contact lenses this late in the day it makes my eyes dry out and the lenses stick to my eyeballs. It just makes me sag, my anger deflating like a punctured balloon. Sometimes Kelly angers me so much, and then he humbles me with the slightest gesture.

He rises, his body close to mine as he clips the delicate latch on the bag closed. Then he looks at me as he hands it over. "Here you go, Chunks."

I take it, trying to pull it from his grip when he doesn't let go. "I'm not Chunks."

"You kinda are."

"One time," I reply, yanking at the bag. "I throw up one time and what, I'm Chunks for life?"

"Babe. You name it, you threw up on it."

"Give me the bag, Kelly."

"I don't wanna fight with you, Ace. You can have the bag, but not until we kiss and make up."

"You're impossible." I yank again and his lips twitch. "You're holding my bag hostage for a kiss?"

"Yep."

"Give him a kiss, love!" someone calls out.

I turn my head. We're being eyeballed by guests walking toward the venue, all of them dressed in suits and glittery gowns, hair and makeup immaculate while I probably look like I rode in on a cyclone. And not only that, I'm here griping at Kelly and playing tug of war with a glittery clutch. "You're so immature," I mutter at him.

"Speak for yourself."

"Fine! Kiss me, then." I close my eyes and pucker my lips.

"Nobody wants to kiss a fish face, babe."

I burst out laughing, so hard I lose my breath and begin to wheeze, and I'm glad I have the bag to hold on to otherwise I fear I'll topple over in these heels.

"You're not going to vomit are you?" I hear him ask, sounding genuinely worried.

THE CEREMONY IS BEAUTIFUL. Held at the Grounds of Alexandria at dusk with pink and orange in the sky and a thousand fairy lights creating magic around us. Even though I don't know them that well, my eyes burn as I watch Grace and Casey exchange vows, Grace saying, "I've seen the best of you, and I've seen the worst of you, and I choose both," and Casey with, "I want to hold your hand at eighty and say we made it." They're both funny and serious, making promises to love each other through sickness and health, for life.

I sniffle quietly.

"You cryin'?" Kelly whispers from beside me.

"Don't judge me."

He grabs my hand and gives it a squeeze, and he doesn't judge me while I swallow the lump in my throat. I tilt my head to look up at him while he watches his brother get married.

Kelly always knows just the right thing to do at just the right time. Comforting me through a tender moment. Making me laugh when I'm angry. Stealing cars with me when I'm in trouble. Taking care of me when I'm sick. Standing up to Mason when my brother condemns me. It all flashes through my mind as he squeezes my hand, and my vision blurs worse.

I look away from his handsome face, blinking madly. He leans in close to my ear, whispering, "You have a tender heart."

For some reason I don't like him thinking me so vulnerable. I don't want him seeing inside my heart when I have no clue what's inside his. "My heart is tougher than old leather, Kelly Daniels."

He snorts. "I have your number, Arcadia Jones."

"And what's that supposed to mean?"

"That you can run, but you can't hide."

His response gives me shivers because suddenly I want to hide. I've never backed down from a challenge, but this is one I'm not ready to face. At least not right now.

Somehow I make it through the rest of the ceremony without tearing up, and after the reception, and after we've eaten dinner and the plates are cleared and speeches done, the first dance between the bride and groom is signalled. Evie, one of Grace's bridesmaids and lead singer of *Jamieson,* and their guitarist, Henry, both get up to sing. It's just her voice and his guitar, both of them crooning a slow acoustic version of "Heroes" by David Bowie.

"Dance with me?" Kelly asks when other couples start joining in.

I'm surprised, not just because we're at his brother's wedding— the very one he was adamant about not attending—but because he actually wants to. He must see it written on my face. "We're not best friends, babe, but it doesn't mean I'm going to ruin his wedding by being a dick, okay?"

The song ends as we walk out and they start a new one: "Dusk Till Dawn." It reminds me of my lunch date with Kelly and how long ago it feels, like I've known him forever. He pulls me close and we start to dance, and though it's just a slow sway, my heart is pounding double-time to the beat. We've not had this before. A beautiful evening with a touch of romance. I want to savour it like fine wine.

I relax into him, allowing him to lead while I sway lazily, happy just to breathe him in. I turn my head, resting the side of my face against his shoulder, and as we turn, my eyes snag on a man seated at a nearby table. He's watching us intently, green eyes piercing and dark hair tousled. He's wearing a tuxedo yet his dress shirt button is undone and bow tie loose, left to hang around his neck.

He swirls whiskey in his glass, saluting me with it when I catch his eye before downing it in one easy slide. Then he rises and I realise he's tall, as tall as Kelly. He starts toward us, his stride just a little off. It's not quite smooth, as though walking doesn't come easy for him.

I nudge Kelly, nodding imperceptibly at the man. Kelly glances over. "Shit," he mutters.

"What?"

There's no time to answer. He's upon us. "May I cut in?"

Kelly's hold on me tightens, making me uneasy. He gives a single shake of his head. "Bad idea, Valentine."

The whole reception appears filled with Valentines. I was introduced to Mac earlier, the youngest, but there are three brothers, the two younger ones work with Casey and I know who they are because I was introduced to them during dinner, so this must be the eldest. And for some reason Kelly is bothered by him.

"Bad ideas are always the best kind, aren't they, Ace?" he says, arching a brow as though we're co-conspirators in a crime.

Kelly releases me, stepping away, though he does it with flat eyes and a deep exhale through flared nostrils.

The eldest Valentine takes my hand, his arm sliding around my waist. The heat from his palm burns against the bared skin of my back. It's unsettling. My eyes search the dancefloor for Kelly. He's gone. They return to the man in front of me, lifting until they reach bright cold green. "Do I know you?" I ask as we begin to move.

"No you don't, but I know you."

I look again for Kelly, my discomfort rising. "Who are you?"

"Now that's a question you probably shouldn't ask, but the answer is one you should probably know."

My expression remains flat but my mind is racing. *What is going on?* "Shall I call you the Riddler then?"

He chuckles. "My name is Mitchell Valentine. My friends call me Mitch."

His name means nothing. "Good you for you, Mitchell Valentine."

My polite sarcasm deflects off of him like Teflon, leaving him unaffected. "So ..." He lifts my hand in his, taking me through a small turn before returning me back to a perfect dance frame. "How do you like to spend your time, Miss Jones?"

"Is that a roundabout way of asking me what I do? Because if you know me like you say you do, then you would already have your answer."

We move slowly about the room. Despite his excellent dance

technique, Mitchell moves with a light degree of difficulty. I almost wouldn't notice except dancing with Kelly was effortless; his proximity making my pulse race and my belly tickle with butterflies. "You study finance."

Trepidation grips me by the spine. "And how do you spend your time, Mr. Valentine?" I ask, battling for composure as I search again for Kelly. *Where are you?*

A smile quirks the corners of his lips. "Is this your roundabout way of asking me what I do?"

"It is."

The song reaches an end and the couples surrounding us on the dancefloor pause, clapping their hands toward the musicians. I step back from Mitchell's hold, swallowing as I face Evie and Henry, clapping alongside everyone else, a polite smile on my lips. From beside me he tilts his head downward, in my ear saying, "I work for the AFP, Miss Jones."

Fear rises swiftly, a dark cloud that chokes the air surrounding me. My hands stutter to a halt, and I can't catch a breath.

The Australian Federal Police.

Mitchell is watching my reaction, waiting for it. I can feel his eyes.

My chest burns for air. It's a battle to keep my expression neutral as I lift my head to look at him. "A noble profession." I swallow, holding on to my composure by my fingernails. "Thank you for the dance. If you'll excuse me."

I weave my way through couples as I leave the dancefloor, no longer looking for Kelly. My stride is slow. Casual. But inside my heart is pounding hard enough to hurt. I keep my eyes focused on the exit door as though I'm in the deep dark waters of the ocean and I'm swimming for the surface, my eyes on the light above and my lungs ready to explode.

I shove it open, gasping as cool night air washes over me. Mitchell knows me. He was *watching* me. And Kelly left me with him. He *left me with him,* handing me over like a lamb to slaughter. Sure, he did it with some reluctance, but he still did it. A sob rises, betrayal burning like a thousand fire ants biting at my skin.

I put a shaky hand to my forehead, unsure if my trust in Kelly has been misplaced. Until now his actions say it hasn't, but suddenly I feel tangled in a web of deceit. The way he railed at me when I questioned his motives in the car. He was so believable, throwing it back on me like *I* was the one who'd *wronged* him, rather than the other way around. How could I be so stupid?

27

KELLY

My eyes follow Ace as she leaves the dance floor. She's moving casually, yet her face is pale and her eyes are fixed on her destination like she's adrift in a wild storm and the exit door is her life raft.

Then my gaze narrows on Valentine. He shrugs at me as I push off from the back wall I was leaning against and follow her out. The door closes behind me as my eyes adjust to the darkness. The muted outdoor fairy lights illuminate her form. Ace is standing by the three-tier water fountain, her back to me and hands shoved in her hair.

She drops her arms and turns, hearing my dress shoes rap against the sandstone tile as I walk toward her. "Is this your plan? To hand me over to the cops on a silver fucking platter?"

Her expression is wild with panic. Damn Valentine for cutting in. Damn him for planting fear in her chest. "Ace—"

"Don't." I reach for her and she steps backward, warding me off. "Don't touch me. I asked if you were hiding something from me and you *lied*." Her voice rises. "I trusted you."

Her accusation is sharp and cuts me to the bone. Not because she's wrong, but because she's right. I didn't outright lie, but I deflected and isn't that basically the same thing?

"Why would you do that, Kelly? Why would you get the police involved? Why?" she shouts, her cheeks flushed with anger and arm thumping the air for emphasis. "All I had to do was deliver the cars and walk away. I was *walking away*. I told you I wanted a new life and you'd rather see me in prison instead?"

"You're not going to prison, babe."

"I'm not your babe," Ace spits, bending as she wrenches a high-heeled, strappy shoe from her foot. "Fuck this." She does the same with the other. Barefoot, she pitches them at my chest like a pro-baller. "Fuck *you*, Kelly," she yells and stomps away, huffing loudly.

I grab her before she gets far, pulling her into me, her back against my chest and my arms wrapping around her front. She struggles to get free, her shoulders twisting and her hands plucking against my arms. "I don't want you touching me," she pants. I pull her closer, my arms tightening around her like a steel band. "Let me go!"

"I can't." I shake my head, my voice a plea because she's asking the impossible. I'm not strong enough. And I don't know how that happened because once upon a time I was in a tattoo shop getting a bear on my arm, choosing solitude over people, and now I'm here, my arms wrapped around a girl I suddenly can't live without. "Don't ask me to let you go."

Her voice breaks. "Please. Let me go. I can't ..." She wheezes, her breath catching. "I won't go back there." Ace is shaking and thrashing like a caged animal, her anxiety escalating. "I won't!"

She wrenches her body so hard her legs give out, and she sags against me. "You're not going to prison, babe. I promise you." I duck my head, pressing my lips to the side of her neck, doing my best to soothe her panic. "*I promise you.*"

Ace takes a ragged breath in, her chest expanding beneath my arms. She lets it out slowly before taking another deep inhale. I hold on, not knowing what else to do. After several moments, she straightens, taking her own weight. She's stopped struggling against me, but she holds herself away, silently denying me the right to comfort her any further.

"Arcadia." I tilt my head, my eyes on the profile of her face. Her lips are pressed tight and her eyes are locked on the sprawling gardens that roll down into the darkness in front of her. She turns her head away from me.

"Don't, Kelly." Her voice is hollow. "I don't want to hear anymore lies. You—"

I turn Ace around, my hands on her shoulders, cutting her off before she says anything too painful to hear. She doesn't resist. Her capitulation should be a relief, but there's no expression on her face. It's empty of all emotion, and that's somehow worse. "Just listen. Will you do that for me? I know I have no right to ask. I messed everything up royally, thinkin' I knew what was best for you, and I need to explain. I need to explain why."

"Everything okay out here, Daniels?" Valentine calls out from behind me.

My body tenses, every muscle quivering with the need to turn around and slam my fist into Mitch Valentine's face. I want it so bad I can almost feel it—the clench of my hand, the throbbing burn of my knuckles as my fist makes contact with his nose, my heart thumping with satisfaction at causing him some semblance of pain. It's what he deserves for playin' a hand that wasn't his to play. A hand that caused unnecessary pain to the woman in my arms, the same woman who won't even look at me.

But I don't and it costs me. My stomach is roiling with built-up anger that has nowhere else to go.

"You need to leave, Valentine," I say without turning around. My voice is controlled, every word low and measured with effort. This is my brother's wedding and I'm determined not to ruin it. Me and black-tie events always end badly, and I won't be that man anymore.

"She needed to know after what happened with Tony," Valentine adds, and Ace stiffens beneath my hands, "your presence doesn't offer protection like we thought. It changes everything."

My anger snaps and snarls against the restraints of its leash. "I won't tell you again, Valentine."

His footsteps fade out until all we hear are the muted sounds of music and conversation and the tinkling of glassware and laughter in the distance.

Ace finally lifts her head and our eyes meet. "You promise?" she croaks.

I'm confused for a brief moment. Then I realise what she's asking, and remember what she said. *I won't go back there.* "Ace, have you been there before?" I ask quietly.

"I have." Her chin lifts, defiant and bold, and I know it's an act because no one goes through something like that and remains unscathed.

"Babe," I say quietly, not prying even though I want to. Tonight has already tested her limits, even when I'm yet to explain what I've done. She'll share when she's ready. "I promise you won't go back there."

Ace gives me a quick nod. I'm not sure she believes me. I've betrayed her trust by keeping her in the dark, so I can't blame her if she doesn't.

"Can we just go?" she asks.

"We can go." I bend, collecting her shoes from the ground.

"I'll put them back on."

We say our goodbyes inside, Grace pulling me in for a hug. I hug back with one arm because my other hand is holding Ace and I'm not prepared to let go. "Thank you, Kelly," she whispers in my ear.

"I didn't do anything," I say quietly while Ace talks to Casey. "I just showed up and ate your food and drank your booze."

"Exactly. You showed up."

I look to my brother. He taught me how to surf when I was ten. How to duck beneath each wave on your board. How to paddle out beyond the wash. How to balance in just the right position as you sliced through the wave. We would sit there on our borrowed boards because we never had our own, and we would talk about what we wanted to do when we eventually got free.

I remember his gaze on the horizon, as if he saw a life beyond the waves that was so much different to what it is now.

"I want to be a cop," he said. "I want to help those who aren't strong enough to help themselves."

Even at ten, his words raised a lump in my throat because he was talking about kids just like us. We weren't strong enough. Not then. Maybe not even now. "You just want to bag the chicks with a uniform fetish."

He laughed, flicking me with water. "What about you, brat?"

I was always *brat* to him. I was the youngest. Mum was a little softer with me. Casey had to grow up faster than I did. Be the man of the house our father wasn't able to be. Dad was always drinking. Most nights would find him passed out snoring on the arm chair in the living room. Vodka was his drink of choice because it was undetectable. He could drink it at work. It's the only reason why I stomach whiskey, because it doesn't raise bad memories—ones buried so deep I know I'll carry them with me to the grave.

I flicked water back at Casey. "I don't know," I replied, even though I did. There was a powerful urge to make my brother proud of me, and telling him all I wanted to do was work with cars seemed lame. He was always better at everything—stronger, smarter, and braver. So much braver than me. He was the one with a thousand friends at school while I had just two. I had to sit at the breakfast table for twice as long to finish my homework because school never came easy for me like it did him.

"I thought you had a thing for cars," he said as we floated on our boards.

I swiped water from my face, snorting. "No. I can do better than that. Maybe I'll join the police too," I lied.

Casey looked across at me, blue eyes the same as mine, piercing me with intelligence as if he saw me better than I saw myself. "You don't need to prove anything to anyone, brat. Whatever you do, do it for yourself."

I'm thrust from the memory when Casey laughs loud and hard at something Ace has said. I blink, my chest tight, because I realise all these years I put him on a pedestal when he was only human too. I blamed him because I thought him better than me, and when he didn't live up to my impossible standards, he fell—and he fell *hard*. And my response was to turn my back and find another family. Shame rises up inside me. I'm an asshole. I'm an absolute fucking asshole, and I need to step up.

"Congratulations, Brother," I say, holding out my hand.

His laughter dies away. His brand-new wife stills beside me, seeming to hold her breath, and Ace shifts closer to my side.

Casey takes my hand, shaking it. If our paths were different, I might have stood there as his best man rather than standing on the sidelines, watching him live the life he always wanted to have. We'll never go back to what we used to be, and only now, as the dark cloud of bitterness has finally begun to dissipate, can I see it, and it hurts. We only have one life as brothers, and we lost our way and fucked it up.

"You did good," I tell him.

"Thanks, brat." He looks from me to Ace and back again. "But so did you."

Ace removes her shoes when we get to the car, though this time she doesn't throw them at my chest. She sets them on the floor of the car before sliding inside. I shut her door and walk around the front of the car, ripping at the bow tie around my neck. I climb in, tossing my jacket on the back seat behind me as I undo the top button of my shirt.

Gravel crunches beneath the tyres as I drive slowly from the parking lot. "Tell me about Mitchell Valentine," Ace says as I flick the indicator on, turning out onto the main road.

"Why?" I ask with surprise. I expected her to ask about the plan, not the man involved in it.

She stares out her window. "Because you're a Sentinel. He's a Fed. Chalk and cheese, yet somehow, you're friends. You trust him enough to put my future in his hands, and I want to know why."

Arcadia

"You've heard of the King Street Boys, yeah?"

I nod. "Yes."

"They were drug runners, Ace. Adam Rossiter ran the show, the half-brother of Elijah Rossiter. Elijah was Chief Inspector with the Sydney Police."

"I know." I remember the scandal. The brothers had the same father, but were raised by different mothers in different states. Yet it came to light that Elijah was actually running the show. The King Street Boys had everyone in their pocket—from celebrities to politicians, even police. And Elijah ran it all.

"Elijah and Mitch grew up together," Kelly says.

"Holy shit," I mutter.

Kelly nods. "Best friends. They went to the same school, they fuckin' double-dated together. And Mitch never knew. Not for a long while. You know what happened when he found out?"

"What?"

"Nothing. He never said a word."

"How is that possible?" Because something like that would break a person. It would be like me finding out that Echo was an undercover agent with the Feds or something.

"Because that's the type of man he is. Loyal to the fuckin' bone. But if you betray him, he'll do whatever it takes to bring you down. And if he has to pretend to be someone he's not, like he did with Elijah, then he'll do it, biding his time for years waiting for just the right moment."

"And he did." Because the King Street Boys were disbanded in a police sting that made international news. One of the biggest operations in Australian history. It was all over the television because of the high-profile members involved.

"Operation Strike. Mitch ran the whole show, and Elijah never knew that he knew."

"Keep your friends close and your enemies closer."

"Exactly," Kelly replies. "Mitch was lead detective with Sydney City Police before his move to the AFP. His woman was a detective involved in the sting too. Gabriella. They both got shot. He lived. She died."

"Jesus, Kelly," I whisper. Hearing that hits hard. It reminds you that no one is invincible—not me, not Echo, not even Kelly.

"I know because I was there. The Sentinels got caught up in the strike because the King Street Boys took a friend of ours hostage. The bullet that hit Mitch was meant for me, but he got in the way. It hit him in the neck, the force of it slamming him into me. We both went down, blood fuckin' everywhere. I stuck my fingers in his neck until paramedics arrived."

Kelly's voice is raspy. He's lived through violence, almost as if it's all he's ever known, yet he got himself involved to help a friend because that's just the type of man he is.

"You saved his life," I say, slowly putting the pieces of the puzzle together.

He doesn't respond.

"And now he owes you one."

Kelly pulls to a stop as the traffic light turns from orange to red. He puts the gear in neutral and turns his head to look at me. "It's not a marker I would ever cash in, Ace. Not with what happened to Gabriella. He was in the hospital for months recovering. But it's you, Ace. It's *you*. And for you I'd ..."

He trails off and the light turns green. We don't move as he stares at me. The car behind us honks.

Kelly changes into first gear, eyes returning to the road as he accelerates.

My heart is in my throat. "You'd what?" I push, because that's what I do. I need to know. I need to know if I can trust him. I need to know if I'm worth the truth.

"Mitch and I have a deal," he answers indirectly. "We hand over Tony and they give you full immunity. He's shipping these cars to the Middle East. He's stripping them and shipping the parts inside containers filled with parts from cars they purchased from legitimate auctions, only to reassemble them when they arrive. He's making millions, and not just on the exports. He's buying cars at a greater price than he's selling the parts for. It's money laundering. They're basically a cashed-up organised crime group. The AFP aren't interested in you. You're just a tiny cog in the Marchetti wheel. But you're the tiny cog that can bring down their whole operation."

My chest tightens. This thing is bigger than me. This whole thing is so much bigger than me. And while his explanation makes sense, there's a question that still needs answering. "Then why keep it from me? If the AFP need me so much, then why not tell me?"

Kelly shakes his head, and after checking his phone and getting the all clear from god knows who that it's safe to deliver me home, he pulls into the drive of my house. "Tony won't let you go. There will always be another car. Another list. He will hold everything you love over your fuckin' head for the rest of your life. Even now, he has eyes on you. Watching. Listening." He switches off the engine and twists in his seat to look at me. "All it takes is one word, one action, one little slip to ruin everything. And if that happens, Tony will take you the fuck out."

"I'm not stupid, Kelly. I wouldn't—"

"Ace! *Dammit!*" He slams his fist against the steering wheel. "Your life is not worth that kind of risk!"

My lips press together, the air between us wired.

"How do you think I feel havin' to sit on my fuckin' hands after what he did to you?" Kelly's jaw ticks with bridled anger. "I'll tell you something, Ace. I got friends on the inside." His blue eyes harden into cold dark steel. "The day he walks inside that prison is the day true justice will be served." Shivers trickle down my spine. The smile forming on his lips is downright sinister. It makes my blood run hot and cold all at the same time. It makes me glad Kelly is on my side. "And I can't wait." He takes my hand and pulls me close, until his lips are a breath away from mine. "You wanna know why I called in that marker?"

My pulse thumps erratically. "Yeah. I wanna know why."

"I've made a shit ton of mistakes, babe. Bad choice after bad choice. But if I ever did anything right in my life, it was givin' my heart to you. You're an all or nothin' girl. That's why I'm in this with you. I'm all in. Your battle is my battle. We fight together."

My breath catches. This was only supposed to be about wild sex with a hot, irresistible man. I should have known. The moment he walked inside Fix, I knew he was a paradox. A puzzle, one I played with, slowly fitting all the broken pieces together until the whole picture now sits before me, a picture so beautiful it steals my breath.

"Kelly." He watches me, his face close to mine. "You were never meant to get involved. It's not your fight."

He draws back like I've slapped him the face.

I fumble for his hand, grabbing it before he can withdraw any further. "It's always been *my* fight. I don't have friends. I don't have boyfriends. I don't sleep around. I've always kept people at arms-length because I don't live a life where I can answer the kinds of questions they ask of me. Then you came along, and I thought maybe this once it would be nice, real fucking nice, to pretend I could have something beautiful for myself. Only you weren't what I expected. You pissed me off. You made me laugh, and you made me ache, and you made me want you so damn much. You did all that and now I can't imagine how I lived a life without you in it. You give so much of yourself without even realising it. Even now, you're taking my fight and making it your own, and I hate myself for being so selfish and letting you."

Kelly stares at me for a long moment, heat building slowly in his eyes until my body hums with anticipation. He reaches for the door handle behind him and gets out of the car. He walks around the front, keys in hand, and opens my door.

I step out, clutch and shoes in hand, the air between us charged with a thousand electrical currents.

"Get inside," he orders, shutting the door behind me. "Now."

I dash up the stairs, fumbling for the key. I slide it in the lock, my hands trembling as though I'm Little Red Riding Hood and the Big Bad Wolf is after me. The door gives and I step inside, leaving it wide open as I go straight for my room.

I toss my heels and bag to the corner, turning, waiting.

The front door closes, Kelly's footsteps coming closer. My breath comes faster as he steps inside, hungrier than I've ever seen him before. He nods his head toward my bed. "On your back."

Kelly's words are short, as though saying any more will make him lose control. My clit throbs as I move to the bed. I sink to the edge while he watches me with darkness in his eyes.

I'll tell you something, Ace. I got friends on the inside. The day he walks inside that prison is the day true justice will be served. And I can't wait.

Kelly is brutal. Rebel blood runs through his veins. He will always be wild. Always willing to inflict damage on anyone or anything that harms those he cares about most. I should stop him. It's the right thing to do, but I'm not sure I'm such a good person either. I don't want to change him. I just want to love him.

Kelly walks over to me. I'm not on my back like he ordered. I'm interested to see what he does with my insubordination. He jams a knee between my legs, spreading them wide. Then he bends, grasping the backs of my thighs. He yanks. Air leaves my lungs in a *whoosh* when my back hits the bed, and my eyes hit the ceiling.

"I said on your back, Ace."

Jesus. My clit is pulsating so hard I think I almost come then and there. He palms my hips, sliding his hands upward, dragging the slippery silver fabric of my dress along with them until my panties are bared and cool air hits my stomach.

Kelly bends, ducking his head and dipping his tongue inside my belly button. "I'm disappointed in you, Ace."

"Why?" I gasp, my head in a fog.

"You got panties on under this dress." He hooks his thumbs in the waistband and tugs them down, painfully—*painfully* slow. "Next time you wear a dress, I want you bare." He leans over me, watching my face as he runs a thick finger through the slick heat between my legs. My eyes flutter closed. It's sweet relief, but only for a moment. His expert touch soon makes the ache inside me grow.

"If we're sitting at a table together," he says in a rough voice, "I want to know I can slide my hand up your thigh beneath it and do this." His middle finger enters me. I moan. "You like that?"

"You know I do."

Kelly plays with me, watching me. It should be awkward, being watched so intently, but it just feels intimate. He's seeing me at my most vulnerable, and he takes pleasure in it. He takes that vulnerability and intensifies it, making my body burn hotter.

He thrusts another thick finger inside, leaving me perfectly full. My head tips back against the bed and another moan escapes me. His breath is coming a little more ragged, and there's less finesse to his touch. He's fingering me harder. Rougher. I welcome it, fucking myself against him. "Wanted to go slow, babe. For you. Make it special. But I need to fuck you."

"Fuck me, please." I need more.

He withdraws and I sit up, whipping off my dress and tossing it to the floor while he unbuckles the belt of his pants. Rising to my knees, I start on the buttons of his shirt, unbuttoning them, yanking when they don't open fast enough. The last two are wedged. The button-holes are too small for the buttons, I have no idea how he managed to fasten them to start with. I give up and tear his shirt apart. They ping across the room.

Kelly ducks his head, his mouth landing on mine. His tongue sweeps inside, his kiss savage as he kicks his pants and underwear away. He nudges me down on the bed, his lips locked to mine.

There's a rustle as I hear the condom wrapper. I couldn't care less if he used one or not. I'm not responsible. Not with him. My head is lost.

His calloused palms grasp me by the knees, and he pushes them toward my belly, lifting my hips. "Put me inside you, babe," he gasps, sweat beading his forehead from restraint.

I grab his cock. It's like iron, thick and pulsing in my hand. He nuzzles my neck as I rub it against my clit for a brief moment. His lips move upward until they're on mine, a deep groan rising from his chest when I guide his cock inside. With his hands on my knees, he thrusts and I gasp, breaking our kiss.

He pulls out slowly, his head tipping down to watch our connection. "Fuck that's hot," he mutters before slamming back in. My hips rise to meet him, his thrusts slow and forceful, building in intensity until I can't catch my breath.

I hug his sides with my knees when Kelly lets them go. His palms land on the bed on either side of my head, his cock moving inside me without missing a beat. I grab the back of his neck and pull his mouth down toward mine. "I love you," I say, breathless, before kissing him.

His tongue rubs with mine, his lips pressing hard as though he's trying to pour every bit of emotion he's feeling inside me.

Drawing away, he lifts an arm and reaches down, sliding a calloused finger against my clit as his cock pumps deep and hard. His eyes are on me. "I only ever want to make you feel good."

I want to tell him that he's doing a great job so far, but I'm too far gone. My body is tingling and I'm coming, my fingers digging into his shoulders as I pull him to me. His thrusts go wild. He comes soon after, burying his face in the crook of my neck.

"I love you too," he whispers against my skin, and I can never remember feeling so scared in all my life as I do in that moment.

28

ARCADIA

"*Y*ou've reached Royal Port Shipping Containers. My name is Rachel, how may I help you?"

"Hi, Rachel," I answer from my seat beside Echo. It's Tuesday, three days after Grace and Casey's wedding, and we have three cars left on the list. A Bugatti Veyron, the '68 Pontiac Firebird, and an iconic '87 Ferrari Testarossa.

Of all of them, the Bugatti is almost impossible. *Almost.* This isn't just an expensive car. It's a car valued in the seven figures. The engine is an eight-litre quad turbo, meaning its performance would be nothing short of explosive. The moment you punch your foot down on that pedal, the torque will compress your chest and push you back in your seat so hard you'll stop breathing. Unfortunately, I won't get to appreciate the religious experience because even though I'm technically stealing the car, I won't actually be driving it. And that's the tricky part I'm trying to arrange now.

I'm inside Echo's apartment, surrounded by four empty packets of Doritos, two half-empty Diet Cokes, and three computer screens. The left screen shows live video feed of incoming and outgoing trucks at the Port of Sydney. The middle screen shows the processed order Echo hacked for the delivery of a shipping container. Echo is working on the one on the right, and she's moving so fast it hurts to watch, so I don't. My eyes return to the middle screen as I continue with my phone conversation. "I'm calling about the delivery of a shipment that my boss arranged through you yesterday. He needs to cancel it, unfortunately."

"That's fine. If you can give me the consignment order number, I'll look it up for you."

I read it from the screen. "It's D-six-five-five G-A-zero-two-seven. It's for George Ashton."

The sound of tapping comes through the screen. "The order has been paid in full. Were you wanting to arrange another delivery day or did you want to go ahead with the cancellation?"

Fark. I don't know. If they reschedule, a new order form will go to George Ashton, but if they reimburse his fee he'll see the credit on his account. I didn't think this through carefully enough. My gaze shifts to Echo. She eyeballs me, slicing a hand across her neck in a throat-cutting motion. "Cancellation, please."

"Not a problem." *Tap, tap, tap.* "We can only reimburse the funds via the same account they were paid from. It will take between five to eight business days for the credit to process."

And this is why I usually leave the finer details to my friend. She knows things. The shipping container, and the Bugatti inside it, will be long gone in five business days. "That's fine, but we're interstate on business at the moment. Can I give you a new fax number to send the cancellation confirmation through to?"

"Sure." She continues tapping. "Just give me a minute to finish processing this."

I wait a few beats and Rachel's tapping comes to a halt. "Okay," she says. "What's the number?"

I give her the fax number direct to Echo's computer and end the call. Then I swivel in my seat and face my partner in crime. "And that, my friend, is how you steal a Bugatti."

She rolls her eyes and sits back, shoving her hand in one of the Dorito packets to scope out the dregs. "You're not that clever, Ace."

My brows rise. "Umm, that's why they call me Ace? Because I'm fucking ace, and you know it."

"Whatever." She licks crumbs from her fingers and points at the computer screen. It shows the image of a plain white tilt tray truck. "Reckon you can handle driving that, *Ace*?"

I've never driven one in my life, but how hard could it be? "Of course I can."

Another eye roll. "That's what I thought. We get the truck the day before so you can work it out."

"I'll need a special licence."

"Already arranged."

The Bugatti is arriving Thursday via a shipping container, making it the only one available in Australia. Our only option once it hits Australian shores is to steal it from the docks. The issue is that only trucks drive in and out, taking or delivering shipments. If I could just walk in there, open up that container, and drive on out, it would be a cinch. But there's also security to factor in, and paperwork, and yeah, the actual owner of the car.

The plan is for me to take the place of Royal Port Shipping Containers and drive the truck in with the original order, the same one the owner doesn't know we just cancelled, have the container loaded on the back, and drive on out. It's almost too easy. I spend another hour looking at it from every angle, making sure I haven't missed any minor but important details.

"What about the container delivery mob?" I say to Echo. "They won't send the cancellation to the ports too, will they?"

She shakes her head. "I already told you the onus is on the owner. Everything is arranged via third party. We're all good, Ace. Stop stressing."

It's so easy to tell someone not to stress, but I've never boosted a car of this magnitude. If you're going to retire, it's definitely a car you want to go out on.

"The uniform's arranged?" I ask, already knowing the answer.

"You pick it up tomorrow."

I take a deep breath. "Okay. Good."

"Have you texted Kelly yet?"

I pick up the phone he gave me on Saturday night to correspond with him. I can't use my own phone to talk to him. Not anymore. And with the police already involved, there's no point in using code. They can see every message I send.

Me: The lady is locked in. Friday. 8:00 p.m.

He replies in an instant.

Kelly: Be safe.

My eyes close, my fingers squeezing around the phone in my hands.

You're not going to prison. I promise you.

Kelly

It's just after 7:00 p.m. on Friday, a full moon already on display, as I slide in the front passenger seat of Mitch Valentine's black Subaru WRX STI while Fox slides in the back. Though I prefer vintage muscle, this is a car I'm itching to get behind the wheel of. It's built for the unexpected. It won't just handle whatever you throw at it, it will go above and beyond it. The Rex is a car forged from rally roots, and it's a fucking beast.

Valentine is in the driver's seat, one hand on the wheel, the other on the gearstick, eyes ahead as he waits.

"I approve," I say.

He turns his head. "I live to please you."

"Good." I nod. "I'm glad we got that out of the way."

He stares at me for a moment before turning his head to Fox in the back. "I didn't say you could come along."

"Yeah?" Fox replies, clipping his seat belt. "That's my brother's old lady boosting a Bugatti tonight. She's out there alone, having to play this the fuck out with us taking a backseat, for me literally, and that means you ain't got a say."

My chest expands. Fox has my back, and I'll be honest, it feels real fuckin' good because I'm on a ledge right now. I haven't seen Ace for a week. I have no idea what she's thinking and feeling.

"Where do we go from here?" she asked me as we lay tangled together on her bed the night of my brother's wedding. She was on her back, one hand behind her head, the other resting on the naked cheek of my ass as she stared at the ceiling above.

I lay on my belly beside her, my head turned her way, my hand slowly trailing over the curve of her tits and stomach, our skin cooling in the aftermath of seriously hot sex. "This is where I leave you."

Her body stilled. "What do you mean?"

"It means I might've been cleared to take you to the wedding because Marchetti's eyes are elsewhere tonight, but we're down to the wire now. He made it clear he doesn't want me involved, so now we make it look like I'm not. It means you go about your everyday life like nothing has changed. You go to class. You go to family dinners. You plan your last three boosts with Echo, and you deliver those cars alone."

My eyes closed at that point. I couldn't even look at her, knowing this was how I had to leave her. I couldn't even look at myself. I knew it was the only way we could end this for good, but sitting on my hands made me feel like a useless piece of shit.

I forced myself to keep speaking. "Someone will deliver a new phone to your letterbox tomorrow. Use it to talk to me. Text only, babe. No conversations."

Ace shifted and I opened my eyes. She was rolling on her side to face me. She tucked her arm beneath her head, looking at me as though she saw right through my controlled façade. "I can do this."

"I know you can," I said, brushing hair from her face. Ace wasn't just cool under pressure, she was ice. I'd seen her in action, and it was beautiful. She was born for a life behind the wheel, but she wasn't invincible. No one was. And this situation she was caught in the middle of wasn't just unpredictable, it was deadly.

There was nothing else I could say, so we lay there looking at each other as the minutes ticked by. "You should go," she said eventually.

My body burned with frustration because leaving was the last thing I wanted to do. But she was right. My palm slid from her chest to the naked curve of her hip, pulling her toward me. I put my mouth on hers, kissing her long and slow, for minutes. Then I shifted to the side of the bed and rose to my feet, finding my clothes and putting them on, the air between us heavy.

Finding my keys, I walked to the doorway and turned. Ace was sitting naked on her bed, one leg tucked beneath the other, lips swollen and hair a tousled mess. Her eyes were dark in the night and watching me silently.

I carried that look with me out the door as I left, and it's haunted me ever since.

"Fine," Valentine says to Fox, drawing me from the memory. His Subaru growls with pleasure as he pulls away from the kerb out the front of the clubhouse—the one place we know with absolute certainty is free of watching eyes. Marchetti wouldn't risk a war with the Sentinels by keeping tabs on us. "But keep your mouth shut."

"The only thing I'll shut," Fox retorts, more aggressive than the engine of this car because he's just as pissed as me about having to sit on his hands, "is your face if you fuck this up."

Valentine glances across at me. "You had to bring him?"

I bare my teeth.

"Jesus Christ," he mutters.

My phone *pings* from the back pocket of my jeans. I tug it free and read the screen.

Arcadia: Thirty minutes.

"Thirty minutes," I say aloud, my blood pulsing thickly through my veins. I roll my neck and shoulders before typing a reply. I want to tell her she isn't alone. If it all goes to shit, I'll be the first one there to get her out. Instead, I keep it short because I'm not the only one reading these messages.

Me: Roger that.

Valentine drives us to the docks. All we can do is wait in the shadows, making sure she enters and leaves the facility without any trouble. We park beneath a leafy tree down a side street, far enough from the entrance to remain undetected but close enough to keep it in view.

He switches off the engine, plunging our surrounds into darkness.

"Waiting is shit," Fox says from the backseat after we've sat there for no more than thirty seconds.

"This whole thing is shit," I mutter, every muscle in my body tensed so tight it's giving me a throbbing headache.

Valentine shakes his head. "You two can walk home."

"We didn't have to come to you," Fox gripes. "The only reason you're getting this collar is because of me and Ace. And Kelly."

"Nice of you to include me," I add mildly.

"I can be nice."

After five minutes of bickering because we're wound up and stressed, Echo's Ford rumbles down the street. She pulls up twenty metres down the road from the entrance to the docks.

We watch silently. A bare minute later, a white truck with a tilt tray arrives. It's too far and too dark for me to see inside, but I know Ace is at the wheel. My heart pounds hard in my chest as the truck starts to slow, the indicator coming on to turn inside the parking lot of the port.

Valentine has binoculars stuck to his face. I grab them.

"Fuck. Kelly!"

I put them to my eyes, adjusting the lenses as Ace comes into focus. Her hair is tied back in a loose knot and she's wearing a long-sleeved collared shirt in pale blue with the Royal Port Shipping Containers emblazoned on the left breast pocket. Black Raybans cover her eyes and earbuds rest in her ears. It's all I get a glimpse of before the truck turns.

The inside of the Subaru is wired as we watch. She passes through the first boom gate because it's always left open. The second boom gate requires a pass card. The truck rumbles toward it, the red brake lights coming on as she reaches the entry point. Her window comes down, and she runs the pass over the scanner. The gate lifts instantly and she's inside.

"I have no idea how she managed to pull that off," Valentine says with a trace of amazement.

"What about the owner?" Fox asks from the back.

"Echo confirmed delivery with him earlier this afternoon. He's waiting at the warehouse," Valentine answers.

I toss the binoculars in his lap and put my hands behind my head, stretching. "He'll be waitin' there a long time."

Fox chuckles.

Valentine's fingers tap against the wheel, betraying his agitation. "He'll get his car returned," he says, his eyes not moving from the spot where Ace's truck disappeared. All she has to do now is hand over the order. They'll direct her to where the container is waiting to be loaded, and they'll set it on the back. Then she just has to drive out the same way she came in and deliver the car to Marchetti.

"Eventually," he adds, "because for now it's evidence in a crime."

Fox sits forward, resting his elbows on the tops of mine and Valentine's seats. "How long do you think it'll take?"

Too long. "Half an hour or so." I hunker down, setting a foot on the dash. Valentine shoots me a dirty look. I drop my foot and tip my head back against the seat. "Maybe more."

Ten minutes pass by. Ten minutes of me checking my watch every thirty seconds. I press fingers to the bridge of my nose. "Fuck being a federal agent," I mutter. I'd rather have a tooth pulled than deal with this *covert surveillance* bullshit every day of my life.

Valentine smirks. "An agent who gets to slap cuffs on Tony Marchetti and put him away for life, you mean? That kind of federal agent?"

"Yeah, but you can't put your hands on him," I point out. Maybe I might not get that chance either, but once Marchetti's on the inside, he's fair game. Fox and I share a mutual glance.

"I'm gonna pretend I didn't see that," Valentine says, shaking his head at the both of us before returning his gaze to the docks.

My brows rise coolly. "See what?"

"Exactly."

I check my watch again. *Fuck.*

"What's the plan for the Firebird?" Fox asks, filling the tense silence.

"They can't find one. They've got two weeks. Ace says they've got their eye on a '69 Pontiac GTO. It's valued higher. Marchetti will probably go for it. That's all I know," I tell him because that's all the information she's sent through. I don't even know if she's scouted the Testarossa yet—the final car on the list. All her focus has been on the Bugatti. One car at a time. That's all she can do.

"As long as it's not located at the docks," Fox mutters.

I'll second that.

The truck reappears fifteen minutes later. Valentine picks up the binoculars before I can snatch them back, holding to them tighter than a squirrel holds his nuts. "Fucker."

I sit forward in my seat, squinting. It may be dark out, but there's enough lighting not to miss the container sitting on the back as the truck rumbles through the exit boom gate.

My chest expands with pride. That's my fuckin' old lady right there, drivin' out of the docks with a goddamn Bugatti Veyron tucked up in the back like a little baby. A grin splits my face wide as she pulls out on to the main road, moving at a slow, steady pace.

"You males and your blazing testosterone. When you think about boosting cars, you picture "The Fast and the Furious," with rubber burning and cars drifting through corners. Ninety-nine percent of the time, this is how it's done. Quietly. Below the speed limit. I'm the best because I fly under the radar."

Ace sure got that right. But she's not just the best, she's a goddamn legend. "There goes my little Chunks."

Fox exhales as we watch her motor up the hill and over a crest. "That was fuckin' hot."

29

KELLY

"You've got to be fuckin' shittin' me," Fox snarls, his eyes glittering with wrath. He rises slowly from his chair beside me.

It's the Sunday after the Bugatti boost, and we're at the clubhouse. We've been kicking back with a beer at one of the outdoor tables and talking smack all afternoon. Work is mostly our topic of choice because any mention of Ace winds me up too much. I almost bit Fox's head off last time he asked about the GTO she was scouting for her next boost. We were sittin' at home on the couch eating Chinese takeout and I stood up and kicked at the coffee table, flipping it over and sending noodles and rice flying clear across the room.

His response had been to mildly lift a brow and say, "This is what happens when you go and catch feelings, you stupid wanker."

And it's clear I'm handling those feelings like a giant man-baby, but we're in a pressure cooker situation. There's only so much I can take right now before I lose my shit and explode.

"What?" I ask, following his line of direction.

My eyes land on Murphy walking through the gates of the Sentinels' compound. She's wearing tight black leather pants and a loose white collared shirt tied at the waist. It's sheer, making it obvious she's braless and tattooed beneath it. Her face still holds the innocence of Bambi, but the bitch has balls just walkin' right on in like she owns the joint.

"No fuckin' way." I stub my cigarette out in the ashtray in front of me, rising as smoke blows hard through my nostrils. I'm not a smoker. I already do my body enough damage with the shit I do, but this forced separation with Ace has me lighting up like my life depends on it.

One of our Sentinel brothers pulls her up before she gets too far. She looks our way as she speaks to him. Then he turns to look at us, a question in his eyes. I give him a short nod. He nods back and walks away, our silent communication finished.

Murphy starts toward us, and Fox takes a step forward. "Let me handle this bitch."

"Have at it," I tell him, watching her approach.

"Fox," she says, reaching us, and then looks at me. "Daniels."

My brother folds his arms. "You got some balls comin' in here, lady. What do you want?"

She replies, flicking at the choppy mess of dark hair that barely reaches her shoulders. "You aren't going to offer me a beer so we can sit and chat about what I want like civilised people?"

Fox gives her a death stare, laying it on hard and thick. "We look like civilised people to you?"

Murphy shrugs, a small smile playing on her lips. "You look like a couple of guys I wouldn't mind having a chat with."

A harsh breath punches out through my nose. "Cut the bullshit, bitch. What do you want?"

She looks at me. "I want to make you an offer."

Murphy works for Marchetti. The only reason she's here is on his behalf, and whatever Marchetti is offering, he can light it on fire and shove it inside his own ass. I pretend interest, folding one of my arms and using the other to scratch at the beard on my chin. "What kind of offer?"

"A monetary offer," she elaborates, keeping her cards close to her chest.

Fox shakes his head. "Spit it out, Murphy. We got shit to do."

Her eyes shift to our half-drunk beers on the table and back to us. "Clearly."

His jaw locks. My brother is usually an easy-going larrikin, while I'm the hothead, but she's riling him with ease. "Don't play games you can't win. Tell us the offer and then fuck off."

She takes a deep breath and divests her flirty cover, folding arms over her mostly exposed tits and flattening her eyes. "Fifty K for the Sentinels to back off."

"Back off of what?' I ask, because we can play cards too.

Her dark eyebrows arch. "Tony thinks you deliberately got yourself involved with Arcadia Jones so you could muscle in on his deal. Maybe cause some trouble. He sees you're not sniffing around her anymore, but he's not convinced you've changed your plans."

"Yeah? And what do you think?"

Murphy takes a step closer. "I think you care about her—a lot more then Tony realises. He believes Ace is just some cheap throwaway whore to you. But I saw your face the night he knocked her around. It was not the face of a man who doesn't give a shit. And after what Tony did, I'm thinking that maybe you want a little revenge, and it wouldn't be above you to piss all over his deal in order to get it."

I laugh. I tip my head back and I fuckin' *laugh*. She thinks that all I want to do after what he did is *piss on his deal*? My amusement dies off, and I'm left with simmering rage, nostrils flaring as I work to contain it. I don't give two shits about his deal. I want the motherfucker dead, and I don't care if that means climbing into bed with the Feds to get the job done. After this is all over and they slap their dinky little cuffs on him and put him behind bars, the only way Marchetti will be leaving that prison is from the inside of a body bag while Ace and I walk away, free and clear.

Fox speaks for me while I stand there, my jaw working as I stare at Murphy. "Two hundred K," he counters.

Her eyebrows skyrocket and my brother smirks. "What can I say? Our compliance comes with a hefty price tag."

"Hefty? Don't you mean ridiculous? One hundred."

"One fifty," he shoots back.

Murphy shakes her head. "One hundred, no more."

"One twenty-five and a fuck."

A burst of laughter escapes me. I should have been expecting that. Fox always gets growly whenever his cock takes charge. And while Murphy's mouth falls open, her face mottling a mixture of red and pink, he remains impassive beside me, hiding the amusement I sense bubbling away beneath his skin.

"Excuse me?"

"You heard," he says coolly. "One twenty-five and my dick in your pussy. And that offer is final."

Murphy's lips pinch, and she looks to me. My shoulders lift, my expression telling her it ain't my circus and not my monkeys. This is the Fox show now. I walk away laughing, leaving him to it.

I resume my seat and kick back in the chair, sticking both feet up on the table and crossing them at the ankles. They argue while I sip at my beer before it gets hot, and I admit it doesn't look good for Fox when she stalks her way from the compound with a face so mottled with anger I wouldn't be surprised to see it catch fire.

He returns to the table, picking up his beer as he sits down.

"I can't believe you. Dirty dog," I say with a laugh, feeling thoroughly entertained. "What was that about?"

"Fuck if I know. My dick was the one doin' the talkin'."

"And?"

A grin cracks his face. "We have a deal."

"Ha!" We clink glasses before I take a hefty gulp. "Brother, I did *not* see that coming."

Fox chuckles. "She's returning tonight with a good-faith down payment and a naked pussy. We're not going to hand it over to Mitch, right?"

"What?" I smirk. "The money or the pussy?"

"The money, idiot."

"Fuck no. We're not handing that shit over."

Arcadia

I WAKE with a start when a hand comes over my mouth, my heart pounding like a jackhammer. Kelly's face comes into immediate view and I blink, sagging back into the pillow behind my head. "You sonofabitch," I gasp, my body trembling uncontrollably from the sudden rush of adrenaline.

He puts a finger to his lips. "Quiet, babe. You got eyes on the house."

"You sonofabitch," I hiss a second time, lifting my head back up to look at him. Time apart has only made him hotter. His hair has already started growing out, the thick tufts appealingly mussed. I want to run my fingers through the strands, tugging on them while his head sits between my thighs. "What are you doing here?"

He leans one hand on the bed, bending as he tugs the boots from his feet. "I'm here to bake you that cake you were talking 'bout, babe," he says with whispery sarcasm. "What do you *think* I'm doin' here?"

My heart is still hammering in my chest. "Besides giving me a heart failure for waking me up that way?" I grouse in my quiet voice. "I don't know whether I want to punch you in the junk right now or ride your face."

Kelly looks directly at me, his eyes so hot it's a wonder they don't burn me to ash. "Babe, I've been dreamin' of you ridin' my face for days," he says, straightening to rip off his tee. "I wanna eat you alive."

He bunches it in his hands and tosses it to the corner, treating me to a delicious flexing of shoulders and biceps and thick ropey veins. Kelly's body isn't chiselled and lean. It's large and wide and thick with bulky muscle, as if his physique is acquired naturally rather than hours spent pumping iron in the gym. It feels good to have those rounded shoulders take some of the load. I didn't realise how much I've been leaning on them until he left. Now those luscious shoulders are coming at me right now and instead of being all sexy like I want to be, my eyes prickle with hot tears.

"No, no, no, no, no, no," he says, keeping his voice low as he climbs on the bed. He collects me in his arms, lifting me against the warmth of his chest. "You are not gonna cry now. Not now. We're almost there, babe. We didn't come this far for you to fall apart when we only have two cars left." I mush my face into his bare skin, breathing him in. "You've been so strong. You've got this okay?"

My inhale is shaky, but I suck in the tears, holding them at bay like a dam holds back the flood. He's right. We've come this far.

Kelly pushes me back, grasping my face in his hands. "You stole a Bugatti, for fuck's sake. That shit is insane. *You're* insane."

A little bit of hysterical laughter bubbles out of me, and he clamps a hand over my mouth.

"Shush," he whispers and removes it.

"No one's going to hear us," I protest. "You're being super paranoid."

"I don't want to risk Marchetti finding out I'm here, that I'm still involved."

"And yet here you are sneaking inside my house."

He walks his fingers slowly up my bare thigh, inching his way closer until his palm cups me between my legs, rubbing slowly. "Because I needed you."

"Needed me?" I ask, my eyes dropping to the intimate placement of his hand. "Or just needed that?"

Kelly stills, and I literally feel the thunder rolling up inside him. "Did you really just ask me that?" He draws back, looking at me as if he doesn't know me at all.

"I'm sorry. Fuck." I cover my face with both hands, feeling like a fool for experiencing even a sliver of doubt. I'm so wound up and exhausted. "I don't know why I said that. I'm all over the place. I feel so much for you so soon. It's scary, and then add everything else going on into the mix and it's made me crazy." I inhale another shaky breath. "My life is a such a bloody *mess,* and I've dragged you right into the—"

Kelly plucks my hands from my face so I can see him. "If we're together, it means I'm in. I'm *all* in. Your mess is my mess. If you have shit in your life, then I'm not going to sit back and wait while you sort that shit. I'm wadin' in to fix it because I have a dick, and that's what any real man would do for his old lady."

"Dick fix it?"

"Damn straight, baby, I'm gonna dick fix your mess."

I laugh. It's a teary one, but I still laugh while I wipe at my eyes.

"Where's the remote?"

His abrupt change in topic throws me. "What?"

"Your remote. For the TV. That *is* a TV, isn't it?" he asks, lifting his chin toward the little box resting atop the tallboy in my bedroom corner.

"It's a TV. But it's old." And a slight layer of dust rests on the top of it because housework is low on my list of priorities at the moment. "I don't have a remote. And the picture only comes in black and white."

"Jesus," he mutters. "Well get up and turn it on."

My brows rise, dubious. "You want to watch TV?"

"No. I want to watch TV with you. There's a difference. So get up and turn it on."

I rise, getting up to turn on the TV like the man wants, halting when he grabs my arm. "Wait. You have to take off your clothes first. I wanna watch you do it naked."

"Watching me switch on the television in the nudie rudie is what gets you off?"

"Anything that involves you being in the nudie rudie gets me off. Does that upset you? I know you got your knickers in a twist when you thought I only wanted your pussy, but I don't discriminate. I need your tits too. And your sexy ass. And you always smilin' at me with that smile. That one right there..." he pokes at my lips while I'm trying to pull them down into a straight line and failing horribly "... that says you're a fuckin' idiot but I love you anyway. You do realise you're a package deal, don't you? I've fallin' so hard for you that I'm here, sneaking into your bedroom after midnight just so I can touch you and hold you and breathe you in like you're fuckin' air." His eyes lose their teasing glint, hardening in the shadowy light of my room. "Don't you ever doubt me, Arcadia."

"I won't."

"Promise?"

I trace a cross over my heart with my finger. "Promise."

"Good. Now get your gear off and turn on the television."

I rise from the bed, tugging my tank top up while he watches me. My hair is out and gets tangled in the folds. I yank, feeling hairs rip from my scalp. It's about as sexy as a dog taking a shit. Seriously. I actually feel a bit sorry for Kelly. I have no moves. I finally free myself and drop the offending garment on the floor beside me. "Why do you want to watch TV anyway?"

"You're right. I'd rather just watch you."

My cheeks flush. "Watch me make an ass of myself," I mutter.

"Babe, you could dance about the room wearing an adult diaper on your head and unicorn slippers on your feet and I'd still find you sexy."

I snort. "Oh my god, that's ridiculous. You would not."

His chuckle is low and deep and washes over me like a hot shower on a cold day. I peel my panties down my legs without any further drama, kicking them off with my feet as I straighten. His gaze slowly runs the length of me and back up again. He exhales deeply as though he wants me with every fibre of his being.

Then he nods toward the television. I walk over to the tallboy, feeling the burn of his eyes with every step. I switch it on and a late-night talk show flickers to life, flooding my room with dim light and the muted sounds of studio laughter.

Kelly divests his pants as I walk back to the bed, pushing them down to the edge with his feet where they go over and drop to the floor. I set a knee on the mattress, climbing on and crawling my way to where he lies.

He tugs at my hand, and I drop on top of him. I scoot off, tucking myself to his side, my arm resting over his belly and my head in the crook of those wonderful shoulders. He tucks one arm behind his head, lifting it a little, and the other comes around my back.

"This is nice," he says, gruff, his eyes on the little black and white screen. It's a crappy show but neither of us seem to care. It just feels so *normal* and just what I need. His fingers play with the ends of my hair while mine scratch lightly through the hair on his chest and lower, where his cock rests at half mast, showing interest in my wandering hands. "We never get to laze about and watch TV."

I find myself starting to doze.

"Babe," he whispers.

"Mmm?"

"We're almost there. Then we can do this whenever we want." The arm around my back lowers, skimming the cheek of my ass and further down. Goose bumps rise on my skin. His hand finds my inner thigh and nudges. I slide them apart, lifting one to rest across the top of his legs. His touch curls inward, stroking the crease between my cheeks.

My breath judders. "Almost there."

"Did you patch things up with Mason?"

"Seriously don't want to be talking about my brother right now."

Kelly stills his hand. "Yes or no?"

"No." Damn him. "Stubborn donkey."

His eyes round like dinner plates. "Did you just call me a fuckin' donkey?"

"Just calling it like it is."

"Oohh, baby, you're askin' for it."

I giggle as Kelly rises up over me and flips me on my belly like I weigh nothing. He grabs my hips, lifting them up and towards him. His tongue comes out and flicks my clit.

My teeth bite down on my pillow to stop the squeal escaping. He teases me like that forever, until I'm feverish, and then he fucks me until I'm limp and it's when we're dozing, tangled naked together in the sheets, that I whisper in his ear, "You're the last thing my heart expected, Kelly Daniels. You make me feel everything. I'm scared of losing that."

"You won't," he replies, his voice low and sleepy and his arm tightening around me, making me feel safe. "Trust me."

"I trust you."

He turns his head. I can feel his eyes watching me in the dark.

"Enough to tell me about your past? You said you won't go back there, Ace. To prison. What happened?"

I clear my throat, the memory sticking in there like a lump. It wasn't the lowest point in my life, but being incarcerated feels shameful. Even though the record was expunged after three years, it still sits like a stain on your clothes you can never get out. "It was a juvenile detention centre. I stole a car and got caught. Grand theft auto. I pleaded guilty."

Kelly pulls me closer, pressing his forehead to mine. "Tell me about the car."

I close my eyes, picturing it in my mind. "It was yellow with black stripes on the bonnet. A Camaro. Rusted. A little beat up. But the tyres were new. She needed work but she was a sweet ride."

"How old were you, babe?"

"Sixteen and twenty-two days."

"Young."

"Yeah," I mutter, opening my eyes.

He draws back a little, brushing hair off my forehead with his warm palm.

"It started when I met Johnny," I tell him. "We hung out. He was my first." He was also my last for a long, long time. "He was actually pretty great, but his best friend was a total ass, always watching me. Not in the way that suggested he liked me, it was more creepy ... like he didn't like me. He resented me because he and Johnny were thick as thieves and then I came along and suddenly they weren't. He went through Johnny's phone, found a picture of my tits, and posted it all over social media."

Kelly's body goes rigid beside me. "He fuckin' what?"

"It didn't have my face in the photo at least, but I was wearing a necklace that everyone knew was mine. Johnny gave it to me for my sixteenth birthday. It was a strip of black leather and in the middle, separated by little knots, were three small silver blocks with the letters A C E stamped on each one. So yeah, everyone knew they were my tits on display."

Kelly dips his head, pressing a kiss to my lips, then he rolls to his back, pulling me on top of him.

Kelly

My eyes drop to Ace's tits as she straddles me, her hands planted on my chest. They're a small handful. The nipples perky and pale pink, so pale the edges almost disappear into the rest of her skin. They're pretty and pucker beneath my stare.

That someone stole a photo of them and then plastered it all over the internet pisses me right the fuck off. It's a violation of her trust by some disrespectful little shit who needs to learn a lesson. Then it hits me and my chest swells with pride. My eyes slice up to hers. "You stole his car. The Camaro."

"Yes," she breathes, rocking a little because my cock is hardening beneath her weight.

I ignore the rising surge of hunger. Ace got her revenge in the best way she knew how. And the way she answers me tells me she doesn't regret what she did. Not for a minute. But satisfaction wars with the anger inside me, because Ace did her time for it. He deserved to lose more than his Camaro, and she was the one that got locked up.

"That's how I met Echo. Ellington Reid. It was her idea to take the car. She was my new lab partner and the one who showed me the photo. She said she'd take it down in exchange for stealing his car."

My brows pull together. "What was her beef with the guy?"

"I don't know."

"You're best friends. How can you not know?"

"I've tried to pry it out of her, but whatever it is, it seems she plans on taking it to the grave."

Her fingers trail over my stomach. It tickles. I circle her wrists with my hands and tug. She drops down against me and I feel the loss of her pussy rubbing against my dick, but I need to focus.

"How did you get caught?"

"We took the car from the school parking lot. Echo disabled the cameras and we drove it through back streets to the chop shop, but the damn thing almost had an empty tank. We had the choice to stop and fill her tank or just abandon her on the side of the road."

"Ace. Babe." I rub the side of my face, knowing what she did before she even tells me. "You shoulda just fuckin' abandoned her."

"I know. But I was so mad about the picture I wasn't thinking straight. All I knew was that I didn't want him to get his prized car back. I wanted it in pieces and sold off to all four corners of the globe."

"And that's how they got surveillance video of you fillin' the tank."

"Yep."

"And why you pleaded guilty when they arrested you because there's no refutin' that kind of evidence."

"Nope."

I swallow. "How long?"

"Six months," she replies. "Plus I had to pay him back for the cost of the car. Even though I didn't feel lucky at the time, I got off light because no one was hurt. There were no weapons involved, and I didn't resist arrest. That wasn't the worst part though."

Her breathing is shaky. I twist a little, grasping the edges of the sheets and pulling them over us. "What was?" I ask, wrapping my arms around her and rubbing her back.

"The first night I was there, they roomed me with another girl. We were pretty much free to roam the facility during the day, but they locked us in our rooms at night. The rooms were tiny and there was a small square window high up with bars on it. I couldn't breathe in there. I was so wound up it was a wonder I got to sleep at all. But I did. I don't know what it was that woke me just after 3:00 a.m, but I remember my eyes blinking open in the dark, adjusting. The girl, my roommate, had used her sheets to ... to ..."

Ace chokes up and I rub her back while my heart pounds a hard, furious beat.

"She was dead, Kelly. And I banged on the door for someone. I banged and yelled until my hands were bruised and my voice was gone. They didn't come until morning. It was the worst night of my entire life. I've never been able to stand enclosed spaces since. Even getting trapped in traffic gives me anxiety."

I'm angry. So angry my whole body vibrates with it. A tear plops down on my chest. Ace smooths it away. "Kelly—"

"Don't," I snap, my arms tightening, my fingers digging in to her delicate skin. Ace doesn't try to pull away. She simply sinks in further, holding me tighter. I'm trying hard to find calm. So *hard*. But I can't. It's rising, building, a tidal surge I don't know how to stop. "Give me his name."

I need to know the name of the fucker who'd sink so low as to post a photo of a young girl's tits on the internet. A little shit who, instead of taking the punishment he deserved by telling the cops it was all a mistake, brought her down with charges and walked away, leaving her to drown beneath the choppy waters he threw her in.

"You don't—"

"His name," I grind out.

"Miles Howard."

"*R*un the name, dammit," I say into the phone, shoving frustrated fingers through my hair as Mitch denies me my request. How is it fair if you have a contact in the Feds and they won't even do one simple thing for you?

"I don't have time to be your errand boy, Daniels."

If I could just reach through the phone and ring his infuriating neck, maybe it would squeeze the information out of him. If I'd entertained for even a single second handing over that one hundred and twenty-five K like an upstanding citizen would, then I surely wouldn't be now. Not that I care about the money. I just want Marchetti to know that not only were Ace and I the ones who parked his ass in prison, we also took his cash too.

"Miles Howard," I reiterate. "I'll even spell it out for you."

"Go ask Echo if you need someone to dig shit up for you."

I huff. According to Ace, Echo is a vault on the subject. You can't get blood from a stone. Approaching her won't just be a waste of time, it will tip my hand. Girls tell each other everything, and Ace's best friend is as loyal as they come. "I'm not askin' Echo. I'm askin' you."

"We have Ace on the GTO in a few short hours. Why don't you

focus on that? Whatever this Howard guy has done to piss you off can wait. I'll see you in a few."

Mitch hangs up, leaving me to feel like a petulant toddler who didn't get the toy he wanted from the store.

I contemplate lighting another cigarette out of frustration, but my stomach rebels at the idea. I may as well just lick the bottom of an ashtray. Instead I send a message to Ace.

Me: All set?

I left her just before dawn the other morning, sleepy and sated. That little furrow of worry between her brow eased. I'm glad I went, even if that meant having to sneak in like a naughty schoolboy. We both needed to see each other. Have that edge taken off. Even if only for a few hours. She needed the reminder that I was there, taking her back. And I needed to make sure she wasn't buckling beneath the crazy pressure she was being put under.

Arcadia: All set.

Tossing the phone to the couch beside me, I rise and walk to the front door, resting an arm up against the frame as I stare out, watching a storm rumbling its way in from the west. Branches are flapping wildly as the wind picks up, sending leaves fluttering through the air and cartwheeling along the road.

Flowers bow beneath the gusty onslaught, fragile, and so unlike Ace, despite their beauty. Ace is strong, and I've never met a strong person with an easy past. She's passionate and fierce. A sinner and a saint. A gift. Something given for me to fight for. To show me that there's still love in the world, even when it's dark and I'm waking from the monsters that choke me in the night. She's there to remind me that life is short, and there's no time to leave important words unsaid.

I return to the couch, picking up my phone, no longer giving a flyin' fuck that the Feds are reading our messages.

Me: You got this. And you got me.

I watch three little dots bobble across the screen before her response pings.

Arcadia: You got me too.

My body gets tight because this time when she says it, I feel it deep down inside. Despite the shitty hand life dealt me, and despite almost folding those cards so many times with my *fuck it all* attitude, I never ended the game, and now I got the ace of hearts in the palm of my hand. She's my trump card.

THE PONTIAC GTO is a walk in the park. We watch from a strategic position inside the Subaru as she eases the car from the garage and down the short drive way. The owners are out. It's a simple matter of getting inside their house and taking the keys.

That's how ninety percent of cars are stolen, because people just toss their keys on the breakfast table, or the kitchen counter, or on a little key nook that hangs from the wall just inside the door. They don't even think twice about it. They don't think someone is going to get inside that quick and just drive on out with their car. But they do. Ace just proved it, driving that stealthy black animal out of the garage, the black paintwork gleaming as she pulls out on to the road.

"Dude's running fifteen wide on the rear," Fox says from the back, and my eyes drop to the tyres. They're large, their tread thick and wide, making them able to hug the corners better because they run at a lower pressure. It plants more rubber on the road, making more contact and increasing cornering grip. *Fuck me* but I'm in love with those beauties. "She looks hot in that car."

My eyes lift to Ace. She's as catlike as the car she's driving, dressed all in black and wearing a bomber jacket with the hood up, keeping her face in shadow. She looks *smokin'* hot. "Keep your dick in your pants," I mutter, watching as she drives down the street, brake lights red as she slows for an intersection before disappearing around the corner.

"You need to buy her a GTO. She belongs in that car."

"She wants a Mustang."

"Yeah Mustangs are cool and all, but that car is a beast."

I shake my head. "The woman gets what the woman wants." I glance to Mitch beside me. "We gonna follow?"

"No need."

My gut gives a niggle. "We should follow."

"We have another Fed on her tail, and we can track her movements right here," Mitch says, pointing to the map screen on the dash and the moving dot. Ace is simply a blip on a screen. It's not good enough. It's not a camera.

Mitch checks his mirrors before pulling out on to the quiet street, doing a quick U-turn and taking us in the opposite direction. "She's being watched, Daniels. Too many cars tacked to her ass will raise suspicion." He looks across at me, changing gears, and it makes me itch to be in the driver's seat so I can take my frustrations out on the wheel. "It was an easy boost. She'll be fine."

Maybe it's because we're near the end, or because there's only one car remaining on the list, that my chest is tight. I sit in the passenger seat, quiet, rubbing at the beard on my chin. Minutes tick by as I try telling myself that everything is okay, that I'm just antsy because the boost went entirely too smooth, but I can't switch the feeling off. It's all just ... wrong. "Nup." I shake my head, even as the dot continues moving calmly toward the Marchetti chop shop, my unease overrides it. "Nup. Somethin' ain't right. Turn the car around, Valentine."

"I'm not turning the car around, Daniels," he says, accelerating through a green light. "They'll check in when the GTO is delivered, and it'll be fine. I'm not risking this operation because you have some random itch."

"It's not an itch," I say, my voice beginning to rise. "My gut is telling me that somethin' is wrong. Turn around."

"I'm not—"

My heart begins to hammer like a hunted animal. Lightning streaks across the sky as though sensing my agitation. "Turn the car around."

"Daniels, calm down."

"Turn the fuckin' car around!" I bellow, slamming my fist down on the centre armrest that sits between us, my breathing harsh and my blood on fire.

"Goddammit, Valentine," Fox interjects from the backseat while a fear that I can't even explain threatens to swallow me whole. "If Kelly says Ace is in trouble, she's in fuckin' trouble. Turn this car around or I'm callin' in every goddamn Sentinel in the city, and I don't give a flyin' shit if that busts your operation wide open. We're not risking Ace for your fuckin' collar."

Mitch's lips press in a thin white line. He looks across at me. *Really* looks. Then he pulls up at the red light of the nearest intersection, hitting his indicator to turn back around.

I give him a short nod and sit back in my seat, feigning a calm I do *not* feel. Then the radio on Mitch's dash comes to life. "Boss, we got a situation."

Tension rises in the car. "Is this your boy on Ace?" I ask Mitch.

He nods and presses the button to answer. "Go ahead."

"The GTO has a tail. It doesn't look like Marchetti's boys."

"Did you run the plates?"

"Running them now. Stand by."

The radio crackles before going silent. I swallow, my jaw tight as we wait. "Fuck it," Mitch says and hits the accelerator. The Subaru shoots forward like a horse at the starting gate. We squeal through the red light, its back end sliding out as he performs a U-turn. "My gut is not liking this either."

The car fishtails forward, leaving rubber on the road behind us as Mitch's boy comes back on the radio. "Car is registered to a Michael Lincoln. Lives at 556 Banksia Road, Parramatta." Who the hell is *Michael Lincoln*? "He's clear."

"Is Lincoln still on her tail?" Mitch asks.

"Roger that."

"Then he's not fucking clear, is he?"

Damn straight he's not clear.

"You want us to pull him over or let it play out? Could be he just has a hard-on for the car."

"Let it play out."

The Subaru roars through a corner. "Play out? *Play out?* If that was your woman gettin' tailed by some unknown, would you—" Shit. Fuck. Shit. Gabriella. I bang the back of my head against the seat behind me. As if that would knock any sense into it. "I'm an asshole."

"You *are* an asshole," he says, grim. "And yes I'd let it play out. Ace can outdrive anyone on the road. If she gets in any trouble, she'll handle it." As if on cue, lightning strikes again, shuddering the earth around us, and the heavens open. Water buckets down and Mitch flicks his wipers on. The blades chop back and forth as we streak along the road. "Even in these conditions."

I open the glove compartment, revealing a forty-calibre semi-automatic and ammunition magazines, a two-way radio, one set of handcuffs, and a torch. Mitch is a regular boy scout. I know for a fact the gun is a spare because Mitch has his gun tucked into the back of his jeans. He looks across, giving me a warning glance. I don't heed it and take out the gun.

The radio crackles. "Boss, Ace has spotted her tail. She's speeding up."

"Did Lincoln respond?"

"Roger that," he says as we hit a stretch of traffic. "He's still on her."

"Man." I grab at the back of my neck, failing hard at containing my stress levels. "I need my bike. I need my fuckin' bike."

"That's it," Fox says, sounding fed up and twitchy. "I'm callin' it in."

"Do *not* make that call, Fox," Mitch warns, eyeing him in the rear-view mirror.

He shakes his head. "You can't salvage this operation. It's already in the shitter."

Mitch gets back on the radio. "Pull him over."

"Roger that."

I drum my fingers against my leg as another minute passes by.

"Boss, he won't stand down. We have another situation."

"What is it?" Mitch barks.

"We have police flooding Marchetti's chop shop. He's getting arrested as I speak."

He slams a hand against the steering wheel, yelling, "On whose orders?"

"We don't know that yet. My gut is that Lincoln is an undercover."

Mitch's jaw works for a moment. "Dammit!"

"What the fuck is going on?"

"Undercover cops are issued with false identities and matching cars. That way if anyone runs their plates, us included, nothing gets compromised. We might have walked in over the top of their operation. If we did, it means we tipped them and now they're playing their hand early."

I'm literally gobsmacked. "How the hell can you not know about another operation?"

"Because whoever it is, they're in deep. My guess is that they're after Ace too. They won't know she's working on our side."

"Jesus Christ!" I shout, hating how out-of-control of this situation I've become. All I can feel is fury, the taste of it bitter and harsh. "This shit storm is on me. You might have fucked this up, Valentine, but it's my fault for bringing you in. Now I've got cops hunting my woman? I swear to *God* if they put her in a cell I will rain down Sentinel hell all over this city!"

I dial Ace's normal phone. There's no point hiding now, not with the cops storming Marchetti's shop. I didn't want her distracted for a single second, but I can't have her thinking she's all alone, that I've thrown her to the wolves. "Fox," I bark as her number rings in my ear. "Call in the brothers. I want my bike."

Arcadia

"KELLY?" I shout into the phone.

The rain is teeming down. I have a tail and I can barely see three metres in front of me. I should have called off this boost as soon as I saw the storm roll in, but half the time they blow right over, unleashing out over the ocean. Instead, I was impatient. We had two cars to go, and I was desperate to have them done with. I wanted that night with Kelly in front of the television every night. I was tired of being kept apart. Frustrated. Angry. And it made me reckless.

Kelly's response is a crackle.

I put him on speaker and set my phone down in the centre console. "What?"

"Do..." *crackle* "...pull..." *crackle.*

"I can't hear you!"

I glance in the rear-view mirror, the car behind me barely visible. Police lights start flashing from its dashboard. My chest begins to pound. The Feds would not be on me like this. *I'm on their side.* My eyes lower, checking the speedometer. I'm driving below the limit, safe and steady like I always do.

"Kelly, I have an unmarked police car on my ass! What is happening?"

"Ace..." *Crackle ... crackle* "...pull over!"

"What?" I shout, my skin prickling with the heat of panic.

"Do *not* pull over!"

I stare ahead as the magnitude of what he's saying sinks in. I have the cops on my ass, and he's telling me to run. There's only one reason why he would be telling me that. My belly knots with fear.

"I'm on..." *crackle* "...way, Ace. Hold..." *crackle.* "I ... my—"

The call cuts out. Breathless, I grab for my seatbelt, making sure it's clicked in place with trembling fingers. Then I put one hand on the wheel and the other grabs the gearshift. With a deep breath, I drop it down and plant my foot.

The GTO surges forward through the storm, my wipers going a thousand miles a minute. All I can see behind me is blinding head-lights and a flashing siren, but their car responds, keeping pace.

I find the nearest intersection and turn, searching for back streets. My ride hugs the corners, gripping the road like a powerful magnet. I don't know whether to head for the city where I can hide in a dingy alley, or find the nearest motorway and open up the car. All I know is that I can't flip a coin. I need to decide *now*.

I glance across at the empty passenger seat, my heart giving a pang that Mason isn't here beside me. He would know what to do.

The Chevelle, Ace. Don't make the same rookie mistake.

Mason was shot because we were ambushed at the end of an alley. Split-second decision made, I check the street sign. I'm on Macauley Avenue in Bankstown. I need to make a right turn up ahead and the traffic light is green. My foot lowers on the pedal. The light turns orange. *Fuck.* I speed up, making the turn, fishtailing through the rain as the light turns red behind me.

I risk another quick glance in my rear-view mirror. The under-cover car has driven through the red light. My heart thunders in my chest. The cop is goddamn barnacle, taking every risk to stay on me.

The drive is a smooth sail on the wider road. I shift my way through the slower cars, braking and accelerating, gears shifting as I put the GTO through her paces. The street sign looms ahead. Sydney Motorway 5. Left hand lane only.

I roar past another car and downshift, sliding into the left lane between a Mazda 6 and a Toyota Hilux. Both cars continue ahead as I take the exit, speeding down the on-ramp and onto the Motorway, merging into minimal traffic.

A text message *pings* on my phone. I grab it, reading the screen.

Kelly: Stay on the M5

I exhale a deep, shaky breath as I set the phone back down, my eyes on the long road ahead of me and my pursuer still behind me. Five minutes pass, five minutes of me angry at myself, cursing, and coming to the stomach-sinking realisation that I need to pull over.

The AFP might have honoured my deal, but these clearly aren't the Feds. And Kelly might be on his way, but he won't catch me. It's not right for me to rely on him, or anyone else, to save me from this mess. The choices I made brought me here. It's only right I take responsibility for them.

Another on-ramp looms head. The rain begins to ease as two police cars shoot down it, reaching me at the same time I pass. One of them doesn't account for the slippery conditions and clips my back end.

I grapple with the wheel as the GTO skids sideways. The tyres catch loose gravel and I spin, the world flying dizzyingly around me in slow motion. Blood roars in my ears and trees come at me with powerful speed. The scream and grinding crunch of metal deafens me, the impact bringing the dashboard toward my face. My head slams into the wheel and I lose consciousness.

"Step out of the car!"

My eyes blink open, my head throbbing. I bring a trembling hand to my face, pieces of smashed glass scattering everywhere as I touch it to my forehead. I pull it away, seeing two bloody palms swim in my vision.

"Step out of the car!" someone shouts again.

I take in a shuddery gasp, trying to fill my lungs as I fumble for the handle of the door. It opens with a jerky, grinding motion. I go to step out and jerk back in my seat. My head swims as I look down. My seat belt is holding me in place. I swallow, tasting blood as I unclip it.

My body freed, I step out of the car, my legs unsteady and my stomach lurching. Light rain pelts my face, mingling with the blood and glass, trailing it down my cheeks. It drips to my clothes as I squint, blinded by the headlights pointed in my direction.

Someone steps toward me, walking slowly, gun pointed at my head. "On your knees." It's a female voice. I blink as she gets closer. "On your knees now! Hands behind your head!"

I sink slowly, lowering one knee to the rocky ground. The other follows, and I sway, woozy as I place both hands to the back of my head. The light at the end of the tunnel darkens, closing in as she steps in front me, gun pointed in my face.

Sobs rise in my chest. I hold them back. Do *not* cry. Do *not* fucking cry. I lift my chin, my eyes slowly rising, blinking against the drenching rain. I encounter tight black jeans, a police badge tucked into the waistband. My eyes lift higher, skimming a wet black tank top, until I reach her face.

My eyes widen in shock, my voice a croak. "Murphy?"

A man steps up beside her, his gun pointing at my head while Murphy tucks hers into the back of her jeans, her hands coming away with a set of handcuffs. My eyes shift to his, and I blink against the rain, my heartbeat erratic as his face swims into focus. It's Miles Howard.

31

ARCADIA

"Is this some kind of personal vendetta?" I say to Miles, my voice a rasp and my wrists handcuffed behind my back. He grabs my arm and drags me to my feet, pushing me toward their car. Murphy walks ahead of us, opening the back passenger door. "Because I did the time for your piece of shit Camaro."

Miles shoves me inside. I fight a wave of dizziness and glare, straightening in the seat. He's grown taller, wider, his eyes dark brown and surly. He ducks his head, leaning in. "You think I have a personal vendetta? I might have you to thank for helping me find a career where I can take scum like you from the streets, but it doesn't mean I'm going to kick back and watch you run loose all over Sydney. Once a thief, always a thief." He arches a brow. "Isn't that what they say?"

"I have a deal with the AFP, you imbecile," I hiss.

Miles straightens, a smirk playing on his lips, so cool and smarmy I want to slap it off. The bully inside him has never left. "I don't care about your deal with the AFP. I have no intention of honouring it. They were moving in over the top of our operation, so we're taking Marchetti out tonight, and you along with him. You're in my jurisdiction now, Jones."

He shuts the door and walks around the front of the car. He slides in the driver's side while Murphy seats herself in the passenger seat in front of me. I scowl at her back and it hurts my head. *Traitorous cow*.

She half turns. "You okay, Ace?"

Murphy is clearly an undercover detective, working her way inside the Marchetti crime group. She knows about the list. She knows I was coerced. I give her a hostile look and face the window. I know better than to say a word, but I am *not* okay. My head is thumping harder and my neck is aching. I feel the hot prickle of tears in my eyes and blink them back.

Kelly

"Pull over up here," I bark at Valentine.

Hammer and four other brothers are up ahead, pulled over to the side of the road, astride their Harley's with mine sitting there waiting.

"You shouldn't have told her to not pull over," he says. "We can sort out the mess at the station and pick her up from there."

"Ace is not goin' in a cell. Not for a single second."

"It won't matter. I'll get her out."

My jaw ticks. "It will matter. I made a promise. I fuckin' *promised*!"

My car door is open before the Subaru even growls to a stop behind my Sentinels brothers. They turn their heads.

Fox and I jump out of the car. "Need your eyes and ears with Mitch," I tell him, tucking the gun from his glove compartment into the back waistband of my jeans.

He nods and climbs in the front passenger seat as I jog to my bike, rain pelting my clothes and face. My brothers don't question me as I reach them. They simply straddle their bikes, engines rumbling, waiting for me to take the lead.

Mitch zooms off ahead of us while I climb on, not wasting the time to put on a helmet. Sparing the barest glance at oncoming traffic, I shoot out behind him, slipping through gears as I overtake and pull ahead.

The last piece of information I have is of Ace heading east down the M5 Western Motorway. I push my Harley to the absolute limit, sliding through corners, my baby struggling to hug the slippery road. Our bikes crest a hill before shooting down, flying around the corner for the on-ramp. I kick it up another gear, opening up the engine as I roar down the motorway.

The traffic is light, yet cars start braking up ahead, building, the red lights illuminating the dark road. I catch the flash of a police siren in the distance.

Fear rises, a living, breathing animal inside me. I shove it down as I shoot forward, leaving the Subaru behind as I weave my Harley through the building cars. A section of the road ahead is closed. There's been an accident. My eyes burn as I blink against the rain, seeing the GTO crumpled against a tree.

Ace. Bile rises. *Baby, no. No, no, no, no, no.*

I reach the scene. I'm off my bike and running before my brothers even stop behind me. Someone tries to push me back, but I shove them away and they go flying as I run for the car. The door is open. Ace is not inside. I turn my head, searching.

My eyes land on the undercover police car. Is that ... *Murphy?* What the hell? I glance to the back-passenger window and see Ace, her arms clearly cuffed behind her back and blood streaked down her face.

"Ace!" I shout, running. "Ace!" She turns her head just as the car pulls out, taking her away. "No! Ace!" I reach the car, jogging beside it as I grapple for the handle.

I'm seized from behind as it accelerates out onto the motorway. Someone's trying to restrain my arms. I shove again, sending them backward as I stare after the car, my stomach sinking. "Motherfucker!" I shout, grabbing at my hair. I'm too late.

I turn, starting for my Harley when my phone rings. I tug it from my back pocket and check the screen. It's Valentine.

"The GTO hit a tree," I answer. "She's injured and they took off with her in the back of their car. Where the hell are they takin' her, Valentine?"

"They'll book her down at the Parramatta station."

I'm ready to hang up, when he asks, "Why were you wanting me to run Miles Howard earlier?"

"Because he's some prick from Ace's past, and I wanted to know where he was at. Why?"

"Because we found out more information about the undercover tail. Howard works the Property Crime Squad Motor Unit. He's the one who just cuffed her."

Suddenly it makes sense why the guy was all over her ass in the GTO. I'm angry. This guy literally has held a grudge all these years because Ace made him look the fool. *Sonofabitch.* "Meet me at the station."

I get back on my phone and make another call.

Echo answers, sounding frantic. "Kelly, what the hell? I've tracked Ace out on the Motorway, and she's not answering her phone."

"She's just been arrested."

There's a pause. "How did that even happen?"

"You wanna know? Miles Howard made it happen."

"Kelly—"

"I have to go. Meet me at Parramatta station. I'm headed there now."

There's not much my Sentinels brothers can do from this point on. I give them a brief overview of the situation as I climb on my bike. They make the decision to follow me to the station and wait out the front, a silent form of support. We head off, and after we park our bikes along the kerb just down from the station, Valentine pulls up behind them, Fox jumping out and jogging toward me as I climb off.

"Did you talk to her?" he asks.

I shake my head. "Sonofabitch was already driving off with her. You know Murphy was in the front?" I say as Valentine reaches us. He falls in beside us as we jog across the road, making our way to the entrance.

Fox's eyes widen in shock. "What?"

"Bitch must've been working undercover."

"Murphy?" Valentine asks, scrolling down something on his phone. "Shoulder-length dark hair? Dark eyes? Curves?"

"Yes," Fox replies.

"This her?" he asks, holding up a picture on his phone as we reach the front door. It's *definitely* her, but she's in full issue uniform, her intelligent eyes severe as she stares down the camera.

"That's her," he confirms.

"It's a classified photo. Detective Hayden Lewis. A finalist for NSW Field Operations Police Officer of the Year this year. She didn't show for the awards ceremony," he says, reading his screen before looking up. "And that would be because she was working undercover and doesn't want her face out there."

"There goes our money," Fox mutters to me, as if I honestly give a shit.

Valentine raises his brows as we jog up the stairs, having heard him. "What money?"

"Nothin'." The automatic front doors slide open.

Fox steps to the side, letting me go first. I walk in and Valentine grabs the back of my shirt, pulling me up. "I'm handling this, Daniels. Keep your mouth shut."

Clearly the man doesn't know me at all. "You've got rocks in your head if you think I'm gonna sit back and let you deal with this."

"Newsflash, Daniels. I'm the one with the badge."

He flashes it at the man behind the front desk like a superior asshat. "We need to speak with Detective Miles Howard."

"I'll call him for you, Agent Valentine."

My chest is tight with impatient fury. I glare at him. "We're in a hurry."

He looks from me to Valentine, his expression unimpressed. Then he nods toward the stairs before going back to his computer screen. "Second level."

We pause at the base of the stairs, turning as someone from behind us flags Valentine down. "Mitch!"

"Alan," he replies, moving away from the stairs and toward the older man. His salt and pepper hair is short, but mussed as if he's had a difficult night. Despite the late hour, he's still in uniform, the shirt slightly rumpled. They shake hands. "Thank you for coming so quickly. Especially at this time of the night."

"I was just around the corner attending to another matter, but when my godson puts in a rare special request, you can guarantee I'll be here."

My lips press tight as the pleasantries waste our time. Alan turns in my direction. He holds out a hand, an essence of power emanating from the man. "You must be Kelly Daniels. I'm Chief Superintendent Alan Rossiter," he says as I shake it, and I'm impressed because this man holds a very high position of authority. It doesn't surprise me that Mitch holds this connection—godson to a chief superintendent. The Valentines have their tentacles woven throughout the entire state of New South Wales and beyond. They're resourceful and smart, and the reason why I brought Mitch in on the Marchetti deal in the first place. They're like the goddamn Avengers of Sydney. "Appreciate you being here."

He nods and introductions are made between him and Fox. "Let's get this done then. Lead the way, Mitch."

We make our way up the stairs. Valentine flags down a passing officer as we reach the top and step inside. "Detective Howard?"

He stops, impatient. "He's in booking. You'll have to wait."

Valentine flashes his badge again as Rossiter keeps behind us, letting him take the lead. "We're not waiting, so point me in the direction of booking or I'll rain down Federal hell on this entire station."

Fox and I share a mutual glance. It grates to rely on an agent with a shiny badge, but it opens doors.

The officer huffs, clearly pissed. "I'm not—" His eyes land on Rossiter and his hand snaps in a brief salute. "Sir. Booking is downstairs at the back of the building."

"Appreciated," Valentine replies as the officer walks away, turning his head back for a second glance before disappearing inside an office. We head back down the stairs and make our way to the back.

"Kelly!"

I pause and turn. It's Echo. She's jogging toward us, her eyes red-rimmed and raw. "Where is she?" she gasps, out of breath as she reaches us.

"Out in booking. We're just headed through there now to get her."

She grabs my arm as I turn. "Miles Howard is a cop."

Echo knew and never said a word? "Yeah, I know that now. A heads-up woulda been fuckin' nice, you know?"

"Why would I do that? It's not a happy subject. We don't talk about it. But I've kept tabs on him on and off through the years. Why is he arresting her?"

"Because he's an asshole. Apparently he was running his own undercover operation on Marchetti and rather than inform the Feds, he got the jump on them and not only did he fuck everything up, he arrested Ace too."

Her face pales. "He's out back booking her right now?"

"Yes," I bite out, impatient. "So if you don't mind, we'd really like to keep movin' so we can get her the hell out of the there."

Echo falls in behind us as we reach the door to booking. The cop on duty is flashed badges, and we step through. It opens to a large wide room with two offices to the left and an administrative counter. It's quiet, with only three bodies inhabiting the area. Murphy is unmistakably one, though she's not Murphy now, is she? She's Detective Hayden Lewis. The other is a uniformed officer, which means the man in the black shirt and jeans, a badge hanging from a small chain around his neck, is Howard.

Fox makes a grab for me, sensing my intentions before I even make a move. "You'll end up arrested too," he says in a quiet, harsh voice.

"I don't care." The need for retribution won't be denied. I start toward him.

"Daniels," Valentine cautions.

Howard looks over, seeing our group before his eyes shift to me. I see a flare of recognition. "You Howard?"

"I am," he says, straightening, chin lifting.

That's all I need to know. I cock back a fist and slam it in his jaw.

My knuckles burn. I shake them out as he crashes backward into the officer behind him. "Where is she?"

Howard regains his footing and rubs his jaw, his eyes narrowed with fury. "Consider yourself under arrest for assault of an officer."

"You're not an officer. You're a fuckin' disgrace." I grab him by his shirt and drag him toward the nearest wall. I slam him up against it, taking great satisfaction in his head smacking into it. Hard. "Where is she?" I shout, having reached the absolute end of my tether.

Valentine and Rossiter grab at me, trying to pull me from him, but rage has me in its clutches, lending me extra strength. I don't budge. "Where, Howard?" I slam him again, harder, and despite the pain I see swimming in his eyes, he still manages a smirk.

Hayden shifts in my line of vision. I turn my head. She nods to the wall behind her. There are two open entrances on either side. I drop Howard like a sack of potatoes and start for the right side because it's closer.

"Cuff him," Howard barks to Hayden.

She blocks me from moving, but she hesitates at cuffing me. He's her partner, clearly she has to back him, but I can see she doesn't want to. I wouldn't be surprised to hear that Howard acted against her tonight. She was the one working undercover. She was the one having to swallow her ethical code and subject herself to Marchetti in order to get closer. And that sonofabitch just goes rogue and prematurely ejaculates all over their operation, all for his own personal gain. It's a wonder she didn't punch him in the face before I did.

Rossiter steps forward as does Valentine. Fox keeps back, his arms folded and eyes on Hayden. "Stand down, Detective."

His brows snap together. "Sir. He just assaulted me in front of all of you. With all due respect—"

"There has clearly been no respect given here," he replies, his voice a whip. "Tonight you have conducted yourself in a manner unbecoming to your partner, your fellow officers, and your entire unit. You received a tip yesterday about the Feds being involved in an operation with the Marchetti crime group. Rather than approach their lead agent..." he waves a hand to Valentine "...about working together, you chose to act outside the parameters of your own opera-tion, discounting all the hard work both you and your partner have made to date, in order to bring in Marchetti and those who work for him before the Feds did. You compromised your fellow officers' lives, and civilian lives, to make this collar for your own personal gain. You acted recklessly, causing a civilian who was working with the Feds injury. Not only that, you arrested her and proceeded to book her and lock her away without medical attendance. I want your gun and badge, Detective Howard. Consider yourself suspended, pending further investigation."

I walk around the heavy, brick wall, wanting to take satisfaction out of Howard's comeuppance, but I'm too anxious to put my eyes on Ace. There are three cells. She sits in the middle one by the wall, her head tipped back against the bricks and her eyes closed. Her hair is wet and limp. They've taken her jacket and her skin appears damp and chilled. The wound across her forehead hasn't been properly attended to, and her legs are spread slightly, a pool of vomit at her feet.

Seeing her so hurt and vulnerable just about breaks me. I've failed her. I've fuckin' *failed* her. "Ace," I croak.

There's no indication she heard me. She doesn't move.

"Ace," I say louder, firmer.

Nothing. She's unconscious. Panic rises up in waves. "Fox!" I roar. "Hayden!"

Hayden is closer and reaches me first. Fox isn't far behind with Echo right behind him. "You goddamn fuckers!" I shout at Hayden, banging my hand against the bars Ace sits behind. They both look inside the cell, Fox visibly blanching, which makes my panic worse because he's seen all kinds of injuries, so he already knows it doesn't look good. "Get her out!"

She wastes precious time running back out for the keys.

"Ace?" Echo cries out.

"I'm okay," Ace slurs with her eyes remaining closed. It's little reassurance because it's clear she's not okay at all.

"You need to call an ambulance," Fox says to Hayden as she

returns, his voice grim. "She has a serious head injury and potential spine and neck issues. We can't move her without a back board and proper transport."

"Mitch is already on it."

I'm so angry. I can't remember ever being so angry. I want to go back and punch Howard until he's unconscious and lying in a cell so he knows how it feels.

"She's going to be fine," Fox reassures me as Hayden unlocks the cell door. I know my Sentinel brother would never lie to me, but I also know he'd do or say anything in this situation to keep me from losing my shit. "Just don't lift or move her."

The door swings open, and I shove past Hayden and crouch by Ace's side, bringing us to eye level. I put my hands on her knees. "Baby?"

Her eyes flutter, acknowledging she heard me, but she doesn't open them. "I'm okay, I promise," she rasps quietly. "My head just ... hurts a bit. I need a painkiller."

"Pain meds are comin', babe. We'll get you sorted."

She swallows. "I crashed the GTO. Damn cop clipped my back end."

I file that information away, knowing it will go in Rossiter's investigative report. It's not looking good for Howard's career. "Fuckers."

Ace nods her agreement and winces from the pain. "Fuckers," she whispers like a little injured warrior. "What about Marchetti?"

"Arrested," I say with satisfaction as I take her hand, giving it light squeeze. "The ambulance will be here soon. We'll get you out of here."

"Don't need ... an ... ambulance."

"You don't get a say."

"Stubborn ... donkey."

She's trying to make me laugh, but it just makes me want to cry because my woman is the one injured and trapped inside a jail cell, and she's the one trying to comfort *me*, even if it *is* just with cheeky insults. "I'm so sorry, babe." The words sound trite and useless. Apologies don't fix anything, especially not this. Not this.

"Don't ... apologise. I've got it handled because I got you." Her eyes blink open and land on me. Their colour is dull and worn, indicating her high level of pain, but they're still beautiful. I want to wake up to those eyes every single day. The realisation makes my heart pound because this isn't just love, this is forever. "Turns out I'm ... stronger than I thought." She takes a deep shaky breath. "Jail is a piece of cake."

32

ARCADIA

I open my eyes, turning my head on the hospital bed. Bad move. It feels like someone's driving a jackhammer through my skull. My accident caused a bleed to the brain, something that can apparently be serious, but mine doesn't require surgery. After a consult with the neurosurgeon on call, we were told the bleed would heal on its own. I touch a hand to my forehead. It's bandaged. I have no idea what kind of mess lies beneath it.

Kelly's behemoth body is crammed in the chair by my bed, his head resting on his hand. He appears to be sleeping despite the uncomfortable position, but the sheets rustle when I shift slightly and his eyes blink open, bleary.

"Where's Echo?" I whisper.

"I sent her home to get some sleep," he replies, his voice croaky. "You okay? You need somethin'?"

"Drugs. Lots and lots of drugs."

"You got it, babe." He straightens, putting hands behind his head and stretching out his wide chest. He groans as veins pop and joints crack. It's hard to not appreciate the sight, even with my head being crushed inside a hydraulic press.

He rises to his feet and presses the buzzer for the nurse before checking his watch. "It's 5:00 a.m."

"Are you sure?" My eyes flick to the window. The blinds aren't fully closed, and I can see through the slats. "It's still dark out."

"I'm sure." Kelly shoves the watch in my face.

It's actually five minutes past. Dammit. "Maybe wait until six."

"Nice try, Chunks, but it's not fair on your family to wait any longer to call them. I promised you I'd wait until at least five, but no longer."

"Whatever."

"Don't whatever me."

"Well, you can't keep calling me Chunks. It's so ... unsexy. I want you to think me beautiful," I say with a pout, which is ridiculous because I'm lying in a hospital bed with my face smashed in and a bandage covering my forehead. There's no hope for me now.

Kelly is in the process of tugging his phone from his back pocket. My comment makes him pause and look at me. "Babe. Your beauty isn't in how you look. It's in how you stood outside of Fix that night where I met you. You turned to look at me with lust in your eyes, which at the time I thought was for me but it was really for Romero's Charger." He keeps talking, not giving me the chance to correct him and say it was lust for them both. "It's in how you found out I was a Sentinel and gave me a chance anyway because you looked deeper and saw somethin' inside of me that I don't even see myself. It's in how you flung that old bra across the room the first night we fucked because you were worried I would think it was hideous, which it was, but all I cared about was what was underneath it." My cheeks burn. *He saw that?* Of course I never did try to recover it, probably because I was hoping it would spontaneously combust. "It's in how you include me in your family, involving me in Racer's greenhouse build and taking me to Sunday dinner, despite it being a shit storm, which we knew it would be, but you did it anyway because I mattered to you. It's in how you attended my brother's wedding with me, wearing a silver dress so sinful I spent the entire night at half-mast, and when you turned around and waltzed inside the docks of Sydney, coming out with goddamn Bugatti. It's in how you're lookin' at me right now like I still mean somethin' to you, despite the fact that I failed and you ended up inside a cell like I promised you wouldn't. It's in how—"

I cut him off, taking his hand and squeezing it. "You didn't fail me. I was barely in that cell for ten minutes, and I handled it."

"You shouldn't have had to handle it for even a second, let alone for ten minutes."

"But I did, and it's because I knew you had my back. It's because I knew you would move heaven and earth to get me out. And you did. You punched Miles Howard in the face. In front of the chief superintendent no less. My only regret is that I didn't see it."

Kelly shrugs like it was nothing, but I can see he's pleased. He likes knowing that I know he has my back. "I can always re-enact it for you."

I chuckle and my head pounds, making me wince. "Maybe when I'm feeling better."

Kelly returns the squeeze of my hand and lets go. "Now stop trying to distract me from callin' your parents."

"I'm not trying to distract you, but I honestly think I'm hungry," I lie. If I ate right now, I'd hurl it across my hospital bed, only reinforcing my horrible nickname, but it's a risk I'm willing to take. "Maybe we could eat something first and call them later?"

He shakes his head and turns his back, moving to the window to make his call. I poke out my tongue because I can be very immature when I feel like crap and don't get my way. "I can see you," he says, putting the phone to his ear. He's looking at me through the reflection in the window.

"I know."

My dad is usually Snoop Dogg in a crisis. He goes preternaturally calm. It's almost eerie. I remember one time Mason and I stole two golf carts at school late on a Sunday night, they ones they keep on site for use during sporting activities. We'd been arguing about speed versus skill, and being the cocky young girl I was, I challenged him to a race through the front parking lot and down through the bush track along the edge of our school grounds. Mason won. He may have rolled his cart in a ditch, but he was able to get out and right it and still beat me, even with an ankle sprain. I may, or may not, have a hit a parked bus. It was never proven, though the bruises and scratched up skin was obvious. We were caught by a passing motorist, who conveniently happened to know my dad and subsequently called him and told him what we were up to.

Dad came down and collected us, tossed the bikes we'd ridden to the school in the back of his wagon without saying a word, and drove us home, also without saying a word, which made it worse because when they don't yell at you, you have to sit there freaking out, stress levels building while you wait for the axe to fall.

It fell when we got home. Dad made us sit down at eleven that night and write two thousand words each on defensive driving techniques. That was that.

Then there was the time Mason shot at me with a nerf gun. The "bullets" were only foam, but they had suction caps at the end of each one. It literally shot out of the plastic barrel and attached itself to my eyeball. I screamed the house down while Mason threw his nerf gun in a panic and ran. Dad simply came in, detached the offending projectile, swiped Mason's nerf gun from the floor, and threw it in the trash.

But then Mason got shot, and I had to make the call. Dad came in acting stoic like he usually does, but I didn't miss the way his hands trembled on the takeout coffee in his hand as we sat in the waiting room. It doesn't seem like much—a hand tremble—but it was *huge*. It was definitely the equivalent of him losing his shit. It reminded me that he was vulnerable, that even though he appeared calm each and every time we pushed him to his parental limits, he was actually a bundle of worry on the inside.

But where Dad shows the bare minimum of emotion, Mum wears her heart on her sleeve. She shares her feelings. She'll be the one sitting beside you at the train station, telling you about her day, even though you don't know her, but she'll do it in a way that makes you actually listen because she makes you feel comfortable with her genuine nature. Mum is the one that hugs us a little tighter before bed at night, gives us an extra kiss, remembers every special occasion, birthday, and every tooth we lost. That's how I knew she'd adore Kelly. Her mission is to always heal and fix people, to rebuild what others have tried to destroy.

"Lydia," he says. "It's Kelly."

Mum has answered the phone. She says something I can't hear.

"Everything's fine. Ace is fine, but she's had a bit of a bump to the head." My heart expands in my chest. He's downplaying it, mindful of making my parents panic, and I love him for that. "I've brought her to the hospital."

She speaks.

"Westmead," he answers.

He's quiet for a bit while she responds.

"We can explain more when you get here," he says and pauses. "Yep. Will do. See you soon."

Kelly hangs up, turning around and tucking his phone away. "They're on their way."

The thought of having to explain everything knots my belly. My dad will do more than just suffer a hand tremble. He'll probably add an eye twitch just to mix things up. Mum is likely to go rogue. People who wear their heart on their sleeves can be unpredictable.

Kelly must see everything written on my face because he says something pretty damn amazing. "I'll talk to them."

"Come here." I crook a finger at him. He comes over to my bed. "Closer." Kelly brings his face in close, his lips a bare inch from mine. "Closer," I whisper.

He ducks his head, his mouth pressing to mine in a lingering chaste kiss. He draws away, being mindful of my injury, but I'm not having it. I slide a hand around the nape of his neck, pulling him in for another one, holding my mouth to his until I'm satisfied. Then I sigh, because even the slightest kiss is everything. I settle back against my pillows saying, "Thank you, Kelly. But I'll talk to them. It's my issue to deal with."

"It's *our* issue," he lectures, just as the nurse arrives in response to Kelly buzzing for my pain medication. "We'll talk to them together."

"Stubborn donkey," I say, my lips twitching.

"Call me donkey one more time and you'll be Chunks for life."

"Donkey," I whisper because I just can't help myself. Don't ever taunt me. I'll rise to the bait and make everything that much harder for myself.

"You've gone and done it now."

I widen my eyes. "Ooohh, I'm scared."

In the end we don't talk to them together. Not because Kelly changed his mind and left me to handle it alone but because my nurse arrives. He's ever so lovely and obliging after checking my chart and my vitals, by giving me enough codeine to fell an elephant. I'm dragged into unconsciousness, blissful and ignorant in sleep as my parents arrive.

The sun is well up in the sky when I open my eyes and see them both hovering by my bedside. Mum looks like she tore out of the house straight from bed. Her hair is puffy on one side and her shirt is rumpled. Dad looks his usual self. I do a quick scan of my room. No Kelly. He might have left to give them a private moment. Or gone to pee. Or get coffee. I have no idea. I'm hoping it's the latter because my head is in a fog.

"Oh, love," Mum says, her expression hurt and kind all at once. "You should have told us."

I blink. "Told you what?"

Dad is further down the bed and places a hand on my shin. It's not trembling but the gesture alone is huge. "About the Marchetti chap. Kelly says he's been arrested? And Miles coming out of the woodwork after all this time when we thought all that was done with." Dad shakes his head. "That little shit needs a *come to Jesus* talk with my fist."

Kelly told them everything rather than wait for me to wake, only it's clear he didn't tell them *quite* everything. The man of the hour walks in the room holding a tray of takeout coffee. Bless him. "Kelly already did that," I say, smug, looking at Kelly as he sets the coffee down on the side unit by my bed. My gaze shifts back to Dad. "And not only does he have a contact in the AFP, his contact has contacts.

Big ones. Ones that got Miles suspended while they investigate the whole thing."

"He had it comin'," Kelly mutters, far too modest of his heroic efforts as he hands a coffee each to my mum and dad.

"Owe you big for that, son," my dad says to him, and my chin wobbles a little because he's never called any of my past boyfriends *son*. I've only ever had two, but still. My dad has *embraced* him whole-heartedly with a single word, and I can't even with that.

Kelly jerks slightly at the use of *son*. It jars him, and I don't know if that's a good thing or a bad thing. After what happened with his own family, maybe getting involved deep in mine might be too much? I tuck it to the side to think on later.

"How are you feeling?" Mum asks in a change of subject, which I'm grateful for because I'm starting to get a bit emotional. She touches her fingers to the edge of my bandage. "The nurse came in while you were snoring and said they wanted to do another head CT to confirm the bleed is going down. They reassured us that if it wasn't, you'd be getting worse, not better, but..." her brows draw together "... you aren't looking so hot."

I give my mother a fixed stare. "I wasn't snoring."

"Whatever you say, love," she says in a dubious tone.

I take offence. "I wasn't."

"You weren't snoring, Chunks," Kelly intervenes as he finds the device by my bed and presses it. My bed starts to rise, bringing me to a seated position. "Your mum was just teasing you."

I frown at my mother. *Hard.* And I'm not going to lie, it hurts my head, but I do it anyway. "That's really uncool, Mum." Kelly hands me my coffee. I pause to take it, muttering a "thanks" before continuing. "I just crashed a GTO and got arrested and hospitalised, and you think it's okay to make a joke?"

"Chunks?" my mother echoes, ignoring my reprimand.

"She throws up a lot," he tells her.

"One time!" I burst out, again, because I know we've had this conversation before. "And I'm Chunks for life."

"Three," he says, raising his brows at me while I take a sip of my coffee and burn my tongue. "The night you called me a fucking Sentinel and stole the Dodge Charger. Then there was the time you were down with the flu for an entire week and threw up on everything and everyone." His voice lowers distinctly, and I know it's because he hates saying it. "And in your cell."

"Well, you called me a thieving whore."

Kelly winces. "Maybe we shouldn't be airing our dirty laundry in front of your parents."

They both appear utterly fascinated.

"You started it," I mutter. "Donkey."

"Chunks."

"Donkey."

Kelly's lips twitch, and I want to pull the sheets up and over my face because I can't believe the immature levels he makes me sink to. It's like I'm ten and fighting with my brother all over again.

"Where's Mason?" I ask Mum, going for another subject change.

"You still aren't speaking? He's back in Melbourne."

"Oh." I didn't know, and it makes my heart heavy because these are the things I used to know back when he talked to me. We shared everything. Now he's living at Racer's house and I have no idea if he ever plans on returning. It's obvious he's still hurting. "Does he know?"

"It's probably best to wait until he gets back on Saturday. In fact..." Mum perks up a bit "...why don't we try family dinner again?"

"Mum, the last one was a disaster."

"Well this one won't be," she says. Her voice is firm, but I can tell she doesn't believe a word coming out of her own mouth because she doesn't blink when she says it. I don't believe her either. Mason finding out about my list of cars with Marchetti? He will lose his shit. He won't talk to me for the rest of his natural life. Maybe we shouldn't tell him at all.

33

KELLY

*L*oud banging comes from the front door of Ace's parents' home. It's Sunday night and family dinner. Lydia's in the kitchen already making a second batch of Jamie Oliver's mulled pear and ginger cocktails because Ace's dad, Ron, has downed two already. Ace watched him do it with increasing agitation, so I'm assuming her dad doesn't normally drink much. I can't blame him, though. These cocktails are the shit. There's a poached half-pear in each, a cinnamon stick, and a liberal dash of rum. The good kind of rum too, not the kind that you'd see Ace buying from the store.

Ron has been commandeered by Lydia to help make more because Ace has been relegated to the couch and told not to move a muscle. Despite the bruising around her eyes deepening, the bleeding went down quickly, and she's been acting her usual self since, though I know she isn't. She's still processing the events of the past week. She needs time, and I won't lie, she needs me too. She also needs her brother, which is why we're all here, again, for round two.

With Ace using the bathroom, no one else is free to answer the knock, so I rise, bracing. Only it's Echo behind the door. My eyes drop. She's wearing a tiny pair of jean shorts and black combat boots, the latter I'm assuming she used to bang on the door with because her hands are filled with a large box.

It's pink and glossy like her hair. "What's in the box, Fairy Floss?"

"Your balls, Nurse Betty," she retorts, muscling her way inside. She frees a hand and dumps her shoulder bag on the arm chair in the living area. "How's our patient?"

Ace was discharged Friday morning, and Echo stayed over both nights, only having left just this morning. She fussed and cooked and did things like laundry and weeding because she's a good friend. The best, actually. But she's also arrogant and cocky, so I like to bring her down a peg or two where I can because it's fun. "She's better since you left."

"She's better because of the healing cup of tea I left on her bedside table."

"She didn't drink it," I lie, lifting my shoulders in a shrug. "It's still sitting by her bed, cold."

Echo huffs and sets her box down on the coffee table. "Where is everyone?"

"Ace is in the bathroom and Ron and Lydia are in the kitchen."

"Oooh, I need to use the loo too."

She makes her way down the hall, and I lift the lid on the box for a peek. A cake sits inside. A large cake covered in thick chocolate frosting. The smell comes at me in waves, making my stomach growl. There's a message piped across the top with icing, the letters wonky which indicates it's not in actual fact a store-bought cake, but something Echo made herself. It reads: *Congrats on your release from jail.*

I shake my head. The woman is ridiculous. "Echo your cake looks like a shit sandwich," I call out, swiping a finger through the top. It comes away with a thick heaping of fluffy chocolate frosting. I pop it in my mouth. It tastes fuckin' amazing. "Tastes like one too!"

"Keep your bear hands off of it!" she yells back. "That's tonight's dessert."

I close the lid as another knock comes at the front door. I brace again and go to answer. Casey and Grace are on the other side, Casey in a collared shirt and pants and Grace in a pretty yellow dress with a bottle of something fancy in her hands. Champagne maybe. My mouth opens and closes and it opens again. "What are you both doing here?"

"Way to lay out the welcome mat," Grace says.

I stand to the side, letting them through, giving Grace a quick half-hug and kiss on the cheek in greeting as she steps inside. "But it's family dinner. At Ace's house."

"We're family, right?" Casey gives me a cool look, daring me to refute him.

"Right," I mutter, knowing I need to be mature and keep a level head because we still have Mason to deal with. The last thing I need is being at loggerheads with Casey too. There's only so many brothers I can fight with at one time, to be honest. Besides, I think we left things at a good place at his wedding. It's like we both know without having to communicate it that we'll never be the best friends we could have been, but we can work toward being something new. Civil acquaintances, maybe.

"I invited them," Ace says, returning to the living area.

She greets my brother and sister-in-law while Grace fusses over her injuries. Echo returns soon after, getting introduced, and more girly fussing commences. At one point Grace touches Echo's hair, and it amazes me how woman can bond over the smallest shit.

"Mitch told us everything," Casey says to me.

"Nice of him to blab," I mutter. Though it doesn't surprise me. Casey is tight with the Valentines.

"It came from a good place. And you did good bringing him in on it. Marchetti would always be a problem if you hadn't intervened and did what you did." He claps me on the back.

I don't know what to do with his praise. I clear my throat. "Yeah, well, Ace is pretty special. Didn't want that asshole causing her any future trouble."

Lydia and Ron return with a tray of drinks. More introductions are made and cocktails are dispensed. My eyes watch Ace as everyone chats and drinks. She's seen the box. She bends slightly and lifts the lid for a peek like I did.

Her lips move as she reads the piped wording. Then her eyes go wide, and she snorts, straightening as she elbows Echo in the ribs. They both laugh and I realise the cake was a good idea. It makes light of a serious situation, but sometimes that can be just what you need to get over something.

Then the front door opens again, this time admitting Racer. He holds it open while Mason wheels in behind him, then he shuts the door behind them both.

Everyone's chatter dies clean away. Then it restarts, a little more awkwardly. Mason's eyes search the room. They land on Ace. And I can tell by the way he's looking at this sister that he already knows. I'm relieved. A big family dinner like this one is the not the time or place to be sharing something of that magnitude.

"Can we talk?" I hear him ask her after he wheels his way to her side.

"Sure." She looks to me as they leave the room, giving me the thumbs-up as she goes to let me know she has it handled.

Ordinarily I'd follow anyway, but when Ace indicates she has something handled now, it's because she knows I have her back. So I stand, sipping at my mulled cocktail, which I'm still lovin' even though it's the kind of classy shit I wouldn't typically drink in a million years.

"That Mason?" Casey asks, holding a mulled cocktail of his own. We stand in similar clothing because I'm wearing a collared shirt and pants too, only my sleeves are rolled up because keeping them buttoned at the wrists makes me uncomfortable.

I don't mind makin' that kind of effort for my old lady when I'm dinin' with her family because it's important. And I remember once makin' a snarky comment to my brother about being pussy whipped because I saw him makin' that exact same effort. He replied, saying I was probably right, but if it meant havin' Grace, then he didn't really give a shit.

I get it now.

"Yeah, that's him."

"They at odds like we used to be?"

A smile tips the corners of my lips, because I know if I, of all people, can sort my shit, then Ace and Mason have a fighting chance. "Yeah," I reply, gruff. "Like we used to be."

Arcadia

WE MOVE out on to Mum and Dad's back deck. There's a wicker outdoor setting in the corner, which is basically a table with a glass top and a low-lying chaise lounge. A chilly breeze is blowing through, making me long for one of Mum's warm mulled pear and ginger cocktails, but I'm not allowed because of my injury, at least not yet. You would think it makes me the designated driver, right? Wrong. Because we came on Kelly's bike, and he wouldn't let God himself touch that ride, let alone me. So he's restricted to one drink so he can drive us home safely.

I don't have my jacket, so I grab the pale blue throw from the lounge and settle it around my shoulders before I turn and perch on the edge.

It brings my brother to eye level, and I wait for him to unleash, the tension between us palpable. He opens his mouth then closes it, as if he's not sure what to say.

I wait, watching my brother, remembering our history and the way we used to be. The way we laughed as we burned rubber around the school in those stupid golf carts. The way he held me all night while I cried and cried after being sentenced to juvenile detention for six months. He was devastated at seeing me locked away. There were nights he would sneak out to see his girlfriend and have me cover for him, though he never let me do the same with Johnny. We were mates. Co-conspirators. Best friends.

And I realise I'm not angry at Mason anymore. I'm just sad. Resigned. I'll hear what he has to say, but if it involves him heaping any more shit on Kelly then he already has, or if he threatens me to choose, then I'm standing up and walking out, and I'm taking that Sentinel biker with me.

Maybe that makes me selfish for choosing Kelly after everything my brother and I have been through. Maybe it makes me selfish for loving him. For refusing to give him up. How could I not? Kelly is beautiful. He deserves everything. *Everything.* But don't I deserve a bit of happiness too?

"I don't want to fight with you, Ace," he says eventually, exhaling a heavy sigh. His gaze runs over my injuries as he speaks quietly. "I'm not angry at you. I'm not angry at Kelly. I'm not angry at anyone else but myself."

"Oh, Mason." My heart sinks. My brother has been hurt terribly. I know he's lashed out unfairly because of it, but it doesn't mean I want him putting everything upon his own shoulders. "Please don't."

"It's true. I was an asshole. I'm your brother. I'm your fucking *brother*, Ace, and when you were at a point in your life where you needed me to be there, to have your back like you always had mine, I pushed you away. I wasn't there, and I'm so angry. *So* angry. And sorry," he chokes out and looks away, blinking, his jaw trembling.

His apology tears me in two. "Stop," I say, my vision blurring. I wipe beneath my eyes. "You'll ruin my makeup." And I applied *loads* because I wanted to cover the bruising.

"You look better without that shit on your face anyway," he says, trying for a teasing tone but failing miserably because there's too much pain, too much emotion, in his voice.

"Don't let Mum ever hear you say that." Mum will probably be buried with her makeup kit.

"She'd shit a brick."

"Yeah."

We sit quietly for a moment.

"Racer told me everything Kelly did. With getting the Feds involved. Punching Miles. Getting him suspended and Marchetti locked up. I'm an idiot, Ace. I painted him with a shitty brush before I even knew him. I was so wrong. I can't even believe how wrong I was."

"Damn straight you were an idiot." We both turn at Kelly's comment. He's standing by the open French doors, a soda water in his hand because when it comes to riding on the road, my man is responsible. "I came to tell you dinner's ready."

Mason nods. "I was just apologising to Ace."

Kelly nods back. *Men.* It's all about the head nod. "Good. I know she'll accept it because that's who Ace is," he says, as if I'm not even a part of the conversation. "But she's built up walls with you now. It's gonna take action rather than words to knock 'em down."

And there he goes again, defending me to the last breath. This man. I just can't. I would never survive losing him.

"Yeah, I get that. I appreciate that you're looking out for her. That you were there for her when I wasn't." My brother takes a deep breath, wincing as he speaks because it's hard for him. "I need to apologise to you too."

"I accept," Kelly says without letting him speak further.

"I don't deserve that."

"You've been through a helluva lot." Kelly shrugs. "I'm not going to rake you over the coals and make it all worse. Yeah, you lashed out. Yeah, you took some time to get over it. So did Ace. But you just had the balls to admit you were wrong and then apologise for it. I respect that."

Mason turns his chair and wheels toward Kelly. He holds out a hand. Kelly shakes it, both of them holding firmly before letting go. "What can I do to make it right?"

Kelly looks at me before turning to look at Mason again. "You could move back in?"

Mason grins. "Deal."

"Good," he says, he's eyes finding mine and holding them, even while he's still talking with my brother. "If you wouldn't mind, I need a minute alone with my woman before we sit down to eat."

Mason leaves, wheeling himself through the French doors and disappearing, and all the while I watch him go, my shoulders feel lighter and my heart fills with hope. I have a future, one with family and Kelly, and Kelly's family, and maybe that future won't include finance anymore, and I admit I won't be crying any tears over that, but I will work it out. Seriously. I have this shit *handled.*

"What are you grinnin' at, babe?" Kelly asks, stalking his way toward me.

I rise from the lounge. "You."

His arms slide around my waist, lowering until the cheeks of my ass are gripped firmly in his hands. My hips are yanked against his body. "Why?"

"Because I'm happy. You make me happy." And I get to go inside and enjoy a Sunday family dinner with everyone I love.

Kelly rubs his crotch against my lower belly. "I got somethin' that'll make you even happier."

My head tips back and I laugh. His lewdness shouldn't make me want him more but it does. His mouth lands on my neck, kissing me there. "Is this why you needed a minute alone with me?" I ask as his lips travel along my skin, sending goose bumps rising. I tilt my head to give him better access. "To make filthy suggestions and grope me at my parents' house?"

"Hell yes it is."

"You're a donkey."

"Chunks."

"Donkey."

"Babe."

EPILOGUE

ARCADIA, SIX MONTHS LATER.

I wake slowly, feeling the bright light of the morning burn my eyelids. I moan and roll over, yanking the sheet up and over my head. Then I yank it back down, suffocated. We're in the height of summer, the type of summer where you need to wear oven mitts to protect your hands from the blistery hot steering wheel of your car. The kind where you crack a sweat at eight in the morning because the sun is up and already on the warpath. The kind where you *cannot* get any sleep because it's just *too damn hot.*

I open my eyes. *Ugh.* It's so bright. I close them and try catching the tail end of the weird dream I was having. Dinosaurs had overtaken the city, and we were fleeing in a beautifully restored Dodge Charger as they chased after us. The upholstery was absolutely mint, and I threw up all over it. "Babe," Kelly had said and I turned to look at him ... only it wasn't him. It was Vin Diesel but Kelly's voice. I *love* Kelly's voice, which is probably why Vin was using it. It's a *man's* voice, all deep and rough and what dreams are made of, literally.

"Ace." My shoulder is prodded. I wobble on the bed. "Wake up, babe."

Seriously? No. *You have a sexy voice, Kelly, in my dreams and out of*

them, and I could lie here all day listening to it, but I'm not waking up for it.
My eyes remain closed as I try sliding back into blessed sleep.

"Ace. It's graduation day." The sheet is ripped from my body and a
slap lands on my bare ass. It's only light but I feel the sting, enough to
want to kick out with my leg in retaliation. But I don't. I'm trying to
play possum here. "You made me promise on the engine of a
Mustang to wake you if you slept through your alarm."

Fuck. I do remember saying that last night. And I remember
drinking with Kelly too, but not enough to give me the hangover I'm
feeling right now. We went to a nearby bar, just the two of us. It was
crowded and rowdy with fairy lights covering the ceiling. I wore a
brand-new black corset top and my black leather pants, thrilled
because it got Kelly all hot and bothered, which was my aim. We
haven't spent much time together of late. Kelly has been working
double-time to finish a restoration, and I've taken on extra course
loads to finish my degree early after changing my major from finance
to management, having discussed taking over management of Rehab
once I gain some experience. I'm not a quitter. Up and leaving my
studies when I didn't have long to go would have been a waste of the
work I'd already put in. And the money.

So last night we drank beers together until the early hours, and
Kelly spun me around on the dance floor until I was drunk and dizzy.
Except now my head is pounding and my stomach is very unhappy. I
don't understand it. Beer doesn't give me a hangover. A bloated belly,
yes. But not this.

"I don't care. I just want to sleep," I mutter, hoping he'll go away,
but my hopes are shattered when I feel Kelly seat himself on the edge
of my bed. My body dips toward him.

"But I have a present for you."

My eyes fly open like he just whispered *abracadabra* and blew
fairy dust into the air around me. I turn my head, my hangover gone
in an instant.

Kelly is grinning at me, clad in nothing but a pair of jeans. His
beard is still short so the dimple pops, but his hair has grown and sits
thick and mussed on his head. I want to open my mouth and tell him

he's present enough because honestly, he really is, but I *love* unwrapping gifts. The anticipation is almost as good as what's inside.

"You do?" I turn and rise to a seated position, a little breathless, my eyes darting about the room. I don't see anything wrapped. "Where?"

"You have to get dressed first."

Say no more. I flee the bed naked, stumbling and hopping as my legs tangle in the sheets. I half drag them off with me as I race to the tallboy in the corner of my room. Then I pause, halfway through opening a drawer, and half-turn, so excited I can barely keep still. "What should I be wearing?"

His eyes rove slowly over me, and they get that lazy glint that warns me he's ready to pounce.

"Kelly! Eyes up here." I point to my face. We had sexy times twice last night. It seems Kelly is aiming for a trifecta. And I can get on board with that. *After* my gift.

"Clothes," he says to my tits, his voice heated.

"Yes, but what kind?" I ask, impatient. "What am I dressing for?" Maybe it's a destination present. A breakfast picnic. Hot-air ballooning. Or one of those zip-lining obstacle course things, which supposedly double as an emotional breakthrough. I've seen the advertisements. You fly through the air in a harness at great heights and basically experience a rebirth. It would make sense because it's my graduation. Today is the first day of the rest of my life. And I love those kinds of gifts—even though there's nothing to unwrap, you have a memory for life.

"Zip-lining?" I question without giving him a chance to respond. "Because you have to dress in heavy gear for that, right?" I turn back to my drawers as I try recalling where I left my boyfriend jeans. They're the most heavy-duty item of clothing I own. "You don't want that harness riding too hard up your clacker," I mutter to myself, shoving clothes aside as I hunt for them.

"Babe." There's amusement in Kelly's voice. "We're not goin' zip-lining. We can do that one day if that's what you want, but I'm just suggestin' you might wanna get dressed before you leave your room."

"My gift is out there?"

"Your brother is out there makin' breakfast."

"Is that my present? Mason cooking me breakfast?" My excitement drops just a little. Not to be ungrateful, but Mason burns toast. And I choked on his last attempt at making freshly squeezed tropical juice because there was a lump of rind in it and some unidentified floating black things.

"No, your present is outside."

"Outside? What is it?"

"A surprise."

Kelly is a vault. It only heightens my anticipation *and* my impatience. I really need a shower, but it will have to wait. After pulling on a pair of panties and jean shorts, I grab the first shirt I see and tug it on. It's a black tank top with white lettering that says: *If everything seems under control, you're not going fast enough.* Racer bought it for me when he and Mason attended the Muscle Car Masters at Sydney Motorsport Park two years ago. I missed it because I had to study. They came home smelling of engine oil and hotdogs, their eyes bright like kids at Christmas. My jealousy raged so hot I wanted to smack the grins from their faces. But then Racer presented me with the wrapped gift of the shirt and it, too, smelled of engine oil and hotdogs. My resentment died a quick death. Not because of the gift, though it helped, but because it was the first time I'd seen my brother so happy in ages. He was *smiling*.

I follow Kelly from my room and realise it's true. Mason *is* cooking breakfast. But Echo is there, helping. And Luke is seated at the kitchen counter, sipping at a mug of coffee. They're all joking and laughing together.

My brother.

Laughing with a Sentinel.

A lump forms in my throat. He has his surgery in two weeks. I'm terrified. Not because I'm worried he won't pull through. He will. But because his hopes are built too high. The surgery may help his range of movement, or it may do nothing at all. Either way, I'll be there for him. I'll always be there.

Mason turns in his chair. "Happy graduation day."

I walk into the kitchen, leaning down to kiss his cheek. "Thank you." I eye the scrambled eggs in the pan in front of him. They look a little rubbery. "But you didn't have to cook."

"He insisted," Echo interjects, pulling something from the oven.

A knock comes at the front door. Three loud raps.

I leap a little with excitement and race to answer it. "Is this my present?" I call out, about to turn the handle.

Kelly's voice is a whip. "Do not open that door."

I freeze as he comes toward me. "Why?"

"Because your present is out there."

"Is my present the person at the door?"

"No," he replies, nudging me to the side so I'm basically *behind* the door as he opens it.

"Kelly," I whine, and I'm not going to lie, I sound like a petulant toddler, but I can't help it. The anticipation is *killing* me.

"What do you want?" he asks the person standing on my front porch, his voice icy cold.

"I want to speak to Ace. Is she here?" It's Murphy. Well, Hayden now. And Kelly sounds pissed. I can't blame him. She was *Mile's* partner. It doesn't speak well for her character, cop or not.

"She's out," he says. A tremor of love runs through me. He doesn't want my graduation day ruined.

But Hayden appears too stubborn to heed his growly tone. "I just heard her talking."

"That was me."

"That was a girl talking. You do *not* sound like a girl, Kelly."

On this, at least, we both agree.

"It was me," Echo calls out from the kitchen, facing Hayden with a mutinous glare.

Luke makes his way over, standing beside Kelly and folding his arms. "You need to leave."

"Ace?" Hayden calls out. "You can call off your dogs. I'm here because I have news."

She must be here about the investigation. Mitch mentioned they were almost done. I actually want to hear what she has to say, but not because I need closure. I don't. I already grabbed a shovel and buried Miles Howard in the past.

"I'm here," I say, stepping around Kelly and in front of Luke. Hayden looks nothing like the detective she is. Her hair is tied in a topknot on her head, likely in deference to the heat, and she's wearing a tee-shirt dress with white Converse. "It's fine," I say and nod to the living area. "You can come in."

She steps inside my house, a little wary.

"Take a seat," I tell her, being a polite host.

"No." Kelly folds her arms, his eyes telling her not to get comfortable. "She can stand."

Hayden's nostrils flare in obvious frustration, but she remains standing. She gives me her attention. "I came to apologise."

"Six months too late," Echo mutters from somewhere behind me.

She frowns, having heard. "I wasn't allowed to approach you until the investigation was over with. Howard has been stood down. This isn't the first time he's pulled shit like this. They pretty much decided it wouldn't be the last until something was done. Something more permanent than a public reprimand and suspension."

Her news is both good and bad. Miles got the punishment he deserved. Maybe *more* than he deserved because his whole career has gone up in flames. But according to Hayden, his behaviour has been cumulative, so maybe it *was* the best course of action. The bad news is that it's highly possible he'll blame me.

I shake my head. "I don't know what to say."

"There's no need to say anything. I just thought you should know."

"Well ... thanks for the heads-up."

"There's nothing to worry about," she reassures me, her jaw a little tight, which I don't understand because she should be rejoicing at the loss of a shitty partner. Miles is not the type of person you want having your back. "He doesn't blame you."

"I call bullshit. Miles always blames everyone but himself."

Her voice is soft when she answers, almost inaudible. "He blames me."

I stand there as her words sink in, and I start feeling stupid. Horribly stupid. Because I know Miles' modus operandi. I *know*. And if I know, Hayden knows. She worked with him ... I don't even know for how long. She came knocking on my front door after I was hurt by Marchetti (which I know about because Echo told me), and she came back again today to personally apologise, knowing she would likely get a chilly reception (which she did). Those are not the actions of someone who's tight with a person like Miles, partner or not.

I remember what I said to her the night we first met.

"I'm trying to get out! And he'd rather burn my family to ash than see me walk away. Is that what you want for yourself? If so, you're an idiot, and you deserve everything you get for crawling into bed with him, knowing the consequences."

Hayden not only had to deal with Miles, but with Marchetti too, doing god knows what to work her way inside. But she did what she had to do without any support from friends and family because undercover work is not something you can share with those who love you, and then Miles shot the operation to hell, risking everything she'd done. *Everything* she'd sacrificed. She's the one who deserves the accolade for bringing Marchetti down. I've no doubt Miles knows it too, deep down, and that knowledge makes him *burn*.

Suddenly Hayden is starting to feel more like a friend than the enemy and that causes worry to bubble up inside me. Worry for *her*. "You need to watch your back."

"I know." She looks around the room as if only just realising everyone else is standing around listening to our conversation. "I should go. I just wanted you to know." Hayden starts to leave. "Oh," she says, pausing and looking at Kelly. "And unofficially warn you to keep your hands off Marchetti."

Kelly raises his palms as if clueless. "Don't know what you're talkin' about."

"He's in the infirmary. I've no doubt you put him there."

"Still have no clue what you're talkin' about," Kelly answers.

"Lucky for you he's still alive."

"It's not luck," he retorts, the subject a touchy one, one she's poked at. "It's—"

I cut him off before he can incriminate himself. "Kelly."

Marchetti has been a subject of much debate between the two of us. My argument being in favour of walking away and letting life take care of him. His argument being life is unfair, and we have to take care of things ourselves. We reached a stalemate and, reluctantly, Kelly compromised. Hence why Marchetti is actually still alive.

Hayden's brows rise coolly. "Someone's turned a blind eye and let you have your fun, but it ends there."

"Enough," Luke cuts in, his expression unreadable, which is unusual because usually you can read him like a book. "I'll walk you out."

Hayden nods, a little too agreeably. My eyes narrow in suspicion. What—

"Oh, by the way, nice car, Ace," she says, half turning, cutting off my train of thought as she leaves. "Happy graduation."

"Nice car?" I parrot.

Nice car? I don't have a— *Your present is outside.* "Holy shit." I race for the door, muscling Hayden and Luke out of the way. Luke's a big guy, and I'm pretty sure I've made him stumble in my haste.

"For the love of ... Bitch, you just ruined my surprise," I hear Kelly growl from behind me, and she really did, because I come to a halt at the top of the porch steps and stare, my mouth open. There is, indeed, a car parked in the drive. It's the '67 Mustang Fast-back. The same one he drove us to Casey's wedding in. Her paint-work is luminescent beneath the morning sun—the blue bright and glittering like the prettiest jewel in the store. Her chrome is shiny and her wheels fat and black. A big red bow rests on her bonnet as she sits there waiting, showing off her beauty like a prized mare.

My breath hitches. Kelly steps up beside me. I tuck my hand in his to ground me, otherwise I fear I'll literally just float away. "You bought me that car," I whisper, my voice wobbly, wondering how on

God's earth he managed to get the owner to part ways with her. This is the kind of car you *never* let go.

"Happy graduation day, baby."

"I can't ..." My voice chokes up. "It's too much."

"You kiddin' me?" he replies, gruff. "You gave me a family. I gave you a car. It's not anywhere near enough."

I squeeze his hand. "I didn't give you anything you didn't already have."

Kelly squeezes back. "I wouldn't have them if it weren't for you." He jingles car keys in my face. "Now go warm her up, we've got somewhere to be."

"Where?" I ask. My ceremony isn't until late afternoon.

"You'll see."

"I know you wanted a Mustang you could make beautiful yourself," Kelly says from the passenger seat as he holds tight to the holy shit bar. "This baby doesn't need any work, but we'll find you a rebuild one day soon."

He says that as if I care. I own a Mustang. I *own* a Mustang. I own a *Mustang*. I can't stop saying that in my head as I screech through a corner, giddy. You can take the car thief out of the girl, but you can't take away her need to drive like one.

"You won't own it for much longer if you keep driving like that," he says mildly, and I realise I must have been saying that aloud. I punch through another gear. "The police will impound it."

"You've got contacts, remember?" I point out, high on the smell of rich leather and brake dust.

"Those contacts don't really condone hoon drivers."

"I'm not a *hoon*," I protest hotly. *Hoons* only care about laying rubber on the road and blowing smoke. There's no skill in that. "I'm simply driving my little lady the way she was born to be driven."

We pull up outside the RSPCA animal shelter in Yagoona that Kelly directed me to. It's right near Bankstown and my motorway accident. The sickening crunch of metal is still fresh in my mind. The pain and fear. The pouring rain and the bitter tang of blood in my mouth. It runs through my head each night as I lie in bed, my eyes closed as I search for sleep. I don't think that's something that ever really leaves you. But Kelly makes it less just by being there.

I take a deep breath, shoving the memory from my mind as I stare at the big building. "What are we doing here?"

"We're here because I love the shit out of you, Chunks. And despite neither of us being ready for kids, I want to start building a family with you."

My lips pull back in a wide, excited grin that will not be contained. "We're getting a dog?"

He shrugs. "Well you can get a mean-ass goat if you want, but yeah, I'd prefer a dog."

It's not until we're inside the facility and walking past cages filled with dogs that I realise how difficult actually choosing one is. My heart wrenches as each and every one of them comes to the cage in greeting, desperate for affection. For someone to take them home and just love them. I want to take them all.

The lady who greeted us follows behind, answering the questions we pepper her way with a quiet calm, leaving us to take the lead rather than influence us toward any particular animal. "You'll know your dog when you see him or her," she says.

And she's right. I see him about halfway down, not jumping and barking at the cages, nor hiding in the corner either. He's a red merle Australian shepherd, his coat a patchwork of red, brown, and white, with pale blue eyes that watch us, not warily, but patiently, as if he's been waiting for us all his life.

My eyes catch his and cling, and I *know*. We reach his cage and I stop, Kelly stopping with me. It's only then I see he's missing a leg. A back right one. We were approaching him from his left side and didn't see it.

"What happened?" I ask the lady.

"Car accident," she answers and my eyes burn instantly.

I see you, I say to him silently as though he can read my mind. *I know what you've been through. I've been there too.* He stares back at me with his beautiful eyes, then his two front paws step forward a little, one after the other, and his single back leg hops once to catch up.

"Hit and run. No one came to claim him. It's possible the owner couldn't afford the surgery so the vet took him on, pro bono. He's been here almost nine months."

As long as I've known Kelly.

The dog waits patiently, watching, ignoring the barks of all the others around him. "What's his name?"

"Maximus," she says. "We named him after the Gladiator."

It's perfect. I couldn't have chosen better. *Falling down is how we grow. Staying down is how we die.* Maximus Meridius. Max. He's the one.

"We'll take him," Kelly says, as if he knows exactly what I'm thinking because he's thinking it too.

She unlocks his cage door and opens it wide, taking a step back. "I'll be down in my office when you're ready," she tells us.

Her shoes slap quietly against the concrete as she walks down the hall while Maximus slowly does his half walk/half hop as he leaves his enclosure. He sniffs at us for a moment then his tail wags as if to say *I'm ready now. Take me home.* My heart is full the moment I crouch and run my fingers through his thick rusty-coloured fur. I have a dog. I *have* a dog. I have a *dog.* And a Mustang. I can't believe that I actually played possum this morning so I wouldn't have to get out of bed. Today has been the best day ever, and I haven't even graduated yet.

"Where will Maximus live? Your place or mine?"

Kelly crouches beside me. "Ours, babe. I'm movin' in."

My mouth falls open in shock, and my hands pause their scratch in Max's fur. "In with me and Mason?"

"Well, the house we've been workin' on is gettin' sold, and Fox can move in to a place with his brother, so yeah, I'm movin' in with you and Mason."

Then my brows draw together in a wobbly line of worry. "It's not because of his surgery, is it?"

"Babe, no. I'm tired of wakin' up and not havin' you beside me every mornin'. If that means havin' to live with your brother, then that's what I'll do."

I lean across, kissing Kelly hard on the lips. He kisses me back, his tongue sweeping inside for a quick moment, a promise for later tonight, after my graduation, and after family dinner with everyone, a dinner that even Lee and Hammer are attending, and after Maximus is settled in the brand spanking new bed we now have to go buy him, and I can't wait.

"You're the best," I say.

"The best you ever had."

THE END

THANK YOU

Thank you so much for reading! If you enjoyed The Thief, please consider leaving a review on Amazon.
Please also tell your friends by recommending or reviewing the book on your blog, Facebook, Instagram and Twitter.

Stay tuned for

THE COP

Luke Fox and Hayden Lewis (aka Murphy)
And if you don't want to miss this upcoming release, or other future books, you can subscribe to my monthly newsletter.
https://www.katemccarthyauthor.com/join-1

BOOKS BY KATE MCCARTHY

The End Game

Fighting Redemption

The Thief

The Give Me Series

Give Me Love

Give Me Strength

Give Me Grace

Give Me Hell

ACKNOWLEDGMENTS

To my readers, I thank you for your constant encouragement, and for reading The Thief. Your support inspires me daily, motivates me, and makes me strive do better with each book. I'm eternally grateful for all of you.

To my darling kids, how loved you are. You (and my writing) are what gives my life meaning. Every day I am grateful for you, the two brightest stars that shine in my sky.

To all the bloggers, reviewers, and bookstagrammers who have helped spread the word about this book. There are no words to express the level of my gratitude and appreciation of your constant hard work and support. Thank you so very much.

A special thank you to Maree Hunter. You have been there for me through every step of this book (and all the others) but we both know it's been an especially tough year, with lots of learning life's lessons, and I just know this book would not be what it is without you.

Thank you to Terrena. Girl! You are my rock and I am your barnacle. I love you.

My editor, Max. I am so thankful and lucky to have you. You are the reason I continue to grow.

Tammy, thank you for being the beta to this book that I needed.

Girl, you scare me, but you are honest, and that is why I appreciate your contribution, and your friendship.

Kimberly Brower, my agent. For all the work you have done for me already. I'm excited for the future and for what we can achieve together!

To Nina at Social Butterfly PR. Thank you for everything you have done for me. You have shared so much of your knowledge, and offered so much support and advice, and for that I am eternally grateful.

Rachel Grey. I am so very thankful for your encouragement, and your advice.

To all my friends and family. Kirsty, Craig, Stephen. I appreciate the shit out of all of you.

And to little Petie, my dashchund, my sweet loyal pup. We went on a journey together writing this book, one in which you lost your leg. But you beat cancer. And now I get to keep you for longer. And while I couldn't write you into this book because you belong to Evie in Give Me Love, I did bring in a very small piece of you. Because you are loved.

ABOUT THE AUTHOR

Kate McCarthy lives in Queensland, Australia.

Website
https://www.katemccarthyauthor.com/

Facebook
https://www.facebook.com/KateMcCarthyAuthor

Instagram
https://www.instagram.com/authorkatemccarthy/

Twitter
https://twitter.com/KMacinOz

Goodreads
http://www.goodreads.com/author/show/6876994.Kate_McCarthy

Lightning Source UK Ltd.
Milton Keynes UK
UKHW020625230819
348409UK00014B/1618/P